Sophie's
Surrender

SAM MARIANO
LAURA LOVETT

SOPHIE'S SURRENDER

A DARK COLLEGE ROMANCE

SAM MARIANO

LAURA LOVETT

This is a work of fiction. Names, characters, businesses, places, events and incidents are either the products of the author's imagination or used fictitiously. Any resemblance to actual persons, living or dead, or actual events is purely coincidental.

Sophie's Surrender © 2022 Sam Mariano
All rights reserved.

——

AUTHOR'S NOTE FROM SAM MARIANO

Hello, dear reader.

All my books come with some type of warning, so if this is your first by me, welcome!

If it isn't and you're well-versed in my shenanigans, go ahead and start reading. There shouldn't be anything you haven't encountered before.

If you're new to me and/or require trigger warnings, please be aware that this story will contain dub-con sometimes right up to the non-con line. There will be manipulation from the romantic hero, and the suggestion of birth control makes him LOL. Silvan is possessive to the point of toxicity. He is also pretty stalkerish. Sophie forgets this sometimes because he gives her enough orgasms to potentially cause brain damage, but if you're **not** into toxic book boyfriends, you might not have a good time here. We are, so we had a great time! :)

If you've enjoyed my heroes before, this book should be right up your alley. If you're a Laura Lovett reader and haven't read *my* stuff before, please be aware that my stuff is darker than hers, so Silvan may be a bit darker than what you're used to. I give my heroines and heroes partners who are built to suit them, but the journey often contains some darkness and depravity.

This story takes place in my Coastal Elite world, but Sophie and Silvan's story can be read as a standalone. If you'd like to start my Coastal Elite series, it begins with Dare and Aubrey's book, *Even if it Hurts*. Next year, Silvan and Sophie's story will join that series as just *Surrender*, but then it will be paired with a short story/series bonus content that will make that book not a standalone. That's one of the reasons I'm releasing it this way now even though I know it will be rebranded later. I wanted the story to be accessible whether you're reading that series or not.

I hope you enjoy Sophie and Silvan's story! I know we did.

Happy reading! 🤍

CHAPTER 1
SOPHIE

I KNEW I SHOULD HAVE BROUGHT AN UBER TO THIS thing.

Sighing, I turn the steering wheel and try to maneuver into a too-small spot in the too-full driveway.

Everyone is here tonight.

The thought causes my introverted soul to shrivel, but after being a hermit the entire last year of high school, I promised Mom I would make an effort in college.

Since school started at the end of August, things haven't been much different from high school—*except for the class schedule*—but when my roommate invited me to this Halloween party tonight, I knew I had to go.

Once I get the car parked, I grab my little denim purse and climb out. Nervously fidgeting with my too-short cut-off jean shorts, I glance around, hoping no one sees me.

These stupid things keep riding up.

I never wear shorts this short, but it's a costume party and I decided to come as a farm girl. It was the best thing I could put together with stuff I already had in my dresser.

I might be willing to put myself out there and come to this party, but I wasn't about to waste $60 on some slutty pirate costume on top of it.

My blonde hair is braided and in pigtails. I'm wearing a flannel top with the front tucked into my tiny denim shorts. The best part of this costume is that, as I enter the sprawling mansion, I see girls in painful-looking heels all over the place, but here I am in a comfy pair of ankle boots.

Nailed it.

I'm not overly stylish, anyway. I prize comfort over beauty, and fashion tends not to. My feet wouldn't even know how to react if I tried squeezing them into a pair of high heels.

The music is so loud it hurts my ears as I pass through the entryway and into the first room full of people. I want to get away from the speakers, so I quickly go deeper into the house.

I search the room full of faces, some I've at least seen before, but others complete strangers. A random guy makes eye contact with me, making my heart beat a little faster and my nerves start to fray.

I veer into a hallway to get away from him.

Am I really ready for this?

Maybe not, but I'm here now. Better make the best of it.

I scan the crowd in this new room for a familiar face, someone safe and comfortable I can talk to.

I should've come with Kendra, but I didn't want to be stuck without a ride in the very likely event that I decide to leave early. Plus, not having my roommate to lean on would force me to socialize.

I haven't really met many people at college yet. There are people in my classes I've exchanged casual smiles with, but I've been too shy to say much outside of the typical schoolroom niceties.

None of these people look familiar, though.

For a panicked moment, I wonder if I'm at the right house. What if I got the address wrong and came to the wrong stupid Halloween party?

Before I can work myself into too much of a panic, I spot a group of girls from my Spanish class gathered near the refreshments table. I paste on a quick smile, but they quickly look away when they catch me looking at them.

My smile droops.

I guess they don't want to talk to me.

I take a deep breath and try to ignore the impulse to take this as a sign and flee. I could so easily turn around and go right back to my dorm…

But no, I promised Mom I would try. I have to give it a real shot.

Forcing myself to socialize makes me anxious, so I focus on the home itself.

This party is being thrown by some rich guy on campus, and he lives in his family's classy old-money Boston mansion. It's decked out for Halloween with candles flickering inside of ornately carved Jack-O-Lanterns and fake cobwebs in every corner, but the home's classical décor has so much history of its own, it lends an air of authenticity to the spooky vibe.

I've never been in a house this grand before, never even seen something so impressive except on the glossy pages of this old Sotheby's magazine I flipped through in the clearance section of a used bookstore once.

The inside of the house is just as imposing as the outside.

This old mansion has real character and a sense of stalwart confidence that tells me it doesn't need to keep up with the times. It may not have all the modern upgrades of flashier homes in a similar price range, but it doesn't need them to be impressive.

This house doesn't need to prove *anything* to *anyone*. It is what it is; like it, or don't.

I like its vibe, so I spend more time exploring the house itself than the party I didn't want to come to. I'm sure I'm not supposed to, but the quiet of the empty rooms provides even more temptation I can't bring myself to resist.

Eventually, though, I make my way back to the rooms crowded with partygoers.

There are people everywhere, mingling and laughing and dancing. Some are paired off in corners, kissing and touching with sly smiles and roaming hands.

My skin crawls in sympathy even though I realize the girl I'm watching is actually into it and wants the attention she's getting.

When I look away from the display, I feel an icky weight in my limbs, a full sick feeling inside me. It should dissipate when I turn away from the stimuli, but it doesn't. If anything, the sensation intensifies.

It feels like I'm being watched, but I know that's crazy. It's just because I feel myself starting to get panicky and it's so embarrassing that I'm worried about someone noticing.

I don't expect to find anybody *actually* watching me, so when I cede to my paranoia and take a look around, I'm shocked to lock eyes with an imposing figure leaning over the railing on the second floor, watching me without distraction from his solitary perch.

His intense gaze is locked on me, and his eyes

are such a piercing green, I can see their color from all the way down here.

Why is he watching me like that?

Because he *is* watching me. It's not like when I happened to meet the glances of the girls from Spanish class. His gaze is trained on me, and I get the feeling it has been for longer than I realized.

Probably because you're being such a socially awkward lunatic, Sophie. Get a hold of yourself.

I tell myself that's all it is, but the knowing smirk that tugs at his full lips makes me decidedly uneasy. It's like he can tell he's making me uncomfortable and he… likes it.

What a creep.

I tear my gaze away from his and turn away like it doesn't bother me, but I can still feel his gaze burning into me until I disappear from the room—and his line of sight.

Everyone else seems to be having fun, but to me, this party feels a little like being chased through a haunted house. Spooks around every corner, and not a chainsaw in sight.

There are a *lot* of Jack-o-lanterns, though. My hands ache for whoever had to carve these elaborate designs into so many pumpkins.

The next room is huge and packed so it's easy to get lost in. I wouldn't normally enjoy such a crowded room, but I feel like I can easily blend in with so many people, and I'm creeped out from that guy upstairs watching me the way he did.

People in costumes are gathered in groups standing and talking, scattered across pieces of expensive-looking furniture, and leaning against walls checking their phones.

Across the room, a girl dressed in a kickass Harley Quinn costume is playing on her phone until Batman interrupts her. At first, it's all in good fun, but I watch as the amusement on her face turns to annoyance. It's easy to surmise she's probably getting attention she *doesn't* want from him now.

I take a step in her direction, intending to pretend I know her so I can offer a convenient escape from the obtuse fake hero, but before I make it more than a couple of steps, my path is blocked by a Viking.

His mantle of fur sways as he stops directly in front of me and crosses his muscular arms. I look up to say excuse me before I move around him, but the words never make it past my lips.

I stop short of gasping when I look up into the handsome but vaguely sinister face of the guy who was staring down at me from upstairs.

He's wearing a great Viking costume with lush fur over his broad shoulders—hopefully *faux* fur—and adornments that look like real gold. Dark-colored clothes cling to his muscular torso and thighs, and there's more fur covering his boots. A sheathed sword hangs at his hip, and his long dark hair is pulled back like the gorgeous Viking from one of my favorite TV shows.

If he told me he was an actual Viking who had stumbled upon time travel and stepped out into one of the rooms upstairs, I might be tempted to believe him.

I appreciate a sexy Viking as much as the next girl, but this one has already set off my admittedly sensitive creeper alarm, and I don't have time to talk to him, anyway. I have to save Harley Quinn from Batman.

His voice is deep and rumbles right through me. "I don't believe we've met."

Ordinarily, my manners would compel me to introduce myself despite how uncomfortable he makes me, but I'm on a mission right now and can't be deterred.

"Sure we have," I say, even though we haven't. "You're Uhtred of Bebbanburg. I've watched many seasons of your show. Big fan. Now, if you'll excuse me…"

I try to brush past him, but he grabs my hip, stopping me right next to him.

My heart nearly stops.

His firm touch should make my skin crawl, but it doesn't. It does make me nervous, and I look up at him with more caution than before.

"You haven't told me who you are," he states immovably.

"A farm girl."

He smirks, his gaze traveling over my body with interest before returning to my face. "Yes, I can see that. Does the farm girl have a name?"

"She does, but she's very busy right now." I push his hand off my hip, relieved that he lets me, then try to move past him.

"Pigs to feed, cows to milk. I get it." Despite saying that, he moves to continue blocking me when I try to walk past him. At least this time, he doesn't touch me. "Are those contacts?"

A wave of annoyance tinged with self-consciousness moves through me. "No. I have heterochromia. One brown eye, one blue. All-natural."

He nods. "I like it. Now, your name."

His command should annoy me, but I realize he won't leave me alone until he has it, so I give it to him. "It's Sophie."

"Silvan," he offers.

I cock an eyebrow. "Your name is Silvan?"

He nods somberly. "My parents are assholes."

Reluctantly, I crack a smile.

"It's a nice name, I've just never heard it before. Silvan what?"

"Silvan Koch. Do I get a last name, too?"

"Sophie Bradwell," I say, since he's apparently obsessed with learning my name. "Now, it's been a pleasure, but I really have to…" I lean over to peer around his shoulder, but when I do, Harley Quinn is no longer being harassed by Batman—she's being ravished by Joker. Judging by the way he has her pinned against that wall and the way her arms are locked around his neck, she is much more amenable to *his* attention.

Silvan glances over his shoulder to see where I'm looking. "Friend of yours?"

I shake my head. "Some creep was bugging her. I was going to help her out."

He smirks. "She must like creeps."

I roll my eyes. "Not the guy she's making out with, some other guy dressed as Batman. I guess Joker scared him off."

"Villains are better. Clearly, she agrees."

I'm taken off guard when Silvan suddenly reaches out and traces the curve of my jaw with his finger. The touch alone causes my breath to catch and my tummy to tumble, but then there's the intense way he's looking at me…

"Well, if you're into villains, I don't know what you'd do with a sheltered farm girl like me, anyway," I say with forced lightness, trying not to let his touch affect me.

He shrugs nonchalantly, but I can see interest glinting in his eyes as he drops his hand. "I've got some ideas."

I bet you do.

Since he's looking at me like he'd like to devour me, I can guess what kind of ideas he has, and I don't want any part of them.

A shiver runs down my spine, and I know I need to get away from him.

"Now, if you'll excuse me..."

I half expect him to stop me again, but this time, he lets me pass.

As I walk away, I can feel his eyes on me, watching my every move. But I refuse to let him feel how uneasy it makes me.

A normal person would feel bad if they made someone uncomfortable, but I still can't shake the sense that he would enjoy it.

CHAPTER 2
SILVAN

I sip the expensive Scotch I stole out of my father's liquor cabinet, letting it burn its way down my throat.

As I drink, I watch from the shadows as the girl who caught my eye earlier wanders aimlessly through my house.

I didn't invite her, so I wonder who did. Clearly not a boyfriend. Maybe a friend, but I haven't seen her spend much time with any of the girls, either. Could be a party crasher, I suppose. I'm sure there are people here who weren't invited, just heard about the party and decided to show up. Doesn't seem like her, though. I don't know her, but just observing her here, I can't imagine her going out of her way to come to a party she wasn't even invited to.

She seems utterly out of place at this party, not at all the charming socialite I'm usually attracted to.

I don't know why she intrigues me so much, but I've been watching her since I noticed her sneaking out of one of the empty rooms… *alone*.

It's not unusual for people to sneak off together at a party to hook up, but as I continued to keep an eye on her, I watched Sophie creep in and out of our private rooms completely alone and for no apparent reason.

Odd behavior, that.

I might think she's here to spy on us, but no one in their right mind would send a girl with such unusual eyes to evade notice. Catching her gaze once means you have to look again, and she's hardly skilled at blending in with a crowd. Sophie stands out like a sore thumb. I can't seem to keep my eyes off her.

I suppose it doesn't hurt that she's wearing that sexy little farm girl costume, but there are plenty of girls here in much sexier costumes and none of them hold my attention.

I keep envisioning getting her alone, wrapping her blonde braids around my knuckles, grabbing her tight ass in those cut-off denim shorts…

Fuck.

The way she would look up at me….

My cock hardens just imagining it.

I want the real thing.

She didn't even want to talk to me, though. Might be a bit of an obstacle.

She felt an attraction, though. I wasn't alone in that.

By the way her gaze lingered, I could tell she liked my costume, too.

And hey, now I know we've seen at least one of the same shows.

I bet we have so much in common.

That doesn't feel like the truth, but I'm still glad I went with this costume. It feels fitting given the filthy thoughts of raping and pillaging the cute little farm girl inspires.

I've been watching her for hours. I can't believe she's still here. She doesn't seem to have any friends here, though she briefly chatted with a guy dressed as the Tin Man from *The Wizard of Oz*.

I didn't like it.

Yet another illogical response.

She wasn't even interested in him.

She doesn't seem interested in anyone.

She doesn't even seem altogether comfortable with being here. Maybe she's uneasy in social situations. An introvert.

Dammit, why am I so curious to know more about her?

My eyes narrow as the pocket of solitude she has been enjoying is interrupted once more by the tenacious Tin Man.

Sophie waited around until a coveted spot on the couch opened up, then she dropped into it and hasn't moved since. It was the first time all night she's looked happy. She pulled out her phone and mentally left the party.

But now, Tin Man is back, forcing a seat for himself between her and the sexy black cat beside her and ruining her good time.

Sophie scoots over as much as she can, seemingly worried about him crowding the cat, but now *she's* trapped. I can practically see the panic swelling up inside her.

I polish off the last of my drink and put my empty glass down on the nearest surface.

I could easily end this for her, but I'm not usually the type to intervene on others' behalf.

I'm not that nice or that considerate.

I'm a Viking, for fuck's sake, not Prince Charming.

So why does the idea of rescuing her fill me with anticipation and relief?

I don't know, but it does.

Since I'm also not in the habit of denying myself

things I want, I abandon my watchful perch and make my way across the room toward Sophie.

Tin Man has his hand on her exposed knee, stroking it slowly despite her obvious discomfort.

Irritation bubbles up inside me.

Stopping directly in front of them, I drop my gaze pointedly to the Tin Man's hand, letting him see that it displeases me.

Without even needing to know why, he stops stroking and looks up at me, his eyes wide with alarm.

"Hey, Silvan," he squeaks.

"Move."

It's not a request.

Tin Man's Adam's apple bobs as he swallows hard, then quickly scrambles to his feet, practically tripping over his own bulky costume in his hurry to vacate the couch.

"Sorry," he murmurs. "I didn't realize she was yours."

Sophie opens her mouth to object, but before she can, Tin Man flees without so much as a backward glance.

A smirk tugs at my lips as I gaze down at her. Her vulnerability bothered me when it was Tin Man taking advantage, but I find I quite like it when I'm the one towering over her.

It's decided.

The girl's spending the night with me.

The decision soothes something inside me, some restless thing that hates the idea of her slipping away from me. I know so little about her. We must go to the same school if she got an invite to my party, but the campus is so sizable, I may never stumble across her again.

As much as she doesn't seem to be enjoying *this* party, I doubt I'll see her at another one.

If this is my only shot, I have to take it.

I wait for her to scold me for "pretending" she's mine or snip at me that she didn't need me to save her and she was perfectly capable of handling herself, but when she looks up at me, despite the wry look on her face, she merely says, "Thank you."

I like her.

Offering my hand, I tell her, "Why don't we go somewhere less busy?"

She eyes my hand with distrust, but the only thing she enjoys less than trusting me seems to be this party, so she takes my hand and lets me pull her off the couch.

Deliberately, I pull her a little too hard so she falls into me.

She gasps, her small hands pressing against my firm chest. Her gaze flickers to mine, full of uncertainty.

It takes all the willpower I possess to remember that we're in a room full of witnesses and I can't lock my arms around her and keep her captive against me.

Yet.

I cannot fucking wait to get her upstairs.

She eyes me with mild admonishment for the stunt, but it only causes my smile to widen.

"What?" I ask innocently.

Once she's standing on her own two feet, she releases my hand.

Don't like that.

I have to be touching her, apparently, so I grab her hip and pull her close under the guise of guiding her through the throng of partygoers.

"Where are we going?" she asks, but I don't answer because I suspect she'll stop letting me guide her if I tell her upstairs.

Her body is so warm and soft pressed against

mine, the temptation to press her against a wall and ravage her right here and now is almost too much to resist.

Sophie looks back at me questioningly, and I clear my throat. "Somewhere less peopley," I say lightly.

She's torn between wanting to be away from people and not wanting to be alone with *me*.

She's polite, though. Doesn't want me to think she's suspicious of me just because she is, so she doesn't speak up about her doubts again until we near the stairs.

"Silvan," she says, mildly distressed as she looks up at me.

I give her a firm but gentle push toward the staircase. I feel like a predator who's just caught his prey, and I'll be damned if I let her get away.

"Where are we going?" she asks again, more anxiously this time.

Rather than answer, I stop, turn her to face me, and look down at her. "What are you afraid of?"

She licks her lips, her wide eyes locked on mine. She didn't expect me to call out her obvious discomfort, and she doesn't know what to do now that I have.

"I... I think I should go home."

She tries to take a step back, but I grab her hips and hold her tightly against me.

"Look at me," I tell her, my voice a warning in her ear.

Her gaze obediently rises to meet mine. I don't know if it's that or the fear in her eyes that makes my cock harden, but cognizant that I can't let her feel what she's doing to me, I loosen my grip and let her have just a little space.

"You're not leaving," I tell her, my voice gentle despite the steel of my convictions. I need to feel her wet heat wrapped around my cock, but obviously, I can't tell her that's the reason. "Not yet. You haven't even seen the coolest room. There's an elaborate escape room set up just for the party. There are too many people to let them all in, but my friends will get to go through it later. If you want to leave, I should probably show it to you now."

Her brow furrows with distrust. "I'm not your friend."

"You can be."

Her gaze flickers to the staircase. "I don't know…"

I grab her hand and drag her toward the stairs. "Come on," I say reassuringly, looking back to make sure she's following.

She doesn't want to.

She looks over her shoulder and around at all the people as if hoping one of them might save her from me.

They won't.

I'm no Tin Man.

Tension tugs at me until she reluctantly puts her first foot on the step.

Then, a sense of victory fills me.

She thinks we're going to explore a room built for escaping, but I know there'll be no escape for her.

CHAPTER 3
SOPHIE

HE JUST WANTS TO SHOW ME SOME COOL, THEMED escape room set up for the party. That's all.

That's what I tell myself as Silvan hauls me up the stairs.

I hope and pray it's true.

My instincts scream at me that it isn't, that I'm a fool for even momentarily believing there might be an escape room, but then I think it's a little conceited to imagine he's doing all this work to lure me upstairs for some nefarious purpose when I'm sure he has his pick of girls at this party.

I have eyes and I can see for myself that Silvan is incredibly attractive—*especially in that costume*—but I've also periodically glanced in his direction and noticed other girls in the room watching *him* the way he was watching *me*.

"If we're not supposed to go to the escape room until later, won't we get in trouble for going up there now?"

Silvan shakes his head. "It's my escape room. I'll go through it whenever I want to."

So, *he's* the host of this party.

I guess that makes sense.

I don't know why it makes me even more nervous. I guess the notion that there's someone here whose authority is above his made me feel safer, but now I know there isn't.

It's *his* house, *his* party, and he'll do what *he* wants.

When we reach the top of the stairs, a fresh rush of apprehension fills me.

"I've never done an escape room before," I say, sure that the best thing I can do is turn around and go back downstairs. To flee this party like the Tin Man fled this guy's presence, if for slightly different reasons.

I can't shake the feeling that *I* might be in danger, too.

"You're in luck," he tells me. "I have."

His tone is light and playful, but I can't shake the instinct that I'm walking into a trap.

"And it'll just be the two of us? Isn't there supposed to be someone outside who... I don't know, operates the thing and lets us out?"

Silvan smirks. "We have to let ourselves out."

"What if we can't?"

He glances back at me. "Well, then you'll be stuck in there with me for an hour," he says, his lips tugging up. "But don't worry," he adds, probably seeing my alarm. "I'm sure we'll find our way out."

Silvan turns at the end of the hall and leads me toward a pair of double doors.

I swallow hard, trying to calm my racing heart.

"Wait," I say, pulling my hand free from his and backing up.

There's an unmistakably predatory gleam in his dark eyes as he turns back. I can see his impatience, feel him closing in on me as I hear the shifting leather and heavy fur of his costume move with him.

It really *is* like being cornered by a Viking.

Maybe that's why I let him back me up against the wall instead of turning and running.

An ordinary man I would run from, but this striking Viking stirs feelings of interest low in my gut right alongside the fear.

He reminds me of the old books I used to read from the library, brutish Vikings rutting their slave girls, and dashing rogue pirates ravishing their pretty stowaways.

I look away from him as he traps me against the wall. His big hand comes up to caress the curve of my jaw and he grabs a pigtail, rubbing his thumb over a chunk to feel the texture of my hair.

"Soft," he murmurs, something like approval in his voice.

I want to tell him once more that I really need to go, but I know the time for that has passed.

We're not downstairs in a room full of people anymore. We're upstairs all alone in a quiet corner of the house.

He presses closer, trapping me against the wall, his hands coming to rest on either side of my head.

"I'm going to kiss you now," he tells me matter-of-factly.

"Please don't," I whisper.

His dark eyes glint with something that feels almost affectionate. I know he heard me, but he doesn't bother listening.

Fear surges through my body as his face nears mine.

I try to be as still as possible. He's going to kiss me, I know it. I just have to get through it.

My heart hammers as I close my eyes, expecting his greedy lips to smash against mine, expecting him to kiss me however he likes, the same way he would kiss any other random girl at this party he doesn't honestly give a fuck about.

Instead, he stops a hairsbreadth away and just breathes me in. "You smell incredible," he rumbles.

My breath catches at the unexpected compliment.

With convincing tenderness, he slides a hand behind my head and cradles my skull in his palm.

I gasp softly against his mouth as his lips find mine. The sudden and unexpected intimacy of it knocks the strength out of my legs and my knees buckle.

I might fall, but Silvan's wedged his knee between my legs. I feel the steady strength of his hard thigh beneath my pussy as he presses it against me, holding me against the wall while he tastes me.

Heat spreads through my lower belly as he moves his leg slightly, using it to rub me between the thighs. I don't want him to, but I'm trapped between him and the wall and can't move. The unexpected friction sends more heat to my core, and I moan helplessly against his mouth, grabbing his broad shoulders for support.

The fur feels soft between my fingers while his muscular shoulders are firm and dependable beneath my unsteady hands.

His mouth moves against mine with a fierce possessiveness and unwavering passion, like he's fighting to conquer me right there on the spot. Mine opens for him like the damn fool thing wants him to, even though *I* most assuredly do not.

As if he can hear me wanting to reject his kiss, his tongue brutally invades my mouth, tangling with mine, overpowering it and leaving me breathless as he claims me for his own.

I've never been kissed like this before. So thoroughly, so tenderly, as if he has all the time in the world to explore me and he intends to use it.

I'm trembling, caught between arousal, fear, and shock. Silvan's body is so hard and insistent, pressing me against this wall, trapping me with his strong body. I should be totally alarmed being so confined, but I feel almost… safe.

I know it's a deception, though. Just my instincts going haywire.

I can feel the bulge in his pants, and I know he doesn't want this to end with a kiss.

His thigh rubs harder against my pussy. The friction has me gasping and clutching his shoulders for support.

Silvan groans into my mouth, his grip on the back of my head tightening as he pulls me closer, forcing me to take more of him than I'm ready for.

I try to pull away, but I can't. There's nowhere to go.

He reaches between our bodies and unfastens the button on my denim cut-offs.

Alarm rings out through my entire body, dousing the flames and sending a chill straight down my spine.

I rip my lips from his just as he tugs down my zipper.

"No. Wait, please." I grab at his hand, but he's too strong. Too hungry, and with an appetite he seems intent that *I* sate.

The denim waistband goes slack, and panic grips me. I expect him to shove down my shorts and force his hand into my panties. I expect him to take his dick out and ignore my struggles as he forces it between my thighs.

I can't breathe.

My vision goes spotty from lack of oxygen, and I have the passing thought that at least if I pass out,

I won't be present for it. He can use me like a doll, ravishing my helpless body until his needs have been met, and when I come around, I won't remember any of it.

Might be a blessing, really.

Instead of raping me, Silvan notices my panic rising. He frowns thoughtfully, then pulls me into the shelter of his strong chest.

I don't even know him, really, but that doesn't stop me from accepting the comfort he offers.

I lock my arms around him and close my eyes, begging my pounding heart to calm down.

He's not going to hurt me.

If he wanted to hurt me, he wouldn't have stopped.

Slowly, my breathing steadies and the panic begins to fade. Silvan doesn't say anything, he just holds me and lets me feel safe, even if I might not be.

It's what I needed to calm down. At least he seemed to care about that.

Eventually, I'm able to pull back slightly and look up at him.

I feel a bit sheepish at first, but he stares down at me with such intensity that my stomach flutters and I forget all about the icky sensation.

I'm tempted to, but I hold his gaze and don't look away.

I expect him to ask what that was all about, but he doesn't.

Maybe he realizes I'm a wreck and not the most stable target for the attention he wants to give me.

It's not too late to take me back downstairs and pick someone else. Someone who isn't such a mess, who would know how to respond to his advances —who would *enjoy* being cornered by him in a dark hallway.

"We should probably go check out the escape room now," he finally says, breaking the silence between us.

Relief trickles through me that I don't have to explain myself. That I don't have to unleash the big, scary ghosts in my past, and instead, we can just move on.

I nod, still feeling a little shaky but much better overall.

I guess my surge of panic didn't scare him off, but he doesn't stop me when I reach down to button my shorts back up.

Once they're fastened and I have at least an illusion of safety, Silvan takes my hand and entwines our fingers.

It's a startling, almost tender gesture for a pushy stranger to make.

I look up at him, and he gives me a look that feels reassuring.

Then he leads me deeper into the darkened hallway, and like a fool, I follow.

CHAPTER 4
SILVAN

I DRAG SOPHIE INTO THE ESCAPE ROOM, MY HEART thundering in my chest.

I'm still reeling from our impromptu kiss in the hallway, and now I'm even more determined to claim her as mine.

I've never been so shaken up by a kiss before.

She was clearly shaken up, too, though I suspect for different reasons.

Not that she didn't enjoy the kiss. She might want to pretend she didn't, but those moans that slipped from her pretty lips as I rubbed my thigh against her pussy told the truth. The way her fingers dug into my shoulders and her eyes drifted closed.

She wanted to be fucked, she just didn't *want* to want it.

My pretty little farm girl is severely repressed. Don't know why. Don't even care. I just know I'm going to have to fix it.

"What are we even looking for?" Sophie asks, her voice soft and a little shy as we make our way through the main entry doors into a small outer chamber.

We spent a good chunk of change building this

escape room in the ballroom, but I don't care if it's just for a party; I don't do anything half-assed.

"This isn't the escape room," I tell her.

"It isn't?" She looks around at the table set up with paper and pens, then at the one to the left which is a water station with disposable cups so people can get a drink before they enter this room they might be locked inside for an hour if they don't solve the puzzles.

I gesture to the liability waiver my family's lawyer insisted on having the guests sign. "You'll have to sign one of those before we go in."

Her eyes widen and snap to my face. "What?"

"Just saying you won't sue for any emotional distress or possible injury you might sustain in the escape room."

"I'm not signing anything," she informs me. "I don't even want to *go* into this escape room thing, but certainly not if there's a risk of emotional distress or possible injury."

I smirk and grab her hand. "You run a risk of that anytime you hang out with me."

"I don't want to hang out with you, either," she mutters.

I laugh and haul her over to the entry doors. I don't care if she signs the waiver or not. "You ready?"

"Nope."

I nod and push the door open anyway.

When we step through the doors, it's like stepping back in time.

Sophie gasps as she steps forward and the floor beneath her feet is no longer even. Massive gray stones cover the shiny hardwood floor beneath this construct. The new floor is dusty stone with walls made of wood and clay.

Mouth hanging open, she walks over and

lightly touches the wall. She looks around at this room that looks like a hulking Viking could actually reside here.

"There are four rooms," I tell her as she runs her fingers across a round shield hung up on the wall. "We have an hour to make it through all of them."

"How do we get out of this one?"

"We have to solve the puzzle. Look around at all the stuff in the room and try to figure out what will open the door to the next one."

Her lips curve up faintly. I get the impression she likes it. "All right."

Sensibly, she grabs the wooden box of trinkets on the table and starts rummaging through it. The box houses kitchen supplies— wooden ladles and dishes, but no eating utensils since Vikings didn't bother with those.

When she notices I'm just standing here watching her, she looks back at me. "Aren't you going to help?"

"Not yet."

Her eyebrows draw together in a frown and her full, pretty lips press together in a pout that sends a rush of blood straight to my cock.

She doesn't bother arguing with me, though. She gets to work herself, turning back to the box, then opening and closing drawers, searching for something that might be useful.

In the corner of this room, there's a wood chair with a fur thrown over it for comfort. I take a seat, lacing my hands together behind my head and relaxing like the master of the house while my pretty slave girl does all the work.

As soon as she notices, she rolls her eyes at me, but doesn't cease searching for whatever the hell she's supposed to be looking for to complain about it.

I haven't made it easy for her, but I wanted to get a feel for how she handles struggle. The party-goers who play in the escape room later will get clues heading in to make the search faster so we can get people in and out of here. It's not meant to be an impossible escape room, but it's a hell of a lot harder when you do it the way I'm making her do it.

She's not a natural leader, she doesn't seize control, but she's smart, observant, and definitely a hard worker. Even without being given a fair toolbox to prepare her, she tenaciously seeks out the key to the next room.

"Finding anything?" I ask.

"Nothing useful," she replies, kneeling on the floor and searching through the contents of a wooden toolbox. She pulls out two axes and flashes me a mischievous smile. "Well, these could prove useful."

I cross my arms over my chest and settle my gaze on her, amusement tugging at my lips as I lift an eyebrow. "Oh, yeah?"

She nods, her eyes glinting with merriment as she subtly threatens to maim me. "I think so."

The axe is a prop so she wouldn't be able to hurt me with it, anyway, but feeling the roleplay, I tell her, "If I were you, I'd think better of it. Unruly slave girls who attack their masters are bound to be *severely* punished."

She cocks an eyebrow. "I didn't realize I was your slave girl now."

"You're serving me, aren't you?"

Her tone is lightly acerbic, but in the damned cutest way. "I suppose so, *master*."

Her sweet tone of voice and playful sarcasm stir my desires.

I shift to accommodate my hardening cock as

she flings a braid over her shoulder and carefully runs her fingers along the prop axe, searching for anything amiss. I watch her test their weights to make sure they're the same, then her lips purse and she looks back at the bin they were kept in with a thoughtful frown.

I watch as she stands with an axe in each hand, then inspects the round shield hanging on the wall. "There are pegs on the shield like maybe it could hold something."

I don't say anything, just watch as she tries a couple of different ways, and finally fits an axe on the pegs on each side so they form a V across the shield.

There's a magnetic click as the connected lock disengages and a key falls out of a chute hidden in the knotted wood wall.

Gasping with excitement, she holds up the key and turns to show me. "I found it! I found the key to the next room!"

Her excitement is adorable.

She runs over and uses the key to unlock the next room.

This one's the storeroom. Now that she has more of an idea of what she's supposed to be doing, she opens the chest to search for items, presses on a round carving in the wall, and lifts up the fur rug on the floor, providing me with a lovely view of her ass bent over in those little jean shorts.

Eventually, she gets to the clue—letters carved into the lamps that if opened and read together give the combination to the lock on the door.

In no time at all, we're in the third room.

The third room is neat. It has a bench for me to lounge on while I watch her search, a mural of cliffs and water painted on the wall as if we live by the sea.

"Why don't you like kissing?"

Perhaps surprised by my question or the casual ease with which I asked it, she answers guardedly. "What makes you think I don't like kissing?"

I smile faintly and look over at her. "You begged me not to kiss you."

Her cheeks turn pink. "I don't think I *begged*. Maybe politely requested."

I can't help but laugh. "Fine. You *politely requested* that I didn't kiss you with the tremoring fear of a virgin right before her first fuck."

Her cheeks flame even more, and she looks away from me. "Did it ever occur to you maybe I just didn't want to kiss *you*?"

"No," I answer honestly.

She rolls her eyes. "I see your ego is immense."

I smirk. "It is, but that's not why. I'm not the only person you've been tentative with tonight. I've been watching you all evening. You're as apprehensive with everyone."

"Maybe I don't want to kiss anyone," she says, but I can tell she knows her argument has lost weight.

"If you don't want to kiss anyone, it stands to reason you don't like kissing."

Sighing, she shoots me an annoyed look. "If you're not going to help us get out of here, could you at least stop distracting me?"

"Tsk, tsk, tsk. Is that any way to speak to your master?"

"You have more audacity than any man I've ever met, and believe me, that is saying something."

Her comment stirs my curiosity. She has the feel of prey that's been caught in a snare before but managed to escape. That's why she tries to manage me instead of telling me to fuck off when I take liberties I have no right to. A woman who has never been prey wouldn't have jumped so quickly to a soft, "Please don't," when encountering the danger I presented.

And then there was that near panic attack.

"Do you have a boyfriend?" I ask, even though I'm sure she doesn't.

"Shouldn't you have asked that *before* kissing me senseless in the hall?" she murmurs primly.

A helpless grin splits my face. "Kissing you senseless, huh?"

She knows I'm just fucking with her, but she still flushes. "I hate you."

"No, you don't."

"What if I do have a boyfriend?" she asks.

"Then I'll have to get rid of him."

"Even if I love him?"

"*Especially* if you love him."

She catches her bottom lip between her teeth, but the expression on her face is unreadable. "No, I don't have a boyfriend." Suddenly, her eyes widen with horror. "Oh, God. You don't have a girlfriend, do you?"

Smirking faintly, I shake my head.

She breathes a sigh of relief. Probably because she didn't want to make out with someone else's boyfriend, but maybe a little bit because she senses that I'd make her mine regardless and she's not up for all that drama.

Her instincts about me haven't been terrible so far.

"When I see something I want, I take it," I tell her, to confirm her suspicions. "Doesn't matter what's in the way."

"That's hardly reassuring," she murmurs.

"I'm not trying to reassure you."

"Then what *are* you trying to do?"

I shrug. "Just being honest with you."

She looks back at me over her shoulder. "Why do I feel like that's a privilege you don't always offer people?"

I smile. "Because you have very good instincts."

She doesn't smile back. "Why me?" she asks soberly.

"Just feel like seeing how it goes. Now, tell me about this other guy."

A frown flickers across her face. I catch sight of it before she turns to focus her attention on searching for clues, but really, she just wants to avoid my gaze. "I told you, there's no guy. I don't have a boyfriend."

"Not that guy. The one that made you hate kissing."

"That is... incredibly personal and none of your business."

"Tell me, anyway."

Frowning, she looks back at me. "I'm not going to dredge up my past traumas for your amusement, Silvan."

"Wasn't looking to be entertained by them. Just trying to understand you better. Bad breakup? Cheater? Just a terrible fucking kisser? What's the deal?"

"It wasn't a breakup. I never actually dated him. We were friends. Or I thought we were," she mutters, looking down.

"Until?"

Her gaze snaps back to me. Anger glints in her eyes, but I know it's not really for me. "Until we went to a party one night without our other friends. He was all over me and I didn't like it, so I left. But he'd been drinking, and I was supposed to be his designated driver. He called me at two in the morning asking me to come back, threatening to get behind the wheel and drive over to my house if I didn't. I was used to him being... pushy when he was single and we hung out while he was drinking, but I didn't want him to kill himself or someone else driving drunk, so I went back."

I don't need to hear the rest of the story to know that was a mistake.

"Did he rape you?" I ask bluntly.

She stares at me, wide-eyed and aghast that I would use that word. "No!" she says, her voice rising in pitch. "I mean... That's... not what happened. He just wanted to get in my pants and wouldn't take no for an answer."

Sounds familiar.

I consider her words. "And did you let him?"

She hesitates for a moment, then shakes her head slowly. "No, but he wouldn't stop, and I was afraid he was going to... Things happened that I didn't want to happen, and afterward, I felt so gross. I couldn't take enough showers to feel clean. I wanted to scrub all my skin off. Then, to make matters worse, he must have realized he'd messed up once he was sober because he decided to get ahead of it. Told our friends we'd hooked up and I'd been into it, but then I got all weird afterward. He made it sound like I just..." She stops talking and shakes her head. "Anyway, I stopped hanging out with all of them after that. I stopped hanging out with everyone. That's why my mom made me come to this stupid party."

That last bit causes my eyebrows to rise. "You live with your mom?"

She shakes her head. "Not technically. I wanted a chance to live on my own when I started college, so I'm staying in a dorm, but I have three roommates and we all share one bedroom. It's difficult.

So, more often than not, I spend the night at home with my mom, anyway."

"You should get your own place."

She cracks a smile. "Sure, let me just dip into my trust fund. Oh, wait..."

Since her comment seems mildly accusatory, I ask, "Do I seem like someone who has a trust fund to you?"

"You do."

She's right, but most of it is locked up until I'm 21 and then 25. "I have other streams of revenue, too. Do you work?"

She messes with the lantern to see if it has any clues like the last room. "I want to, but I haven't found anything yet."

"What do you want to do?"

"Well, I'm majoring in environmental science and minoring in chemistry, so if I could find something entry level in a lab, that would be awesome. Even a research assistant. I'd just like to find something that will help prepare me for my career going forward, not just waiting tables, you know?"

"Smart," I remark. "You're clearly a big picture kind of girl."

She shrugs off-handedly. "I guess so."

Finally, she locates a small key tucked away inside a hidden compartment on the lantern. She grins triumphantly as she holds it up. "Two lantern keys in back-to-back rooms? And here I thought your escape room was supposed to be hard."

Her teasing makes me smile.

I rise as she unlocks the door, and as we venture into the next room, I admire her ass, filled with anticipation.

Sophie halts just past the door when she realizes what I already know.

The last room is the bedroom.

CHAPTER 5
SILVAN

A soft "oh" of surprise slips past her lips. She looks back at me and swallows, more guarded now that we're entering a room with an actual bed in it.

It's a Viking's bed, so it's not all that comfortable. Made of straw and covered with animal skin just like a Viking's would be.

Sophie steps forward, then seems to decide her best bet is to keep her distance from me. She approaches the right wall with what looks like a window outside, but it's actually an LED light, the only light in this room. It casts shadows on the walls as we move.

Sophie is intensely more aware of me in this room than she was in the others.

Smart girl.

"Um, maybe you could look over there," she says, gesturing to a spot farthest away from her in this small room.

I smirk. "I haven't helped you up to this point. What makes you think I'll start now?"

She glances over at the bed. On top of the animal skin there's a sword. Just a prop, like the axe, but she picks it up, anyway. She eyes me wordlessly, then inspects the long blade. "It's quite nice.

The Viking who owns this place must have a trust fund, too," she says somberly.

A laugh bursts out of me and she smiles.

I take a step toward her and much to my pleasure, she takes an answering step back. All her response does is fuel my interest in chasing her, so I step closer until the wall is at her back.

She holds onto the sword between us as if it's a real weapon, but when I grip the hilt and give her a light shove, she's too startled to react, and I get it from her easily.

She tenses at the noise as I drop the prop on the floor and close the distance between us.

She wants to keep backing away, but there's nowhere for her to go. This room is the same size as the others, but since there's a full-size bed in it, the space is much tighter.

Unless she wants to get on the bed, she doesn't have much room to get around, and obviously, she doesn't want that.

"Um, we need to look for the key," she says, a transparent and useless attempt to dissuade me, but damn, do I enjoy the way she tries to maneuver around me.

"What do I need a key for?" I ask her. "I'm exactly where I want to be."

She stares up at me. I see her throat work as she swallows, hard.

I'm invading her personal space in a big way, but she doesn't bother pointing it out. She knows I'm well aware of what I'm doing.

Her breath catches when I reach out and run the edge of my finger along her jawline in a feather-light caress. Her eyelids droop, but she valiantly keeps her eyes open, as if that act alone might be able to stop me.

She's wrong. I very much enjoy the tremulous

look in her pretty different-colored eyes as she gazes up at me, her eyes glinting with accusations her mouth can't seem to release.

It's dickish to do this to her, especially after the story she just told me.

In truth, I'm no better than the asshole who came before me. Just a better kisser, apparently.

Her body tenses when I grip the side of her face, simultaneously moving in so my body cages hers against the wall.

"Silvan," she whispers.

I keep my touch gentle and almost reassuring even as I ignore her desire for me to stop. "I don't want to hurt you," I tell her.

"But you will anyway," she says resentfully.

I lean in, brushing my lips against the corner of her mouth. "Only if you make me."

"That's not fair," she whispers.

"I know," I murmur with false sympathy, my other hand sliding down to grip her hip. "Should we move this dance to the bed?"

Looking away from me, she says, "I want to leave."

My lips tug up. "Then you'd better find the key."

She lets me grab her arm and haul her over to the bed, but as soon as we get to it, she has second thoughts and turns around. "Wait," she says, reaching up and caressing my jaw with her soft hand.

The sensation sends a jolt of electricity straight through my core. I grab her hand, pressing it closer. "If your intention is to make me want you less, touching me is probably the wrong tack."

"I just... I don't understand. We're strangers, what's the point in getting to know me and acting like you like me if all you want is... this?"

"Who said this was all I wanted?" The words tumble from my mouth from a place I don't even fully understand. I don't know *why* I'm so drawn to this girl, I only know I am. The notion of never seeing her again after this feels absurd.

I want more nights just like this one, and while I realize fucking her when she doesn't really want me to isn't the *best* way to accomplish that, I'm not enough a fan of anticipation to deny myself the pleasure.

I also have a sense that even if I did wait, as tentative as my Sophie is, I'd be waiting forever.

No, I have to be the one to set the pace. Hers won't work for me. It can't be working for her, either, unless she wants to die a virgin.

Is she a virgin?

She never said she was, only that the scumbag who pretended to be her friend to get in her pants hadn't fully raped her.

"Have you been fucked before?" I ask, suddenly needing to know if anyone else has been here with her.

She shakes her head no and my chest fills with something strangely possessive.

All mine.

My lips curve up. I release her arm so I can use my hands to untie the knotted bottom of her blue flannel top.

She turns her head, unable to watch.

I make quick work of it, then I press my hand against the smooth, warm skin of her stomach.

The touch is too much. She grabs my wrist, looking up at me, a pleading look in her eyes.

She knows she shouldn't have to plead with me, but she does anyway.

I like her.

"I've never met anyone like you before," I tell her.

My words must ring hollow to her.

It probably sounds like a line, but it's not.

I don't need to lie to her to get what I want, after all. I'm prepared to take it.

When I reach down to unbutton and unzip her shorts for the second time tonight, she tries again, grabbing my wrists with a soft, "Come on, Silvan. You know I don't want to do this. Stop it."

I don't. I like her hands on me, though, so I pause a couple of times to let her think maybe I'm reconsidering.

She licks her pretty lips, and fuck.

I know she's not trying to entice me, but she's doing a damn good job of it, anyway.

"Get on the bed."

She shakes her head no.

I grab one of her braided pigtails, wrapping it around my fist, then using it to force her face closer to mine. She cries out when I tug her. "I can take what I want from you without the bed, if you'd prefer it," I offer smoothly. Then, lightly tracing the curve of her plump lower lip with my thumb, I tell her, "Such a pretty mouth. It will look so goddamn good wrapped around my cock."

Fear glistens in her eyes, but she doesn't say a word.

I let go of her hair and give her a good, hard shove back onto the bed.

With a gasp, she catches herself on her elbows, then promptly rolls toward the other side of the bed. "Are you crazy?" she demands when I grab her ankle, giving it a good yank and flattening her on her tummy so I can drag her back.

"Perhaps." I grab her other leg and turn her over on her back so she's looking up at me.

"Let go of me," she demands.

Rather than do as she asks, I draw out my sword.

Not the prop on the bed, but the real one hanging from my hip. Her eyes widen at the glint of steel. Before she can do a damn fool thing like grab it to push it away, I tell her, "I should warn you, this one isn't a prop."

She swallows, watching the blade as it nears her, her chest rising and falling rapidly, but her body otherwise motionless.

"My blade is sharp, so I wouldn't advise touching it." I lower the blade as I warn her, pressing the tip against her breasts and forcing her back down on the bed while hardly exerting a bit of force.

Physical force, anyway.

Her words lack confidence, but they come from a place of common reason. Of course, what she says should generally be true, she's just not sure it's true for me. "You're not going to hurt me with that thing. You're not a real Viking. We live in a civilized society. You might be able to get away with raping me in the fucked-up world we live in, but you damn sure won't get away with running me through with a sword."

My lips tug up. "Oh, I wouldn't run you through. Just nick you. I don't mind going deep, though. I like the idea of my mark on your body long after you've left my house. If I cut deep enough, it'll scar. Then, you'll wear a memory of me for the rest of your life."

"You'd still get in trouble," she says uneasily.

"You think so? See, I think it'd be pretty easy to claim there was a mix-up. We were playing around with the Viking stuff, and I thought I grabbed the prop sword. Grabbed the real one instead." She must have buttoned her shorts when she was on her belly trying to roll away from me. The zipper is still down, but the button is secure again, as if that flimsy little thing might stop me from taking what I want.

To stop her from being able to close it on me again *and* to illustrate how sharp my blade is, I bring the blade down toward her hips, line it up with the button, and neatly slice it off her shorts.

She gasps as the button rolls off onto the bed beside her.

Eyes wide with horror, she looks up at me. "You're fucking crazy."

"I'm glad you understand."

She might have had her suspicions before, but now that she's certain I'm a fucking lunatic, the playfulness goes out of her.

Composing herself, she licks her lips, then softly says, "Silvan, I'm... I'm going to say this one more time. Let me go."

Her voice is shaking when she says it.

I like her voice shaking.

I like her fear.

I like the way she's still looking up at me with those wide eyes like she can't quite comprehend the man she sees. Or maybe she can, she just doesn't want to.

"I won't tell anyone about this or anything," she adds, as if that might be a concern for me.

It's not.

If she knew all the fucked up shit the men in my family have gotten away with for generations because we had enough money to make our problems go away, she'd lose all her faith in this so-called civilized world she's so certain she lives in.

I don't tell her, though.

I like her naivety and want her to hold onto it for a while longer.

"I just want to go home," she finishes softly.

"And I'll let you," I assure her. "As soon as I'm finished with you."

I keep the sword at a threatening distance without pressing it to her skin so I can climb on the bed without harming her. She scoots back away from me, toward the pillows where she can rest her pretty little head while I fuck her.

"Silvan, please..."

I like my name on her lips, but I don't tell her that. She might opt to deprive me the pleasure as a punishment if I do.

My costume is elaborate which looks fucking cool, but is a bit of a pain in the ass now that I need to undress with a reluctant partner who poses a flight risk.

Granted, she can't get out of this room until the door opens, so I have her trapped here for a good amount of time, but I—

My thoughts are interrupted when the girl sees her chance—me attempting to disrobe—and tries to roll off the damn bed again.

I grab one of her long blonde pigtails and give it a sharp tug. She yelps as I drop the sword on the bed and drag her little ass back over to me, then cries out when I grab her wrists, forcing both of them behind her back and shoving her down on the bed. I hold her wrists behind her with one hand. Aggravated, I toss the sword on the ground behind me.

"All right, I see we're doing this the hard way."

"Get your hands off me," she says, fighting my hold on her.

This is not how I wanted to do this.

Since she's fighting me now, I hold her down

with one hand and push down her shorts with the other.

"No," she cries, twisting and trying to break free.

I dig my fingers into the waistband of her white cotton panties, causing her to gasp at the roughness. I yank them down and she lets out an agonized cry as her pale, lovely ass comes into view.

Fucking Christ.

I want to bite it.

I run my hand over her soft flesh, then grab a nice handful of her ass and squeeze.

Her ass is fucking perfect. My cock was already hardening, but the sight of it, the feel of it in my hand...

I need to be free of the constraints of this godforsaken costume. Her ass is hard to let go of. I want to explore her body more, so much more. I want to touch and taste every inch of her, but I settle for one more caress. I slip two fingers between her thighs and feel her pussy. So fucking soft, so in need of my attention.

My cock pushes at the fabric of my breeches, trying desperately to break free, and reminds me it is *also* in need of attention.

"Christ," I curse lowly, shifting the wiggling girl and my weight on top of her so I can reach down and free my cock.

Relief fills me as soon as it drops free from its fabric prison and hangs heavily between my muscular thighs.

I can see for all my relief, Sophie's feeling exactly the opposite. Her eyes are wide with absolute horror as she stares at it.

I don't know if she's seen a cock before.

Mine's a good nine inches, thick and veiny when I grasp it in my hand. The sight of it sends her scooting back on the bed, eyeing it like a monster that's coming to get her.

Which I suppose is fair.

"No, please," she says with renewed vigor, shaking her head. "Please don't hurt me."

Please falls from her lips like a Sunday morning prayer, over and over again, more and more desperate as I shove her panties lower and make room for myself between her thighs.

Her desperation intensifies.

"Please, please don't do this."

I ignore her protests, though I do enjoy them. I wish I had more time with her tonight. I haven't even been inside her yet, and I'm already regretting knowing I won't be able to explore every hole or taste every inch of her. My time is limited—literally. When those doors open, she's getting the hell out of here. And if she has her way, I know she'll never see me again.

I don't like that at all.

I want her hair loose and sliding between my fingers as I palm her skull, pulling her into my chest as I drive into her. I want to feel her weight in my arms as she sleeps beside me, know what she looks like in the morning when she first wakes up. I want to taste her, dominate her mouth *and* her scrumptious ass.

I need... much more time than what's left of an hour.

Gazing down at her, I see tears glistening in her eyes.

"Will you have dinner with me?"

Her eyes widen. "What?" she whispers, utterly dumbfounded.

"If I stop now, or even if I don't. Will you have dinner with me? I'll take you somewhere nice."

"No," she says immediately, too floored by my

insane request to even think before she utters the word.

My brow furrows. I suppose it makes sense, but it was *not* the answer I wanted.

My gaze flickers to her braids and all I can think is that I'm so fucking limited on time, I can't even spare a minute to unbraid her hair so I can see it loose.

I need to see her breasts, at least, so I unbutton her shirt and push it open. She's wearing a white bra. I shift her weight and reach behind her to unclasp it.

She squeezes her eyes shut as the fabric goes slack. I want the bra all the way off, so I have to release her wrists.

Of course, she starts fighting me again, so I have to get a little rough with her to get her undressed.

Her tits jiggle as I shove her back down against the bed, my eyes devouring every inch of her exposed body. Her tits aren't large, barely a B-cup, but her nipples are a perfect dusty pink and I very much want them in my mouth.

Not one to deny myself, I lean over and dip my head, flicking my tongue across one soft pink tip. Sophie cries out in protest, struggling against my renewed grip on her wrists.

"Stop," she cries, but I don't.

I stroke her nipple with my tongue, then suck it into my mouth. She gasps and bucks her hips, trying to get me off her, but it's a useless waste of energy.

I bite down on her nipple and she cries out, her body stilling beneath mine.

Good girl.

Keeping her pretty pink nipple between my

teeth, I give it another warning pinch as I slowly let go of her hands.

It's meant to let her know that, while I'm releasing her hands, I can still hurt her.

She seems to get the message because she hasn't suddenly been overcome with desire for me, but she remains still and doesn't try hitting me again when I release her hands.

Now that mine are freed up, I let one hand roam over to squeeze and caress her other tit until I can get to tasting it. This one is just so fucking delicious; I can't tear myself away.

I hear little gasps and groans of protest from her as I grope and tweak her nipples with my teeth, but she's too afraid I'll bite her again to put any muscle behind trying to fight me.

My cock is a log of fucking steel in my pants after tasting and teasing her tits. I kiss my way down her torso, making my way toward her pussy, but now that I don't have a sensitive part of her between my teeth to threaten her with, she grabs my hair and yanks, roaring like a magnificent Viking queen as she tries to hurl me off her.

I think it should annoy me, but I seem to love every fucking thing she does.

Besides, I don't mind having my hair pulled.

I smirk to let her know it, then I grab a handful of her braids and give her a much harder yank than I did before.

She cries out, her neck naturally angling as her head is pulled back. I take advantage and bury my face in that sensitive nook, kissing and nibbling on her as I force her back on the bed and plant myself between her thighs.

She squirms, pushing at my chest and moving her hips to try to unseat me.

All she does is make me fucking harder.

Cognizant of the timer literally ticking as I fuck around with all this foreplay, I reluctantly decide to skip the rest in favor of driving inside this perfect body writhing beneath mine.

Since her thighs are already spread, her pussy is easy to get to. She cries out when she realizes it, trying to squeeze her legs shut, but she can't; I'm wedged between them.

"No, no, no. Please," she cries again, her voice wavering because, like me, she knows she's running out of time.

She just hasn't accepted that she's *completely* out of time.

I bring my aching cock to her entrance and shove into her the first couple of inches.

She yelps and her body tenses.

My entire brain experiences a total white out as my cock is squeezed into the tightest fucking hole I've ever breached.

I don't know if it's because she's fighting me or because she's a virgin. Maybe it's just the way she's built. All I know is it's fucking ecstasy and I need more of it.

"Holy fuck," I groan, my entire body strained as I push forward another inch into her resisting heat.

I'm barely inside her, and it's already the most intense thing I've ever felt.

"Silvan, wait," she cries. It's not the idle begging and pleading I've halfway tuned out in the throes of this immense pleasure. She's desperate now, and her desperation is urging her to reconsider what she has to offer. Her voice is so uncertain, so shy, she can hardly get the words out. "Can... can I suck you instead?"

It's tempting, but I don't want a blowjob. I want in this pussy. I want to feel her heat all around me. Fuck, I want it so bad.

I notch my hips forward, pushing more of myself inside her, but I come up against a barrier and I can't get any deeper.

Well, I can, but I'll have to break through the fragile barrier of her innocence.

"Please, Silvan."

I have her clutched tightly against my body as I maneuver into her resisting tightness, so her face is near mine when I meet her gaze. Tears wet her long, dark eyelashes and her lovely cheeks as she makes this humiliating request.

"I want to," she whispers, even though we both know it's a lie.

I have no desire to humiliate her, so I kiss her cheek reassuringly, following the cool path of her tears. I only mean to dole out a little reassurance, but I enjoy my lips on her skin so much, I kiss the side of her mouth, and then I want more.

When I get to her lips, she kisses me back softly and whispers, "Please."

Fuck.

I can't resist that.

She's begging to have my cock in her pretty mouth, and even though I know it's only to avoid having her virginity ripped away from her... hell, I can't say no.

Since I haven't said yes yet, but she sees me deliberating, she tries a little harder to sway me. "Please, Silvan," she whispers. "Let me suck you."

Fuck me.

If I ever say no to that, she should take that sword I dropped on the floor beside the bed and slice my dick clean off.

My cock throbs at the thought of having her lips wrapped around it even as it instantly misses her heat when I withdraw from her pussy.

Sophie breathes an audible sigh of relief as I ease

her back on the bed. Her eyes close briefly and she releases a shuddering breath, trying to get her bearings and prepare herself for what she has to do next.

She knows she has to deliver on her offer, or she'll be right back where she was a moment ago.

She reaches for her discarded shirt, but I stop her.

"What are you doing?"

"It's cold," she lies. "I wanted to put my shirt back on."

I smirk faintly, then I unfasten the gray fur cloak from around my shoulders.

"Get on your knees on the floor."

Eyes wide, she climbs off the bed and does as I command.

Once she's down there looking up at me, I drape my fur around her to keep her warm.

It's not what she wanted and offers her tits no coverage whatsoever, but she looks up at me like a fucking angel and says, "Thank you," like I gave her something.

Warmth fills my chest. I fucking love the sight of her on her knees wrapped in nothing but my fur, ready to please me.

I cup her jaw in my hand and tilt her face up to make her look at me.

Vulnerability glints in her eyes. I could do anything I wanted to her right now, and she damn well knows it.

"Looks better on you than me," I tell her wryly.

Her shy gaze leaves mine, but she lets me hold her jaw until I'm ready to let go.

The small gesture heats my blood. Then, when I release her, she gently removes the lush pelts of fur tied around my boots. She doesn't have to be gentle, but she is.

My pants come off next, and the black boxer-briefs I wore beneath them.

Now that I'm undressed where she needs access to me, she scoots forward on her knees, planting her hands on my muscular thighs and casting an uncertain look up at me.

I'm curious to see where she's going on her own, so I don't offer her any direction.

I am surprised and pleased that she looked to me for it, though.

It's on the tip of my tongue to ask if she's sucked a cock before, but given what she told me earlier about the last guy who got her in this position and things happening that she didn't want to happen, I wonder if this isn't the first time she has evaded rape with a compromise she thought she might be able to live with.

I don't want confirmation if I'm right.

I don't want the two experiences linked in her mind, though I know I don't have much control over that.

She clearly didn't enjoy her last experience, I know that much.

So, when she shyly reaches for my cock and takes it in her hand, I allow myself a moment of mindless pleasure, but then I reach down and grab her tits.

She gasps in surprise and looks up at me.

"Keep doing what you're doing," I tell her.

She licks her lips, then gently tugs on my hard shaft.

I tweak her nipples and feel them harden beneath my fingers.

"Mm, that's it, baby. Now, lean in and take it in your mouth."

I feel her breath on the crown of my cock a moment before her perfect lips wrap around it. I groan, my eyes rolling back in my head.

I release one of her tits so I can grab her head, needing control of her clumsy, uncertain movements.

She doesn't fight me. She doesn't mind having her movement controlled. Maybe she even prefers it.

Her mouth is wet and hot as my cock fills it, pushing deeper. I feel her start to panic as she gags, but I give her skull a reassuring rub and murmur, "What a good fucking girl. Your mouth is perfect, baby. It fits me like a glove. Relax."

She does as she's commanded, relaxing her throat and opening her jaw to take me.

"Christ." I can feel my cock at the back of her throat.

My hand on her tit hasn't moved, but it hasn't done a damn thing, either. I got so caught up in feeling her take me into her mouth, I forgot I wanted to make her feel good while she pleasured me.

I remember now, rubbing my fingertip over her nipple. It pebbles again, so I rub it harder, circling it and then tweaking the sensitive nub.

Sophie moans around me, the vibration traveling up my dick and sending a tremor of pleasure clear down to my toes.

My eyes drift closed, and I continue to mindlessly caress and tease her tits as she sucks me. She's doing a good job, she's just not taking me deep enough. I want to grab her skull and drive my cock so deep into her throat that she cries and gags around me, but I don't want to traumatize her, either.

Well, more than I already have.

If I weren't so committed to the cause, I might

drag her pretty little ass up here, plant her on my cock, and fuck that sweet pussy I got such a tantalizing taste of.

But no. Here I am, being a good guy.

More or less.

Her tongue swirls around my shaft, reminding me that my compromise has brought me a nice little reward. I love her efforts to please me. Yes, I want more, but I love what she's giving me as much as I enjoyed taking from her.

It's her I want; the method doesn't seem to matter.

I have half a mind to tell her as she sucks my cock that it's unfortunate for her she's committed to never seeing me again, because I'm just as committed to having another night like this one, and between the two of us, it's much more likely I'm going to get what I want.

No need to alarm her.

Not right now.

Not when she's doing such a lovely fucking job laboring over my cock.

I caress her hair tenderly, almost lovingly, as I work my hands around her head. It's to reassure her that everything is fine and she's doing a great job, but once I have her skull cradled in both hands, I force her to take me deeper.

She cries out, startled. Her nails dig into my thighs as she holds on, but I murmur reassurances and remind her to breathe.

Her throat is fucking heaven as I push into it. I've had a lot of mouths around my cock, but I've never enjoyed one as much as this one. They've all been much more willing, too. Hungry for it, even, not begrudgingly offered to avoid a worse fate.

I look down at her now, her pretty blonde head in my hands, moving at exactly the pace I want. It's fucking criminal what I've done to her tonight, but you'd never know it from the loving way her tongue wraps around my cock and her lips suck as I pull her off.

Her mouth makes a wet sound when I break the suction. She looks up at me, confused, silently vibrating with uncertainty and inexperience.

Did I do something wrong?

She doesn't ask the words, but I answer her anyway.

"You're perfect."

Relief hits her eyes, and a little smile curves her lips before she remembers she doesn't even want to be doing this, so she shouldn't care how I'm judging her performance. I see the way her brow furrows and long to smooth it out, to assure her that wanting to please me is the right instinct and she should follow that one.

I'm tempted to finish on her tits. I want to mark them, mark her. I want her to have to make an effort to remove every remnant of me from her body, and then I want that effort to fail, anyway.

"Do you swallow?" I ask her.

Her dainty shoulders shrug. "I can if you want me to."

What an angel.

I smile, tenderly caressing her cheek with approval, then I push her forward. She takes the hint, opening her mouth and gripping the base of my cock as she takes me deep into her mouth.

The sensation of thrusting into her pretty mouth is so intensely pleasurable, and paired with the command I have over her body as I push her face back and forth over my cock...

It's hard to imagine anything better, but then I remember those all too brief moments when my cock was in her pussy.

The memory of that feeling pushes me closer to the edge. I grab her neck and feel the spark of fear in her when I do, but I ignore it. One hand braced on her neck, the other on the back of the head, I pound my cock into her throat so hard she cries out and grabs my thighs tighter as if for help.

"Almost there," I bite out, forcing her face closer to my pelvis.

She cries out around my cock but I'm too lost to the pleasure of possessing her this way. "Swallow it, baby. When I come, you better swallow every fucking drop."

Pleasure erupts and rips through me with a loud groan as I force my cock deep, shooting hot cum down her lovely throat.

My muscles feel hollow in the aftermath, but I keep holding her face close, her lips still wrapped around my shaft. I want to prolong the sensation of her mouth around me since I'm not sure when I'll feel it again.

With my fingers wrapped around her neck, I can feel her pulse hammering. She's afraid, but she accepts my control and stays there until I ease up the pressure on the back of her head and allow her to pull back.

"Suck me clean."

Her mouth is still full of my cock when she looks up at me.

Christ.

Obediently, she wraps her tongue around me and eases back, licking and sucking me clean as she does.

When she pops off, I want to marry her.

I want to be trapped in here for a hell of a lot longer than an hour with her.

I want her naked and wrapped in my fur.

I want her forced to be in my presence, wrapped in my arms after a good fuck.

I want to know what she sounds like when she comes, and I desperately want to fuck that pussy I only got a little taste of.

There's not a shot in hell tonight can be my only taste of her.

She stays kneeling like an angel, but because she does, she frowns at the straw that makes up most of this Viking bed.

Then she reaches toward it and draws out a seax.

A traditional Viking fighting knife hidden between the haystacks.

Like the other weapons in the escape room, it's just a prop.

Still, I watch her curiously to see if she might try to maim me with it.

She doesn't.

She looks it over, then stands, dropping my fur from her shoulders.

She's completely naked now and I very much enjoy the sight. I expect her to be bashful, but she must be too focused on getting away from me because she doesn't even seem to notice her nudity. All she can focus on is finding where she's supposed to stab this knife into to unlock the door.

She's right, of course.

That's the last puzzle.

She walks around the room looking for its perfect sheath as I pull my clothes back on. Finally, she gets to a little wooden pumpkin on a table in the corner. She removes its lid, and sure enough, there's a slot. She turns the knife and starts to push in the blade.

"You might want to get dressed before you do that," I advise her.

Her gaze snaps back to me, eyes wide. "Is this it? This is the way out?"

I nod wordlessly.

Her face lights up with relief and victory. She puts the seax down and rushes over to gather her clothes and pull them back on.

Her braids are messy from me manhandling them so much. Her lips are swollen from sucking my cock, and her jean shorts won't button since I sliced the button off.

I grab my sword and replace it in its scabbard at my hip.

"So, about that dinner..."

She scoffs, smashing the blade down into the pumpkin. "Yeah, right."

"We could do a movie instead."

The lock disengages and the door opens.

Her whole body floods with relief, then she looks back at me. "I never plan to see you again. Ever."

"I see."

She nods, then pushes the door open.

"And if I told you that wasn't an option, you..."

"Would tell you to fuck off. You don't have me locked in a room with you anymore. We're back in the real world, and you can't force me to do anything with you ever again."

Oh, how adorably wrong she is.

I smile faintly and let her have her moment, though.

She'll figure out the truth soon enough.

CHAPTER 6
SOPHIE

I cannot get out of that godforsaken mansion fast enough.

Silvan Koch is fucking crazy.

I'm never going back there.

I'm never going *anywhere* ever again.

I was right and Mom was wrong; going places is terrible.

Hermit life is the life for me.

At least at home, I'm safe.

Safe from Silvan's wild eyes, safe from his dangerous touch.

Safe from the things he wants to do to me.

I try not to think about it as I return home to a dark house and lock the doors.

It's impossible.

When I strip off my clothes and take a quick, scalding hot shower, it's like I can still feel his depraved kisses peppering my skin. The imprint of his lips might as well be burned into my flesh, inked there like a tattoo for all the world to see.

I scrub harder but only succeed in agitating my skin, not ridding myself of the feeling of being touched by him.

Touched *everywhere*.

The man had no shame whatsoever.

I tell myself it doesn't matter, that I'll never see that creep again.

I pull on a pair of plaid pajama pants and a T-shirt and curl up in my old bed.

I tell myself I'm not dirty and I'm not marked, and I try to believe that come tomorrow, Silvan Koch will be so insignificant to my life, I'll practically forget him.

I don't know him, anyway.

He's a stranger I spent a scary evening in an escape room with, nothing more.

I'll never see him again, and after tonight, I'll never think about him again, either.

He may have stolen access to my body, but he doesn't deserve to live in my mind.

Settling into bed, I pull the warm down comforter around my body, snuggling up beneath it to stave off the cold.

I can't shake the memories, though.

He was inside me.

Inside me.

I may have managed to stop him before he went deeper, but he still invaded my body in a way I've never let anyone before.

And then the bastard asked me to dinner.

I might think it was a cruel joke coming from anyone else, but there was something shockingly genuine about his request, as if he actually wanted to hang out with me after what he'd done.

What a psycho.

Shaking my head to clear it, I try to push Silvan far from my mind so I can get some sleep.

I wake up in the middle of the night, my heart pounding in my chest.

I'm sweating, and the sheets are bunched up around me.

In my dream, I was trapped in that room with him again, and even though I'm awake now and alone in my bedroom, the panic won't leave me.

It feels like he's here with me right now.

I close my eyes and breathe, trying to slow my heart down, but it's no use.

I don't feel safe like someone who managed to escape.

I still feel like I'm in his clutches.

Helpless anger wells up inside me. I refuse to be so fragile that some stranger at a party can make me feel like this.

It doesn't matter, I tell myself.

He doesn't matter.

I desperately want that to be true, but no matter how thorough I was with my toothbrush, I can still taste him in my mouth. No matter how roughly I scrubbed at my hair and skin in the shower, I can still feel his firm grip on the back of my head, his warm hands cupping my breasts.

Dammit.

I all but throw my comforter aside and get out of bed.

I head to the kitchen for a glass of water, turning on every light as I go and flinching at the brightness of the first one. If Mom were awake, she would yell at me for wasting electricity, but I can't stand to walk around in the dark right now.

It's absurd, but I feel like he's still lurking, watching me like he was earlier at the party.

I sit at the small kitchen table with my glass of water. My gaze drifts to the windows. It's so dark outside, I can't see anything. Rationally, I know there's nothing out there to see, but a chill travels down my spine, anyway.

I'm being silly. I'm safe here, in my house.

No one can get in.

No one is out there *wanting* to get in.

Just to be safe, though, I get up and double check the locks on the front door.

Feeling marginally safer, I go back to the kitchen table and grab my water. I don't want to be out here anymore. I feel exposed out here, even though I know I'm not.

I shut off all the lights on my way back, then I close my bedroom door and cross the room in the dark, carefully setting my water down on the end table.

The glass doesn't go right down. There's something under it, but it's dark, so I can't see.

I touch my phone on the nightstand to light up the area and gasp when I see the severed button from my shorts beneath the glass.

Where did that come from?

A fresh wave of terror floods my body, but I try to keep it at bay.

I tell myself I must have grabbed it, maybe I mindlessly shoved it in my pocket, but I know it's not true.

I couldn't find that button.

I would have brought it home to see if Mom could sew it back on my shorts so I can still wear them come summer, but I wasn't about to spend more time on that bed trying to find the severed button.

My heart slams in my chest because there's only one other person who could have put it there.

"Hello?" I say, hating how my voice shakes as it breaks the dead silence.

The room is dark. I sense no movement.

No one answers.

My chest constricts.

I tell myself I should walk over and turn on the light to make sure the room is empty, but I'm too damn afraid of what I'll find.

I swallow, listening again for movement. The sounds of someone breathing. Surely, I would be able to sense a person in this room with me.

I'm too afraid to listen for long, though.

As if ignoring the monster can make it disappear, I climb back into my bed like a kid after a terrifying nightmare. I pull the blankets around myself protectively and squeeze my eyes shut.

Please don't be in my room.

I feel safer curled up in bed under my blankets, but I have no idea if I really am.

If he's in my room, I can guess why he's here.

At best, to finish what he started in the escape room.

At worst, to silence me permanently.

Please, please don't be in my room.

I wait for the monster to emerge. For the bed to dip with his weight as he climbs on it with me, or the door to creak as it opens and a sliver of light spills in.

But nothing happens.

The air around me doesn't seem to move.

No monster joins me on the bed.

My heart beats more regularly and my eyelids grow heavy.

I'm safe in my bed, I tell myself.

He can't get me here.

I wish it felt more like the truth.

I didn't feel like this after my run-in with Dylan. I felt sick and disgusted, of course, but I didn't feel his presence hanging around me like Silvan's fucking fur around my shoulders.

I didn't feel *haunted*.

Not like this, anyway.

Not by *him*.

It isn't what happened to me that's keeping me from sleep tonight, it's fear of the man who did it, it's a feeling that he won't go away as easily as Dylan did.

The thought passes through my mind that maybe I should go to the police.

I didn't with Dylan. It was hard to even be sure he'd done anything wrong that night as I left, unable to focus and with trembling hands. I knew how I felt, but I didn't know if maybe it was somehow my fault. If I couldn't even fully believe what had happened to me and I'd been there, why would complete strangers?

I shouldn't have gone there that night.

Rationally, I know I should be able to go anywhere I want with the expectation of safety, especially when I'm there with a friend. He certainly could rely on being safe with me.

I should have been physically stronger, fought him with more force so I wouldn't have been in such a vulnerable position.

Rationally, I know I shouldn't have to physically fight someone off to avoid something I don't want from happening. Not wanting it should have been enough.

But it was hard to see it all clearly in the moment after it first happened, when I was freshly traumatized, and my brain couldn't comprehend what my *friend* had done to me.

After all, don't most people feel a sense of denial when someone they like does something truly horrible? They don't want to believe it when they hear about it, and I didn't, either, after experiencing it firsthand.

I had the same initial impulse that all our friends had after it happened when they decided to believe him and vilify me.

The difference is, I wouldn't have done that to *them*.

I like to think if a male friend of mine started cagily generating the story that a female friend of ours had been *totally into it* when they were hooking up, but then she changed her story later, I would at least *talk to her* instead of automatically believing him.

After all, only one of us had a possible motive there. Only one of us needed to get out of trouble, and it sure wasn't me.

I hadn't done anything wrong.

It took me some time to accept that, but I finally got there.

It freed me of some of the burden I carried, freed me from him completely.

Sure, I still have symptoms.

I still can't stand to be touched, and my sense of trust in men is all but gone. The ability to feel safe with them is utterly obliterated...

I frown, thinking back to earlier this evening when, ironically, I felt safe with Silvan's strong arms wrapped around me.

He had just kissed me, and I hadn't wanted him to, but when I panicked, he didn't get turned off and leave because of my strange reaction. He pulled me into his chest and held me. He calmed me down and reassured me, and even if it was just so he could lure me into his own trap...

It worked.

Granted, I've never let a man *try* to calm me down when I've felt panicked since everything with Dylan. Since then, if my fears get triggered, I flee the scene and avoid the situation going forward.

Silvan didn't let me.

He made me stay through the swell of panic, and sure, I may have been lulled into a false sense of safety thinking him responding to my panic with comfort meant he wouldn't push me any further, but even if the safety was a lie, I felt it. It's the first time I've felt safe in a man's arms... well, ever.

That's a jolting realization.

Even though I know it's a little crazy because I'm definitely alone in this room, I say softly as if he can hear me, "I felt safe with you when you held me. I've never felt that before. It was nice."

I'd never tell him that, anyway, but I feel a little lighter saying it out loud in my own company.

Knowing I felt safe with him even when I wasn't opens up possibilities I had quietly given up on.

Maybe someday, when I meet the right man, I'll be able to feel safe with him.

CHAPTER 7
SOPHIE

Dark dreams keep me firmly in their clutches all night long. After a fitful night's sleep, I wake up with a massive headache and eyes that feel achy behind the lids from lack of proper rest.

Rather than stay in bed like I'm tempted to, I get right up.

I know if I linger in bed, memories of last night will catch up to me.

Mom's in the kitchen with a cup of coffee. "Good morning, sleepyhead."

Her words cause me to frown mildly. I was in such a hurry to get out here, I didn't grab my phone when I left my room, so I can't check it for the time. My gaze flickers to the small black microwave on the counter. It reads 10:13.

That can't be right. I left the party early, so I didn't get to bed super late. I shouldn't be so exhausted if I got that much sleep.

Retrieving a mug from the cupboard, I pour myself a cup of coffee. I'm not a fan of the taste, so I leave plenty of room for the flavored creamer to top it off and make it more palatable.

"Did you have fun at the Halloween party last night?"

My stomach bottoms out at her conversational question.

The headache seems to intensify, so I grab a second cup to get myself a glass of water. I swallow a couple ibuprofen and gulp down the water hoping at least it'll cut through the headache.

Mom's an early riser, so she's always early to bed, too.

"Not really," I murmur without offering any details.

I know she'll likely ask, though.

"No? Did you mingle and try to talk to the other kids?"

Sighing, I stir my coffee to mix in the creamer. "I don't want to talk about the party, Mom."

"I just want to know if you gave it an honest try to have a good time, or if you went with the mindset you'd hate it and hid in some corner the whole time. If you don't give things a chance, then you'll end up missing out on a lot of experiences, honey. You can't be so close-minded."

"I am not close-minded," I snap, looking at her over my shoulder. "Maybe I'm just not as social as you, have you ever thought of that? Just because you're outgoing and you enjoy meeting people and going to parties doesn't mean that I have to. We're different people, and I shouldn't have to keep doing things I hate doing to please everyone else."

My heart hammers in my chest and my stomach feels rocky. I don't like snapping at my mom, but I'm so sick of being pushed into things I'm not ready for.

"I just don't want you to waste your college years like you did the high school ones, honey. You had friends, you did enjoy going out. You shouldn't stop doing those things just because you had a falling out with those guys. Some people aren't meant to stick around in our lives, but if you keep nursing your heartache over the ones it didn't work out with, you'll miss out on moving on with your life and meeting new people, some of whom just might stick around."

I shake my head, annoyed, but I know it's not fair. Mom doesn't know what happened that led to that "falling out." I never told her. Never told anyone until Silvan asked about it last night.

It doesn't matter. What matters is that Mom is so relentless that in the end, I always end up trying to prove myself to her.

But I'm done.

After last night, there's no way I'm putting myself in another situation like that just for it to turn out the same way again.

"You know I just want you to be happy, honey," Mom says softly, ratcheting up the guilt roiling in my stomach.

I am happy.

My lips part to let out the lie, but I shut my mouth before a sound escapes.

Maybe I'm not the happiest right now, but I will be, someday.

I want to make her feel better, so even though I'm hesitant to talk about the party and especially Silvan, I turn around to face her as I wait for my coffee to cool enough to sip it. "There was one thing that was kind of cool, I guess."

Mom perks right up. "Yeah?"

I nod. "The guy who threw the party lives in this big mansion and has a trust fund, so I imagine his family is stupid rich."

"Sure."

"So he had a whole escape room built inside his house for party guests to go through."

"No way," she says, her eyes sparkling with pleasure. "Well, that sounds like fun."

I nod, even though it makes my stomach ache. "He was dressed up as a Viking. You know the guy in *The Last Kingdom*?"

"Uh, yeah. He was my phone wallpaper for a solid month last year when I went through that dry spell."

I crack a smile and nod. "Well, he was dressed up kinda like him."

"Nice. He must be a fan. We still have to watch the last season. You should see if he wants to come over and he could watch it with us!"

My smile falls. "Oh. No. Definitely not."

Mom glances around our small house, then says, "I suppose you're right. If he lives in a mansion, he probably wouldn't be impressed with our digs."

"That's not why," I assure her quickly, shaking my head. "Anyway, the escape room was Viking themed, too. That was pretty neat."

"What's his name?"

I don't want to tell her, but I guess that would be weird. "Silvan."

"He's the one who threw the party?"

I nod wordlessly.

"Did he seem nice?"

"No," I answer honestly.

Mom laughs at the deadpan way I say it, probably thinking I'm joking. "Rich guys are weird."

"He was definitely weird." Bringing my mug to my lips, I test the temperature, then take a careful sip. "Anyway, I did give the party a chance, but I don't think I'll have much time to do stuff like that this year, anyway. The workload for my classes is a lot, and I want to get a job."

"You should at least make time for a couple of friends."

"We'll see," I say, just trying to placate her.

Come evening, I'm so deep in my books that I don't even notice the doorbell ringing. I know Mom's home from grocery shopping, so I know she'll answer it.

I figure it's for her, anyway. The door is always for her. It's probably some guy here to pick her up for a date she forgot to tell me about.

I usually enjoy having the house to myself for the evening, but tonight, I don't relish the thought of being home alone. The sun will set soon, and once it's gone, I might start imagining monsters in the dark again.

The human kind.

Those are the only ones I'm afraid of.

"Sophie," Mom calls out.

"Yeah?" I call back.

"It's for you."

What's for me?

I almost ask, but then I realize she obviously means the door.

What?

That's no less confusing. I don't have a single friend in this town, and if I did, they'd be text-only friends, people I see in class or around campus, definitely *not* people who would show up unannounced at my mom's house.

A sick feeling hits my gut, but the thought is too depraved. There's no way.

Slowly, I slide my page of notes between the pages of my textbook and close it so I don't lose my place.

He's not here, I tell myself.

There's no way he's here. How would he even know where I live? Where would he get the audacity to show up on my doorstep after last night?

I know it's not him. I know it can't be.

I still half expect to see him when I round the corner and see the front door cracked open, Mom standing there chatting with whomever is on the other side.

I try to gauge who it could be by her posture and smile, but Mom is so friendly, just because she's visiting with them doesn't mean she knows them. She gets overly chatty with the pizza delivery guy and I have to drag her away before our food gets cold.

My heart pounds as I near the door.

Despite all logic, I expect to see the Viking who has haunted my thoughts since last night. He asked me to dinner or a movie after our encounter in the escape room, so honestly, would showing up at my house be such a stretch?

I'm almost anticipating seeing his roguish smirk when I get to the door, so when I finally get there and pull it open, I feel Mom's smile like the sun on my face, but my blood runs cold.

"Surprise!" Mom says cheerfully.

Oh, I'm surprised, all right.

I was prepared for a twisted Viking when I opened this door, but I was not prepared for a ghost.

CHAPTER 8
SOPHIE

DYLAN PRESCOTT STANDS ON THE FRONT PORCH NEXT to our old friend Elle, her dark hair pulled up in a ponytail and a tentative smile on her face.

On one hand, he looks exactly the same as the last time I saw him. His curly, dark hair is a little disheveled, but there's a natural charm to that, and his brown eyes are just as warm and inviting as they always were. He has this way of looking at someone and instantly putting them at ease.

Only it doesn't work on me anymore.

It's a deception, one I'm all too aware of at this point.

Since I'm not speaking, Mom laughs a little uneasily. "Well, you two come in."

"No." I find my voice just as everyone is about to move. I can't believe they have the audacity to try to come into my house.

A confused frown flickers across Mom's face.

Without another word or moment's hesitation, I slam the door in their faces and turn the lock.

Beside me, Mom gasps in horror. "Sophie, what are you doing? That was so rude!"

My blood seems to be running hot and cold at the same time, sending chills dancing up my spine but making my skin hot as I turn to look at her. "You knew they were coming? You invited them here without checking with me?"

Her eyes are wide with shock. "They were your friends! After our talk this morning, I was thinking about how you still miss them and your heart's still sore over that stupid fight last year, so I poked around on social media, just curious, wondering what they were up to. Well, wouldn't you know, Dylan and Elle are in the city for a concert this weekend. I guess they're dating now. I always knew she had a thing for him."

The ringing in my ears is almost too loud to absorb the words she's saying. Horrors from last year flood back. I remember him holding me down, forcing my pants down as I fought to get away.

Fought.

I did more than say no, I fucking tried like hell to get away from him when it became clear he knew I didn't want to, he just didn't care.

"I cannot believe you did that."

"I thought maybe it would be nice for you guys to catch up. If you patch things up with them, honey, maybe it will help you to move on—"

"Stop saying that!"

Too frustrated to stand here and keep talking to her about this, I turn on my heel and go back to my bedroom. I grab my school bag and start shoving in my books.

There's laundry in the dryer I did here since I don't have a washer or dryer in my dorm room, but I don't take the time to get it out. I'll have to come back for it when I'm calmer.

"Where are you going?" Mom asks as I come flying back down the hall.

"Back to school."

"Sophie, I wasn't trying to upset you. I thought—"

"Doesn't matter. I have to get back, anyway. I'll see you next weekend."

"Sophie, come on."

I step into my shoes and fling open the door. My heart stalls when I see Dylan and Elle are just getting to their car, but they've seen me now, so there's no way I'm going back inside and waiting for them to leave.

Tipping my chin up and hoisting my bag over my shoulder, I pull the front door shut behind me and make my way down the porch steps.

Dylan is on the passenger side about to get in and Elle is driving him, of course. Such a dutiful chauffeur.

Anger surges up inside me. Since he's on the other side and Elle is closest to me, as I walk by her, I say, "Your boyfriend's an attempted rapist, just so you know."

Her jaw drops open, and Dylan decides to speak up. "Wow, I see you're still smarting from that rejection, huh, Bradwell?"

Rejection? I almost laugh. "Is that the story you're telling? Coward."

"At least I'm not a bitter cunt who makes up lies about guys who didn't like her."

His words cut straight to my bone. That this is the narrative he's selling... I can't even stomach it.

"That's a really serious accusation, Sophie," Elle calls after me. "Regretting hooking up with someone is not the same as being raped, and it's really messed up that you would lie about something like that when there are real victims out there."

The muscles in my legs turn to jelly. I've never enjoyed confrontation to begin with, but this is so fucking unjust, I feel like hurling. "You deserve each other," I tell her.

"And you deserve to be lonely and friendless for telling such hateful lies," she yells back.

Angry tears threaten to fall, but I don't let them. I would die before giving either one of them the satisfaction.

I throw my bag in the passenger seat and slam the door closed. My hands are shaking so badly, I can hardly get my seatbelt fastened.

It can't be safe driving back to school in this headspace. When I get there, I find I can't even remember half the drive.

Just like last night.

I'm going to get in a car crash and die if I keep letting all these people fuck with me.

It's a dreary day to match my mood. The sky is gray and cloudy. Looks like it might storm.

I hope it does. A thunderstorm would be nice. I only wish I had my own quiet bedroom to enjoy it in.

I was right about the storm. By the time I get my car parked and I'm heading into my building, a few raindrops hit my exposed arm.

By the time I get the apartment unlocked and myself inside, rain pelts the windows.

One of my roommates is on the couch eating a bowl of cereal. Another is in the kitchen fixing herself a snack.

"Hey," Sabrina says cheerfully. "Boy, you just made it in time. Rumi just went out to get an iced coffee. Her ass is going to get soaked."

I'm starving. Now that the nausea has subsided and I see Sabrina munching on cinnamon toast, I'm realizing I was supposed to have dinner with Mom, but then I stormed out.

Seeing me eyeing her snack, Sabrina holds up her toast. "Want some?"

I shake my head. "I'm okay, thanks. Just realizing I should have gone grocery shopping before I came back."

"Too late now," Kendra says, nodding at the window.

That's too bad. I like to cook when I'm upset. Provides a nice distraction, and I could sure go for some comfort food right now. Maybe a nice flaky chicken pot pie.

Dammit.

My tummy rumbles but I shake my head no. "I'm okay. I've got some homework to finish."

I head to the bedroom, but when I get there and unload my books at our shared desk, I can still hear them talking in the other room. The walls are thin, the room is shared. This is why I wanted to do my homework at Mom's house.

All my safe spaces seem to be disappearing.

Sighing, I take out my headphone case, but when I turn my noise-cancelling headphones on, the battery is dead. They're so old and "well-loved," the damn things don't hold a charge anymore.

Deflated, I plug them in to charge, but it will take a while, and I'll never be able to concentrate when I can hear Rumi talking about the barista she wants to bang like they're standing in the same room with me.

Since I know I won't be able to study and I feel icky after the day I've had, I abandon my things in the bedroom and go to take a scalding hot shower.

It doesn't take a lot to make me feel frazzled these days, but today is really taking the cake.

By the time I get out of the shower, the rain has stopped. I'm a little bummed, but I towel dry my hair and change into a baggy T-shirt and a pair of sweats.

I'm still emotionally exhausted but feeling a bit better as I step out into the hall.

"Um, Soph, there's some guy here for you."

You have got to be kidding me.

"No. No more guys today. I'm closed for business."

"He's like... someone's dad or something," Sabrina says. "I don't know, he's old."

A frown of confusion flickers across my face. That throws me off, so I follow her to the front door to see who it is.

A man in a neat black suit stands just outside the door looking dutiful. I get the impression he wouldn't come in even if we invited him.

"Can I help you with something?" I ask him.

"Ah, yes. Are you Miss Sophie Bradwell?"

I nod.

"Perfect." He hands me a garment bag. "This is for you. Mr. Koch requests that you change into it so that I might drive you to dinner."

"Mr. Koch?" Sabrina questions.

Eavesdropping, Rumi asks, *"Silvan Koch?"*

Sighing, I hold the dress bag back out. "I'm sorry to have wasted your time, but I told him last night I don't want to go to dinner with him, and my answer hasn't changed."

My rumbling stomach chooses now to stage its protest, growling so loud that everyone in the room must hear it.

How embarrassing.

Ignoring the rising heat in my cheeks, I offer the gentleman a polite smile and go to close the door.

He puts out a hand to stop it. "I'm sorry, I explained that poorly. Mr. Koch isn't in the car. I'm here to take *you* to dinner. Just you."

I blink, my arm going slack and the dress bag drooping to touch the floor. "What?"

"He understands you didn't want to dine with him this evening, but he wants to buy you dinner, anyway."

"What?" Rumi demands, slamming her iced coffee down on the counter. "Sophie gets a sugar daddy who doesn't want sugar *and* it's Silvan Koch? What kind of fairytale did you fall out of?"

If only she knew.

I still feel obligated to say no just because it's coming from Silvan, but... I mean... it's not dinner with Silvan. It's just dinner alone.

"Then what's with the dress bag?" I ask, holding it up again. "Why buy me a dress if he won't even see me in it?"

"It's a comfortable style," the man assures me. "Not for his viewing pleasure, he just thought he would send you something suitable to wear in case you didn't have anything. You'll be dining alone, and then I'll bring you back here when you're finished. You won't see Silvan this evening," he specifies, since that's clearly a concern for me.

That's a little harder to say no to.

I'm famished, and I suppose he *does* owe me dinner.

Well played, Silvan.

Not that he gets anything out of it, so I don't really understand the gesture.

"If she's still saying no, I'll go," Rumi volunteers. "I'll wear whatever he wants me to wear, *and* you can take me to him. *I'm* not stupid."

Sliding her a sideways look, I murmur, "Thanks, Rumi."

"Anytime," she says cheerfully.

Kendra pipes in from the couch. "Mm-hmm. I knew something happened between you two last night, sneaking up to the escape room before the rest of us were allowed to go."

"There was an escape room?" Sabrina bemoans. "I love escape rooms."

Kendra nods. "He had it built just for the party in case anyone was wondering exactly how rich his family is."

Rumi stayed home to study like I should have, and Sabrina had to work, so even though Kendra invited all of us to the party when she got the invite, only I went.

Scrutinizing the driver to make sure it doesn't seem like a trick, I ask, "And you're positive Silvan won't be there if I go with you?"

"He wanted me to assure you that you wouldn't have to see him at all this evening. He just wants to make sure you're fed."

"Oh my god, he's *so* sweet," Rumi says, clutching her chest.

Sweet, my ass.

But the driver seems to be genuine, so without further interrogation, I head to the bedroom to change into whatever Silvan sent from me.

Unless I hate it, of course. Then I will change into something of my own.

I still think it's a little odd that he sent me a dress if he doesn't plan to see me in it. When I unzip the garment bag, I find a soft cashmere wrap dress inside. It feels so nice when I run my fingers across the soft fabric. I'm definitely wearing this.

I grab my cosmetic bag and make quick work of brushing on some mascara and a coat of lip gloss, then I look myself over in the mirror on the closet door. The dress is very comfortable, but the soft white fabric clings to my curves and—I have to admit—looks really good on me.

I grab a little cream-colored purse from my

corner of the closet and slip on a pair of nude-tone flats.

My coat is definitely not appropriately classy to match the cashmere dress he sent over, but it's the only one I have, so I pull it on, anyway.

My roommates play up their jealousy as I leave —well, all but Kendra who watches wordlessly like she has something to say, but she never says it.

Once the door is closed behind me, I ask the man in the chauffeur's get up, "So, what's your name?"

"You can call me Hugh."

"It's nice to meet you, Hugh. I'm Sophie."

He cracks a smile beneath his mustache. "Yes, I know."

"Right."

Despite his casually friendly demeanor, Hugh's body is stiff as he stands in front of the elevator watching the numbers tick by. The doors open and he gestures for me to step into the empty elevator first.

Once we're inside, he presses the button to close the doors.

I peek over at him. "So, you work for Silvan?"

"His family, yes."

A moment later, the elevator doors open, and we step out into the quiet of the lobby. He guides me to the front door and opens it for me so I can step out onto the sidewalk.

I'm stunned when I see a long, black limousine is parked in front of the building. Even though rationally I know it must be what he's driving, I'm still floored when he approaches it and opens the back door for me.

My gaze flickers to his face, my jaw practically on the floor. "This is just for me?"

He smiles faintly. "He wanted you to be comfortable."

"Wow," I say softly as I step toward the car.

I've never been in a limousine before. When I was in fifth grade, my school had a fundraiser and the four kids who sold the most got to ride in a limo with one of their parents. It was near Mother's Day, and I so desperately wanted to win it so I could take Mom. I spent every day after school going door-to-door with my fundraising flyer and my biggest smile. I made it into that top four, and I was so excited.

Then, when the day came for our limo ride, I had the flu so we couldn't go.

I duck my head and climb inside, pulling my dress in behind me and scooting over a bit so I'm not right by the door.

It's so spacious with soft leather upholstery and a small bar running along the side the car door is on. A flat-screen TV is mounted above the bar and the driver already has a glass of champagne waiting for me.

Ducking down, Hugh tells me, "I've poured the first glass for you, but help yourself if you'd like more. The bottle is chilling right down there."

I think about telling him I'm not old enough to drink, but I've never had champagne before, and I suppose one glass couldn't hurt. "Thank you," I say instead.

Hugh closes the door and walks around to the driver's side. As soon as he gets in, he looks back and asks, "Would you like the privacy divider up, Miss Bradwell?"

I shake my head with a faint smile. "That's all right. Thank you, though."

With a perfunctory nod, he buckles in and starts up the car.

While I sip my champagne, I sit back and gaze at the passing city as Hugh drives me to the restaurant. I don't know where it is, so I don't know how long it will take to get there. I suppose I should have asked more questions.

Just to be safe, I open my purse to grab my phone so I can text Sabrina my location just in case I go missing.

When I light up the screen, I see I have a new text message from a number my phone doesn't recognize.

The message reads, "So, how was your day?"

A frown flickers across my brow as I text back, "Who is this?"

"Your favorite Viking."

My eyebrows rise. "Alexander Dreymon? How did you get my number, and does your girlfriend know about this?"

"Very funny," he texts back.

I laugh because I somehow doubt he's amused. "How did you get my number?"

"I have my ways," he answers. "You didn't answer my question."

I have to glance up at his first message to remember what it was. "My day has been trash. Yours?"

"Not bad," his next text reads. "Would've been better if I were joining you for dinner."

His comment causes my guards to rise. "I have it on good authority you won't be. That's the only reason I got in the car."

"That's correct," he assures me. "You won't be seeing me this evening."

The surge of anxiety that spiked a moment ago goes back down. Even though it's absurd, I find myself typing back, "thank you," because I know he could have easily been lying to set me up. Evidently, Silvan has no problem forcing his will on others, and he made his desires clear enough last night about wanting to have dinner with me.

I know there were other things he wanted from me, too.

The memory surfaces of when he practically had it. His cock was inside me... just the tip, but all he had to do was push past that fragile barrier...

My skin is flushed from thinking about last night.

Clearing my throat, I try to shake off the memory as I look back down at the phone.

His last text reads, "You're welcome."

As if he's actually granting me a privilege.

I suppose he is.

"Thank you for dinner," I type back, my manners getting the best of me. "It was loud at my apartment, and there wasn't much to eat there, anyway."

"Anytime," he says. "Though, typically, you'll have to accept me as part of the deal," he adds with a winky emoji.

I never plan to accept an invitation from him again, but there's no point telling him that now.

"Where's Hugh taking me?"

"A restaurant my family has owned since the roaring twenties," he answers.

"Wow, that's a long time. So, you come from a restauranteur family?"

"No. The restaurant was more of a meeting place than an enterprise in and of itself. Opened up at the start of prohibition. My great-grandfather had business dealings with, uh... questionable friends, so they needed somewhere more private to meet and entertain, but not as private as our home. The restaurant has a cellar underneath where they used to meet. That's where we eat when we go there. It's where you'll be eating tonight."

I like the idea of privacy, but a private cellar makes me a bit nervous. Not sure about the place's history of shady dealings, either. "Is it actually the restaurant? Will any other people be there? You're not trying to kidnap me, are you? If I end up chained to some wall in a cellar beneath a restaurant, I am going to be pissed."

"If I wanted to kidnap you, I'd probably be a little more discreet than this," he assures me. "After all, I'd expect to get away with it."

Ugh. I roll my eyes in disgust and text back, "You're terrible."

"But not stupid, so you can rest assured, no one's trying to kidnap you this evening."

I like how he had to add this evening, as if it might be on the menu later.

"Almost there, Miss Bradwell," Hugh calls back.

"Thank you, Hugh." I look back down at my phone. "Well, I should probably go. Hugh said we're almost to the restaurant."

"All right," he answers. "Enjoy your meal."

CHAPTER 9
SILVAN

She orders a charcuterie board to start, then a grilled baby pear salad with roasted pecans. For her main course, she gets chicken—a nice safe choice, like most of the choices she makes.

I am not a safe choice, so that might present a bit of a problem.

Nothing I can't get past, of course. Just a small obstacle. Every relationship has them.

I look forward to getting past it.

I come from a long line of very certain men who tend to know the moment they get a taste of what they desire that they must have it forever, no matter the cost.

This very restaurant was the beginning of that cycle.

While it was my great-grandfather whose name was listed as the proprietor of this restaurant, it was my great-grandmother who ran it. It was a labor of love. She was adventurous and intelligent and different, the kind of woman plenty of men fell in love with. She was destined for greatness.

But then she met him.

She was only 19 when they met. It was a whirl-wind romance that knocked the sense right out of her. Within three months, he'd impregnated her, but she wasn't worried.

They loved each other madly, and though he couldn't marry her right then, he promised he would once he'd made his mark in the business world. The "friends" he met with at the restaurant got him a lucrative opportunity to make money in the Soviet Union.

She didn't want to go with him. He was only in Boston for school, but she'd grown up here, had family here. Plus, she had some concerns about the kinds of people he was associating with in his efforts to amass himself a fortune. Moral reservations about the work he was doing and who he was doing it for.

She stayed behind with their son, James, and ran the restaurant.

He went off to see the world and make his money.

When he finally came back, he brought his new wife with him.

Mary was by all accounts the perfect woman—educated, athletic, creative, and gentle. She came from a wealthy, prominent family and didn't pay any mind to my great-grandfather dirtying his hands; she simply used his fortune to bolster the arts and culture scene, donating blood money to fundraisers and collecting humanitarian awards for her efforts.

According to him, it was love at first sight. That's why he married his wealthy young bride only a month after they met.

It's why it was so easy for him to forsake the love of my grandmother who was still running this restaurant, raising their child, waiting for the day he would come home to her, and they would be a family again.

It may be true that he loved my great-grandmother the way she swears he did, and it may be true that he fell in love with Mary as soon as he met her and realized all she had to offer him.

But it wasn't any woman my great-grandfather wanted most.

It was his money.

Because of his greed and ruthlessness, money's no concern for me. It wasn't an issue for my father, or his father before him. Though my great-grandfather married and started a family with someone else, he made sure to provide financial support to my great-grandmother and his firstborn son. After all, money was what really mattered, wasn't it?

My grandfather James always felt he had something to prove to his estranged father. He was thirteen when his father's first *legitimate* heir was born. At that tender age, he started helping his mom out with the books at the restaurant so his father would see them succeeding when he made his way to Boston and stopped in for a sporadic visit. Turned out, James Koch had a head for business.

They say he "had a way with the ladies," too.

When their father's eldest *acknowledged* son started attending Harvard, Grandpa James was a 35-year-old businessman in Boston. As much success as he'd had, there was still something missing. He still felt he had something to prove.

With his father's other son in Boston, he saw his opportunity and began to stalk his prey.

In watching his brother, he discovered the younger man had fallen hard and fast for a gentle young woman named Katherine. She worked at a bookshop, and he was a collector of rare books.

From afar, my grandfather watched his brother's wholesome courtship with Katherine. He even arranged a meeting between him and his brother (his father's second family knew nothing of the first, so he pretended to be a stranger) at a bar one night where the younger brother professed his excitement—he'd bought Katherine a ring and was just waiting for the right moment to ask her.

Grandpa James was suitably convinced that what his brother wanted most in the world was Katherine.

And then, because my grandfather was an asshole, he swept in and seduced her. She didn't love him, didn't really even want him, but he was older and more experienced than she was, so he was skilled enough to confuse and trick her. All he needed was a brief opening to strike, and when he got it, he did.

Katherine was mesmerized by James, completely out of her depths with him. He was cunning and got her pregnant quickly so that she would marry him instead of his brother.

She did, and in doing so, shattered her lover's heart.

Grandpa James got a bouncing baby boy, a brand-new bride, and the thing *he* wanted most of all.

Revenge.

As a result, *my* father grew up with parents who didn't love each other. The generational trauma of abandonment had finally been resolved, but his mother was a lonely woman who could hardly endure my grandfather's cruelty. He never stopped treating her like a tool he could wield to wound his brother, so he spent their entire marriage hurting *her*.

It was a relief when he died of heart failure at the age of 83. She was 66, young enough to perhaps find one last love to end her life with, but she never did.

Her first love had been so hurt by losing her to my grandpa, he never married or had children of his own.

Family urged her to reach out to him after my grandfather's death hoping for a reunion that might heal both their wounded hearts, but she was too ashamed, so she never did.

After watching his parents' miserable marriage, when my father met my warm and loving mother, he knew immediately he had to lock her down. Warmth was the one luxury he never had access to from his cold, wealthy father or his lonely, destroyed mother.

My mother filled that empty well deep inside him until it overflowed, and for that, he loved her immensely.

The problem was, in his gratitude and appreciation of my mother, he let her have more freedoms than I think he should have. My mother *is* a warm and loving woman, but her love and warmth isn't just for him.

Over the years, I've watched him ignore countless affairs as my mother's *friends* have become more than that.

She's not a cruel woman, just weak and unable to control her own whimsical desires.

My father isn't the sort of man you'd ever imagine suffering such an insult without punishing everyone involved and ensuring it never happened again, but he's weak when it comes to her.

Over the years, I've watched him love her, and I've watched her hurt him. She's always immensely sorry for the pain she's caused when her affairs crash and burn, and his arms are always open for her to run right back into.

I understand my father's appetite for warmth, but not his tolerance of her misbehavior.

I can understand loving someone with little self-control, but perhaps I have a streak of my grandfather in me, because if I were him, I'd have made damn sure she could never run off again after the first time.

For me, there will be no first time.

Once I have my sights set on a woman I'm actually serious about, she *is* effectively mine, whether she has agreed to it or not.

Tonight, Sophie won't even endure my presence at her dinner table, but if another man's gaze swept over her lovely tits, if they so much as shared a smile of mutual interest, I'd have his heart in a fucking box before night's end.

Sophie is mine, apparently.

Because that's what I want, and the men in my family *always* get what they want—whether we deserve it is frankly irrelevant.

CHAPTER 10
SOPHIE

Sighing with contentment, I rub my belly and lean back in the leather-upholstered booth.

I just ate way too much food.

It was so delicious, and since I knew Silvan was paying, I even took the liberty of ordering a second dinner so I would have leftovers for the next couple of days.

Ha, take that, rich boy.

I know he probably won't bat an eye at the bill, but it still makes me feel better to think I'm getting one over on him.

"Thank you," I say to the server as they hand me a to-go box with my second dinner inside. It's still warm, and I'm still feeling the effects from the champagne I consumed in the car on the way over, so *I'm* feeling rather warm, too. Pleasantly so. I pull on my coat and make my way out of the empty cellar dining area.

Even though it hasn't been a true speakeasy for a long time, the area looks untouched. If handsome men in pinstriped suits and hats came strolling in with beautiful women wearing flapper dresses and feathered headbands, I wouldn't be surprised.

It reminds me of when I saw Silvan and thought he could be a time-traveling Viking.

Clearly, there's something about this family. It's like they can freeze time wherever they fit best and preserve it forever.

Then again, as I pass the gleaming mahogany bar, I know it's no coincidence or gift of fate that the place is so well-cared for after so long. Effort is put into stopping time, that's why it looks like this.

Effort.

Silvan certainly put in effort for me tonight. The whole time I was eating, I kept waiting for him to pop up. It was like last night in my bedroom. I could feel his presence even though I couldn't see him.

I guess I was wrong about him being there both times.

He didn't assault me in my bed last night, and he didn't join me for dinner this evening.

It seems he truly just wanted to make sure I was fed, and sure, it's probably the champagne softening my brain so much that this thought can even burrow into it, but it's surprisingly thoughtful.

I shake off the unwelcome thought.

It's not thoughtful, Sophie. It's probably strategic. He's trying to play the nice guy and get you to lower your guard so he can swoop in...

As I step out of the restaurant and onto the sidewalk, it occurs to me I don't know what to do. Hugh dropped me off at the door, but now that I'm finished eating, I have no way of summoning him. How will he know when I need him to come back?

The thought hardly has time to finish passing through my mind and I see the gleaming black limo turn the corner on the next street up. I feel strangely content as I wait for it.

I guess it's not all that strange. I just had a delicious meal I didn't have to pay for, I have dinner for tomorrow in a box, and now I don't even have to drive myself home; I get to ride back to my dorm in a limousine.

The vehicle glides up to the front of the restaurant and stops. On instinct, I step forward and reach for the door, but before I can, Hugh races around to open the door for me.

He looks mildly panicked that I thought I had to open the door for myself. God forbid I be so put out!

"I'll get that for you, Miss Bradwell."

"Thank you, Hugh. You're so nice."

He chuckles, then opens the door. "Did you have a pleasant dinner?"

"Oh, yes. Everything was delicious. And I do mean everything. I'm pretty sure I ordered half the menu."

I climb in, put my dinner box down on the bar, and sink into the soft black leather. It's a chilly night, but Hugh already has the car warmed up so I'm nice and toasty.

This is the life.

When Hugh gets back in the car, he puts the partition up.

A frown flickers across my brow and I sit up a little straighter. My guards have risen a bit since I told him before I didn't need the partition up, but maybe it was something he did out of habit. Maybe Silvan or whomever he usually drives likes to have the divider up.

Even though I'm sure it's nothing, my uncertainty makes me more aware of my surroundings. I glance at the bar where my champagne glass sits empty, the bottle still chilling in the bucket from earlier. I probably shouldn't have more, but it was so good, and I don't know when I'll have champagne again.

I pour myself one more glass, then sit back in my seat. As I take a sip, I become aware of a little white box sitting on the seat beside me and nearly choke.

Where did that come from?

It certainly wasn't there on the ride over to the restaurant.

Warily, I grab the box and pull it closer to me. A note on top reads, "Sophie," so I know it's for me.

My heart starts beating faster. I don't want to open it, but I suppose I should.

It looks like a bracelet box, but wider. When I take off the lid, I see a silk blindfold on a bed of black velvet and my heart stalls.

The note from the lid flutters down on my lap and I see that the back reads, "Put it on."

Uh-oh.

Suddenly, the word choices Hugh used come flooding back to my mind.

He specified over and over again that I wouldn't have to *see* Silvan tonight.

Now, I'm holding a blindfold.

Goddammit, he did trick me after all.

I don't want to put it on, but the thought of seeing Silvan makes me feel sick. Crushing the scrap of silk in my hand, I lean forward and knock on the divider.

The partition doesn't move.

Sinking back in my seat, a sense of foreboding washes over me. I'm tense as I lift the silk to my face just to see if putting it on triggers anything. It doesn't seem like it should since Silvan can't see me, but there's a sense of him seeing everything that I can't seem to shake.

Swallowing, I slide the band down over the back of my head and settle the mask on my face. The silk feels smooth and cool as it falls across my cheek.

Like a fool, I wait for some magical change, but nothing happens. I'm just sitting in the backseat of a strange man's limo wearing a blindfold like a lunatic, so after a moment, I rip it off and toss it on the seat beside me.

I look around for locks, but I don't see them. Maybe only the front partition where the driver is has the ability to lock and unlock doors in this thing.

That realization makes me feel more like a prisoner than a pampered guest.

I'm about to start banging on the divider again when I feel the limo slow and come to a stop. A stop alone wouldn't be suspicious. I can't see with the partition up, but maybe we're stopped at a traffic light.

Foreboding sweeps over me when I hear a sound that's suspiciously like Hugh's door opening. We've only been on the road for a minute or two, so we're definitely not to my destination.

Trying to ignore my racing heart, I tell myself it's nothing.

It feels like a lie, though. I think I'm in trouble.

In hindsight, I definitely shouldn't have gotten in this car. Hugh seemed so nice, I can't believe he's complicit in a thing like this.

Extinguishing the last of my thoughts that perhaps I'm overreacting, the limo door swings open, letting a gust of cool air into the cabin.

I stiffen at the sound of Silvan's voice. "Thanks, Hugh."

I'm angry at myself because I knew better.
Again.

When will I ever learn to listen to my damn instincts?

For a moment, I'm frozen as Silvan climbs into the car. He's tall and broad-shouldered so he cuts an imposing figure despite being dressed much more casually this evening. His hair is still long, his facial hair still trimmed in the style of Uhtred since he was just dressed up as him last night.

His mouth tugs up with pleasure at the sight of me. Or maybe at the sight of my palpable fear.

I like to pretend I look cool and collected, but I know I'm only fooling myself. My mind keeps generating memories of last night when I was alone with him in that Viking bedroom.

I stop the thoughts before they can get more intimate.

"I knew this was a trick."

Silvan shakes his head. "It wasn't a trick."

"You said you'd leave me alone tonight, that's the only reason I came."

He cocks a dark eyebrow. "Actually, I said you wouldn't have to *see* me tonight, and that was true. If you'd been obedient and put the blindfold on like I told you to, you wouldn't have had to see me."

"That is a very technical loophole."

He smirks. "Should've had your lawyer look it over before you agreed. Too late now."

"I don't have a lawyer," I mutter, even though I know he was joking. "Maybe I should get one," I say, hoping to sound at least mildly threatening.

"Sure," he says, leaning back in the seat and making himself comfortable. "You can use mine."

"That would definitely be a conflict of interest, and I'm fairly sure anyone working for you is outside of my budget."

"Damn. Guess you'll just have to rely on my honesty, then."

"That's like relying on a dinosaur not to eat me," I mutter.

His smile widens, his dark eyes glinting with amusement, then he playfully gnashes his teeth.

"See?" I shake my head. "Cannot be trusted."

"If the worst thing I do to you is eat you, then I don't know what you have to complain about."

My face heats as soon as I realize the *double entendre* in what we're talking about, and he laughs.

"Better watch that pretty mouth around me, farm girl," he says, still amused. "You might give me ideas, and I assure you, I have enough of my own."

"I am not interested in any of your ideas."

"And I'm not interested in your denial," he shoots back.

"That makes one of us disinterested in something and one of us a criminal," I inform him.

"Are you attracted to criminals?"

"No."

"Damn. Well, I'm only technically a criminal if I get caught, right?"

"You and your technicalities." He scoots closer on the seat, and I scoot away. "Besides," I say, trying to buy myself some time since there's only so much space to run away. "You don't seem to care whether or not I'm attracted to you. You seem intent on forcing yourself on me either way."

"I already know you're attracted to me," says the cocky bastard.

"Whatever you have to tell yourself."

He smiles as he reaches out and grabs my neck, causing my heart to hammer and my breath to catch. "I don't have to tell myself anything, pretty girl. I want you, so I'll have you. It's that simple. I won't lose a blink of sleep."

I should knee him right in the groin, but my body won't cooperate. With his hands on me, all my muscles have turned to jelly. A scream I can't release is stuck in my throat. I want to call out for help, but I don't even know if Hugh can hear me, and if he can, I have a hunch he still won't intervene.

"Silvan," I whisper, my voice softening from the surge of fear and vulnerability.

"Yes, baby?"

A shiver dances down my spine at the tenderness in his words despite the brutality of his hold on my throat. "Please don't hurt me."

"No," he murmurs reassuringly as he leans close and kisses the corner of my mouth. "I won't hurt you."

He's hurting me now by doing this to me, but he doesn't seem to get that.

Or maybe he does, and he just doesn't care.

Whatever the case, I have to placate him. He's bigger and stronger than me. Physically, I'm no match for him and I know he can overpower me easily. Dylan was shorter and far less muscular than Silvan, and he managed it.

For him it was at least a struggle to control me, but for Silvan, I'm not sure it would be.

His green eyes are dark with desire when I meet his gaze. Whatever he sees in mine pleases him, and he rewards me by caressing my face in a reassuring manner.

It feels nice, but it's a lie, so I'm not reassured.

Slowly, deliberately, he brings his face closer to mine and kisses me.

I try to pull away, but the only place to go is back against the seat. I panic when he pushes me back while he kisses me, slickly maneuvering himself between my thighs as he does.

My heart races because now I'm on my back on the seat of the car and he's on top of me, between my legs. "Silvan, please..."

"Sh," he murmurs soothingly, kissing my lips. "You're okay, baby."

"No." I push at his chest, panic gathering in mine, but he's immovable. "Please get off me. I just want to go home."

"We're on the way now," he tells me. His fingers slide through my hair as he cradles my skull to keep a firm hold on me. "I'm glad your hair's down tonight. I want to feel it in my hands while I'm fucking you."

That confirmation of his intentions sucks the breath from my lungs. My brain whites out for a moment, panic buzzing in my ears.

"Help," I shout loudly. "Hugh, please—"

Silvan's hand clamps down over my mouth, hard. He doesn't look worried, just annoyed as he leans down. "Now, now. If you're going to be a bad girl, I'm going to treat you like one."

My eyes widen in alarm. I'm not sure what that entails, but I can't imagine it's good.

"Should I do that, Sophie? Hm? I can silence this pretty little mouth with a gag. I can tie you up so you really can't move and take you somewhere no one will ever find you. I can keep you there for as long as I want to, do whatever I want to you, and you'll be entirely at my mercy. Entirely mine."

Fear shoots through me and intensifies more and more with every brush stroke of the horrifying picture he creates for me. I shake my head no, unable to summon a single word.

"No?" He cocks an eyebrow. "You don't want that?"

I shake my head no.

He runs a finger beneath my chin in a deceptively sweet caress. "Then I guess you'd better play nice and give me what I want. Maybe then I'll play nice, too. Not take as much as I intended to."

Hope sparks to life, easing some of the hopeless fear I was just getting lost in. I still have some control here. I can stop him from taking everything from me, I just... I have to negotiate. I have to buy my freedom.

I shouldn't have to, but right and wrong don't seem to matter to him.

I have to work with the reality I'm experiencing, not moral parameters he clearly doesn't give a fuck about.

I have an idea of what he likes because of last night.

Even though it kills me to give him anything more, I tell myself this is the last time. Obviously, I'll never go anywhere near him again, so I never have to do this again. I just have to escape him one last time with my virginity intact, and in order to accomplish that... I have to stall.

After all, we're on our way to my place. The drive isn't that long.

I bring my hand toward his face, but he grabs my wrist. I gasp, my heart pounding. "I was just going to touch you," I whisper.

He watches me carefully, but releases my wrist to see what I'll do.

I bring my hand closer and caress the side of his face the way he caressed mine. His posture is rigid, his guard still up. He expects me to fight him, and I could, but that will deplete my energy quickly. I won't be able to fight him off, and then he might decide to hurry things along and get straight to fucking me.

If I'm soft and pliant and I play along, I can burn up much more time with much less physical effort.

So, I caress the monster, then I bring him closer for a kiss. My heart flutters madly when his lips touch mine, the breath abandoning my lungs yet again.

Why is it always so intense when he kisses me?

I lose control of the kiss immediately. His hand in my hair makes a fist, then he uses it to pull my head back, angling my neck so he can greedily kiss his way along my jaw and then enjoy that sensitive nook. I can scarcely breathe, and he makes it worse when his scruff scrapes the sensitive skin and then his soft lips soothe the burn.

The way he's holding my hair, I can't really move without hurting myself. I'm pinned beneath the weight of his body, held by my hair like a puppet by its strings.

And he's the puppetmaster.

I only dance when he wants me to.

CHAPTER 11
SILVAN

HER SKIN IS FUCKING DELICIOUS.

I bite and suck like a starved man encountering his first meal, intent on completely devouring her.

I can't get enough of her.

Each taste only seems to further whet my appetite.

She cries out when I bite too hard, so I soothe her soft skin with a kiss.

Beneath me, she moans, whines, and whimpers like absolute fucking perfection. She lets me do what I want to her, but it's a struggle for her.

I consume her like a burning flame and let my hands roam her body, squeezing every curve, exploring every dip, every valley.

When my fingers caress her pussy through the fabric of her panties, she squeezes her eyes closed.

Her reluctance doesn't bother me. I've already determined she's mine, so I paw at my property like it belongs to me.

Because it does.

She does.

The more I call her mine, the more I seem to like it.

Eventually, I'm sure she'll get on board.

Until then, I'll enjoy this unconventional phase of our relationship.

The chase.

I'm not usually much of a chaser. Everything is different with her.

I tug down her panties and she instinctively squeezes her legs closed, but I'm between them, so it does no good.

"Silvan, please."

Her words are like gasoline thrown right on the flames.

"You said you wouldn't…"

She trails off, probably realizing I never promised not to fuck her if she gave me something, I only tossed the bait out there and let her wrap her pretty little mouth around it.

It got me some kisses, so I regret nothing.

"I love the sound of your voice," I tell her, releasing her hair so I can use both hands to untie the comfortable wrap dress I put her in tonight. "I love your skin and your smell. Your fucking taste. Everything about you is…" I trail off, squeezing her tits through the fabric of her bra, then moving lower and kissing her soft stomach.

My cock was already hard just kissing her and toying with her, but the sight of so much bare flesh makes the ache fucking painful. I long to sink inside her, but if I do it right now, she might panic. I don't mind calming her down, but I'd prefer her not feeling that way in the first place.

It's no hardship to continue kissing her beautiful body, and I find I quite like kissing her stomach. Her skin is so soft, and I love the way I can feel her muscles tense each time I kiss her.

I make my way lower and lick her hip bone, my mouth moving closer and closer to paradise.

"Oh, no," she murmurs, embarrassed. "Don't—"

I grab her hands in one of mine when she reaches down to push me away, then I pull her panties all the way off with the other one.

"Silvan…"

"You've never let a man eat your pussy before, huh?"

"Please, I'll die."

I crack a smile at my pretty little virgin. So fucking innocent.

I can't wait to tongue the fuck out of that sweet pussy. I want her whining and whimpering; I want to feel her tummy muscles contracting as she struggles to breathe through the ecstasy.

Fuck yes.

Ignoring her virginal dismay at the idea of my face between her thighs, I position myself between them, keeping one hand firmly locked around a thigh and using the other to spread that pretty pink pussy open so I can have a look at my meal before I devour it.

"Silvan, please. Let me suck you. Please? I'll swallow for you. I'll suck you clean like a good girl."

Christ, that is tempting.

She knows it, too. My clever girl collected all the things I said to her so she could deliver them back to me in an offer too good to refuse.

But I summon some willpower and shake my head. "It's your turn. I want to taste you tonight."

"But—"

I stop her words with my mouth, latching onto her pussy and savoring the sound of her gasping, then moaning when my tongue teases her sensitive clit to give her a taste of what's coming. Her thighs squeeze my head tight, but I have all the space I need to spread her pussy lips wider and dip more of my tongue inside her.

"Oh, God," she murmurs weakly, clutching at the edge of the seat. "Silvan…"

My cock throbs with need as I feel her wet heat all around my tongue. There aren't fucking words for how badly I want to feel it around my cock.

First, I want to taste her. Every fucking inch of her.

"Silvan," she cries, reaching down and grabbing my hair.

I pop up to let her know I like it. "Fuck, yes, baby. Tug on my hair all you want while I'm eating this perfect pussy."

Her face is flushed, but I can see the sheen of pleasure over her unique eyes.

I flash her a smile, then dive between her thighs again, taking a mouthful of sweet pussy and fucking her with my tongue like I so desperately want to do with my cock.

I tease her clit, paying careful attention to her gasps and moans so I can learn her body. I caress her tummy, feeling the way the muscles contract and using her body's responses as a map so I know exactly where to spend more time.

When I think she can take it, I take her clit into my mouth and suck. She nearly shoots off the seat. "Oh god, oh god, oh god," she cries as I gently suck on that sensitive little nub. "Oh my god, Silvan."

Her thighs tremble, and I know she's on the brink of coming. She's so inexperienced, it won't take much stimulation, so I slide a finger inside her to let her feel the fullness in her pussy—and so I can feel the convulsions when she does.

Her breathy little cries drive me fucking crazy. My hard-on is aching, but I stay focused on her pleasure, gently finger fucking her wet heat as I suck on her clit.

She struggles against my grasp, her body twisting and her hips thrusting against my face as she chases the rapture she must know she's close to.

And then she explodes.

She's fucking gorgeous like this—her head thrown back, her eyes tightly shut and her lips parted as she cries out in ecstasy.

I feel her pussy spasming around my finger. I think about *how fucking good* that's going to feel around my cock.

I wish I could record her coming so I could watch it later, jerking my cock to her perfect little fucking sounds.

For tonight, I guess a memory will have to suffice.

Maybe next time I'll plan a little better.

It's my first taste of her pussy, but it's not nearly enough to satisfy my hunger.

Her body is spent in the aftermath. She lays there spread open for me, too blissed out to fight me. If I shoved my cock in her right now, I think she'd let me. At the very least, she wouldn't have the energy to fight me. I could drive deep inside that hot pussy and use her perfect body to get myself off even if she wouldn't participate.

I want to. I really fucking want to.

But I force myself to take a look at the big picture.

Just a few minutes ago, Sophie was intent on never being anywhere near me ever again.

Maybe if I let her have a taste of the pleasure I can offer her without demanding anything in return, she'll change her tune.

Short term, fucking her now makes the most sense, but I'm playing the long game this time.

I don't just want a taste of Sophie, I want the smorgasbord. I want her on the menu every fucking night. I want her in my bed, in my *life,* and while I can force myself on her for a time, eventually, she has to accept me or she's going to end up my prisoner.

I'm looking to make her my girlfriend.

I might take her as my prisoner if I have to, but I'd like to give this a shot the right way first.

Her breathing steadies, but she still lies against the seat like a broken doll. One hand rests on her tummy, the other hanging off the seat. I can't bite back a smile at how fucking spent she looks.

I want to make her come again and again, but that's probably enough for her first time.

Besides, I want to hold her.

I ease down on the seat, careful to adjust my aching cock, then I grab my pretty broken doll and tug her against me.

She's still feeling out of it after that orgasm, so she curls her legs up on the seat behind her and rests her head on my shoulder.

I feel it in my fucking chest when she does.

I fight the instinct to grab her and pull her closer. This is a good first step, but she's vulnerable right now. I don't want to scare her off.

I do want to touch her, though. Can't *stop myself* from touching her. I caress her face and slide a hand down her neck. I pull her close and she nuzzles my neck, and my heart nearly fucking stops.

I can't be in love with her already, but I don't know how else to explain what I feel right now.

I've never been in love with anyone, so I guess what the fuck do I know about how fast it can happen?

All I know is I'd rather die than leave this embrace, and when the car rolls to a stop in front of her apartment building, I curse myself for not having the foresight to tell Hugh to drive around the city before we took her home.

To be fair, I wasn't sure how this would go.

I know last night she went soft on me once things got sexual, but I wasn't sure if it was a fluke or if I'd get that side of her again.

Sleepily, she starts to sit up. "Are we home?"

God, I wish.

I have half a mind to tell Hugh forget it, to take us back to my place so she can spend the night, but I don't want to do anything to fuck up this perfect end to the evening, either.

I don't know if it feels as good to her as it does to me, but if it does, surely, she'll want to feel it again, too.

"Yeah," I say gruffly.

Her gaze meets mine briefly, but she looks away just as fast. Her cheeks are rosy, her gaze still a little hazy.

I watch her hastily wrap the dress around her body and tie the little belt.

"I'll walk you inside," I say.

She bites down on her bottom lip uncertainly but doesn't argue.

Hugh opens the door and Sophie stumbles out.

I smirk with satisfaction at her wobbly balance and grab her extra dinner box off the bar.

I know her apartment is empty—*I made sure it would be*—and as we head into the building and make our way to her dorm, I'm sorely fucking tempted to invite myself inside.

I imagine pushing open the door when she tries to close it, dropping her dinner box on the counter and picking her up, wrapping those pretty legs around my waist and carrying her down the hall as I tear off her new dress. I imagine taking her to her bed and throwing her down, freeing my aching cock and fucking her senseless.

Then we get to her door.

She stops and looks up at me, biting her bottom lip and looking shy.

All I want right now is to kiss her, so I do.

She gasps softly against my mouth, but she doesn't fight it. She lets me push her back against the door and tangle my fingers through her loose hair. Her hand slides around my neck and she lets me plunder her mouth like I want to plunder that sweet fucking pussy.

Maybe she knows I'm fighting a war with myself, so she's sweet and permissive and gives me just enough to get me through the night.

When I finally force myself to break the kiss, I press my forehead against hers, trying to calm my racing heart.

"Thank you for dinner," she says softly.

My lips tug up with wry amusement. "Thank you for dessert."

Her cheeks flush a pretty rosy color, and I can't help laughing as I hand her the box she brought from the restaurant.

She unlocks her door and steps inside.

"Your roommates are gone," I tell her, shoving my hands in my pockets and leaning against the doorjamb since I know I'll have a hard time making myself leave if I come all the way inside.

She turns back to frown at me in confusion. "Where are they?"

"I sent a second car for them after you left. They're at some trendy bar I knew you'd hate. This way, you can finish your homework."

A soft smile plays around her lips, albeit reluctantly. "How thoughtful."

"I'm a thoughtful guy."

Her smile widens a bit. "Well, thank you."

I nod. "I should probably leave you to it, huh?"

She nods, too. "Probably."

"Goodnight, Sophie."

"Goodbye, Silvan."

I watch the door close and crack a smile when the lock immediately engages.

It's cute that she thinks she can keep me out.

It's not lost on me that her response was much more final than mine. It's not ideal that she's still planning to be done with me, but I don't pay it much mind.

Regardless of what she wants, I know I'll see her again soon.

Sooner than she knows.

CHAPTER 12
SOPHIE

It feels like much more than a weekend has passed since I last stepped foot on this campus.

Everything feels different even though I tell myself nothing has changed.

There's a sense that Silvan is lurking even though I don't see him anywhere and we don't have any classes together. Knowing he's likely somewhere on campus taking his own classes makes it difficult to concentrate on mine.

When I got home last night, my place was empty, so I was finally able to finish studying and relax a bit. The girls were still out when I went to bed, and for a fleeting, crazy moment as I tried to fall asleep, I worried something might have happened to them.

Considering Silvan lured *me* under false pretenses, it's not like the notion should be impossible or even unlikely, but I can't explain my certainty that his depravity is isolated to me and me alone.

Maybe I'm fooling myself.

When we were all getting ready for class this morning, the girls were all there in one piece, though. More than that, they couldn't shut up about how amazing Silvan is. He had a limo take them to a trendy downtown bar like he said, and then he paid for all their drinks.

"If you're not interested, I'll happily take him off your hands," Rumi said as she poured herself a bowl of cereal, a starry, faraway look still lighting her dark eyes.

I'm *not* interested, obviously.

I mean, I'd have to be *crazy* to be *interested* in him.

Sure, the thought of him makes my skin burn, but that's only because he's stolen so much access to me, made me experience intimate things with him I should only experience with someone of my choosing, and because I want to.

I know it should feel exactly like when Dylan violated me back in high school, but for some reason, it doesn't.

I don't know what it is about him, exactly, but he feels like once in a lifetime. An experience that's more like a fever dream, and when it's over and you try to explain it to someone, you can't.

He's like being Wendy, kidnapped by Peter Pan and flown to Neverland, but the next morning when he returns you home with no evidence he was ever there, everyone insists you imagined it.

The difference is, Peter Pan wasn't a monster, was he?

He didn't invite himself to feast on Wendy and give her confusing, passionate kisses in the hallway before leaving her to come up for breath when he could have easily invited himself into the apartment he arranged to be empty and helped himself to much more.

He's confusing.

I'm confused.

I've never met anyone like Silvan.

I'm certain I never will again.

That's probably a good thing.

After spending the entire day restless and on edge, my last class comes to an end and the room fills with the sounds of students all around me packing up their things to leave. I look at my notes. All I wrote down was "misattribution of arousal" and without context, I can't even remember what it means.

I spent the whole class doodling. Stars in the sky around a massive clock tower with two figures flying past it.

"Nice work."

I look up in surprise at the professor standing in front of my table, gazing down at my paper.

"Wh-what?" I stammer, embarrassed to have been caught not taking good notes.

He nods at my paper. "Your sketch. I assume you were illustrating an example of misattribution of arousal."

"Oh. Yeah, of course," I fib, my face flushing an even deeper shade of red.

The professor smirks, the tilt of his lips telling me he knows I'm full of shit. "If you need to go over anything you might have missed, I have office hours from three to five."

I don't want him to think I'm some day-dreaming slacker and I'm sure I can find my answers in the textbook, so I shake my head. "Oh, I think I'll be okay, but thank you."

"This will be on the exam, so you'll want to make sure you're familiar with the material."

"I will," I assure him.

Quickly, I gather my things since mostly everyone else has already left.

I'm frustrated with myself as I make my way out of the building. I'm a good student, always have been, though last year was a little rough.

After everything happened with Dylan, I couldn't concentrate, either. I had to put in an immense amount of effort just to focus on things that used to be a piece of cake, and knowing the timing couldn't be a coincidence made it that much worse. I wanted to be fine. I wanted to put it behind me and forget it. I wanted to fucking erase it from my past and go on like it had never happened.

I just couldn't.

The reason I can't concentrate is different this time, though. It's not the trauma fucking up the wiring in my brain, it's... him.

As I make my way off campus, I find myself anticipating returning home, but it's not the simple act of returning I'm thinking about.

I told Silvan goodbye and I swear he smirked like he considered it a challenge.

Some part of me expects to go home and find him leaning against the wall outside my dorm, a smirk on his handsome face.

He's a bastard, but he *is* handsome.

The sight of a sleek black limousine pulling up to the crosswalk makes my heart stop.

I thought I'd probably see him again, but I didn't think he'd be so bold as to...

Hugh leaves the car running, checking behind him as he gets out and then walks around to my side. "Miss Bradwell," he says with an amiable nod of his head.

"What are you doing here? Is Silvan...?"

Hugh shakes his head as he opens the door. "Master Silvan sent me to pick you up. It's a chilly day, he doesn't want you walking."

"I..." I look at the car, a frown flickering across my face. "No. Last time, this was a trick."

"It's not a trick," he assures me. "No loopholes.

Silvan won't be meeting you this evening. The car is just for you."

"No," I say, shaking my head. "I'm not risking it. I don't mind walking."

"He thought you might say that. He wants you to text him."

"And I want him to leave me alone. I guess neither of us will get what we want."

"I see," Hugh says, though he sounds disappointed.

A car pulls up behind his limo—since he wasn't supposed to stop where he did to pick me up—and leans on the horn.

"Miss Bradwell, I'm afraid I've been explicitly instructed not to leave without you. I'm not sure if I'll get in more trouble for disobeying Master Silvan or for disobeying traffic laws, but if you could just get in the car while we figure this out, I would be immensely relieved."

My stomach sinks at the notion of getting Hugh in trouble. At the same time, I don't want to fall into another of Silvan's traps.

And he probably expected I would feel that way.

I'm a bit miffed and also mildly impressed that he tailored this to put the responsibility on me to save Hugh from whatever trouble he'll get into if I hold my ground.

"He's such a jerk," I mutter, grabbing my phone and tapping the message we exchanged last night. "Tell your driver he can leave," I type, then press send.

"Nope," he responds instantly. "Not without you."

"I am not getting into your rape-mobile and being delivered to you like a lamb to slaughter," I inform him. "I fell for that once. It won't work again."

"It's not a trap this time," he promises. "Not a technicality, either. I swear I won't be meeting you there or along the way. I have family business in New York today. We won't even be in the same state until you're safely sleeping in your bed."

I narrow my eyes at the screen. "I'm not taking the chance. I don't need a ride that badly."

"Have I ever lied to you, Sophie?"

Maybe it's his deliberate use of my name, but the words make my stomach sink.

He has definitely deceived me, but has he *actually* lied to me? I can't easily pick out a lie from my memory, so maybe there isn't one. Maybe he's just very, very slippery and adept at navigating all the loopholes in the things he says.

A minuscule part of me is impressed by how deliberately he puts together words to reassure me with untruths and get exactly what he wants. I can't lie to save my life, and he's turned it into an art form.

"You're very manipulative," I tell him.

"Thank you."

I almost laugh. "My god, that wasn't a compliment."

"Anyway, it's not just a ride. I put you through a lot this weekend. I think you deserve a little pampering today. Hugh will take you shopping."

"I don't have money to go shopping."

"I know, that's why Hugh also has one of my credit cards. Buy whatever you want. Perhaps a warmer coat," he suggests. "You seemed cold last night."

"I can buy WHATEVER I want?"

"Yep. Get yourself some dinner, too. He's taking you to Newbury Street. If you don't know where to eat, Hugh will have some recommendations for you."

"And I'll be dining alone, correct?"

"Correct."

An idea strikes me. It's probably not a good one, but God knows he has enacted his bad ideas on me for the sake of *his* own pleasure. It's my turn. "What if I want to bring a friend?"

"One of your roommates?"

"No."

I deliberately don't give him more than that.

"Harley Quinn?"

"No. No one you've encountered. A male friend."

"Oh, I wouldn't recommend that."

I think he's a bit of a madman and I would never *actually* endanger a male friend just to taunt Silvan, but he doesn't know that. "Why not?" I ask innocently.

"Because unless his exclusive sexual preference is other men, he'd have a very unpleasant encounter with me following the shopping trip and that would probably be awkward for you to explain. Unless, of course, you're exceptionally comfortable speaking to corpses. Even so, the idea of you apologizing to another man... rubs me the wrong way. Let's avoid it."

"That's an insane thing to text someone."

"All in good fun," he replies, but I don't entirely believe him.

"You can't be possessive of my apologies."

"Oh, but I can. All your apologies belong to me. I think you owe me one right now for pretending you'd invite another man into my car to take you on as shopping spree I'm paying for."

"I think you're crazy if you think I owe YOU an

apology for anything after the things you've done to me."

"I'll take it, anyway. You repentant and on your knees. I'm getting hard just thinking about it."

"Okay," I say, ready to cut off this interaction before it goes even more off the rails. "I'm done with this conversation."

"Just take the car. Have a nice evening. I won't be there. Like I said, I'm in New York. I'll be in New York while you're out and about. By the time I'm back in Boston, you'll be in bed."

"You SWEAR you're in New York?"

A moment later, he sends a picture of himself holding up a Post-It note he wrote the date on and a view of the Manhattan skyline out the window behind him.

"Cross my heart. Let me do a nice thing for you."

An idea hits me as I look at the limo. "I was joking about the guy, but would I be able to bring someone?"

"Who?"

"My mom. When I was a kid, I won this limo ride from my school fundraiser and I was going to take her for Mother's Day, but I got sick the day of the limo ride and we couldn't go. I know it's silly, but... I don't know, it'd be kind of like a raincheck."

"It's not silly at all," he texts back. "Yes, of course you can bring your mom. Buy her something, too."

A smile tugs at my lips, accompanied by a burst of excitement. I'm not as worried he's tricking me if he's fine with me bringing my mom, and this would be so much cooler than a 30-minute limo ride around our old town. "Thank you," I text back.

"You're welcome, beautiful."

My cheeks flush, and not from the nippy fall weather.

Since there are now three angry drivers slamming on their horns behind us, I drop my bag from my shoulder and quickly get into the car.

My heart races when Hugh closes the door and I know I'm trapped inside again. It could be another deception. A bigger one. He might have agreed to me taking my mom so easily because he knew I would never make it back to my dorm, let alone to her house to pick her up. I could be on my way to him right now.

But then I'd never be able to trust another thing he says.

Maybe he doesn't care, but I think... I think he does.

The partition is down so I can see Hugh, and there's no reason he can't hear me. "We're going to pick up my mom," I say tentatively, watching carefully for some sign he's not going to do what was promised.

"Very good. What's her address?"

I give it to him, but I'm still on the edge of my seat as he gets back on the road and presumably starts toward my mom's house.

When he takes a left I'm not expecting, my heart accelerates. "We're going straight to her house, right?"

He meets my gaze briefly in the mirror before returning his to the road. "Unless you'd like to stop at your place to drop off your schoolbooks, yes."

I glance down at the bag leaning against the seat. "That's okay. I'd just like to pick up my mom."

He nods. "We're heading there now," he assures me. "I was just avoiding an accident on the route," he adds, perhaps realizing my anxiety is because he took a wrong turn.

"Oh," I say, relief washing over me as I sit back in the seat. "All right. I should probably text her to let her know we're coming then, huh?"

Hugh nods kindly. "Yes, I imagine you should."

Reassured that we really *are* going to pick her up, I finally text Mom to let her know I'm coming to get her, and I have a surprise.

"What is it??" she asks.

"You'll never guess," I tease. "Just clear your schedule and be ready to go in ten minutes."

"Ohh, I love surprises! Best daughter ever," she sends back with a smiley emoji.

I smile, too, because I love being *able* to surprise her like this.

CHAPTER 13
SOPHIE

AFTER A FULL EVENING OF SHOPPING, WE LEAVE THE last store with bags bursting with new clothes and a new winter coat for me.

I don't feel guilty indulging in a shopping spree on Silvan's dime. I wish I could buy more. He owes me a little something for the pain and suffering of having to endure his tenacious presence.

"Remember those Christmas trees with hanging wishlists from families in need they used to have up around the holidays? Do they still have those? It's been years since we've been able to grab a tag and buy them some stuff. We should find one while I have Silvan's credit card."

Mom smiles faintly. Obviously, I couldn't tell her the real story, so I told her Silvan lost a bet with me and that's why we're out on the town on some rich boy's dime. "I don't think they put those up this early in the year. I feel like we used to get those around Thanksgiving."

"Too bad," I murmur, stopping on the sidewalk where Hugh dropped us off. I glance over at Mom. "I don't know about you, but I'm starving. Are you ready to get some food?"

Mom nods and Hugh pulls up to the curb. Like

always, he gets out and comes around to open the door for us, but I feel so awkward standing there waiting for him to serve me, I say, "Don't worry about it," and open the door myself.

Or, I try to anyway.

I'm expecting an average car door, but when I go to open it, it's like pulling on a wall of cement.

What the hell?

"I've got it, Miss Bradwell," Hugh says, grabbing the handle and pulling the heavy door open.

Why is it so heavy?

Mom climbs in, but I remain on the sidewalk, frowning at the thick door, noticing things I didn't last night. I knew it was thick, of course, but I didn't think much of it. I've never been in a limousine before, so I figured it was standard. Maybe it is. Are all limos like this?

"Is that... armored?" I ask, glancing at Hugh.

His lips thin and he gives a curt nod. "Yes, ma'am."

I've heard of like presidents and dignitaries having armored cars, but I can't imagine Silvan needing something like that. What did he say his family did? Shady business in the 1920s, sure, but did he specify what they do to make so much money *now*?

Not for the first time, an awareness that I don't really know anything about this guy washes over me. I glance down the road in the direction Hugh came from absently, torn between asking more questions and knowing he likely won't answer if I ask anything too juicy, anyway.

Hair stands up on the back of my neck. I don't know why, but then I turn my head and my heart stalls as my gaze locks with Dylan Prescott's.

He's standing on the sidewalk a few yards down, outside a candy store. He's talking on his cell phone, but rather than do the polite thing and look away so we can pretend we didn't see each other, he starts walking in my direction.

Is he seriously coming over here?

Panic swells up and I feel sick at the thought—and even worse because Mom's in the car. "Hugh, can you please close the door for a moment?" I ask, barely able to keep the panic from my voice.

A frown flickers across his face, but he obeys without question.

"Thank you." I try swallowing, but my mouth is dry. "Can I also get some privacy?"

"Privacy?" he questions, his gaze flickering as Dylan approaches.

"Yes, can you... leave us for just a moment?"

He straightens, directing his gaze forward. "I'm afraid not, Miss Bradwell. I'm under strict orders to ensure your safety while you're out with me this evening. One can reasonably surmise that pre-cludes leaving you alone with strange men."

I shoot him a look, doubtful that his orders to keep me away from strange men has anything to do with my *protection* and everything to do with Silvan's ridiculous and utterly baseless possessive-ness over me.

There's no time to argue, though.

"Nice ride," Dylan says, his gaze sliding down the gleaming black stretch limo.

A grudging, polite 'thanks' tries to escape, but I bite the word back just before it can slip past my lips.

"Certainly an upgrade since last time I saw you," he says, his gaze flicking to me. "I thought you were a scholarship student."

And I thought you were a decent human being.

One of us was wrong.

"My financial situation is none of your business," I inform him. "In fact, everything to do with me is none of your business, so if we ever encounter one another in public again, I would very much like for you to keep walking and pretend you didn't see me. I'll offer the same courtesy to you."

The corners of his mouth tip up. "Yeah, you're already being real courteous to me, aren't you? Like telling my girlfriend I'm an attempted rapist?"

My heart stalls and my gaze jumps to the window. They're tinted so I can't see inside, but panic swells up at the thought of my mom overhearing.

Grabbing his arm, I pull him away from the car. "We both know that wasn't a lie."

He glances back at the limo. Ignoring my comment, he brags, "Yeah. My financial circumstances have improved since last time we met, too, that's why Elle and I can have little getaways like this. Got a good job working for my uncle's company, 80k to start, benefits and tuition reimbursement while I'm in school." He waits for me to be impressed, and when I'm not, malice flickers through his eyes. "There was some fucking specialty chocolate shop over here Elle wanted to come to. Expensive as fuck, but I'm a nice guy," he says, smiling cruelly. "I take my woman's wants into consideration."

"Unless what she wants is not to fuck you, right?" I ask innocently.

"Eh, you were never really mine, were you? Could've been if you hadn't been such a headache after we hooked up."

God, he is disgusting.

"We did *not* hook up," I say carefully.

"That's how I remember it." His gaze drifts

down my body, lingering on my breasts as he reaches for my arm. "It was hot, too."

"Fuck off," I snap, jerking my arm out of his grasp. "I haven't even been the same *person* since that happened and you have the fucking audacity to say that to me? Fuck off, Dylan."

"You don't have to be so pissed." He tries to grab me as I turn away, and his hand on my arm makes my skin crawl. "What's the story with the limo, anyway?"

"It's my boyfriend's," I snap, the words bottoming out my stomach even though I know I don't mean it and I'm only saying it to get at him. "He's out of town on family business tonight, but he *takes his woman into consideration*," I say scathingly, echoing his own words back at him, "so he gave me the car and his credit card and told me to have a good time."

Rather than feel like an itty-bitty inferior man like he should, he smirks like an asshole. "Sounds desperate."

"Desperately in love," I bite back. "And very possessive, so if my desires aren't enough for you —*and we both know they're not*—next time you see me out in public and think about approaching, consider that he might be with me, and if I told him what a fucking creep you've been to me, he would break you in half."

His smirk widens. "Aw. Yeah, I'm real afraid of your big bad boyfriend. So insecure he has to buy you with limos and shopping sprees. See, I know Elle isn't going anywhere simply because she doesn't want to, Sophie. Sad that you're with some fucking dork living on daddy's dime and treating you like some whore he has to pay for."

Blood surges through my veins so violently, I hear buzzing in my ears. Heat rushes my body, a mix of anger and embarrassment heating my cheeks.

I wanted the last word, but right now, I want to get away from him much more.

"Goodbye, Dylan."

"Hey." He grabs my arm again to stop me, and anxiety surges as I try to tug it free.

A second later, he releases my arm. I jump when I hear him slammed up against the car door beside me, and stumble back a couple of steps when I see Mr. Proper Hugh standing behind Dylan with his arm locked at an agonizing angle that has Dylan's face twisted with pain.

"The lady has asked you on multiple occasions not to touch her."

"Let go of me, you fucking—"

"I will release you as soon as you assure me that when I do, you'll apologize to the lady and walk away without another word to her."

"What-the-fuck-ever, man. Get off me!"

Hugh releases Dylan who takes it sorely, shaking Hugh off a moment after he's been released and turning to glare at him.

"I should call the fucking cops."

"I concur," Hugh says brightly. "Miss Bradwell might wish to report your relentless harassment. Will you call, or should I?"

Dylan shakes his head, muttering, "Bitch isn't even worth it," as he walks away.

"I believe you forgot to apologize to Miss Bradwell," Hugh calls after him.

Dylan turns around to flip us off as he backs into the street.

I fantasize about a bus hitting him Regina George style, but sadly, it doesn't happen.

"What horrendous manners that boy has," Hugh remarks.

I crack a smile and look over at him. Hugh has a lean build, so I definitely didn't expect him to go all bodyguard. "You're kind of a badass, Hugh."

Hugh smiles, his chest puffing up with pride. "I'm trained in evasive driving techniques as well, though hopefully you'll never have need of those."

"Does Silvan's family have a lot of enemies or something? I thought you were just a driver."

"Men in families like Master Silvan's always have enemies, Miss Bradwell." Turning and reaching for the door handle, he says, "Shall I?"

I nod and thank him, so he opens the door.

Mom waits inside, wide-eyed. "What the hell was that?"

Trying for glib, I tell her, "I don't like surprises as much as you do."

She continues to stare at me, but when I don't offer another word and I take out my phone, she seems to take the hint that I'm not going to expand upon that thought.

My phone vibrates and a text from Silvan appears on the screen. It reads, "Having a good time with your mom?"

My heart jolts and I glance up front to see if it looks like Hugh has told on me, but I can't tell. All I know is Silvan hasn't checked up on me before now. I thought he was letting me enjoy time with my mom uninterrupted.

"Yes," I type back cautiously. "Thanks again."

"Anytime."

I swallow, waiting a second to see if he types anything else. When he doesn't, I ask, "Are you still in New York?"

"Yeah. About to catch a show with my mom before we head back."

"On Broadway? That sounds like fun."

"I'll have to bring you sometime."

I'd like that.

My fingers freeze when I realize the thought that just flitted through my mind.

No, I would not. Am I crazy?

Shaking my head to clear it, I try to think what to type back, then I decide I should probably type nothing.

I need to stop talking to him. He's making me feel strangely comfortable with this profoundly dysfunctional relationship he's trying to lure me into, and I need to put a stop to it before it goes any deeper.

I can't bring myself to cut off the conversation at such an unnatural place, though, so I type back, "We're heading to dinner now, so I should probably go."

"Okay," he responds. "Enjoy the rest of your night."

"You too," I answer politely, without thought.

"I will," he answers with a winky face.

My eyes narrow with suspicion, but I suppose he was only responding in kind. Maybe the wink is because I was being polite to him when he knows I shouldn't have been. Sometimes it occurs to me a moment too late.

My rationalization makes sense to me, but I still feel uneasy as I tuck the phone away inside the new Marc Jacobs purse I bought myself at the first store we stopped at.

"Everything okay?" Mom asks.

I look up, startled.

For a second, I completely forgot she was in the car with me.

Silvan has a way of making the rest of the world melt into the background when he has my attention.

"Yeah," I lie, trying to feign nonchalance. "Everything's fine."

After a delicious dinner, Silvan has one last surprise for us.

I expect Hugh to take us home, and I tell him I'll just stay the night at Mom's so he only has to make one stop, but rather than to Mom's house, he takes us to a movie theater where Silvan has rented out one of the screens.

Mom and I get drinks and a small popcorn to share, and then we go to our own private screening of the first episode of the season of *The Last Kingdom* that we haven't watched yet.

I can't help but to grin when Uhtred comes on the screen, memories of my own crazy Viking stirring to mind. I fight the urge to grab my phone and text him even though we're the only ones in the theater, so it's not like I'd be disturbing anyone's viewing experience.

As soon as we're back in the car, I dig out my phone and text Silvan.

"You rented out a theater for me."

His response comes promptly. "I thought it might be more your speed. You've given the impression you're not fond of crowds."

He's right, I'm not.

I can't believe he's figured that out about me already, though. In more than a year, my mom hasn't figured that out. My roommates don't get it at all.

I just met him, and he already gets it.

I've never met anyone who paid such close attention to me.

"Thank you," I type.

"You're welcome. Did you and your mom enjoy the show?"

"Very much. I don't remember telling you where we were on our watch, though. How'd the guy know which season to play?"

"At my party you said you'd seen 'many' seasons of my show, not 'every' season of my show," he returns. "Stood to reason you hadn't started the last one yet."

"You pay attention to everything, don't you?"

"Everything involving you, absolutely."

His words should probably alarm me. It's not normal to be so preoccupied with me. Nothing about him seems particularly normal.

But rather than alarm me, it feels oddly comforting. It's like when I felt safe in his arms even though, practically speaking, I wasn't.

The ground feels too slippery to respond to his last text and we're almost home, anyway, so I tuck my phone away and enjoy the rest of the ride.

Despite the craziness of this whole day, I feel somewhat relaxed.

Last year, even last week, I couldn't have envisioned a day where I ran into Dylan Prescott when I wasn't prepared to face him and managed to feel relaxed later that same evening.

What was once unfathomable now feels almost… natural.

My impulsive words to Dylan on the sidewalk were fueled by fury and a sense of helplessness I've lived with for far too long. Wielding Silvan like a round shield made me feel impenetrable if only for a moment.

It wasn't real, though.

I was just Wendy, lost in a daydream with a familiar but made-up friend.

A protector.

Even knowing it's a fiction, the idea makes me smile.

When we pull up to Mom's house, Hugh lets us out of our prison chariot and Mom thanks him with enthusiasm before we head into the house.

I think about asking Hugh not to tell Silvan about the run-in on Newbury Street, but I'm realistic about where Hugh's loyalties lie, so I don't bother.

CHAPTER 14
SILVAN

I watch my phone for hours. During the quick flight home and then the ride back to the house; before I shower and as soon as I get out.

I'm waiting for a goodnight text of sorts, but one never comes.

I suppose my hopes were a little high, but it would have been easier to plan the rest of my night if my lovely Sophie had told me what the fuck *she* was doing. It's pertinent information, but like any pertinent information, I can get it another way.

Hugh told me she'd be spending the night at her mom's, so the cameras I had installed in her dorm while I had the place empty are of no use to me. I toggle between feeds to make sure she didn't just say that to throw me off her scent, but once I've confirmed she didn't make it back to her dorm, I begin to formulate my plan.

When I was in her room the other night, I didn't plant anything. Wasn't prepared. I didn't know I'd meet her, let alone that I would feel the need to monitor her every move once I did.

I'll have to work with a limited toolbox tonight and prepare better for next time.

Before I leave the house, I collect a few things to take with me.

Spy pen? Of course. In fact, I grab two. One for her school bag, one for the desk in her bedroom. These are cheap ones just to use in a pinch, but they'll do until I get some better equipment.

My grandfather was a big believer in having gadgets like these as soon as they came available to him. Before tech was as advanced as it is now, he and his father before him had sneakier ways of making insurance policies for themselves, making sure they had evidence they could use against their friends should those friendships ever go sour.

I'm not looking for anything to use against Sophie, it's just the only way I can find out things I want to know about her since she refuses to spend time with me voluntarily.

Plus, all right, I want to keep an eye out for any potential competition.

Not that I consider other men to truly be competition, but if she has any little crushes on anyone else that might be preventing her from spending time with me... well, I'll have to handle it.

Once I have what I need, I head out.

I don't drive much, but I drive myself tonight. I park in the street and walk to her house just in case anyone's awake.

The house is dark. I check all around it to make sure no one's hidden in some back room. It would be a fucking catastrophe to get caught by her mom, but I was in and out easy enough the other night, so as long as no one's awake, I'm not too worried about it.

I draw my lockpick set out of my left pocket and finesse the cheap lock. It's no challenge at all, but I've been picking locks since I was 10 years old with an "inappropriate" crush on our maid's daughter. Her mom bought a lock for their door when I kept sneaking in, so I had to figure out how to get past it without a key.

The daughter liked me, but the maid didn't. She didn't work there for much longer after that.

Sophie's house is dark when I slip inside. I lock the door behind me since we're in a shitty neighborhood and I wouldn't want any unsavory characters getting into my girl's house while she and her mom are asleep.

I make my way down the dark hall and carefully twist the knob to let myself into Sophie's bedroom.

The room is completely dark, but I still brace for the sound of her voice, perhaps a startled cry if she wasn't completely asleep yet.

She is, though.

It's late.

I close her door and turn the lock just to make sure we're not interrupted.

I feel at peace just knowing I'm in the same room with her.

Once my eyes adjust, I walk closer to the bed so I can look at her. It's too dark to see her face. All I can make out is the shape of her lovely body beneath the covers.

I wonder what she would do if I climbed into that bed with her and wrapped my arms around her waist. If I pulled her back against my body, her perfect ass wiggling against my cock as she sleepily settled in.

That's probably not how it would go.

She'd likely scream, then her mom would come. Not the best way to introduce myself, I suppose.

I have work to do before I can get to the pleasure part of the evening, anyway. I have my phone, but I don't want to risk waking her up, so I move around carefully, searching out the things I need.

Her schoolbag is on the floor against the wall. Hugh took a picture of it earlier so I'd know which one it was since I haven't actually seen her at school, and I wasn't sure how many bags she might have laying around.

I ease down on the floor, keeping an eye on the bed to make sure there's no movement, then I open her bag and start going through her things.

I could get her class schedule and syllabus digitally, but I prefer the personal touch of going through her copies of her papers. More informative, it turns out, because Sophie's a doodler.

I have to turn the flashlight on my phone to read them, but as I flip through Professor DeMarco's psych syllabus, I don't just see the suggested reading and weekly breakdown of the textbook. I also see how she highlighted *his* office hours and email which she didn't do on any of the other packets she has from other professors.

My eyes narrow as I see the copious highlighting she's done to this syllabus. Far more than she has done to the others. I suppose she could just be inordinately interested in the class, but she's studying the actual sciences, not the social sciences. I expected her to be more interested in Darwin than Jung and Freud.

Not to pigeon-hole her, of course. Sophie can be interested in whatever she's interested in.

Just not Professor DeMarco.

I'm probably overthinking it, so I pull up the university website and search up DeMarco to see what he looks like.

Well, that's unfortunate.

He's not some stodgy old bastard like I was hoping he might be. Instead, he's young and handsome, radiating the kind of smug arrogance I could easily see my Sophie falling for.

Well, that won't do at all.

With renewed interest, I slip the spy pen in her bag with the rest of her pens and highlighters. She has a little case of them, so I expect she takes the whole case out of her bag when she's preparing for class.

I take quick pictures of each page of her marked-up syllabus just to be thorough, then I flip through the rest of her notes before closing her bag and putting it back exactly where I found it.

I slip the second pen in a little rose gold pen holder on her desk in case she comes back here after school tomorrow instead of her well-sur-veilled dorm room.

I'd like to get into her computer as well, but I don't know the password yet and I don't want to risk the brightness of the screen waking her up.

I don't love leaving so many corners of her life unmonitored or only poorly monitored, but this will have to suffice until I can make more suitable arrangements.

When the work is done, I kick off my shoes and lift the covers so I can slide under them with her. This is risky as hell, and I really don't want to wake her up… at least, I don't think I do.

No, I don't.

I'm not prepared.

I even drove myself here, and if the absolute worst came to worst, I don't know how I'd get her out of the house and back to mine without her waking someone up or getting us killed on the road.

Definitely not prepared to take risks like this, but perhaps the risk-averse part of my brain is more relaxed than it should be because I do it anyway.

Maybe she can ask her fucking Professor De-Marco about it, I think sourly.

The sourness doesn't last, though.

It's impossible not to get lulled into the peace of lying next to her in bed. She smells fucking fantastic. I don't know what kind of scent she rubs on herself or soap she uses. I caught a faint whiff of it in the escape room and in the limo last night, but here, in her bedroom? It's everywhere. I inhale the scent like a fucking addict, my eyes drifting closed and my fingers itching to reach out and touch her.

I want to press my lips to her skin and drink her in. I want to dive beneath the covers, between her pretty legs, and bury my face in her pussy. I want her to wake up flushed and confused and then be consumed by pleasure and happy I'm here.

Probably a long shot, so I don't take things *that* far, but I can't resist touching her.

My eyes have fully adjusted to the dark now, so I can see her peaceful face as she sleeps. I can see the mounds of her lovely breasts somewhat flattened since she's lying on her back, the pale blue cotton of her sleep shirt laying against her bare flesh.

A swatch of her stomach is exposed above the waistband of her shorts.

Her nipples are visible through the fabric and make my cock harden even though she's fully dressed. She sleeps without a bra on, and the knowledge tempts me to slide a hand up under her shirt so I can feel the warmth of her tit pressed against my palm.

She's not a light sleeper, thankfully.

Even though I know better, the tantalizing glimpses of her smooth skin entice me to rip open the tank top she's sleeping in so she's completely bare before me. I want to squeeze her flesh, taste it, too, but I know that would surely wake her up.

I try to satisfy myself with just a touch, lightly running my fingertips across her collarbone, then down her shoulder. I slide a hand down her bare arm and enjoy the peace of her sleeping and not fighting me for once.

I glance at her face to ensure she's still sleeping soundly before I peel up the bottom of her shirt to expose more of her smooth stomach. My cock jerks at the mere sight of it.

Splitting my attention between her face and her torso, I carefully push my hand past the waistband of her navy-blue sleep shorts. The temptation is too much to bear, and I can't stop myself from leaning over and leaving a soft kiss on her belly.

I want to leave much more than that.

A brand for all the world to see.

Seeing her in this vulnerable state, unaware and unable to defend herself from me, a dark idea passes through my mind.

I fucking like it, though.

I'm careful as I slide my hand between her thighs and palm her pussy through the fabric of her panties. She's hot against my palm and my cock instantly hardens with anticipation.

Carefully, I move the material aside and slide my finger against her entrance.

I'm tempted to draw off her shorts and panties, to lick that perfect pussy until it's wet and ready for me, but I'm certain she wouldn't sleep through that.

My cock throbs at the notion of her waking up with me inside her. Would she even bother to fight me at that point, or would she just let me do it?

I need her surrender. I need her to let me be inside her like I need to fucking breathe.

If I felt confident she'd stay sleeping until I could get firmly inside her, I think I'd do it.

I don't want her to wake up and ruin this lovely session, though, so I don't undress her. Instead, I carefully draw my hand out of her shorts and push a finger into my mouth, wetting it and then sliding it back between her thighs.

A faint noise escapes her when I push my wet finger into her pussy. Her tight heat around my finger alone is enough to turn my cock to molten fucking steel in my pants.

Needing relief, I use my other hand to push down my fitted sweats just enough to get my cock out. I palm it, closing my eyes and stifling a groan at the sensation of touching myself at the same time I'm touching her.

I rub her pussy gently, using a second finger to massage her clit. In her sleep, she moans, and the sound goes straight to my cock.

I stroke it, imagining her hand wrapped around me instead of my own. Running my palm over the crown, I catch some precum on the end of my thumb, then I reach over and rub the salty cum on her exposed stomach. My cock jumps seeing my seed on her soft belly. I rub it in gently, barely resisting the urge to lean down and lick her.

Fuck, she is beautiful.

And mine.

So fucking mine.

Whether she likes it or not.

Her lips are slightly parted. I know I'm pushing my luck, but I don't care at this point. If she wakes up, she wakes up. Then I can fuck her, so it's a win-win for me.

I push lightly on her bottom lip, opening her

mouth just enough to push my thumb in and leave the taste of my cum on her inner lip.

Once I've marked her, I extract my finger from her mouth and my hand from her shorts.

I look down at my work, at my beautiful girl with flushed cheeks and a peaceful face, her tummy marked with my cum and the taste of me in her mouth. I rub it in a little better on her stomach, then decide I better leave before I lose control and fuck her senseless, uncaring of the details.

I don't want to leave any hints that I was here tonight since I don't want her to be suspicious of the pens, so I make sure everything is as it was when I got here, then I slip out.

Goodnight, sweet Sophie.

I'll see you soon.

CHAPTER 15
SOPHIE

"Sophie, you're going to be late," Mom calls down the hall.

"I know," I call back, my face hot as I search for my class schedule. I know the general time all my classes are, but I'm not the best with directions so I still have to check it for the room numbers when I'm on my way to class.

I swear I tucked it in my psych notebook with my useless notes yesterday, but I can't find it anywhere.

I'm already running late, so I don't have time to stop by the office to have another one printed. I planned to get to class a little early today so I could review some of the material before the pop quiz I'm expecting in my first class. Nothing is going to plan.

I finally manage to rush out the door with my bag and a granola bar since I didn't have time for breakfast. I look up to head for my car, and I'm startled to see a familiar stretch limo parked in front of my house, Hugh waiting by the door.

"Good morning, Miss Bradwell. There's break-fast and a hot latte waiting for you in the car.

Caramel apple spice. That's what your roommate said you'd prefer."

I blink, fleetingly think about saying no, but there's no time for a debate today.

I'm starving, I'm running late, I'm hot and cold at the same time from rushing around, and relaxing and being driven to class today actually sounds magnificent. I can study in the car, so I'll probably do better on my test, and the promise of a caramel apple spice latte has my mouth watering.

I change directions and lug all my crap to the limo instead of my car. "Thanks, Hugh. You're a lifesaver."

"Happy to be of assistance, Miss Bradwell."

The car is toasty and comfortable as soon as I duck inside. I drop all my stuff on the seat and sink back into the warm leather. Are these heated seats? It feels magnificent.

Every bit of the stress I've felt since my eyes opened this morning melts right out of me.

Once the car is moving and I've taken a moment to catch my breath, I lean forward and grab the tray off the bar.

A hot breakfast sandwich on a buttery croissant, a bowl of fresh fruit, and a cold bottle of water await me. I realize as soon as I see it that I completely forgot to grab myself a bottle of water on the way out the door.

I wolf down breakfast. It's *so* good, infinitely better than the sad granola bar I abandoned on the seat beside me.

Once my belly is full and I'm relaxed, I turn my attention back to the stuff I dropped on the seat. I sort out my purse and tuck the granola bar inside in case I get hungry later, then I open my schoolbag and take out my notebook and textbook so I can go over my notes.

When I get to school, Hugh pulls me right up to the door. Since I don't have to park and hustle to my class, I end up making it on time.

"All right, everybody. Pop quiz!"

I smile faintly as a few people groan. I don't know why they're surprised. We've had a "pop quiz" every Tuesday since the second week of classes. Seems like they'd know to expect it by now.

I draw out my pencil pouch and put it on the table next to my bottled water. The teacher walks down the middle of the room, handing piles of papers to the first student in each row and they pass them down until there are none left.

I'm at the end of the table against the wall in this class, so I get the last one and thank the girl who handed it to me.

Once I have my test and the professor starts telling us how long we have to complete the quiz and what we should do once we've finished, I unzip my pen pouch to draw out two pens. I always grab two in case the first one dries up on me or something.

A frown flickers across my face.

Where did you come from?

A black and gray pen I've literally never seen before is the first one in my pouch. I guess I must have accidentally stolen it from somewhere, but I can't think when I last even used a pen that wasn't mine.

"All right, and… begin."

My gaze flickers to the teacher, then I zip the pouch, deciding not to worry about the pen. It's a clicky pen with a nice matte finish that feels good between my fingers, so I click the top and decide to try it out.

Ooooh.

It *glides* across the page as I write my name at the top of the paper.

This is a great pen.

I don't remember stealing it, but I can see why I did. It writes like a dream.

I'm a total school supply nerd, so the good pen gives me a little happiness boost as I start answering the questions on my test.

I finish early and just as enamored of the pen as I was when I first picked it up, so I inspect it more carefully, looking for a brand name so I can order a whole pack of them.

Hmm, no brand name, but what's that little circle on top of the clicky part? Looking at it closely, the inside has sort of a screen texture, almost like the microphone on my iPhone.

"All right, everybody. Time's up. Pass your papers back to the front, please."

I put down my pen and hand my test to the girl next to me. The lecture portion of class is about to start, so I draw out my notes and my textbook.

I guess I'll try to figure out where I can get more of these pens later.

I arrive early to my last class of the day which makes me really happy. I always worry about running late to this one because Professor DeMarco is *not* kind to kids who show up late.

When he's nice to you, it's like sitting in the sun on a warm summer day.

When he's cold to you, it's like being stranded in a tundra wearing nothing more than a bathing suit.

The only time I got here late, I left feeling sick

to my stomach, so I've made an extra effort to get here on time since then.

Since I get myself set up for class early, I grab my phone to check it quickly.

I haven't texted Silvan all day despite my manners urging earlier that maybe I should thank him for sending the car since it has made my day immensely better. I keep waiting for something to pop up from him, but there's still nothing.

"No phones in my classroom, Miss Bradwell."

My heart jolts and my cheeks burn with embarrassment as I glance up at Professor DeMarco. "Sorry, I'll put it away."

His lips tug up as he walks over to the table. "I'm just teasing you. Class hasn't started yet. You're free to check it until you're on my time."

"I always feel like I'm on your time when I'm in your classroom," I murmur, smiling faintly.

His smile widens. "Good. Did you find time to go over the material on misattribution of arousal last night?"

"I did. I even went over it in the car on the way here." My heart thuds and my skin heats because even though I *did* go over it, I know I'll panic and probably forget how to word if he quizzes me on it right now.

"Good. I hope you're prepared. My tests tend to be brutal."

"I am. I will be." I fumble for the right phrasing and lack confidence that I nailed it even though I've sputtered the only two options I can think of.

He gazes at me, still managing to make me feel like I failed to find the right one.

Without another word, his gaze leaves me, and he walks back to his podium at the front of the class.

I breathe a sigh of relief and grab my pen with

shaky hands. The nervous sensation lingers since I still felt like he was unconvinced when he walked away, but I try to shove it down and focus as he tells everyone to open their textbooks to page 77.

When class is over, I make my way out of the building prepared to encounter Hugh and the limo, but unsure how I should respond.

This morning, I was desperate.

I was also confident that he would take me to school without any chance of encountering Silvan because Silvan probably has classes starting around the same time, so surely, he knew I needed to get to class.

But now the school day is over so I'm less certain Hugh would take me straight home.

I'm also not sure if I should go back to my dorm so I can get started on my homework or go to Mom's house. I can do my homework there, and I do need to get my car.

I grab my phone and text her to see if she'll be home tonight.

Hugh isn't waiting by the curb, but it doesn't occur to me until I've been standing there waiting for several minutes... Could it be he's not coming? He never actually said he would pick me up after school.

I'm horrified to realize I just *assumed* Silvan would send the car for me.

That is an embarrassing realization.

My cheeks flushed from more than the chilly weather, I hoist my bag on my shoulder and start to make my way home, the whole way there trying to understand how I let myself get so wrapped up in Silvan's peculiar courtship.

Because that's what this is, isn't it? It's the strangest courtship I could ever imagine, but he's not doing all of this out of the kindness of his heart.

He wants something from me.

His actions the night we met made it extremely unlikely he would ever get it, so he's taken steps to erase the difficulty from my life and make me... start to rely on him.

And it's working.

Without even realizing it, he has made me comfortable enough to get in that car this morning with almost no hesitation, and it was just this past weekend that he locked me in an escape room and nearly raped me.

Wow.

It feels crucial that I get a breather from him, so instead of heading straight home, I decide to go somewhere he wouldn't be able to find me even if he wanted to.

There's a little coffee shop I've been meaning to stop at on my way home, anyway, so I stop in and order myself a hot chocolate. I set up at a table in the corner and get started on my homework.

My head feels clearer than it has in a while with this little pocket of independence from Silvan. I don't understand why I had to make an effort to find a Silvan-free corner of my world, anyway, since I never agreed to be in any kind of dysfunctional relationship with him, but I feel like he has access to me in all the places he has sent Hugh to pick me up.

Not here.

I'm free here in this little coffee shop.

It feels good.

Right.

I feel like my own person here. Like no one knows who I am, so I could be anybody.

A girl without a dodgy past and far too much baggage.

I could start over and be someone new.

"Sophie?"

My heart stalls as I hear a familiar voice behind me.

I turn to look, and my heart melts into a puddle and pours down my legs when I see Professor De-Marco standing there in a brown coat with his briefcase in one hand and a cup of coffee in the other.

"H-hi," I stammer awkwardly. "What are you doing here?"

His lips tug up. He glances around the coffee shop which I didn't realize had filled up with the post-school crowd. "Just coming in for my usual cup of coffee before I head home, but it seems someone has taken my table."

My tummy flutters at the teasing censure in his gaze when he looks at me. "Me? Oh, I'm sorry," I say without thought, turning and grabbing for papers so I can put them away and leave him to his spot.

A firm hand comes down on the papers and he meets my gaze, leaning close enough that I can smell him. "You don't have to do that," he says.

I swallow.

"But," he continues, his tone light since he can see how nervous he makes me, "maybe I could join you?"

Oh, Silvan wouldn't like that.

I don't know where that thought comes from, but it *infuriates* me and solidifies my decision.

I sit back down, my heart hammering and my

skin hot, and nod my consent for him to sit with me.

My area is a mess of open textbooks and scrambled notes. I clear a side for him, pushing my notebook, pens, and highlighters over to my side so he's not crowded.

Professor DeMarco's lips quirk as he watches me. "Not comfortable taking up space in my presence, hm?" he murmurs.

I feel woefully *young* around him, like a little girl without a single clue.

Like right now.

My trusty brain absolutely fails me, and I can't for the life of me figure out the answer he wants.

"I'm an introvert," I mumble by way of explanation, but like anything I ever say to him, it feels inadequate. "I'm not overly comfortable around anyone."

He watches me as he takes another sip of his coffee. "Does that make college challenging?" When my gaze flickers to him, he adds, "I mean socially. You're clearly an intelligent girl, so I'm sure the academic aspects are no trouble for you."

Even subtle praise from him feels like Uncle Scrooge handing over a bagful of money, so I find myself glowing under it. "Thank you. Um, I don't know. The social aspect doesn't matter much to me, but I guess it's a bit harder. My mom has been on me to put myself out there and make friends, but I just... don't really want to."

"Have you always been that way? Must have been a constant struggle if she pushed you in an unnatural direction."

No.

I don't like admitting it, have made it a forced habit not to, actually, but for whatever reason, when he asks, I tell the truth.

"No," I say softly. "I wasn't always like this." I swallow, the words feeling unusually thick and heavy as they roll off my tongue.

The admission causes an uncomfortable stinging sensation behind my eyes. Light moisture gathers, but it's not enough to form tears, so I'm not worried I'll start crying.

"Sometimes I feel like I was meant to be someone else. I *wanted* to be someone else. I think I was on the path to be, but... my natural inclinations tend to lead me toward bad situations where I get... hurt. I can't always trust my instincts," I say, shaking my head. "They're not very good."

His brow furrows with concern, but he doesn't say anything.

"I guess it's just easier not to let anyone close, you know? Anytime I do, I get hurt, and I just... I'm tired of hurting."

Self-conscious of the deeply personal thing I just revealed to my professor, of all people, I grab my hot chocolate and gulp down the rest.

"Well, I better go," I say, not waiting for him to say anything else. "I have a ton of homework and I need to go to my mom's tonight, so..." I keep my gaze directed away from him as I gather up my papers.

"Sophie, if you ever want to talk—about *anything*, not just the course material—my office is always open. I'm generally in there all alone during office hours, anyway," he says with a faint smile as he catches my gaze. "I wouldn't mind the company."

My stomach rocks when I meet his eyes. I nod, but I look away quickly, clumsily shoving papers into my bag. "Thanks. I might take you up on that."

"I hope you do."

His words feel intimate and make my stomach rock even more.

By the time I flee the coffee shop, I don't know what to feel, what to think. I'm still a bit raw from the admissions he just dragged out of me, and I'm a little worried what he might manage to draw out if I saw him again.

The truth is, before I met Silvan and he turned my whole world topsy-turvy, I was starting to develop a bit of a crush on Professor DeMarco. I literally fantasized about an opportunity to have a moment alone with him, but with the nervous feeling he gave me, I also wasn't sure I'd be able to survive it.

I feel like I barely made it out alive today. I don't manage to entirely calm myself down until I make it back to my dorm, but I'm distracted enough thinking about Professor DeMarco's apparent desire for my company that I forget to be paranoid about the possibility of Silvan lurking in my hallway.

He's not there, anyway.

I make it back to my empty dorm and secure the lock, and I feel a flutter of hope that maybe this is it.

Maybe it's over.

I can't explain why he would give up on me so abruptly when he just sent a car for me this morning, but I've been abandoned at the drop of a hat before, so I don't feel terribly shocked.

Just relieved.

Sure, maybe in a deep dark corner of the most broken part of my psyche, there's a tiny flare of disappointment. To be chased so relentlessly and then dropped like nothing would be jarring and confusing, but what prisoner questions their luck when the shackles come undone?

I wait all night for him to reappear in my life, but there's no text. No car.

Mom comes to pick me up and take me to her house where we have dinner and I get my car back.

I watch the headlights in my rearview and still feel a sense of paranoia as I make my way back to the dorm, but there's no sign of him. When I turn out all my lights and climb into bed, I don't even have that same feeling I've had before of his presence lingering in the air around me.

I feel free.

I don't know why, but I don't care.

It was an odd chapter in my life, that's all.

Now I can turn the page and see what comes next.

When I close my eyes, I'm filled with a sense of anticipation I haven't felt since the very start of the school year. Maybe I even feel a little lighter because of what I told Professor DeMarco at the coffee shop, I don't know.

All I know is I feel a little bit like who I was supposed to be before people started breaking me, and it feels damn good.

CHAPTER 16
SOPHIE

I walk to school on Wednesday, and then I walk myself home.

There's no sign of Silvan, no sign of Hugh.

If I feel slightly abandoned, I tell myself that's insane and shove it down.

I'm free.

That's a good thing.

No more looming presence, no more feeling of my space not being entirely mine.

It's as if Silvan has disappeared.

As if he's a monster I dreamt up, banished by the light of day.

I'm happy about it.

Happy.

Not at all confused or disappointed.

Definitely not.

Thursday is more like my Friday because it's my last day of classes before the weekend.

Professor DeMarco's words from yesterday hang in my mind as the end of class approaches. I catch his gaze a couple of times and think it's on his mind, too.

He has office hours Tuesdays and Thursdays, after all.

I could go to his office.

I'm all jumbled up wondering if he wants me to, if *I* want to when class ends and students begin to file out. I take my time putting my things away just in case he wants to come over and talk to me like he has been.

I don't get to find out, though, because Shelby Cunningham approaches his podium and starts asking a million questions.

I can't stall long enough to wait her out, so once the last pen is tucked away in my pouch, I hoist my bag and make my way out.

I catch the professor's gaze as I head for the door, and I swear he looks a bit disappointed.

That I'm leaving?

Maybe he really does want me to come to his office.

I can't decide if *I* want that, though I did enjoy our brief conversation yesterday.

At least, I think I did.

I don't know, he makes me feel immensely confused about everything.

My steps are slow as I make my way down the hall. I end up stopping a few classrooms down.

I don't know what I'm stopping for, exactly. It would be so obvious if I actually waited for him to leave the class, wouldn't it?

Before I can decide what to do, Shelby comes out of the classroom. Her pace is brisk, but she slows down when she sees me standing in the hallway.

"Sophie, right?"

My eyes widen in surprise and I nod.

She holds out a folded sheet of white paper. "I was asked to give you this."

What?

I take the paper, but my confusion must be clear on my face.

She flashes me a smile, then turns and continues down the hall.

I swallow, glancing back at the classroom where I know Professor DeMarco is alone now, but going back feels about as subtle as waiting for him in the hall.

I open the sheet of paper and my heart stalls when I read the message typed inside.

Sophie,

I enjoyed seeing you yesterday after school.
Don't come to office hours today.
Come to my house tonight.
I'll be eagerly awaiting your company.

-Professor DeMarco

My jaw drops open.

"Tonight" is underlined with three bold strikes, and below that, he wrote a time and his address.

It's all typed, but those three bold strikes... he writes those below his comments at the top of tests.

He wants me to come to his house.

That's... insane.

I can't go.

Right?

This bold invitation changes my tune about wanting to see him after class. If I do, I'll have to give him an answer, so I pick up my bag and hurry down the hall so I'm gone before he gathers *his* things and leaves the classroom.

All night, I agonize over whether or not I'm going to go.

On one hand, he's my professor. If I *don't* go, won't that be incredibly awkward come Monday morning?

But on the other hand, what does he expect to happen if I *do* go over there? A brief chat in a coffee shop is leaps and bounds away from going over to his house.

I don't get the vibe that Professor DeMarco is a creep, so after much anxiety over the decision, I finally decide to go. I tell myself it's okay because I'm probably overthinking it. It's college, not high school. Maybe professors and students are allowed to be friends.

Nothing will happen that I don't want to happen.

He's not some creep like Dylan, he's a respected professional.

And it's not like he's definitely going to come onto me just because I'm at his house.

And if he does…

I'll just tell him he needs to pump the brakes a little. No big deal.

Yeah, because you're always able to keep your head clear around him.

True, he does scare me a little…

But that bit of common sense isn't helpful, so I toss it out and proceed to tell myself it's perfectly natural to shower, shave, and pick out a cute outfit different from the one I wore to school today.

I'm so preoccupied with the craziness of this whole thing that it doesn't occur to me to feel guilty or paranoid until I'm halfway to my car.

A creepy feeling passes over me like I'm being watched. I turn and survey my surroundings, but I don't see anybody.

As soon as I get in my car, I press the lock button.

Paranoia still lingers and I find myself checking the rearview mirror and the traffic around me on the whole drive over to Professor DeMarco's house.

When I get there, I park in his driveway and turn off the engine.

I take a breath and grab my purse, but I have to ignore the pang when I realize I'm still using the purse Silvan bought me on that shopping spree with my mom.

It feels somehow wrong to bring that purse here. I should have changed it before I left.

Stop it, Sophie. You don't owe him a thing. What he got from you, he stole.

That perfectly rational thought does little to chase away the memory of how solid he felt in the limo when I leaned on him on the way home after he…

I squeeze my thighs together, forcing the thoughts from my head. *Banishing* them.

I didn't want that.

I didn't want *him*.

This is better simply because I'm choosing to be here. Even if it's the biggest, dumbest mistake of my life, at least I get to choose it.

I push open the door and step out onto the gravel driveway.

I wore a cute pair of black ballet flats and a pair of fleece tights beneath a burgundy corduroy skirt. I'm also wearing a white button-down top and a pink infinity scarf to complete the look.

Under the coat Silvan bought me because he thought I seemed cold the night before.

He was always noticing things about me.

Because you were new and shiny and unattainable.

*You haven't heard from him in days, so clearly you
didn't hold his interest, anyway. Now, stop it with the
Silvan crap.*

Tamping down my nerves and all my stray
thoughts with them, I slide my purse strap over
my shoulder and slowly make my way to the front
door.

Ordinarily, I would ring the doorbell, but
there's a note stuck to the mahogany wood that
halts me.

Sophie,

The door is unlocked.
Please let yourself inside.
I'm waiting for you in the bedroom.

-DeMarco

My eyes widen and my heart slides down into the
pit of my stomach.

He's waiting for me in his *bedroom*?

That puts big dents in all my reassurances to
myself that this probably wasn't even romantic in
nature, and I shouldn't be so freaked out about it.

It's also quite presumptuous.

I frown, glancing back at my car and considering bailing on this whole night. In a way, this
note feels like a warning. He's letting me know
what he expects if I step over that threshold, and
this is more than I thought I was signing up for.

It's one thing to be open to getting to know
each other and seeing where it goes, but to think I
would just... sleep with him?

Not cool.

Not in my plans, either.

I'm sorely tempted to flee the scene so I can skip the confrontation, but I still don't think Professor DeMarco is a creep, and I don't want to make things weird for the rest of the semester. Maybe there's some other explanation. Even if there isn't, I shouldn't stand him up. I can go in and then if this bedroom thing is what it sounds like, I'll simply explain that I'm not comfortable with it.

Not that doing that would make things immensely comfortable come Monday, but maybe less awkward than standing him up?

I can't decide what to do but I'm tired of thinking about it, so I do the thing I can't take back.

I open the door.

My heart thunders as I ease open the door and step over the threshold. The foyer is all dark wood and masculine energy, but not bachelor pad masculine energy. It's like the home of a well-educated, cultured man. The kind of man I still think I'd like.

It reminds me why I came here in the first place.

Not for a crude hook-up, but Professor DeMarco... he struck me as someone I might like.

Swallowing a lump of uncertainty, I call out a bit timidly, "Professor DeMarco?"

I don't even know where his bedroom *is*.

I'd also much rather he meet me out here, somewhere safe with windows and books... Oh, he has such a nice book collection.

I wander into the living room, gazing lovingly at the beautiful built-in bookshelf. I move closer and run my hand gently along the spines of some of them.

The floor creaks and I nearly jump out of my skin.

My heart beats so loudly I feel like he must surely hear it, but that movement definitely came from upstairs.

I guess his bedroom must be upstairs.

My crummy instincts whisper that going up there is a bad idea. They're the same ones that told me not to go back for Dylan, the same ones that told me not to go upstairs with Silvan.

I should listen to them, but I don't want to believe them this time. Not about Professor DeMarco. I don't want to believe *all* men are like that, but I don't have a great case with the evidence I've gathered so far in my lifetime.

You can't disprove a hypothesis if you're too big a chicken to run the damn experiment.

Besides, I've survived the failed experiments in my past. If I'm wrong, I'll survive one more.

The old wood creaks as I ascend the staircase. I keep a hand on my purse, cognizant of the pepper spray inside.

Not that I want to pepper spray him, but I'm betting everything on the hope that he's *not* a fucking creep, and I could be wrong.

Please don't prove me wrong about this.

I'm so tired of constant diligence. It shouldn't be so fucking hard to just exist in the world and not be used and tossed aside.

Perhaps it's the environmentalist in me, but I loathe this culture of easy disposability. Everything can't be replaced, and even the things that can be… should they be? I don't think so. Not always. I believe in the value of people and things, and I believe some things are well worth the effort of fixing them up instead of throwing away.

A flash of Dylan with Elle surfaces but I stomp it down with more force than any of the other memories.

He doesn't deserve to have someone loving him when I'm trapped in solitude, unable to trust or let anyone in because of what he *did to me.*

I wish I wouldn't have come here, but I'm here now. It's too late to turn back.

I *want* to go back to my safe little bubble. I don't want to unearth any more unpleasant truths or bet on the decency of any more people.

I'm tired of being alone, but alone is… safe.

If you don't have anyone, then you don't have anyone to hurt you.

Only that's not fucking true either, is it? Because I sure as hell have been hurt by men who weren't mine.

My face is warm by the time I reach the top of the stairs.

I'm fighting back anger because I know the hope I'm clinging to is fragile and it won't take much to snap that thread.

Please be decent. Please be decent.

If he's not, I might push him down the stairs.

Time slows as I walk down the quiet hallway. My stomach rocks with nerves. Ahead of me, there are closed doors on both sides of the hall, but one is cracked open.

An invitation?

I suppose so.

The tension inside me pulls tighter, but I straighten my shoulders and lift my chin and force one foot to go in front of the other.

I feel sick by the time I stop outside the door.

I close my eyes and take a breath.

Please.

"Professor?" I call softly.

The floor creaks on the other side.

I shift my weight, glancing down and tucking a chunk of hair behind my ear.

I clear my throat. "Should I wait downstairs?"

"No."

The word is terse and sounds strange through the door.

A frown flickers across my brow, my instincts trying once more to get me to turn around.

I wish he'd say more, anything to ease my mind, but the idea that he's angry at me does more to get me in the room than anything else.

The nerves I always feel in class start to flood my system, washing out the anger and doubt. The pepper spray in my purse might as well be a bottle of bubbles for the threat it poses as I walk inside his bedroom, my stomach rocking with the idea that I've displeased someone.

The lights are off, but it's around sunset so there's still some light coming in through the windows.

The bed looms large on the right wall.

I don't see him.

I expected him to be sitting on the bed, I guess. I don't really know what I expected.

Not for him to be mad at me, I know that.

Why is he mad at me? I've done exactly what he asked me to do. He doesn't know I've gone back and forth about it, that I was mad and scared coming up the stairs. All he knows is that I came like he told me to, so why—

The door slams shut behind me, and I jump.

On instinct, I turn around, and when I do, my heart nearly drops out of my body.

Because it's not Professor DeMarco darkening that closed doorway.

CHAPTER 17
SOPHIE

SILVAN.

My mouth goes dry at the sight of him, all broad shoulders and chiseled features. He's made of granite as he stalks toward me, and without thought, I back away from him.

"Wh—what are you doing here?" I stammer, confused.

He's wearing jeans and a black T-shirt stretched tight over his well-muscled body. He seems to grow larger as he closes in on me. My chest tightens when I feel the wall at my back and realize there's nowhere left to run.

"Silvan, please." The words tumble out without thought. I don't know why, but I know I require mercy right now.

He grabs a fistful of my pink infinity scarf and yanks me close. A startled cry slips out of me as he grabs my jaw, using his grip on my face to push me back against the wall.

"Tell me you're sorry," he says evenly, but despite his tone, I can feel the danger radiating off him.

I don't even think, I just obey. "I'm sorry," I whisper tremulously.

For what?

It doesn't matter. Whatever he wants me to be sorry for.

"Such pretty words," he murmurs, his gaze dropping to my lips. "Do you mean them?" he asks almost absently.

"Why are you here?" I whisper.

His lips tug up, but not with any real humor. "Why are *you*?"

My stomach bottoms out.

I know in reality I haven't done anything wrong, but he makes me feel like I have.

His tone is frighteningly calm despite the anger I can feel burning inside him. "I can't decide if I'm angrier that you accepted his invitation and showed up in his fucking bedroom, or that you exposed parts of your soul to him when I thought I'd made it clear *I* was fucking hungry for any single little thing about you that you'd be willing to share."

His grip on my jaw eases, but only so he can wrap his hand around my throat instead.

On instinct, I grab his wrist as if that might keep him from hurting me.

"Tell *me* who you wanted to be, Sophie. Tell *me* what you're afraid of, what makes you uncomfortable. Tell me everything about you, because I want to know."

My heart hammers and my skin feels hot. I swallow, and I can feel the shackle of his hand locked around my throat. "You disappeared," I say softly.

"I had to see what you'd do without my interference." His fingers move and he presses his thumb against the thundering pulse in my neck. "See, there are things I didn't want to be, too."

Keeping a firm grip so I'm trapped against the

wall unless I want to choke, he leans in, inhaling my scent and closing his eyes.

His voice remains calm, but his words still make my heart skitter. "I thought the last thing I would ever want to be is my father. He loves a woman who can't be trusted, but he loves her with everything he has. It sounds sad, doesn't it? I always thought it was. Fucking pitiful. But I'm learning something tonight," he murmurs, his grip on my throat tightening painfully.

My grip on his wrist tightens, and when he leans into me, I grab his side, desperate enough for his goodwill that I'll... I'll do anything for it.

He sees it.

"Unbutton my pants."

Struggling to breathe with his grip on my throat, I drop both of my hands and unbutton his pants.

"Good girl," he murmurs.

A jolt of electricity pierces the desperate fear, but it's too confusing to process.

"I like you desperate."

My heart sinks, but I can't speak and I don't try to.

"You're damaged goods, aren't you, Sophie?"

I flinch at his words.

"I don't mind," he continues smoothly. "I like broken things. And I like inflicting my wrath on the things that caused that damage, too."

Fear numbs my mind, and my eyes go wide.

He took control of me with fear the moment I stepped inside this room, so it never even occurred to me...

"Where... where is Professor DeMarco?"

He shrugs but it feels like a lie.

Panic grips me. "Silvan... Silvan, where...?"

My voice shakes, but I don't even know what to ask.

My god, he didn't hurt him, did he?

I can't breathe.

"Silvan, he—he didn't do anything. Please tell me you didn't…"

It shouldn't even be in the realm of possibility he might have hurt him, but Silvan is *not* normal. He doesn't operate in the realm of normal expectations.

I just don't know how far he would take it.

He might be torturing me on purpose because he's jealous and I made him mad, but surely, he didn't really do anything to him.

Maybe he's just trying to scare me. To punish me. Silvan is very manipulative with words. He keeps a clear head and uses his words carefully while my mind blanks with fear and I can't think straight, so he's probably just fucking with me. Trying to scare me. That's all it is.

I still feel sick.

I don't know what's real and what was Silvan.

Maybe none of it's real.

I play it all back, and when the girl handed me that note, she said she was told to give me the letter. She didn't say Professor DeMarco told her to give it to me.

Maybe this was all a trap.

"Is this even his house?" I whisper.

Silvan smiles, but it's not a nice smile. "Oh, yes. This is his house." He keeps one hand around my throat, but brings the other up to grip my jaw, turning my face and making me look at the bed. "And that *is* his bed. But he is not the one who's going to fuck you in it."

My heart stops.

Fear claws at my insides.

"Silvan, no," I whisper.

He leans close and kisses the corner of my mouth, still holding me in place. "You wanted to give it up to a manipulative bastard tonight, Sophie. Who am I to stop you?"

"No…"

"It's ironic how he was asking if you understood misattribution of arousal, isn't it? When he uses his authority over you to make you nervous, to get you all hot and bothered so you think you might be into him. He was practically rubbing your fucking face in it even as he was using it to fuck you. I've gotta tell you, Soph, I think he's a fucking asshole. I'm not impressed."

"I wasn't going to—"

"Don't bother denying it, beautiful." He lets go of my throat so he can unbutton my skirt.

I squeeze my eyes shut and swallow. "Silvan, please…"

"It's all right. I'll let you make it up to me."

I open my eyes. I know it's a risk even letting on that I care when he's being so unreasonable, but I have to know. "Please tell me you haven't done anything to him."

"I haven't. Not yet."

There's eagerness in his last words, a sense of malice that makes me really fucking nervous.

"He didn't—he didn't do anything to me. I don't like him like that," I say pleadingly, meeting his gaze.

His green eyes are so dark, in this light they could be black.

"I'm sorry," I whisper, since he liked that word on my lips last time I said it.

He likes it now, too.

He grabs my throat and pulls me away from the wall, into his hard body. "Say it again," he murmurs as he kisses my lips like he can taste the flavor of my remorse and he wants a stronger proof.

"I'm sorry," I whisper.

His lips crash against mine and he pushes me back against the wall. I cry out at the impact, then gasp as his hard body presses into mine.

I'm caged against the wall as he ravishes my mouth with such possessive greed, such raw hunger that I can scarcely breathe. I push against his chest, but that only seems to intensify his appetite for me.

When he breaks away from my lips, I suck in air like a drowning person breaking the water's surface.

"You came here to see him, but you're getting me."

I shake my head in denial, but he doesn't give me a chance to speak.

"Tell me you want me, Sophie."

That demand feels like a blade he wants me to turn on myself.

He slides a hand around the back of my head, then grips the strands of my hair and yanks my head back, baring my neck moments before he latches on. I cry out as he roughly kisses my neck, pushing me hard against the wall, but using his hand as a cushion so I don't bang my head.

"I'm still deciding what I'm going to do to him, Sophie. If you want me to be merciful, you better fucking beg for it."

My heart stutters to a stop, then races to catch up. "I... I..." The words won't leave my lips, so he bites me. I cry out at the bite of pain, grabbing his side and bracing one hand on his muscular shoulder. "Silvan, please."

My skirt is on the floor, so when he pushes up

my shirt, he easily grabs the waistband of my tights. I gasp as he tears through them one-handed, ripping them away from my body with a loud tearing sound that seems to echo off the walls.

He leaves the ruined tights hanging around my thighs, then slides his hand up my trembling body to cup my breast.

"Silvan," I whisper. "Please… I'm—"

"You're what?" His eyes burn into mine with such intensity, I can't look away. "I want to hear you say it."

"I'm scared."

He caresses my jaw almost lovingly even as he revels in my fear. "Of me?"

My heart thunders, but I nod my head.

His lips tug up faintly, then he pushes a hand between my thighs and rumbles, "Is that why you're so fucking wet for me, Sophie?"

I squeeze my eyes closed.

Humiliation ripples through me. I want to shove his hand away, shove *him* away. I want to run and never see him again.

"This pussy's just begging to be fucked, pretty girl."

No.

I bite back the denial because I know it doesn't matter.

He'll do what he wants to do to me.

He doesn't even need justification.

I knew coming here tonight was a risk, but I didn't think I was meeting him.

I would have had a better idea of my odds if I'd known it would be him.

With his palm resting possessively between my thighs, he has to let go of my face to unbutton my shirt. I could fight him, but there's little point, so I just close my eyes and refuse to participate.

The cool air hits my flesh when my shirt falls open. Silvan presses a hand against my belly, then slides it around my side and grips my waist.

"I fucking love your body," he tells me. "The feel of it beneath my fingers. The look of it. Your taste. Every-fucking-thing about it is perfect to me."

His words send a shiver down my spine.

His hand presses at my waist until I let him move me down the wall closer to the dresser.

"Get on your knees."

My knees feel weak, anyway. I don't want to, but I don't want anything worse to happen, so I fall to my knees.

"Such a good girl," he murmurs, looking down at my teary eyes. He caresses my jaw briefly, then lets go and grabs a condom off the dresser.

I swallow as he holds it out for me to take it.

I do, my heart sinking.

He didn't put a condom on last time he wanted me to suck him. I'm on my knees, so I thought... but maybe...

"Silvan..."

He grabs a small camcorder off the dresser, flipping open the side and removing the lens cap.

I shrink away, unsure what he's doing.

"Now open it, Sophie."

My fingers shake as I slowly tear open the foil packet.

I don't understand why he's recording me doing it, but I don't like it.

"Look up at me."

He's towering over me. I wonder how vulnerable I must look down here.

His lips tug up and he presses a button. "That was perfect, baby. You're such a good girl. Give it to me."

I do, and confusingly, he puts the open packet on the dresser.

"Now, when I turn this back on, I want you to take off those ripped up tights and then look up at me."

I sniffle, shifting my weight and sitting on my butt so I can peel off my shoes and the ruined hosiery.

"Perfect. Up on your knees. Unzip me."

Moisture leaks out of the corner of my eye. I dash it away before getting up on my knees. The hardwood floor is too hard, and the room is too cold. I shiver, my shirt hanging open, but I guess at least it gives me a little coverage.

Gripping his hip for stability, I try to ignore the feel of him solid and real beneath my fingertips. I tell myself I just have to get him off and then he'll leave me alone, but I don't think it's the truth.

I tug down his zipper and feel his huge cock straining against the fabric. Drawing in a shaky breath, I look up at him. "Do you want me to pull them down?"

His lips tug up and he presses a button on the camcorder. I watch, confused, as he closes the screen and sets the camera aside, but I'm still waiting for an answer.

He offers his hand.

Tentatively, I take it.

He pulls me to my feet and I feel an initial burst of relief before I realize I may be getting ahead of myself.

He walks me over to the bed and stops at the foot.

"Turn around to face me. When I get the camera and start walking over here, you're going to keep your eyes on me and take off your panties."

"Silvan, I… I don't want anyone to see a video of me."

He ignores me, his attention caught on my lips. His brow furrows and he murmurs, "We need to rough up this mouth a little first."

My heart stalls because I'm not sure what that means but my brain goes straight to violence.

Would he hit me?

I can't imagine he would, but I don't really know him that well.

I lurch away as he reaches for me, but he grabs my neck and my waist, pulling me in and trapping me. I struggle to get away, but his mouth crashes into mine with startling brutality. I cry out and gasp at the force, still struggling to break free as he holds me captive and ravages my mouth more savagely than when he's kissed me before. It feels less like hunger and more like an assault.

I'm shaking when he finally breaks the kiss.

I want to curl up in a ball in the corner and find safety, but he won't let me cower. He won't let me go.

"Silvan, please. I just want to go home," I whisper.

He keeps me pulled against his chest. He's solid and unyielding, but right now it feels more like a wall I'm chained to than a haven I can count on for safety. "First, you're going to do what I told you to."

I lie to myself that maybe if I do what he wants, he'll let me go.

I can't make myself believe it, though, so my body trembles in the sudden cold as his body heat leaves me and he walks away to grab the camera.

CHAPTER 18
SILVAN

She's shaking as I stalk toward her with the camcorder on.

Doing her best to please me, though, she pushes her panties down past her lovely thighs. A tear streaks down her cheek as she bends to shove them below her knees, and then the fabric pools on the floor at her feet. Her tremulous gaze meets mine and then, when she thinks it's what I want, she steps out of them.

Such a good girl.

The heartless lens of this old camcorder might interpret her as pitiful, but to me, she's a goddess. An angel. The loveliest sacrifice I've ever seen.

The woman of my fucking dreams.

It's no wonder I'm fucking obsessed with her. She's perfect. I'd have to be a fool not to be, and I am no fool.

I turn off the recorder and chuck it on the bed, catching Sophie's waist and sliding my other hand around her neck. She gasps as I pull her in for a kiss, her hands naturally rising to push at my chest, but I ignore the pressure and walk her back until her legs hit the mattress.

Her lips are soft and pliant beneath mine. She

tastes like cherries. I fucking love cherries, especially mixed with the natural flavor of her skin.

I want to devour her, to fucking consume her, but if I completely consume her, there will be nothing left.

Her breath shudders as I release her from the kiss and press my forehead to hers, just breathing her in. I steal another couple of soft kisses on the corners of her mouth, but I let her catch her breath.

"Touch me," I tell her.

Her gentle hand trembles, but she slides it down the front of my pants and cradles my cock in her hand. I bite back a groan because that wasn't what I meant. I just wanted her hands on my body, but I'm damn sure not going to turn down her hand on my cock.

I listen to her breathing as she caresses my cock through the fabric of my underwear.

"I want your skin touching mine," I say, my voice rough and demanding.

She flinches a little. I hear her swallow, but then she tugs the waistband of my boxer briefs and pushes her hand down inside, gently handling my cock when she could be rough and petty.

I kiss the side of her face as she takes me in her soft hand and strokes my aching cock.

"Like this?" she whispers, sounding so scared but eager to please me.

She's so close I can feel her breath against my neck, feel her body trembling against me when I tip her head back so I can see her face.

If she looks up at me like this when I'm fucking her, I don't know how I'll ever stop.

"Just like that," I rumble reassuringly, smoothing back her blonde hair so I can kiss her temple. "Your hand feels so good, baby." I pull her close and she turns her face so her breath rushes against the crook of my neck. She's hiding, but that's okay. I'll protect her from anything, even me.

Downstairs, the pretentious fucking grandfather clock this prick keeps in his living room chimes, reminding me that as much as I'd like to take my time enjoying her, I do need to move things along if I want to finish before the fucker gets home.

Though it does bring me some measure of enjoyment imagining him coming home to find me fucking her in his bed.

I'll get more enjoyment out of actually doing it, so it's time to stop her. I grab her wrist lightly and her hand stops moving. I draw her hand out of my pants and feel precum on her palm, so I lift her hand, turn the palm to face her, and tell her, "Lick."

Her lips part and her tongue darts out. My cock jumps as I watch her lick my cum off her hand, her gaze never leaving mine.

"Jesus Christ, you're beautiful."

She averts her gaze shyly, but I grip her chin and tilt her face up so she has to look at me again. I never want to stop looking at her lovely face. I want to paint it with my cum and make her walk around like that so everyone knows she's mine.

"Get on the bed," I tell her. "Scoot back to the middle."

Her voice is tentative as she pulls a trusty tool from her limited arsenal. "Silvan, can't I just… please let me suck you. I don't want—"

I press my finger to her lips, stopping her objections before they can escape. "I don't care," I tell her firmly but gently.

She bites her lip, looking conflicted, but after a moment's hesitation, she sits on the edge of the bed.

The camcorder tips in her direction and her

gaze jumps to it, then she quickly scoots away from it, back on the bed. Once she's where I told her to be, she pulls her knees up to her chest and hugs them close.

That's a perfect fucking shot, so I grab the camera and turn it back on.

She watches me with big fearful eyes as I climb on the bed with her. Her grip on her knees tightens as she tries harder to protect herself. I pause the recording and tell her, "There's a present for you beneath the pillow. Grab it."

I start the recording again and watch through the small screen as she moves his pillow and finds a leather cuff connected to a chain beneath it.

Sophie gasps in horror, dropping the cuff right where she found it. Her gaze darts to me, her eyes wide and fearful, then she abandons her course of trying to placate me and launches herself off the bed.

Adrenaline surges through my veins as her feet hit the floor and she runs for the door.

It's a pointless effort since she has to run behind me to get there and I'm faster than her even if she didn't.

I toss the camera on the bed and lunge for her, grabbing her around the waist and hauling her back.

"No!" she cries, fighting in earnest to get free. "Let me go. Let me *go*! Please!"

"Now, Sophie," I murmur, my arms tightening around her waist as she struggles and claws at my hands. "Be a good girl."

"Let go of me, you psycho! I'm not letting you tie me up. You're crazy if you think—"

"You don't have to *let me* do anything, pretty girl. But I'm going to tie you up either way."

"Please," she says, her voice wobbling with fear. "Silvan, I won't be able to…"

"Move? Flee?" I finish, running a finger along the curve of her jaw. "Yes, beautiful, I know. That's the point."

Since fighting me is getting her nowhere, she turns and looks up at me with those big imploring eyes of hers. "Breathe! Silvan, please. I'll have a panic attack. I won't be able to take it."

I caress the curve of her jaw. "I suggest you remember that next time you think about meeting another man because this is more of a gentle warning than a punishment as far as I'm concerned."

Her eyes widen. "I am not yours."

My lips curve up. "I'm afraid we disagree on that point."

"And I'm afraid that's an irreconcilable difference in this relationship," she snaps back.

I smile at her spunk. "Lining up your divorce defense already? We're not even married yet."

"Yet," she mutters in disbelief. "You're a madman."

"Perhaps, but I'm *your* madman."

"Silvan, don't you dare," she says as I retrieve the leather cuff off the pillow.

"You want to know what's funny? This isn't even my equipment. The toys I use on you will be, of course. But this rig was already here when I came to check the place out. Your professor has a kinky streak. Are you disappointed you didn't get to explore it with him?"

"That is *not* why I came here."

I believe her, but I have to ruin him for her regardless, just to be safe. "You're not his first, you know. He has an entire cabinet full of fuck tapes he's filmed of former students. He may have been interested in making you his latest acquisition, but he's not like me. He's not only interested in you. He wouldn't have kept you."

Sophie falls silent. Fear of abandonment is a sleeping giant among her issues, so I know I'm drilling into the right stud.

He's not the only one who understands her mind well enough to fuck with it.

"Maybe you don't believe me," I murmur. "You think I'm being jealous and possessive, that I'm only saying this because you might have liked him. But you're wrong, and whether you like it or not, Sophie, I'm going to protect you."

"I don't need protecting," she says guardedly, yanking at her wrist as I grip it tight and slide the cuff around it.

"You do. From men who want to use and abuse you. From yourself. I don't know if you know this about yourself, sweetheart, but you have shitty fucking taste in men."

"Do you hear yourself?" she demands wildly. "*You're* the one who wants to use and abuse me. *You're* the only one I need protecting from."

"We both know that's not true," I say patiently, securing the Velcro strap, then slipping the leather through the buckle to make it more secure. "There's predator catnip running through your veins, Sophie. You're delightful prey to hunt and trap, and if you hadn't met me, I'm sure your professor wouldn't have been the last man to notice."

"I am not prey," she says, yanking at her wrist.

"I didn't mean it as an insult," I assure her, pulling her shirt aside so I can kiss the cute little freckles on the ball of her shoulder. "It takes all sorts to make up the food chain. No need to be ashamed of where you fall on it."

"You're a lunatic," she mutters. "If you think I'm seriously not calling the police after this…"

"You won't." I peel her shirt off so she's down to her bra before I push her on the bed and wrestle her onto her back. I grab the cuff on the other side and stretch out her other arm. "See, we're making a sex tape tonight, Sophie, but it's not really ours. I'm not going to be in it. I spent a little time studying your professor's previous sex tapes so I could imitate his style. The rest of the world will believe he filmed you here tonight, and I'm not sure if you know this, sweetheart, but our interactions tonight? They haven't appeared entirely consensual. I'm guessing this next part won't, either."

Her eyes are wide with horror as she looks up at me. "You wouldn't. You can't. He didn't *do* anything."

"But he tried to, and you thought about letting him. That's enough for me."

"Silvan, I did not," she says, yanking at her wrist with renewed force since she knows if I get this one secured, she's fucked.

Literally.

"Silvan, please…"

"Now, you might not be as enamored of your professor now that you know you were just one planned exhibit in his collection, but I'm guessing you don't want me to frame him for rape."

"You're sick," she hisses.

"Perhaps. But who would believe you?"

Her face goes white.

A pinch of regret squeezes me. It's the truth, but perhaps that was a little far.

"What reasonable man would go to such efforts to frame some random professor of a class he doesn't even take? It doesn't make sense, Sophie. And sure, you could claim it's jealousy over you, but we only met this past weekend, and I don't have a history of doing deranged things in fits of jealousy. I could come up with plenty of girls to attest to my lack of jealousy when I was with them. The truth doesn't check out, and I assure you, by the time my family's lawyers chew up the facts and spit them back out, not a soul will believe you. You might even start to doubt yourself."

I don't enjoy when she stops fighting me now, but she knows I have her.

The cuffs are secured, both literally and figuratively.

Her watery gaze meets mine and she whispers, "Why are you doing this to me?"

I trace the curve of her jaw with my knuckles. "I think I'm in love with you."

The news doesn't seem to please her.

She swallows and watches me carefully like I've just said something crazy.

I suppose that's fair.

"I know, it's fast," I tell her as I move down the bed, spreading her smooth legs and feeling a burst of annoyance when I realize she must have shaved before she came to see him. I'm a little rougher when I strap the cuff around her leg, then lift it so I can attach it to her wrist cuff.

"Silvan, what are you doing?" she asks, her voice wobbly with concern.

My gaze flickers to her.

The only clothing left on her body is the pink lace bra that matches the panties she took off.

I'm not sure I believe she's the sort of girl who matches her bra and panties when she doesn't intend for anyone to see them, but the sight of her naked and vulnerable, tied up and nearly ready to be used for my pleasure... well, it soothes the sting of whatever she might have been considering.

After tonight, she'll damn sure know what's expected of her, and if she's smart, she'll fucking obey me.

With so much of her body exposed, I can't resist running my hand over her smooth stomach. She draws in a breath when I do, and a surge of excitement shoots straight to my cock.

I don't have her other leg secured yet so she's not entirely helpless, but I find I'm impatient and can't resist a little taste to hold me over. I grip her free thigh and lean down, ignoring her cry of protest and covering her pussy with my mouth.

She squirms to try to get away so my fingers bite into her flesh. I flick her clit with my tongue and enjoy the breathless cry that escapes her when I do.

This is going to be fun.

Once I've had a little taste of her pussy, I unlatch and finish my job of restraining her knowing once I do, I can help myself to her body and there's not a damn thing she can do to stop me.

I debate whether or not I want to put the ball gag on her. I brought one just in case, but I enjoy her little mewls and cries so much…

Then again, now that she knows I'm taping her to frame that fuck DeMarco, she might make sure to use my name a lot so I have a hell of a time editing the footage.

I guess I better put it on.

Next time I fuck her, there will be nothing to stifle her cries.

She doesn't want it, shakes her head and begs some more as I slip it over her head and secure it around her pretty mouth.

The other annoying thing is that because I am framing her professor for my crimes, I'll have to use a condom. As much as I enjoy marking her with my cum, I'm desperate to fill her pussy with it, but that's not what tonight is for.

Once she's properly bound and helpless, I grab the camcorder and walk around the bed, filming her from all the angles he likes. She's camera shy, turning her head since that's the only part of her body that can move freely.

I shouldn't have tasted her pussy and left my saliva on her, but I think my threats will suffice. I don't think she'll report any of this.

If she does, I'll just have to say I ate her out before she came here.

The important thing is I use a condom so it's not determinable who fucked her.

It's not time for that yet, though.

I grab the leather bag of my own toys and debate what I want to use on her. I'll claim all of her holes eventually, but the butt plug is probably too much for her first time.

I grab the black magic wand so I can make her come a time or two first.

Her pussy is so unused that she came quickly last time. I don't know if she uses a vibrator when she's alone, but I didn't find one in her room.

Her eyes widen with horror when I hold it up for her to see. "Have you used one of these before, pretty girl?"

Her cheeks burn an even deeper shade of red and she shakes her head no.

I turn it on, guiding the bulbous head to her forcibly spread pussy and letting it vibrate against her slit. Her whole body jerks, her stomach muscles contracting and her legs moving as she tries to move away from the stimulation.

She can only go so far, and my range of motion is uninhibited, so I push the vibrating head against her clit.

She cries out, jerking more violently. I grab her pussy, spreading her open and holding the intense vibration against her, not letting her escape it.

Her agonized cries make it through despite the ball gag. I can feel the way her inexperienced body trembles under the strain of this forced pleasure, the way she trembles and begs me to make it stop.

I swear I hear her crying, "Please."

My already boiling blood heats and I angle the head a little differently.

Her desperate cries intensify.

Silvan, please.

I can hear it in my head even if I can't make it out through the ball gag. I know she's begging for mercy, and I appreciate her efforts, but this pussy belongs to me, and I'll torture it as I see fit.

"You know how much I enjoy you begging," I tell her, so she knows I understand. "You also know it won't get you anywhere."

She moans and cries as I hold the buzzing head against her spread pussy, her thighs trembling and her helpless cries getting my dick even harder.

"Just give in. Come for me, pretty girl."

She cries miserably because she doesn't want to.

My lips quirk because I know I won't give her a choice.

I press the head deeper and the broken cries that slip out of her are fucking beautiful.

I can tell by the way her responses change that she's losing her battle against the orgasm. Her desperate cries pour out of her and her body bucks against the mattress.

Please, please, please.

"Don't worry, baby. I've got you."

Helpless tremors wrack her body. I shove a finger into her pussy as she cries and the moaning intensifies, her eyes closed, and her head thrown back against the pillow.

Her pussy pulses around me as she comes, crying and writhing against the bed.

Fucking beautiful.

Her body is too overly stimulated to bear the vibration now so I pull it away and turn it off. I keep my finger in her pussy because I just like being inside her, then I move so I can straddle her torso. My cock nestles between her tits and I'm tempted to take it out and fuck them, but right now my pretty girl just came and she can hardly breathe.

"You did so good, baby," I tell her, reaching behind her head to take off the ball gag. I'll have to put it back because she came so fast, I didn't get to film her, but I need to check on her first.

She's breathing hard when I take the gag off. I grab a fistful of her hair and pull her up so I can kiss her. She's too boneless to fight back and lets me ravage her mouth. She's always soft after she's been used, so when I squeeze her tit, I catch her helpless moan in my mouth and my cock tries to rip through my jeans.

"That was so good, baby, but we have to do it one more time. I forgot to film you."

Her eyes widen and she shakes her head. "Silvan, no, not again, please. I can't. I'll die."

I crack a smile and caress the side of her face. "You won't, I promise. It's just an orgasm. They're not fatal."

"My body can't handle it."

"I'll give you a minute to recover."

She shakes her head, but she knows arguing won't get her anywhere, so she uses her brain and lifts up to catch my lips with hers.

Fuck, she knows how much I enjoy kissing her.

I don't care that her pretty little ass is trying to wheel and deal and get out of another orgasm, all I care about is that her lips are soft beneath mine and her hair feels like silk between my fingers. Everything about her is fucking perfect, and right now her body is spread open for my enjoyment and there's not a damn thing she can do about it but bargain and beg for mercy.

Her mouth is much more persuasive when it's surrendering to mine.

My free hand roams down to squeeze her tit again and she moans. I squeeze the peak, teasing her nipple between my thumb and forefinger as she whines.

Her body is so fucking responsive.

I want to kiss and touch her all goddamn night, but I need to resist her sweet charms and get back to business.

Since I know she doesn't want it back on, I pull her close and kiss her deep so her eyes close and she can't tell what I'm doing until the last moment.

She gasps when I yank her back from the kiss and slide the harness over her head again.

"Silvan—"

I push the gag into her mouth and secure the strap as she rages at me. A little smile tugs at my mouth.

"Don't worry, baby. I'll make you feel much better in a minute."

CHAPTER 19
SILVAN

By the time I've wrung two more orgasms from her body, Sophie is exhausted.

I film the second and third one, but set the camera aside so I can just focus on her for the fourth.

She whines miserably when she comes, but her body jerks more violently and I can tell by the dazed, almost delirious look in her eyes, that one's even better than the three that came before it.

She's spent, though.

She can't take much more.

I take the ball gag off her and feel how broken she really is when she whispers against my chest, "Please, Silvan. No more. Please. I'll do anything."

"Are you my girlfriend?" I ask.

She falls silent.

I caress the side of her face tenderly and kiss her temple. "Maybe you need one more."

"No," she cries quickly, shaking her head.

"Are you my girlfriend?" I ask more firmly.

She sighs heavily. Her eyes close. "Yes," she whispers. "Okay."

I smile, pleased that we're finally on the same page. "Should I take the restraints off now?"

"Please," she says softly.

"Anything for my baby."

I release her legs first, then her wrists.

I wait to see what she'll do, and much to my surprise and pleasure, she rolls over and curls up against me.

I know it's not because she wants to cuddle with me, but she needs comfort, and I'm the only possible source of it right now.

God, I love when she's like this.

I kiss her forehead and hold her close as her body recovers from the intensity of those unwanted orgasms. I caress her back and tell her what a good girl she is until I feel her body completely relax.

I only intend to hold her for a few minutes, but she's so tired, she falls asleep in my arms.

I decide then and there I'll have to take her back to my place. I've only done about a tenth of what I wanted to do with her tonight, but she's a virgin, so I should have realized she wouldn't be ready for a marathon fuck.

I also know that while I have to fuck her here and finish this task, it can't be the only time I fuck her tonight. Sure, I could go to her place, but it won't be enough.

I remember the last time I got my cock in her pussy, and I would've given everything I own just to stay there.

I want to spend the whole night with her. I want to fuck her again, and I want her to fall asleep in my arms when she can stay there. I want the scent of her shampoo lingering on my pillow long after she's left.

For now, there's something else I've wanted to do, and while I didn't plan to tonight, I see my chance, so I might as well take it.

My pretty girl is fast asleep in my arms, but I have to jostle her a bit to free my cock and push down my pants. On impulse, I decide I need her tits free, so I reach behind her back and unclasp her bra.

That wakes her up. At first, she clutches the material against her chest, but seeming to realize I'll get it off her with or without her help, she lets go and slides her arms out of it.

I smile when she tosses it off the side of the bed, then lean in to bury my face in her pretty little tits.

Her fingers slide through my hair. I kiss and suck and bite and earn a few moans as I do. I need to spend the rest of the night fucking her, but my aching cock wants its first taste of relief now.

I kick off my pants now that she's awake. My underwear, too.

I roll on top of her, positioning myself between her spread thighs and guiding my cock to her entrance.

"Please don't hurt me," she whispers.

I kiss her pretty lips, but she doesn't kiss me back. "I won't hurt you," I promise.

Her pussy is slick after all those orgasms, so when I push into her, the passage is tight, but not as impossible as it felt last time I inched inside her.

She must not entirely believe that I won't hurt her because her body tenses up and her nails dig into my shoulders as she holds on tighter.

"Relax," I rumble, kissing the corner of her mouth. "It'll hurt more if you're tensed up."

"Silvan," she says, her voice small. "I don't want—"

I kiss her lips, cutting off her words. "It's okay," I tell her.

Her breath hitches and she gasps against my lips as I push a little deeper. I hit the barrier I hit before and she rests her head against my shoulder, holding on tight and tensing up even though I told her not to.

She's not listening, and I've already made her a promise I intend to keep, so as much as I enjoy her clinging to me in her time of need, I grab her hair and pull her off me, pushing her down on the mattress and wrapping my fingers around her throat.

Fear leaps to her eyes and her hands grab at my wrist.

"I said, relax."

Her tits look magnificent from this angle, and that fear looks so good on her lovely face, I decide to keep her here as I ease forward and butt against the flimsy barrier that presents her body's best effort at keeping me out.

I watch the pain transform her lovely features as I shove past it, feel her desperation as she clutches my wrist.

Summoning every fucking scrap of willpower I possess, I manage to ease into her tight resisting heat, but it feels so fucking incredible to be inside her, it's nearly impossible. I want to slam deep and feel her around every inch of my cock. I want to lose myself in her.

I can tell by her shuddering breaths and fearful little noises she's not having an equally pleasurable experience, though, and I don't want to make it worse for her than it has to be.

I've never fucked a virgin before, but I read up on it a bit in preparation of fucking her.

"Just relax, baby," I tell her, maintaining my grip on her throat and using the other one to caress her face.

"It hurts," she says softly.

"I know. I'm sorry. It'll hurt less if you can relax."

She closes her eyes and a tear leaks out of the corner. I use my thumb to swipe it away, then I slide my hand down to palm her tit. She liked when I played with them while she blew me, and I can feel her body start to respond now as I finger her nipple until it's hard and ready for me.

A soft gasp escapes her when I lightly squeeze, then roll the sensitive nub between my fingers. While she's distracted, I push another inch into her tight heat and she tenses.

I release her tit and slide my hand to her hip, holding her firmly as I push more of my cock into her. She cries out but I'm gripped by a primal need to claim her completely and I can't wait anymore.

"Silvan," she whimpers, her breath hitching as I stretch that sweet pussy with my bare cock. "Please. You're hurting me."

Fuck.

It's like pushing into paradise.

"Oh, baby, you feel so fucking good," I tell her, shoving deeper. I'm almost fucking there. I couldn't stop now if my life depended on it. I can't even breathe until my cock is all the way in, surrounded by the tight hotness between her thighs.

Fucking fuck, I can scarcely think.

Men would commit an awful lot of atrocities for a pussy this good.

At least, I will, apparently.

Perspiration trails down my muscled back as I hold myself over her, barely managing not to pump in and out of her sweet virgin pussy despite her cries of distress. I want to give her a minute to adjust, but I also want to feel her squeezing me as I move inside her.

"You're doing so good, baby," I tell her as I notch my hips and ease back. The pleasure is mind-numbing, and I swear to fuck, I nearly black out. "Jesus Christ. I was joking earlier about the whole marriage thing, but what do you think?"

"That's not funny," she says, her voice strained.

"I wasn't joking." I feel bad for her sigh of relief when she thinks I'm going to pull out of her.

I don't. I groan as I push back in. Sophie cries out and her nails bite into my skin as she grips my back.

"That's it, baby," I tell her, releasing her throat so I can brace my weight on the mattress beside her.

"Silvan," she whines.

"You're doing so good, baby," I tell her. "So fucking good. You're perfect."

My words seem to help even if she's still reluctant and extremely uncomfortable. She swallows, then wraps her arms around me to hold on tighter as I invade her sweet body again.

She stops pleading with me to stop, but with her clinging to me, I can hear her sexy little noises in my ear as I fuck her. Every cry sends a sharp jolt of pleasure coursing through me, every whimper makes me feel like I'm on fucking fire.

I've never wanted a woman like this before, never felt so hungry for her even as I drive my cock deep into her body.

I can't get enough of her even as I'm consuming her. My hands roam and grab at her tits. I bite her neck and kiss her jaw with reverence. I kiss the corners of her lips and plunder that perfect fucking mouth. The entire time, her pussy never stops feeling like a vise around my cock, clenching and squeezing, fighting me off and trying to keep me out long after *she's* given up the fight.

And victory as I take her anyway never ceases to feel like I'm conquering the whole fucking world.

I am. She's the whole world. The only part of it that matters, anyway.

My pretty girl is so exhausted, her lovely body covered with perspiration, her blonde hair an absolute mess from me handling it so much while I'm fucking her. Her hands slide over my shoulders, her fingers clutching me tight and her breath coming in quick little bursts as I drive into her body.

I've been so lost in my own pleasure claiming her body for the first time, I haven't even put in any work on hers. But now I see that despite the pain and turmoil, her body can't help responding to the domination. When I grab her tit and slam into her pussy, she cries out and throws her head back against the pillow.

"Does my baby like it rough?"

She doesn't answer and I don't need her to. Her desperate grip on my shoulders, the way her breath rushes in and out of her... her body tells me all I need to know.

I move my hand under her ass to support her better and get her at the right angle, then I draw back and slam my cock deep in her pussy. A trembling cry slips out of her, so I do it again and again and again. Harder each time, her cries growing more and more desperate, louder and needier with every forceful stroke.

"Fucking perfect, Sophie. You're fucking perfect." I can barely grunt out the words as I slam my cock into her tight heat again and again. Even when she comes and I feel her pussy convulsing around me, even as she cries and moans and arches like the most magnificent creature I've ever seen, I don't stop. I can't stop. But I can't hold on, either. Not with her pussy squeezing me like that, begging me to join her.

I keep fucking her through my orgasm, straining as hot jets of cum fill her sweet pussy.

When I collapse beside her on the bed, it doesn't matter that it's someone else's bed.

It doesn't matter that she didn't even want to be there.

Her body knows it's mine, and she's vulnerable in the wake of all the pleasure I forced on her, so she yearns for my embrace. She turns and rolls over on the bed so she's closer to me.

Not close enough. I grab her around the waist, yanking her in as close as I can get her. She snuggles in like an angel, nuzzling her face in the curve of my neck.

I've never felt peace like this before.

I kiss her wherever my lips can reach and lock my arms around her body, holding her tight.

I know it probably wasn't how she imagined her first time, but it was the best fuck of *my* life.

CHAPTER 20
SILVAN

SOPHIE FALLS ASLEEP IN MY ARMS.

I wish we'd have already gone to my place so I could let her stay there, but since we *are* in this prick's bed, I'll have to disturb her.

Loathe as I am to let her go, I ease out from under her, grabbing a blanket and draping it over her naked body. It's drafty in this room, and without my body heat to keep her warm, I don't want her to catch a chill.

I collect my clothes off the ground and pull them back on, mentally taking inventory of all my fuckups and deciding how best to tweak my plan.

I didn't bother with a condom and came inside her, so I fucked that part up, but it was well worth it. I had a back-up idea in mind to buy me a little time if this got messier than I intended, anyway.

I'm not worried about Sophie reporting me now. She's coming home with me tonight, so I don't have to worry about what she does when she leaves.

She's leaving with me.

That feels right.

Too right.

I never want to let her leave my side again.

I want her body curled up against mine every time she falls asleep.

I am gone for this fucking girl.

A fond smile tugs at my lips just looking at her sleeping on the bed.

I need to get it together and get out of here, though. We've stayed longer than I intended to, and I don't know what her mental state will be when she wakes up, but in case it's bad, I don't want her driving herself to my house.

I grab the burner phone I brought here with me tonight and draw out my wallet so I can make sure I'm remembering the phone number right. I'm not in the habit of memorizing my friends' numbers—*I don't even know my parents' numbers by heart*—but I didn't want to program any numbers into this thing, either.

Unfolding the scrap of paper, I tap the flashlight feature on the phone. Once I've got it, I enter the number on my empty messages app and shoot one off to take the temperature and see if he's free.

"You around?"

I give it a few seconds, but nothing comes back.

That's all right. I go over to the closed cabinet in the corner where Professor DeMarco keeps his sex tapes so I can get what I need.

The tapes are all kept together on a shelf and neatly labeled in bold black Sharpie. He doesn't label the tapes by the girls' names, but by the general mood of the movie he's made.

Lust. Anticipation. Desperation. Ambivalence.

This one will be called Reluctance.

I won't write it myself. Just in case my pretty girl proves disobedient and the police end up involved, I can't risk being sloppy with the details. My friend has a contact he claims is an expert at forgery, so I grab a couple of blank labels and take pictures of the others so she'll have all the letters she'll need to copy and in the correct case.

The phone lights up and I glance at the display. The text back reads, "Yeah. You need something?"

I type back, "Remember what we talked about earlier? I'm at the house now. Any chance you could meet me for a pickup?"

"Maybe. What exactly am I picking up?"

"Date night with my girl ran long," I tell him. "I'm gonna take her to my place, but I need someone to drive her car back to her dorm."

"That's it? Just a simple delivery? You don't want me to get rid of it? You don't need my help carrying anything heavy?"

Is it just me, or is he asking if I killed her?

"No, nothing crazy," I assure him. "Just need you to drive the car to her place so it'll be there for her when I return her home."

Apparently satisfied that she's still alive, he texts back, "All right. Be there in a few."

"Thanks."

I shake my head as I tuck my phone away, then I get back to what I was doing.

I finish up at the cabinet, swiping through photos to make sure I have what I need, then I tuck the blank labels in my pocket and grab my backup plan—a tape that was once labeled Passion, but he put a bold strike through it and renamed it Vengeance.

I head back over to the bed and drop the tape on his pillow. I didn't have a lot of time to re-search, but his affair with Passion went sour, hence the rename of her tape. I want to put it in his mind that maybe *she* broke in and fucked someone else in his bed. Given the crazy shit she did when he stopped seeing her, it should check out.

Just long enough to make sure he doesn't go to the police before I have what I need to frame him.

He can't go to the cops if he thinks it was her. Passion was the youngest student he fucked with —an advanced student, only 16 years old. The law might consider her of consenting age, but I have a strong hunch the university faculty would feel differently if they found out about it.

It's only a temporary smokescreen, so it doesn't have to hold up.

Eventually, I want the fucker to know it was me.

Just not until I'm ready.

Besides, I'd like to use it against Sophie for now, see what I can make her do to protect the slimy fuck.

I put Sophie's clothes on the mattress, and when she doesn't wake up, I take a seat and reach out a hand to caress her face.

Her eyes open and her sleepy gaze meets mine. Confusion briefly causes her brow to furrow as she looks around, trying to figure out where she is, maybe even why she's somewhere she doesn't recognize.

I watch as realization settles over her and the unguarded moment comes to an abrupt end.

She realizes she's naked and clutches the blanket against her tits, but then she realizes it's her professor's blanket, and her alarmed gaze shoots back to mine.

"I need you to get dressed so we can leave," I tell her.

I watch her try to process everything. She looks lost as she releases the blanket and sits up.

Her lovely tits beckon me. I want to grab her and climb on top of her. I want to fuck her again already, even though I know she was a virgin, and

I should probably leave her alone for the rest of the night.

"What's... I don't..." She rubs her eyes, then looks around the room again.

"It's time to go," I tell her, taking her hand.

Her gaze jumps to my hand covering hers. She still looks reluctant, but she lets me tug her toward the edge of the bed.

"Get dressed," I say, kissing the back of her hand before releasing it. "We're leaving."

This time, she manages to stand and stretch. I admire the view as she does, and continue to watch her as she pulls on her panties. I relish knowing she must still feel me between her legs, coating the inside of her pussy. I can't wait to take her home and clean her up before we go to bed.

Once she's dressed, she looks around for her coat. I hold it up for her, and she's startled when I help her into it.

"Thank you," she murmurs, her gaze not meeting mine.

I grab the back of her neck and pull her in, kissing her pretty lips as she gasps, then draping her scarf around her neck. "You're welcome."

She looks around as we leave the room, paranoid that we're leaving something behind.

I made no effort whatsoever to fix the bed, and I smirk imagining his horror when he comes home to find her virgin blood and my cum all over his bedsheets.

Fucker.

I lead Sophie out to my black BMW. She's so fogged from everything I've done to her tonight, she doesn't even think to object until I open the passenger side door for her.

A frown of confusion flickers across her face.

She looks back at her beat-up Honda. "I drove myself tonight."

"You're going home with me," I tell her.

"I can't. I can't just leave my car here."

"We're not leaving your car."

Her eyebrows rise, but before she can ask, a tall dark-haired man emerges from the driver's side of a car parked in the street.

He must trigger her prey instincts because fear leaps to Sophie's gaze and she unconsciously moves closer to me for protection.

"He's all right," I assure her. "He's with me. He's going to drive your car back to your dorm."

"I don't want him to take my car home for me. I want to take it there myself. I want to go home."

"You're going home with me tonight, Sophie. End of discussion."

"Silvan…"

I hold out my hand. "Give me your keys and wait for me in the car."

She looks uncertain and more than a little unhappy, but I can tell she's wary of another man being here. Especially one who came at my behest.

To me, it's crazy she even imagines I would ever let another man hurt her, but I take advantage of her old fears for now because it makes her capitulate to my demands much easier.

She hands me her keys, then gets into my car without further protest.

Dare hangs back while I get Sophie in the car, then approaches when he sees I'm finished. We meet behind her car in the driveway, and I hand over the keys.

"Thanks, man. I appreciate your help."

"Anytime," he says wryly.

"I owe you one."

"Aren't we up to two now?" he shoots back, his

tone light enough, but I know it's no joke. He's keeping track, and someday he'll cash in on every favor he's owed.

That's how it is with most friends in my circle, whether or not they're honest about it. I'm used to it.

"Of course. Speaking of that first favor..." I draw out the burner phone and the blank tape labels. "I took pictures of the other tapes so she'd have a good sample of his handwriting. Looks like he uses a well-worn black Sharpie."

Dare glances over his shoulder before grabbing the phone and the labels.

"All right," he says, tucking them into his jacket pocket. "It'll take me a week or two to get it done. I'll have to do this in person, and that means flying back to Baymont. I've been thinking about making a trip home, anyway, but it's not a comfortable favor to call in. I have to get some things in order first."

"That's fine." I glance back at my car, at Sophie curled up in the passenger seat. "Sooner is better just to be safe, but I don't even know if I'll end up using it. For now, I think just the threat of it will prove a useful tool in working around my girl's reluctance. I want to do it right and have the insurance policy in case this guy turns out to be a problem, though."

He nods without the faintest hint of being bothered by my methods. "I get it. I'd do the same thing."

I figured.

That's why he's the one I called.

"I appreciate it."

He nods, turning and heading for Sophie's car. "I'll be in touch."

CHAPTER 21
SOPHIE

THE CAR IS COLD.

Silvan took both sets of keys. I don't know if he just didn't think about it, or if he took them deliberately so I couldn't drive away without him while he talks to his scary friend.

There's something familiar about the guy, but I can't quite place him. He's tall and handsome with a face I wouldn't think I'd forget.

When I look at the car he came in, I see there's someone else inside. That's when I realize why he's familiar.

The girl has dark hair tonight, so I guess she's not actually a blonde, but that's definitely the girl who was dressed as Harley Quinn at Silvan's Halloween party. I guess that makes the guy talking to him the Joker who was making out with her.

I wonder if she's a willing accomplice to whatever this is. She never got out of the car, just scooted over from the passenger side to the driver's side. She could leave, but I get the impression she's waiting for her boyfriend to make sure everything goes okay here.

Her gaze catches mine and she smiles. It's a feeble smile, more a gesture of friendly solidarity than any kind of happiness. I wave, and she gives me a little wave back.

Prisoners in nearby cells, reminding each other that we're not alone.

Maybe it only seems that way to me.

Maybe she's free, and I'm just looking at her world through my own broken lens. The same one that makes me feel sympathy for girls at parties when I see them being kissed.

The guys separate, Joker getting into my car and Silvan coming back to his.

I avoid looking at him when he opens the door and slides in.

Instead, I focus on Harley and Joker.

I think I was right about her protectiveness of him because now that she sees everything is fine, she cuts the wheel and drives away.

I guess she isn't a prisoner, after all.

I guess only I am.

I wrap my arms around myself, watching out the window as we leave my professor's house.

I feel like such a fool for falling into Silvan's trap.

Again.

I don't know how I could have known better this time, but I should have.

Silvan starts the engine. Air blows out of the vents, but it's cold, so I wrap myself up tighter. Off-handedly, he notices and reaches over to close the vents on my side.

"They'll warm up in a minute," he tells me.

I finally dare a glance in his direction. "You didn't tell me you knew that guy."

Silvan glances over at me, but doesn't say anything.

"He's the Joker from last weekend, right?" I'm second-guessing myself, but I'm sure he is. I only saw him from behind, but I definitely recognized the girl as Harley.

"Of course I know him. He was at my party, wasn't he?"

"I was at your party," I mutter. "You didn't know me."

He smirks faintly. "*He* was invited. *You* were a plus one. I'll have to send your roommate something nice to express my gratitude."

I focus my gaze out the front windshield and stifle the urge to cast a longing look behind us to see if my car is still in view. "I know you want to take me to your house, Silvan, but… I don't want to go there. I want to go home."

"I understand. Unfortunately, that's not an option."

His words make my insides feel cold.

Especially after what just happened at Professor DeMarco's house.

What he took from me.

I lick my lips, unsure of my next words, but feeling the need to put them out there anyway since I don't know what happens next. "Look, I won't… tell anyone what happened. I just want to sleep alone in my own bed."

"No."

The startling simplicity of his response makes my eyes widen. I turn my face to look at him, but his gaze is fixed on the road. "Why?"

"Because I want to spend the night with you, and I don't *want* you to spend tonight alone. I want you with me."

"Why? So you can keep an eye on me? You said whatever you did to me you'd expect to get away with."

His brow furrows, but his gaze doesn't leave

the road. "I think you're paraphrasing pretty generously. I said that about a specific instance."

"You came inside me," I say accusingly.

"Yes, I know."

"You made me open a condom and then you didn't even use it. I'm not on the pill."

"I know."

"I don't get the shot or anything. No IUD."

"I get it, Sophie."

Maybe he does, but now that I'm actually thinking about all this, I'm beginning to panic. Spoiled rich boys like him might like to dally with girls like me, but they certainly don't want to deal with any unwanted repercussions.

He's proven tonight he's willing to commit crimes to get his way, to cover his tracks. I've seen that he apparently has friends who will help him clean up his crime scenes.

What else might he do?

What might he do to *me*?

"So, you got what you wanted. Why won't you let me go home now?"

His gaze flickers in my direction, but there's a car coming in the other lane, so he doesn't look at me for long. "I already told you. I want to spend the night with you."

"Then you'll let me leave in the morning?"

He doesn't answer that question.

I wait for it, thinking perhaps… I don't know what, but he has to answer me.

Because it's an easy answer.

Yes.

Of course I'll let you go home in the morning.

If he just wants to use me one more time to satisfy his urges and then he'll let me go home, I'll stop complaining and let him have his way, but so much has happened tonight that's swirling through my mind.

He asked if I was his girlfriend.

I would have never said yes to that, but I was desperate to stop him using that toy on me. My body couldn't take much more. I felt like I was losing my mind, and the shame that came with the physical release...

I didn't *mean* it.

He knew I didn't mean it. Everything I've agreed to, I've agreed to under coercion. He's always making me do things.

A new, scarier question occurs to me.

When will it stop?

I thought it was odd how quickly he dropped me after coming on so strong, sure, but it was a relief as well. It meant I could get back to my life and stop looking over my shoulder.

Clearly, I wasn't looking over my shoulder *enough*.

"How did you know I'd come to his house tonight?" I ask softly, remembering some of the things he said to me earlier. "How did you know what I even talked to Professor DeMarco about?"

"You shouldn't ask questions you don't want answers to, Sophie."

"I *do* want answers. If I tried to tell anyone the truth about you, they'd think *I'm* crazy. I don't even understand it myself. Why are you doing this to me? Why won't you leave me alone?"

"I will never leave you alone," he snaps.

My eyes widen and I rear back, alarmed at the frightening intensity of his words.

I can tell he didn't mean to say it, at least not like that.

He lost his temper.

My questions made him angry.

I swallow, hugging myself tight as if I can stop myself from unraveling, but I'm not sure I can.

When he speaks again, his tone is more controlled. I can tell he didn't mean to scare me. "Just stop asking questions, Sophie. You're coming to my house. You're going to spend the night. I didn't mean to snap at you, but it's been a long few days for me, too."

I don't say anything for a moment. Can't decide if I should.

But finally, I decide to tell the truth. "I'm afraid you're going to hurt me," I say softly.

I feel his gaze on me, but I don't turn my head to return it.

"I told you I wouldn't," he says solemnly.

"I know," I whisper.

But I don't believe you.

CHAPTER 22
SILVAN

I CHANGED MY MIND ON THE WAY HOME.

I *did* plan to let her go home tomorrow, but Sophie's reaction in the car made me realize something.

She needs firmer boundaries.

She doesn't understand her place right now so she's spinning around trying to find it.

Until she does, she won't be able to feel secure.

Sophie needs a firm hand right now.

I need to let her know exactly where she stands, conventionality be damned.

I want her to give up on this foolish notion that she'll ever get away from me. I want her softness back, and I always get it once I've trapped her and she knows she has to rely on my mercy.

She needs to learn to rely on me.

So, she can't go home tomorrow.

She can't learn it as quickly from so far away.

Giving her space now would just lead to us going around in circles, and I don't enjoy this path. I'm sure she doesn't, either.

She's quiet as I park the car and take her hand to lead her into the house.

"My parents are home," I tell her.

Her gaze flickers to mine, startled. "Will I meet them?"

"Yes. When you do, it would be easier for me if you didn't mention that you're a little reluctant to stay the night with me."

"A little reluctant," she mutters. "What if I tell them I'm 'a little reluctant' about the whole of our acquaintance?"

I crack a smile. "I'd prefer you didn't."

She's quiet again as I lead her into the house. She's been here before, but it looks a bit different. Our housekeeper has already removed the Halloween decorations in favor of Christmas décor.

"Favorite time of year?" Sophie murmurs, eyeing the twisted garland of faux pine tree with lights and a sprinkling of pinecones and red berries twisted around the staircase railing.

I nod. "My mom's favorite holiday."

"Not yours?"

"Mine's Halloween," I tell her.

She nods. "So, you didn't just throw the party to see a bunch of girls in skimpy costumes."

I crack a smile. "I don't need to throw a party for that. If I want a bunch of girls at my house in skimpy costumes, I can just tell them to show up that way and they will."

I can't help the faintest swell of pleasure when her nose wrinkles up as if she finds the idea of my having a bunch of scantily clad girls over distasteful.

"What about you?" I ask. "What's your favorite holiday?"

Her gaze drifts to the pine tree garland hanging over the arch we're about to walk under. "I like Christmas. I'd say Thanksgiving is my favorite, though."

I cock a brow. "Thanksgiving? Really?"

She nods.

"I wouldn't think you'd like that one. Big family gathering, lots of people. You must really like turkey."

She cracks a smile. "That's not how we do Thanksgiving at my house. We don't have a big gathering at all. When my mom's dating someone, she might invite him and any kids he might have over, but usually it's just the guy. One time, one of her boyfriends brought his 12-year-old son—*I was around the same age*—and he was cool. He didn't like to talk. He liked to sketch. We snuck out back while our parents were being gross together, went for a nice walk and sketched the pretty fall trees."

"That sounds pretty chill."

She nods. "Thanksgiving is usually a pretty chill holiday for us. We make pumpkin pie and homemade apple sauce. We make a big batch and freeze a bunch beforehand. It was my grandma's recipe. Then, on Thanksgiving Day, we make turkey with all the typical holiday foods. We make a big batch of yummy dinner rolls and we snack on them all night while we watch Christmas movies. We watch the Thanksgiving Day parade in the morning and do some online shopping for Christmas presents in the afternoon, and then, after a nice relaxing day, we drag the tree box out of the attic and put up our Christmas tree."

"Not a real tree person?"

She shakes her head. "I'd like to be. I know buying real Christmas trees is actually *better* for the environment—especially when you recycle them after the holiday—but, unfortunately, buying a tree from a tree farm every year isn't in the budget right now. We've been using the same artificial tree since my mom got it on clearance in July when I was 10 years old. We have a container of those scent sticks to hang in it, so we still get the pine smell."

"Nah, that's an artificial smell. Gotta have the real thing. My mom loves Christmas trees. She practically butchers half a forest for all the trees she puts up at Christmas. None of them are up yet, but as soon as she can get away with it, she'll have trees up and decked out with different monochromatic décor. Red, silver, gold, blue; every tree gets a different color scheme."

Sophie smiles faintly. "How many trees does a person need?"

"To be fair, we have a lot of rooms."

"Well, I hope you recycle them after you take all the tinsel and stuff off. Christmas trees have lots of uses once we're done using them for the holiday season. They can help fisheries, be used to rebuild sand dunes and riverbanks, or they can just be chopped up and used as mulch."

To be honest, I have no idea what happens to our trees after Christmas. "You'd have to ask the housekeeper," I tell her.

She shoots me a look to let me know she is *not* impressed. "I will," she says primly. "If you're going to kidnap me, then I'm going to make sure you're disposing of your Christmas trees responsibly."

I smirk. "That seems like a fair trade-off."

"Sure, for *you*," she murmurs, but her voice lowers as we enter a room where we aren't the only occupants.

In the main living area, we find the lights dimmed and my mom and dad on the couch in front of the fire.

Mom is curled up next to Dad with his hand on her waist. She pops up when she realizes I'm home, then straightens a little more when she sees I brought a guest.

"Richard, honey, Silvan has a friend with him," she says, trying to peel his hand off her waist.

Dad's hand doesn't budge. He's enjoying a nice cognac and a nice cuddle with his wife, and I'm damn sure not going to interrupt it. At her behest, he glances over at us. "So I see."

"Mom, Dad, this is Sophie. She'll be organizing our Christmas tree disposal this year."

Beside me, I hear Sophie groan, "Oh my god," and I can't help grinning.

Mom blinks, confused.

Dad cocks an eyebrow. "Bit early for a consultant in that particular area, isn't it?"

"He's kidding," Sophie says.

I open my mouth to tell them she's actually my girlfriend, but despite our playful banter just a moment ago, Sophie decides to narc on me.

"Your son has actually kidnapped me a little bit. If you could help me out, I'd like to go home."

"How do you kidnap someone a little bit?" Mom inquires, sounding merely curious. "Is this another joke?"

I grab Sophie's waist and tug her close, seeing the need to get out of here quickly. "Yeah, Mom, it's a joke. Don't mind her. We're going up to my room. Sophie's spending the night."

"I'm not kidding," Sophie says. My warning grip on her waist tightens, but she keeps talking. "I really do want to go home."

"Very funny, baby," I say, grabbing her arm and turning her in the direction I want to go, my other hand still at her waist. "We're in love," I assure them.

"No," Sophie says, looking back at them. "No, we are not."

"Beauty, brains, *and* a tenacious sense of humor," I say, shaking my head. "Surely, you can see why I'm so taken with her."

"Your son has been *stalking* me, and I am not here of my own free will."

I drag Sophie out of the room, shooting her a look as I do. "Remember when I told you I'd prefer if you didn't do that?"

"Yes. I paid it as much heed as you do when I tell you *I* don't prefer things to happen," she answers.

Sighing, I pull her closer and haul her toward the stairs.

She's such a *lovely* pain in the ass.

She doesn't say much as I haul her up the stairs, but I can feel the tension in her body when she realizes she's been this way before. Her alarm grows when we come to the ballroom doors and her gaze darts to me, but I don't return it.

"I thought we were going to your bedroom."

I don't answer, just drag her little ass inside.

Her brow furrows as she looks at the escape room that hasn't been decommissioned yet.

"What are we doing in here?"

I open the doors and give her a little shove into the first of the four rooms we had to go through the night we met. I step inside with her, but only long enough to grab an axe.

Sophie is confused and doesn't catch on until a moment too late.

"Silvan, wait!"

Taking the axe with me, I pull the door shut and the lock engages.

"You brought this on yourself," I tell her.

"You took half the key! I can't get to the next room. I'll be stuck in here for an hour!"

"I'll release you when I come back up. After

that little performance downstairs, I have to talk to my parents—alone."

"Silvan," she calls, beating on the door.

I take the axe with me and start to make my way back the way we came.

I only make it to the stairs. Mom is heading up, but she stops short when she sees me coming down alone. "Where's the girl?"

"I put her in the escape room." I hold up the axe. "She can't get out."

Mom shoots me a disapproving look. "Silvan, you can't kidnap people."

I ignore that and continue down the stairs. "Dad still in the living room?"

"He's waiting for you in his study. He'd like to talk to you."

Yeah, yeah, yeah.

I head to Dad's study with Mom right on my heels. When we get there, he's waiting inside, finishing up his cognac in the chair behind his desk.

When I was a kid, I thought he looked so imposing in that red leather chair behind his desk.

I guess he still does, I'm just not a kid anymore.

"You rang," I say lightly.

"What's this kidnapping business the girl was going on about?"

Without having to ask if he wants her to, Mom grabs the empty glass and goes to the liquor cabinet to get him a refill. My gaze flickers back to Dad.

I could keep up the story that it's a joke, but my actually locking her in the escape room upstairs pokes holes in that story, so I decide to tell the truth.

"You don't have to worry about it," I assure him. "I have everything under control."

Mom comes back and slides Dad's drink in

front of him. "But you *have* kidnapped her?" she asks to clarify.

"A little bit. It won't be a problem," I assure them. "She's malleable, just still resisting a bit right now. I'll wear her down."

"This doesn't sound like a very typical courtship," Mom says as she sits on Dad's lap behind the desk.

I shrug. "She's not a typical girl. She likes me, she just has issues. Like I said, no need to worry about it. I'll handle it."

"When you say you'll handle something like a kidnapping, I have some questions," Dad says. "You've never handled a kidnapping before."

"It's light kidnapping."

"You're perceiving a lot of different degrees of kidnapping where the law doesn't," he advises.

"The law will never be involved," I assure him.

"Yes, I know." His gaze meets mine meaningfully. "I won't have you putting the family at risk over a fling, Silvan."

"She's not a fling." The words are out before I think them through, but they're the truth. "I'm in love with her. It's taking her a little longer to return the feeling, but she'll get there."

Mom with her soft heart and lack of anchor in the real-world smiles over at Dad. "Aw, Richard, he's in love."

"With a girl he kidnapped."

"A little bit," Mom adds, like that makes it okay. "Even the girl said only a little bit."

"Melanie, you cannot slightly kidnap someone."

Mom's cheeks pinken at his admonishing tone and use of her name. Usually, it's her own foolishness that brings out his sharper side, but since it's mine this time, she decides to leave me to it and butt out.

Her gaze drops to Dad's desk for some distraction to let him know she's letting him handle things. She finds the morning newspaper and grabs it, but as soon as she does, Dad stops her, planting a hand on the paper to keep her from taking it.

I try to imagine what Sophie would say if I did a thing like that.

Mom just smiles and looks at dad with a glint of love in her eyes, then teases, "Guess I'm not reading the paper today."

"No, I guess you're not." Perhaps to soften his admonishment, he dips his head and steals a neck kiss, then he kisses her jaw. She smiles softly as their lips meet, but we're in the middle of something, so he doesn't linger.

Mom's attention flits back to me once she doesn't feel shut out of the conversation anymore. "How did you two meet?"

I hesitate to tell the truth since it hasn't been long, but there's little use complicating things with lies.

"I met her at my Halloween party."

Most people might find the timeline alarming, but the men in my family have a tendency to move fast once their gaze locks onto the prize they want, so Dad doesn't bat an eye.

"And you're sure you're in love with her? It's not just lust?"

I nod. "She's all I can think about. I want to make her smile even when I'm not around to see it. I'm completely gone for her, Dad. It's not lust. I've felt that plenty of times. This is different."

He and my mom exchange a look.

I keep going. "I'm not going to hurt her, I just

need to keep her in close quarters for a while so I can batter at her resistance. The foundation is there. She likes me, she just... doesn't want to. She'll give in eventually. I won't give her a choice."

"Is there anyone who will notice her missing?"

"Yes and no. She lives in a dorm room so her mom will just think she's staying there. Her roommates like me, I could tell them she's with me and they'd think it's romantic. I've laid all the groundwork for this to go smoothly," I assure him.

"She goes to school with you? What about classes?"

"She doesn't have any until Monday. I'll figure it out before then. I have some shit I can blackmail her with if need be. I don't see it being a problem."

"Is she close to her mom?" Mom asks. "She might consider it strange if she doesn't hear from her daughter all weekend."

"I'll let her text her mom and roommates so I can control what she says."

"You didn't leave her with a phone up there, did you?" Dad asks.

"Yes, but she can't use it." I hold up the axe. "She's trapped in the escape room."

Dad nods. When we had the escape room built, I knew it wasn't feasible to collect everyone's phones, so we had a signal blocker built in to turn the escape room into a quiet zone. It fit the theme, anyway. Vikings didn't have fucking cell phones.

"Rather convenient that we built you a prison before you knew you'd have a captive," Dad remarks, watching me closely. "You're sure you didn't plan this?"

I shake my head. "Happy coincidence."

He scrutinizes me for a moment longer, but since I've been so honest about everything else, I guess, he decides he believes me.

"Well, I suppose we don't need the ballroom back until the Christmas party. I can contact the builders and delay having the room taken down to give you a little more time. You can't have long, though. If you're wrong about the girl and this isn't going to work out, I need to know sooner rather than later so I can handle it."

My spine stiffens but I nod tersely. "I'm not wrong. Sophie's it for me. Everything will work out. No one else needs to get involved."

"You have the weekend," he states. "If she still wants to leave come Monday, we have to reevaluate. I'm trusting you on this, Silvan, but I won't let some random girl endanger the family, and I trust you won't, either. If she won't play ball, she has to go. You'll meet plenty of women who will."

That's not much time, but I guess I'm not really in a bargaining position here.

I'll have to make it work. I'm confident I can.

After all, I fell for her in the space of an evening. Surely, I can make her love me in a weekend.

"She will," I assure him. "Sophie isn't replaceable," I add, just so he knows where I stand and that I'm serious about her.

He nods, his gaze watchful. "Then I hope you're right and she falls in line—quickly."

I didn't need the added stress of Dad watching over me this weekend, but I know he won't bend on this, so I don't try to negotiate for more time. Doing so would only make him think I'm not as confident as I say I am about being able to convince her.

Locking my jaw, I give him a terse nod of understanding, then I turn to leave.

"Silvan," Dad says, causing me to turn back around.

"Yeah?"

He holds out the newspaper Mom tried to read. "Can you toss this for me before you head back upstairs? It's old news. I don't need it anymore."

I walk over and grab the paper. "Sure."

Mom's gaze flickers to it, but Dad grabs her waist and tugs her legs across his lap, murmuring, "We're going to stay in here for a while longer."

Mom smiles playfully. "Oh, are we?"

I shake my head at them and hasten to leave the room before I hear something I don't want to hear.

I pull the study door shut behind me and consider stuffing the newspaper into a waste can in the nearest bathroom, but then I consider Sophie's enthusiasm about recycling the Christmas trees. I'd never hear the end of it if she caught me not recycling a fucking newspaper.

I head to the kitchen instead so I can put it in the recycling bin. I should probably grab a couple of bottles of water out of the fridge to take upstairs for us, anyway.

I toss the paper in the empty bin for the housekeeper to take outside tomorrow, but when the newspaper lands, I catch sight of something that snags my interest.

I retrieve the folded-up paper and unfold it. Frowning faintly, I flip it over to the article Dad had it open to.

The headline reads: **Investment Banker Found Dead of Apparent Suicide**

Accompanying the article is the man's picture.

My frown deepens because I recognize this guy.

Mom would have, too, which I'm guessing is why Dad didn't want her to see it.

I don't always know who Mom's fucking aside

from Dad, but I do know she was involved with this guy a few months ago—the affair is why they're so loved up now. Dad was pissed at her because she was more careless than usual. A friend spotted them out together and asked him about it.

Fucking someone else is one thing, apparently, but embarrassing him is unacceptable.

I didn't know the guy well and didn't like him since my loyalty lies with my father, but he's the last person I would expect to off himself. He was new-money and acted like it. Cocky and self-important, always telling stories about his travels and boasting about his accomplishments every chance he got.

Suspicion stirs in my gut.

I suppose it could be a coincidence, but is it?

Maybe I'll ask him about it tomorrow.

Maybe I won't.

Right now, I need to go let my lovely little captive out of her cage and make her start falling in love with me.

CHAPTER 23
SOPHIE

When the lock disengages, I'm sitting on the fur-covered chair Silvan sat on last time we were in here, when he had all the answers, so he sat back and watched me do all the work.

I don't rush to jump up. I don't even know if he's letting me out or if he's coming in.

There's no bathroom in here, so surely, he doesn't mean to keep me locked in here the whole time.

I'm relieved when he drops the axe on the ground inside the room and offers his hand.

"Am I free now?" I ask, a bit sourly.

"No," he says, his green eyes glinting with mischief. "Just moving you to a comfier cage."

"What a prince." I take his hand anyway and follow him out of the escape room.

"I think you'll change your tune once you're in my bed. It's extremely comfortable."

"For you, maybe. I don't have any of my stuff. I don't have my books or clothes. I have homework, you know."

"I'll send Hugh for your things tomorrow," he assures me. "As for clothes, I like buying you things, and I have plenty of gifts I haven't given you yet." He slides a hand around my waist and tugs me close, pressing a kiss to my temple. "Not that you'll need them most of the time. We'll sleep naked and tangled together."

"Sounds hot."

He smirks. "I agree."

My cheeks warm. "That is *not* what I meant."

"Obviously, I didn't have time to get your toiletries from your place, so I stole some of my mom's for tonight. I'll have Hugh bring that stuff tomorrow, too, but for tonight you'll have to make do."

"I don't really think I need all my stuff," I say a touch hesitantly. "I'm not moving in."

He falls quiet for long enough that I start to worry, then he says, "You'll be staying here for the weekend."

I don't say anything right away. Knowing he just talked to his parents after I specifically told them he kidnapped me... I'm not sure what that means. I guess he lied to them.

"Will I see your parents again?"

His lips tug up faintly as he twists a doorknob and pushes open what I presume is his bedroom, then he tugs me inside. "Yes, but don't bother telling on me anymore."

"Because you've already convinced them I'm a jokester and they won't believe me?"

"Because they won't be of any help to you, and all you'll do is make it awkward," he says vaguely, backing into the room.

It's still dark. He didn't turn on a light.

My senses are off, and I feel uneasy in the dark with him. I think about feeling along the wall for a light switch and turning it on myself, but before I can, he tugs me through the dark room and I'm so disoriented, I have to stay close to him.

Presumably, he knows where we're going and won't let me trip on anything. I grab his muscular shoulder, moving close so I'm right on top of him as he leads the way.

I can tell he likes that. He doesn't say anything, but I can feel it in his energy. Then he expresses his pleasure physically, curling an arm around my waist and pulling me against his chest. I stumble over something—his foot, maybe?—but he doesn't let me fall. I brace my hands on his firm chest and look up at him, even though in this light, he's all dark shadows.

"Are you afraid of the dark, pretty girl?"

"The dark? No. What might happen in the dark… maybe."

His hand cradles my face, then his fingers burrow into my hair. Once he's cradling my head in his hands, he forces me to stay still while he leans down and kisses me.

My tummy flutters at the way he holds me captive so he can steal a kiss. My heart skips a beat as his lips find mine, and my lips part naturally to receive him despite my reluctance.

I should push him away, but I know there's little point.

My hands remain planted on his firm chest, my eyes drifting closed as he forces his way into my mouth. He keeps my head cradled in one palm, but his other hand slides to my waist, then lower until he's cupping my ass beneath my skirt. Without the flimsy protection of my tights, there's no barrier but my panties. My breath catches as his finger flirts with my pantyline, casually threatening to push that last defense aside.

I try to pull back, but he lets go of my ass, locking his arm around the small of my back instead to keep me close.

"Where do you think you're going?" he murmurs, but his voice is tender.

I let him hold me to pacify him, but only so he's feeling generous when I say, "You said something about borrowing your mom's toiletries, didn't you? Can I assume that means you'll let me shower before bed?"

"Of course. I'm not a beast."

Aren't you?

I don't say that, though.

I say, "Thank you."

His lips tug up and he leans down to give me one last kiss, then he lets me pull away from him, but his hand lingers in mine for a moment more before he lets go. "I'll grab us a couple of towels."

I nod and follow him into the bathroom, but then his words sink in, and my heart skitters. "Wait, us?"

He's opening the linen closet but spares me a glance over his shoulder as he reaches in for the towels. "Yes."

"Can't I shower alone?"

"I'm sure you're capable of it," he says lightly. "But I've spent just about every moment since I met you wanting as much access as I have to you now, so I can assure you, you will not be showering alone."

My lips purse as I look over at the shower stall. I've certainly never showered with a guy before, and though he's seen me naked and I've seen plenty of him, there's something much more intimate about the thought of showering together. It's the sort of thing lovers do, and I don't know what we are exactly, but not that.

Girlfriend.

The agreement he coerced me into earlier tonight flashes back to my mind.

It wasn't long ago, but it feels like it's been days. I can't believe I met his parents tonight. Maybe I should have tried harder to plead my case to them. Surely, if they thought there was any truth to Silvan kidnapping me, they would have put an immediate stop to it.

Thoughts of the armored limousine surface.

I look over at Silvan with the intention of asking him about it, but my brain freezes when I see his hands on his jeans.

He undoes the button, and I bite down unconsciously on my lower lip at the sight of the gray waistband of his boxer briefs. My nerves tense as he pulls down the zipper revealing more soft gray fabric stretched over the bulge between his thighs.

I turn away, my chest starting to feel tight.

This is too much.

I can't do this.

I spin in a circle, scattered, then finally find the direction of the door so I can flee.

I'm nearly to the door when Silvan grabs my arm, gently but firmly pulling me back into the bathroom.

"Where do you think you're going?"

"I can't do this." I tug at my arm, but he doesn't release it. Instead, he turns me around to face him, then grabs my hip and pulls me closer.

"I'm not going to hurt you," he says, gazing down at me. "I just want to get you clean so we can go to bed."

"You've already hurt me," I tell him, my heart in my throat.

A frown flickers across his brow almost like he doesn't see it that way. He reaches out and touches the side of my face, caressing my cheek before sliding his hand around the back of my head so he can force me in against his chest. "I would never hurt you."

He sounds so sincere, I think he must be quite insane. How can he say he would never hurt me when he has so many times already?

He drops his hand and takes mine, pulling me back into the room and over toward the shower. "Come on. Let's get undressed so we can clean you up."

I don't want to, but I don't think there's a way out of it, either. And I do want to get clean. The bastard came inside me back at Professor DeMarco's house, so I can still feel him between my thighs.

I make quick work of undressing. The house is warm, but it's a cold night so there's still a slight chill in the air. Maybe that's why I shiver, but it's probably something else. It's probably being here with him, feeling his hot gaze on me as I step out of my panties.

He comes up behind me the moment I'm completely naked and locks an arm around my waist, pulling me back against his strong body and gazing at me in the mirror. I look up, meeting his gaze in the reflection, but quickly dropping it. I look at his strong arm locked around my waist, the way he holds on like he'll truly never let me go.

But then his grip loosens and he kisses the hollow between my neck and shoulder. He takes my hand—probably so I don't try to flee again— and leads me to the shower.

The hot spray has already made the glass steamy. He steps in first and I follow, letting my gaze get caught on his muscular back since he can't see me. Silvan has an incredible body, so sturdy and reliable. I'm attracted to the visible strength he possesses, and as attractive as he is fully clothed, he's about a thousand times hotter without any on.

My skin feels warm, but I tell myself it's from the steamy shower.

He releases my hand and turns back to close the shower door, reaching across me and making my heart skip several beats.

He's still in my space as he leans back. He does it slowly, seeming to enjoy crowding me. My heart hammers and my gaze flickers to his. Wry amusement tugs at his perfect lips.

"Are you afraid I'll bite?"

"I know you bite," I murmur back, feeling my cheeks heat more as I drop his gaze.

I don't know if the shower is too hot or he's just too close, but it's hard to breathe.

"Come here."

I flinch as he grabs me, but I don't fight him as he pulls me in front of him and sticks me under the hot spray. It feels good as the water beats down on me. I'm cognizant of him right behind me, so close I can feel the heat of his body, but he won't let me move very far, so I turn only as much as he lets me and get myself all wet and my hair soaked through.

I gasp and jump a little when Silvan gathers my wet hair in his hands. He pops open the shampoo bottle and, a moment later, I smell a lovely fragrant scent as he runs his fingers through my hair, massaging my scalp as he spreads the shampoo.

My eyes drift closed. My scalp tingles pleasurably, and I'm surrounded by a cloud of that incredible shampoo smell.

This feels really, really nice.

He must think so too, because once he's finished working the shampoo through my hair, he pulls me back against him and hugs me around my waist from behind. He bends to kiss the side of my face, and I think I should feel differently with his face so close to mine, but... I feel cherished. Loved. I know that's crazy, but I've never felt such warmth before. Such absolute adoration. He holds me and kisses me like I'm the most precious thing he's ever touched, and I feel ridiculous when tears well up in my eyes.

His deep voice rumbles through me. "Turn around."

I do as he says, my throat clogged with emotion. I keep my eyes down so he can't see it in my face. He notices everything, but with the hot shower, I don't think he would be able to tell there's moisture coming from my eyes, too.

"Come here."

He pulls me against his chest, and I go willingly, wrapping my arms around his torso and hugging him. His strong body feels warm, comforting in a way that I need right now when my emotions are in tatters.

He holds me tight until I can breathe again, then he takes my face in his hand and tilts it so I have to look up at him.

His lips meet mine and my heart flutters wildly in my chest. I grab onto his shoulder as he backs me up against the wall. I don't think he means to ramp things up, but then he reaches down and takes my thigh in hand, lifting it so I can wrap my leg around his hip. I break the kiss to look up at him uncertainly, but when I see the hunger in his eyes, I know he means to have me again.

I open my mouth, but anticipating my possible protest, he crushes his lips to mine again, silencing me. I cry out against his mouth, but he ignores it, grabbing my ass and easily lifting me off the ground.

Fear slices through me and I grab onto him, terrified he'll drop me. I know he's strong, but my body is wet and slippery.

My fears are for naught, though. He has a firm grip on me as he walks me back and plants my back against the shower wall. The wall feels cool, but my body is on fire. Silvan tears his lips from mine just long enough to look me over, then he grabs his cock and guides it to the opening between my spread legs.

"Silvan—"

He silences me with his mouth again, kissing me aggressively as he shoves his cock inside me.

I cry out and he kisses me harder, but doesn't stop forcing his cock into my resisting body. I try not to tense up, but he was so rough with me before, my pussy is sore. He's also not wearing a condom again, and my body stretches as he forces himself deeper until I'm so full of him, I feel like I can't breathe.

He fits so tightly inside me, once he's fully impaling me, he stops and just holds himself there, trying to let my body adjust to his size. For just a moment as I try to breathe through the pain, his kisses gentle. He's still the conqueror acquiring land he is certain should belong to him, but he's trying his best to reassure me despite his brutal invasion.

My pussy aches and throbs around his hard length, but after a moment, the pain becomes more of an intense discomfort.

It's a wild feeling to be so full of his cock. I've never felt anything like it. I've touched myself before, of course, but my finger did not remotely prepare me for *this*.

"I need to move, baby."

His voice sounds strained like I'm not the only one feeling discomfort right now.

I bite my lip, nodding and sliding my hands around his neck as he adjusts his hold on me. My pussy burns, but I don't stop him as he pulls almost all the way out and then pushes his cock back inside me.

Silvan groans and kisses my neck, murmuring against it, "That's it. Take it, baby. You're doing so fucking good."

I don't know if I am or not. My body still rejects him, making it tight as fuck every time he pushes back into me. I can see the strain in the corded muscles along his neck each time he shoves in.

The intense discomfort is fading, though, my body giving a little to accommodate the intrusion. It's still a foreign feeling to have his cock filling me up like this, but as it gets easier to take him, the friction of him moving inside me starts to make breathing harder for a whole different reason.

I don't want to come. I really don't. After he weaponized orgasms against me earlier, I'm terrified he won't stop until I feel like I'm going out of my mind, but the inevitability starts settling around me as my heart pounds and my tummy muscles tighten, the building sensation in my pussy starting to feel so good. I let go of his shoulder with one hand to hold onto the wall behind me, tipping my head back and closing my eyes.

Silvan shifts his hold slightly to accommodate this new position, holding me against the wall by my ass, and starts thrusting into me again with more force.

One hand moves from my ass to my breast, squeezing it and pinching my nipple until I cry out. Pleasure and pain tingle through me as he moves roughly inside my sore pussy, but maybe I'm sick, because my body wants more of it.

"Harder," I say breathlessly.

Silvan growls, his hot breath gusting across my tits, making my nipples pebble. I whimper as he draws back and drives into me again, harder and faster than before. "Fuck, you're perfect," he rumbles, his fingers biting into me and probably leaving bruises as he holds me tight and pounds into my sore pussy.

Oh, god.

My body is on fire, and it's not because of the hot water. His thick cock rubs against my walls, hitting something deep inside that makes me feel hot all over. And desperate, so desperate.

Silvan moves faster, grunting and pummeling my pussy until I can't hold on anymore. I cry out as pleasure erupts inside me, releasing the shower wall and clinging to him as rapture ripples through my system. I feel the shaking in my thighs, the trembling in my whole body, and then all I feel is shattering ecstasy. Pure fucking pleasure.

My limbs go weak. I can't hold myself up anymore, but Silvan's strong arms hold me up easily. He's still fucking me, holding my ass and forcing his cock deep as my pussy convulses and squeezes him.

He groans as he shoves deep and I feel a jet of warmth as he pumps me full of his cum.

In the aftermath, he leans us against the shower wall, bracing one arm on the cool gray tile and resting his head against my left tit. I try to let myself down so he doesn't have to hold me up anymore, but when I try, his fingers bite into me and though he doesn't verbally tell me to stop, I do.

He holds me there, holds himself inside me even though he's finished. Once he's recovered, he finally pulls his cock out, but even then, he seems a little reluctant.

My limbs feel hollow when he finally lets me down. He holds me until he's sure I can stand on my own two feet, then he drops his hands, but still lingers close to me.

I don't know what to say or do. My heart is still beating faster than it should be. My pussy feels his absence, a feeling of hollowness that was never there before he forced his way inside me.

He made space for himself, and now... it feels strange not to have him there.

I shake it off, knowing this strange feeling will pass.

It has to.

CHAPTER 24
SOPHIE

As the fuzziness of being thoroughly fucked begins to wear off, Silvan—now satisfied—returns to worshiping me.

He stands behind me again with my body pulled close. He lathers up a white washcloth and works his strong hands all over my body. He cleans my tits, squeezing and enjoying them a bit as he does. He washes my stomach, then lets his cloth-covered hand slip between my thighs.

I close my eyes as he pulls me back against him, sliding his finger out from beneath the cloth and using it to tease my clit. I sink against him and let my eyes drift closed. I don't want to come again, but he makes me, anyway.

At least this time, he only makes me come once.

I'm dazed and sleepy as hell by the time he finishes cleaning me.

My eyes close as he grabs the conditioner and works it into my hair, then he moves me to stand behind him so he can make quick work of cleaning himself.

Now that we've been so intimately connected and it wasn't like at my professor's house, I let myself look at him. I watch him take his cock in his hand and clean it. I watch the lather as he drags the cloth over the ridges of his abdominal muscles and over his firm pecs.

His gaze meets mine as he lifts his arms and continues soaping himself up, but this time, I don't look away.

Maybe it's all the orgasms, but something feels disconnected in my brain. It's like he rewired something, made me feel like... I want him.

Because I do strangely feel in this moment like I want him.

Once he's done showering, he pulls me back under the spray and rinses all the conditioner out of my hair. It makes the floor slick, so he takes my hand as he leads me out of the shower.

The cool air hits my skin and some of the fog clears. Reality begins to trickle back in, but I kind of don't want it.

"Here you go."

I look up as Silvan hands me a fluffy towel. "Thank you," I say softly.

We dry off and he gives me a toothbrush so I can brush my teeth. I wait for him to give me clothes since he assured me he had some here for me, but he doesn't. He takes my hand, flicks off the bathroom light, and drags me into the dark bedroom completely naked.

Since I can't see anything, I have to rely on him to lead me. I stay close and wait for him to stop.

"On the bed," he commands.

I'm relieved when I put my hand down on soft bedding. At least if I'm on the bed, I know I won't trip over anything.

My hands and knees sink into a lush fur blanket as I crawl across the bed. I don't crawl far because I'm not sure how big his bed is, and I don't want to fall off.

He climbs on behind me, planting his hands on my ass and pushing on my back until I lower myself so my tits are on the bed, but my ass is still up in the air.

Running his hand over my ass, he murmurs, "Fuck, I want to take you again."

"Please don't," I say softly. I don't know if my pussy can take another pounding right now.

I'm still a little confused by how I felt watching him in the shower, but now that we've emerged from the steamy, confusing shower stall, my head feels slightly clearer.

I just know there's not much I can do if he wants to fuck me again. I'm naked in his bed. He'll do what he wants with me.

He pushes my face into the mattress. My heart slams because I'm afraid that means he's going to do it, anyway, but I don't fight him.

His hands roam over my ass, massaging and squeezing my flesh.

"I can't get enough of you. You know that? I don't know what it is about you. I'd sleep inside you if I could."

Despite his words, he lets go of my ass and the bed dips as he crashes down on the mattress. He grabs me, pulling me over so I'm snuggled up against his body.

"I should probably let you get some sleep before we go another round, hm?"

I nod even though it's dark and I'm sure he can't see me. He can hear the pillow rustling beneath my head, and he knew my answer before he asked the question.

It's a strange new world as I lie here in his bed after having had him inside me twice tonight. I'm not a virgin anymore. He took my virginity with a vengeance, but at least I have the time in the shower to cushion the brutality of that initial claiming.

I shiver thinking about how scared I felt when I walked in that room and *he* was there.

"Are you cold?" He grabs the soft lined fur blanket and pulls it up over me, settling it around my back and shoulders. My front is already warm from being pressed against his chest.

"Thank you," I murmur.

In the dark, I can make out his little smile. He leans in to press a soft kiss to the corner of my mouth. "Of course. You're my girl. I'll always take care of you."

I *feel* a little like I belong to him now.

I didn't feel that way at all when I said it at Professor DeMarco's house, I just wanted him to stop torturing me. I would have said anything to get him to stop.

But after the tender way he washed me in the shower, after he fucked me again and this time it didn't feel like a punishment or even an intended violation.

I don't know.

My brain is tired, and my emotions are fried. I need to get some sleep, and it turns out he was right: his bed *is* extremely comfortable.

Aware of my exhaustion, he strokes my hair, kisses my forehead, and says, "You should get some sleep, baby. We can talk in the morning."

My eyes feel heavy, and my body is quiet and still. I feel Silvan's chest rise and fall beneath my cheek and its strong, steady rhythm further relaxes me.

Part of me doesn't want to go to sleep because I don't know what tomorrow will bring, but the pull of exhaustion is too strong.

My eyes don't open immediately when I drift out of sleep. I'm too cozy. Warmth has enveloped me from the impossibly comfortable blanket draped over me to the strong arms locked around my body.

That's a startling realization. I've never woken up to a man's arms locked around me before.

My eyes open a bit reluctantly. I don't want to leave the blissful warmth of oblivion, and the moment my eyes open to a room I've never seen before, the reality of my situation crashes down on me.

Last night, Silvan sorta kidnapped me.

I think I left my purse in the bathroom. Maybe if I could roll out of bed without waking him up, I could go get it. My phone's inside. I don't think I want to tell anyone something as dramatic as "I've been kidnapped" because I'm truly not out to get Silvan in trouble, but I don't want to be kept here against my will, either. I want to go home.

I could text my mom or Kendra and ask them to pick me up. Kendra already knows where he lives, so it would probably be easy for her to come get me.

The house is huge, surely if I'm careful, I could sneak out the front door without anyone even noticing.

I shift in his arms, trying to move gently so as not to wake him. It seems like it should be easy since he's sleeping, but his arms don't budge. A frown flickers across my face as I try again and his grip on my waist tightens.

Eyes wide, I turn my head to look back at him over my shoulder and find him looking much like a sleepy Viking with a smirk on his handsome, fully-awake face. "Where do you think you're going?"

My cheeks warm at the sensation of being caught doing something I'm not supposed to—even though I could argue escaping my kidnapper is something I am very much supposed to do.

He's too crazy to agree with me.

"I have to pee," I say instead.

"Oh, yeah?" he murmurs, sounding somehow unconvinced even though that's a perfectly natural thing to need to do after a long night's sleep. One hand slides up from my waist. He cups my tit, squeezing softly before his blunt fingertip passes over my nipple. "You're sure you're not just hoping to make a phone call on the cell phone you left in there last night?"

"Of course not," I answer.

"Mm-hmm," he murmurs, less convinced than before.

"That you would assume that just proves you're a psychopath," I state primly. "I was going to *text*."

He laughs, giving me a squeeze and kissing my exposed shoulder. "I'm not a psychopath," he assures me.

"You're awfully comfortable with kidnapping for someone who isn't a psychopath."

"I'm a man in love," he states. "Haven't you heard? All's fair in love and war."

"Well, you may be in love, but I'm at war, so does that mean I can play dirty, too?"

"Sure," he says far too easily. "As long as you're prepared for the consequences when you lose." He lets that threat hang in the air for a moment, then he nuzzles his face into my neck. "Personally, I'd much prefer we be on the same team than at war with each other."

"You say that, but what you mean is you want

me to concede to all your wants and desires and just abandon my team for yours."

"There's only a 'your' team and 'my' team because you're still resisting. Stop that and then it's *our* team and we do what's best for both of us."

"But I don't get a choice whether or not I want to be *on* the team."

"Correct. I'm afraid you're stuck with me. You should learn to live with it."

I shake my head. "Then it's not a team. You have to agree to be on a team."

"I think you'll find your contract extremely generous. My father will insist on a prenup, but it's a formality, and I'll include terms you'd find acceptable so you know I'm not trying to screw you over."

My heart jumps and I look back at him. "Do you hear yourself? Prenup?"

"My future inheritance is too much to marry without one. Like I said, it's just a formality. More for your protection than mine. If I told my father to fuck off with the prenup, I'd be worried he might take things into his own hands if he saw any turbulence in our relationship. It's a risk I can't take."

I can't believe he's talking about our marriage as if it's a foregone conclusion.

"I'm not going to marry you."

"Yes, you are."

"No, I'm not."

"You didn't think you were going to go out with me, either, and now here you are, my girlfriend."

My eyes widen. "Because you blackmailed me and forced orgasms on me until I agreed!"

He shrugs. "Still counts."

"You're crazy."

"Crazy in love." He grins and kisses my cheek,

then he lets me go and smacks my ass. "Go pee if you need to, but don't bother with the text." He rolls over, grabbing his phone off the nightstand on his side. "Breakfast will be served here in the next ten minutes, so we should probably go downstairs. You want a robe or an outfit?"

"An outfit, I guess. Will your family be down there? I don't want to see your family barely dressed."

"Your future in-laws will be eating with us, yes."

I shoot him a look over my shoulder as I roll out of bed and stand, but he's too busy looking at my ass and the rest of my naked body to notice. "We're not getting married," I tell him.

"We'll see."

WHEN SILVAN FIRST FOLLOWS ME INTO THE bathroom, I am annoyed.

He snatches my purse off the sink and takes it with him to the walk-in closet, but he's still far too close for comfort. The toilet is in its own little room with a door that closes so I'm at least allowed some privacy for that, but as soon as I emerge from the toilet room, I'm aware of Silvan in the closet.

I wash my hands and keep an eye on the mirror. By the time I'm drying my hands on the hand towel, he emerges.

My tummy flutters at the sight of him. He's still got messy bedhead, but he's wearing a pair of black slacks and a forest green button-down shirt with the top couple of buttons undone.

He hands me two shopping bags. I put them down on the counter and open the first one. There's a black pencil skirt and a soft off-the-shoulder sweater the same shade of green as his shirt. The fabric feels incredible to the touch and I find myself actually eager to put it on.

Stepping to the left, I open the second bag so I can pull out a bra and panties, but all I find is a black Yves

Saint Laurent purse with gold accents and a shoebox. I pull out the shoe box and peek inside to see a stylish pair of black kitten heels. Still a little higher than I prefer, but I'm relieved it's a low heel and not a high one.

Glancing over at him, I say, "You didn't give me a bra or panties."

He wets his hairbrush, then starts pulling it through his long dark hair. His lips tug up, but he doesn't look at me. "Damn."

My eyes widen. "I can't wear the panties I came in! You... soiled them."

"Guess you'll have to go without."

"And I need a bra. Mine has pink straps. You really need a strapless bra for a shirt like this."

"If you're a good girl, maybe I'll take you shopping later and you can pick out whatever you need."

I narrow my eyes at him. "You want me to go downstairs right now and face your father with my nipples poking through my shirt?"

He puts the brush down on the counter. "You don't have to worry about him looking. He only has eyes for my mom." His gaze shifts in my direction. "*I'll* be the one looking at you, and I quite like your nipples."

I hesitate for a moment, but I guess I don't have a better option.

I'm self-conscious about going panty-less around his parents, but at least the pencil skirt is long enough that I don't have to worry about anyone seeing. Only he and I will know I'm not wearing panties.

I pull on the soft green sweater and try not to be too self-conscious about going bra-less. I did tell them I was here against my will and they didn't help, so if they have a problem with my inappropriate breakfast attire... well, they'll just have to deal with it.

I shouldn't care what they think of me, anyway. Usually, I want to make a good impression on people, though, and even though he's nuts, Silvan talking about them as my future in-laws bolsters the desire to make a good impression.

I have to remind myself it's not real, that they're definitely not my future in-laws. If anything, they're accomplices in my kidnapping, though I figure they must have taken what I said last night as a joke since they let Silvan haul me up to his room and never even tried to come help.

If they believed me, surely, they would have helped.

When I'm done brushing my hair, Silvan says, "Ready to go meet the in-laws?"

I shake my head, setting the brush down and giving myself a once-over to make sure I'm as prepared as I can be without all my stuff. "They are not my in-laws," I say, more to remind myself than him. "I am not your wife."

My heart jumps when he crosses the room and stops beside me. On instinct, I turn to face him, and gasp when he reaches for my face with one hand and my waist with the other. He turns me and walks me back, trapping me against the sink. He caresses my face, then leans in until his mouth is a breath away from mine. "You will be one day, Sophie."

Then, he kisses me.

It's a hard kiss, demanding, hungry, and it sucks the breath right from my lungs. I grab his shoulder with one hand and the edge of the sink with the other. I'm helpless as his tongue slips between my lips and invades my mouth. His hand at my waist slides around to my back. He slides it between me and the sink to cushion me from the possible discomfort as he ravishes my mouth.

When he finally pulls back, I'm breathless and my heart beats fast. I feel bashful as he looks down at me, then briefly confused when he smirks.

But he's looking at my breasts, and when he murmurs, "That's why I like you bra-less," I realize my nipples hardened to pebbles while he kissed me.

My cheeks heat and I shove against his chest. He chuckles but lets me push him away. His hands take their time releasing me, and when he does, he still takes my hand.

I've never actually held hands with a guy before him. On the face of it, it seems like such an innocent thing to do, but it sure doesn't feel that way when he does it.

I don't know what to expect of breakfast with his family, so I'm a little on-edge as we head downstairs.

Silvan leads me to a stately formal dining room with lots of light shining in through the massive windows on the far wall. They have luxurious-looking window treatments in a creamy shade of yellow that matches the room. Between the windows is a painting so large it fills most of the wall. Overhead is a gorgeous, expensive-looking chandelier. The dining table is long, built more for entertaining than for an intimate meal for a family of three.

It's a gorgeous room. A fancy table.

And today, it's set for four.

Silvan's mother and father are already seated on their side of the table. Two more places are set directly across from them.

"There you are," his mom says, her voice lyrical and lovely to listen to. Her eyes are warm and her smile is so genuine, you'd really think I'm a guest here and not a captive. "We set places for you two, but I didn't know if your guest was left-handed or right-handed, so I hope you won't bump elbows. We can switch you if we need to."

Silvan glances over at me. "I don't know that, either, actually."

"Left." I clear my throat, feeling his father's gaze on me and feeling profoundly self-conscious because of the way Silvan has me dressed. The clothes are beautiful, of course, but I hardly look like anyone's prisoner. "I'm left-handed."

"Why don't you sit across from Richard then?" she says, indicating the chair across from Silvan's father.

That is not where I wanted to sit.

Last night, I got a certain vibe off the man, but he was relaxed, at the end of his day enjoying some peace and quiet with his wife.

This morning, he's fresh and ready for a new day. The quiet sense of intimidation that rolled off him last night is much louder this morning.

It's unsettling.

He doesn't say anything, but I can feel him watching me. He might be Silvan's dad, but he's a man all the same, so my anxiety begins to spiral like it did the night of the party when a guy looked too long at me. I want to flee, but there's no crowd to get lost in.

I'm so anxious and distracted, I gasp when Silvan places a hand on my shoulder. He frowns, and I blush furiously, my face feeling so hot, I want to press my hands against it.

"Sorry," I say on impulse.

Silvan isn't scattered and nervous like I am. He's calm and steady as he pulls out my chair for me.

My gaze flickers to Silvan. He's the devil I know, so I feel safer with him, but if it came down to it, would he defy his own father for me? Things he said when he was being crazy about marrying me slide back to the forefront of my mind, things like his father might take things into his own hands if he considered me a threat to the family wealth.

He doesn't regard me with any softness or sympathy because his son might be preying upon me. He regards me as if he's considering whether I'm *already* a threat he needs to take care of.

I'm very confused because I thought Silvan's father was a businessman of some sort, but now the armored car comes to mind, and I'm starting to wonder who the hell I'm sitting across from.

My stomach rocks with nerves. He's still watching me. I want to throw up and also crawl out of my skin.

Silvan's rumble pulls me out of my rising panic. "Are you all right?"

"You do look a little warm," his mother agrees. "Are you warm? I always think it's a bit drafty in here, but I can have Ilona turn down the heat if you're too warm."

I shake my head, glancing at her with a forced smile. "I'm okay, thank you."

Just my chest feeling like it's about to cave in. No big deal.

"Ilona," she calls out, glancing at the wall behind us. "Bring in some water, please."

His father finally breaks his silence to ask, "Rough night?"

Again, there's no hint of sympathy. If anything, I think I sense a quiet taunt in his words.

My stomach sinks and I have to fight every instinct I have not to get up and run away from this horribly uncomfortable sensation.

Silvan's mom puts a gentle hand on the man's shoulder and leans in to whisper, "Be nice."

I feel his gaze finally break away from mine, that's the only reason I look up to see him glance over at her, his lips tugging up ever so slightly. "I'm always nice."

She smiles and leans in to kiss him. "That's not true at all," she teases.

An older blonde woman in a traditional maid's uniform comes in with a pitcher of water and distracts me from Silvan's dad for a moment. She goes to their side of the table first and fills water goblets for his dad, then his mom. Then she comes over to our side of the table, but she reaches past me to fill Silvan's glass before she fills mine.

"Thank you, Ilona," his mom says. "We're ready for breakfast now."' Her gaze flickers to me. "You don't have any food allergies, do you, dear?"

I shake my head, but her asking me a question brings Silvan's dad's gaze back to me, so I keep my head down to avoid looking at him.

When Ilona comes back, she has another younger woman with her. Ilona puts plates down in front of Silvan's parents, and the younger one brings plates to me and Silvan. When she puts his plate down, he says, "Thank you, Olena."

The maid blushes prettily and shoots him eyes like the girls at the party did.

I forgot how women reacted to Silvan. I usually have him all to myself.

My attention drifts to my plate when the aroma hits my nostrils. Breakfast is Belgian waffles with fresh fruit and scrambled eggs that look so fluffy, my mouth starts to water.

I didn't realize how hungry I was, but my

stomach rumbles at the sight and smell of all this delicious food. I grab the gleaming fork and butterknife from my place setting and start cutting up my waffles.

I'm so famished, I practically inhale my food. When I drag the last bit of waffle around the plate to soak up the juices and pop it into my mouth, I'm remorseful about eating it so fast. Now it's gone and everyone else is still eating.

Well, this is awkward.

Silvan's father notices my empty plate, but doesn't remark on it. He takes a long sip of his coffee, then puts the mug down with a dull thud. He doesn't say anything, but his hand moves and seems to settle on his wife's thigh under the table. As if signaled, she drops her fork and reaches for the silver carafe on the table. It's between them, as easily accessed by him as it would be her, but he waits for her to fill his cup.

I search her face for some sign of displeasure or annoyance however minute, but nothing registers. In a house with at least two servants and him being entirely able-bodied himself, she seems genuinely content to be serving him.

Maybe she is.

Despite the sense that he keeps some level of control over her at all times, she has a friendly, approachable air about her, like she genuinely wants to make things nice for her husband. There's no resentment, no sense that they're used to or desensitized to each other even though they must have been together for a long time since they have a grown son.

They still gaze at each other with such warmth. His dark eyes dance when he watches her put the pitcher back down. He still enjoys watching her.

I wonder if Silvan would still look at me *like that in twenty years?*

My tummy jumps when the thought passes through my mind. It's the way he looks at me now. I thought that must always fade, but his parents seem to have found a way to keep the spark alive.

Maybe that's why Silvan is so confident when he says crazy things about marrying me like we'll spend our whole lives together. Marriage must not seem daunting when you have parents who still adore each other after decades together.

When she sits back down, I'm curious enough to finally summon the nerve to speak. Keeping my gaze trained on his mom like a horse wearing blinders, I ask, "What is it you do? I don't think Silvan has mentioned it."

She cocks her head curiously, like my question doesn't compute.

"For work," I clarify.

"Oh." She laughs. "I don't work. I mean, I'm involved with philanthropic work, of course. The women in Richard's family have been for generations. But aside from running the house and my family..." She trails off, shaking her head.

I'm not judging her—it's hardly my business what she chooses to do with her life—but I get the impression Silvan's father thinks I am, because he says sharply, "Pride in working yourself to death to make someone else's fortune is a working-class value. I assume you don't come from money, Sophie."

My cheeks heat. I feel like I've been punched in the stomach, even though I'm hardly ashamed of my background. "No," I say, shaking my head. "I wasn't... I don't..."

Silvan's voice is hard. "It doesn't matter what kind of background she comes from."

His father lifts his fresh cup of coffee and takes a slow sip, making all of us wait for his response. When he's damn good and ready, he says, "That's naïve, Silvan. It certainly can matter. If you come from different worlds, you both have to be willing to compromise and learn from one another. She's been brought up one way, you've been brought up an entirely different way. It won't be the most harmonious union."

Clearly, his dad doesn't approve of this relationship.

Not because Silvan kidnapped me, but because my bank account is too empty for his liking.

I feel ridiculous *caring* when his approval should be the last thing that concerns me, but I hate that feeling so much, his withholding of approval makes me... sort of want it.

To my surprise, Silvan's mom jumps to my defense. "She's young, Richard. She can learn to fit into a different lifestyle from the one she was brought up in." Her voice lowers and she leans in to murmur, "I truly don't think she meant any offense."

"I didn't," I say quickly. "I was just curious."

I make the mistake of meeting his gaze, so I feel like a spotlight is shining down on me when he asks, "Do you think a woman should work?"

"I... I think a woman should do whatever she wants."

"Do you consider it debasing for a wife to take care of her husband?"

Eyes wide, I shake my head no.

"Good." That word should bring some relief, but it doesn't. Without tearing his gaze from mine, he says, "I believe Silvan's cup is a little low."

My jaw unhinges, but I catch it before my mouth can open to convey my shock.

Does he really expect me to…?

"Dad," Silvan says, a low warning in his tone.

But his father doesn't waver. He holds my gaze, and only drops it to glance pointedly at the carafe on the table between us.

My stomach drops like a rock, but against all sense, I find my unsteady hands reaching for the silver pitcher.

There's no time to consider what I'm doing. My chair makes an embarrassingly loud noise to draw more attention—*as if it's not already on me*—as I gracelessly rise and my legs push it back. My cheeks burn as I grab the carafe and turn toward Silvan.

What am I doing?

I'm shaky and unsettled until Silvan grabs my hip with one hand, pulling me in closer to him. My gaze jumps to his, and where I feel frazzled and uncertain, he looks calm and comfortable.

His energy overpowers mine and his calm seeps into me. I get my perspective back and realize it's just a cup of coffee. I can even see amusement dancing in his pretty green eyes, reminding me of his teasing about me being his slave girl in the escape room.

When I'm just focused on him, it doesn't feel so embarrassing to refill his coffee cup. Once I've put the carafe back down on the table, he even pulls me into his lap—something I'm certain I should find embarrassing right in front of his parents—and settles one hand around my waist to keep me there as he grabs the mug and takes a nice, slow sip.

I don't know if it's being on his lap or the suggestive way his mouth moves as he takes a sip of the coffee I just poured him, but when he murmurs, "Mm. Perfect," I feel his words and the approval in his voice pour through me like warm honey. It settles low in my gut, and I become achingly aware of him. The feel of his strong thighs beneath my butt, the glimpse of skin with those top two buttons undone.

Maybe the subservient act of filling his coffee tripped triggers in my brain or something, I don't know, but there's tension in my pussy that should not be there.

For a moment, it feels like just us in the room, then his mom attempts to bring things back to a much more pleasant level. "So, do you two have anything planned today?"

Silvan nods, his grip on me tightening when I instinctively start to move off his lap. I'm a bit embarrassed, but I stay put. "Yeah," Silvan says easily. "We're going to do a little shopping."

"Oh, that'll be nice."

"Mm-hmm," he murmurs, setting the cup down but meeting my gaze. "I love spoiling my girl."

CHAPTER 26
SILVAN

I HAVE HUGH WAITING OUTSIDE AS SOON AS breakfast is finished.

My dad was a lot this morning and I want to get Sophie out of there before he makes my job even fucking harder this weekend.

The good news is, by casting himself as the bad guy, he seems to have thrust me into the hero role—which isn't the one I've really had the chance to play since Sophie has made me chase her so relentlessly. Maybe he knew what he was doing, or maybe he was just being an ass. Whatever his motives, the result is a much more pliant Sophie than I expected to have on my hands today.

I'm liking it.

When we slide into the back of the limo, she scoots in right next to me.

The way she looks up at me, if I didn't know any better, I'd think she wants to be fucked.

Maybe she does and she just doesn't know how to ask for it.

That's all right. I don't need her to ask. I'm more than happy to play the aggressor, so I do, testing my theory and lifting her up, pulling her on my lap facing me and yanking up that tight little pencil skirt.

Since she's not wearing any panties, her pussy is fully exposed and the sight of it makes me growl.

She tightens her thighs, embarrassed, and starts to shift away.

I grab her hips, holding her tight against my cock, then slide one hand to the small of her back to pull her even closer. She gasps when I butt my cock against her through the fabric of my pants. I hold her hips and force her close again, using my grip on her to make her grind her pussy against me.

A helpless moan slips past her lips before she can stop it.

Fuck me.

"Silvan," she says softly, her eyes closed. I think it's a half-assed plea for me to stop, but I also think it's only something she's saying out of habit, so I don't. I pull her against me again, moving my hips to force her to rub against my cock through my pants.

She groans and drops her head to my shoulder, her hair falling all over my neck. The way she's breathing in my ear and clinging to me is getting me so fucking hard right now.

"Does my pretty girl wanna get fucked?"

She'd never admit it if she did so I don't expect her to now. Without waiting for a response, I slide my hand under her skirt and tease her entrance.

"Kiss my neck," I tell her, since she's right there and I want to feel her lips on me.

I'm not sure she'll do it since I'm not threatening her with anything, but my heart thuds in my chest when she turns her head and I feel her soft lips press against my skin.

To reward her obedience, I slide my palm under her pussy and push my thumb up to brush her clit. I feel her breath rush against my neck as I circle that sensitive nub, teasing it with my thumb until she's restless and writhing in my lap.

With her words, she'd never admit she wants me, but she does with her mouth. Since I asked for kisses, she starts kissing my neck with renewed desperation, giving me what she knows I want so I'll give her what she wants but is too afraid to ask for.

I don't know why she's so ashamed of her own desires, but I could feel it last night when I was fucking her at her professor's house. She didn't want it until she did, but when I gave her what she needed, she came so hard, she nearly cried.

Lucky for her, she's got a man who has no fucking problem playing the forceful bully for her. I slide a hand into her silky hair and fist it. "More. Kiss me like you fucking mean it, Sophie."

She already is, but she tries harder at my command, gets a little dirtier. She doesn't know how to please me or what I want, but when her tongue darts out and she licks me, my cock nearly rips through my pants.

"Fuck, Sophie." I pull her back by her hair.

She groans, just a little bit. I'm holding her head too tightly for her to move her head much, but she looks down so she can meet my gaze.

"Unbutton my pants."

"Silvan," she pleads, her cheeks flushing the prettiest fucking pink. "I'm sore."

Her voice is tentative, but I still don't buy she doesn't want me to fuck her. Maybe she's nervous about it because she knows it might hurt a little, but she knows her pussy can take it.

"You're gonna have to get used to it, baby." I release her hair and grab her neck so I can pull her in. "I plan to make this pussy sore pretty fucking regularly. It'll have to learn to take a beating."

She whimpers against my mouth when I claim hers, but the noise just makes me want her more. I keep a firm grip on her neck, but pull my other hand from her pussy so I can grab her hand and guide it to the button of my pants. With tentative fingers, she unbuttons my slacks, then unzips me without even being told.

That's my girl.

I shift her on my lap and reach down to free my cock, then I slide my hand under her ass and pull her forward, guiding my cock between her spread thighs.

"Silvan. Wait..."

She tries to pull back, but I tighten my grip and keep her pressed close as I push my cock into her. Her pussy is still so fucking tight, it takes some effort to breach her walls.

Sophie whimpers against my neck as I shove deeper.

"It's okay, baby," I tell her. Now that I'm inside her, I can bring a hand up to squeeze her tit through her soft green sweater. "You're such a good girl, you know that? I fucking love you." Her nipple hardens as I tease it, so I give it a rewarding tug and she gasps.

I force my cock all the way inside her and nearly black out from the fucking pleasure as her pussy squeezes me.

I close my eyes and take a second to regain my composure, then with a firm hand on her ass to keep her where I want her, I move my hips and start fucking her. She holds on tight as I draw back and slam my cock deep into her body. I'm too fucking greedy for her to start slow. I want every inch deep in her pussy, I want to feel her body stretching to fit me, hear her little noises moaned and whimpered close to my ear.

The way she's holding onto me makes this time feel intimate despite everything else. Her tits bounce as I fuck her and I can feel the tension in her body, hear the changing of her moans and whimpers as I pound into her.

"You like that, baby?" I growl, catching my breath. "You like how hard I'm pounding into that sweet pussy?"

She does, but she doesn't admit it.

I kiss the side of her head and murmur, "You want it harder?"

She doesn't say yes, but she doesn't say no, either.

I think my pretty girl likes to have her pussy battered, and I'm not one to not give my girl what she wants. So, I grab her hair and pull her off my lap, throwing her down on the seat of the limo. She gasps at the impact, but I'm between her spread thighs before she can even try to sit up.

I slide my hands up her smooth legs, then jam my cock back into her pussy. She cries out and arches against the seat, reaching overhead for something to hold onto, but there's nothing.

I lean down over her, bracing one hand on the edge of the seat. "Hold onto *me*."

Her gaze meets mine, but she averts it quickly.

She obeys nonetheless, her hands tentatively coming to rest on my sides as I slide deep into her sweet pussy.

Oh, fuck.

"You feel so fucking good, Sophie." I shove my free hand up under her shirt, palming her tit, then pinching her nipple.

She hisses something that sounds distinctly

like, "Fuck," but when I look down at her, she looks too much like an angel to believe she just swore. I pull back and drive into her, finding my pace from a moment ago now that we're in this new position. Sophie twists and arches, her eyes closed and her tits eager as I pinch and tug on her nipples.

My thrusts rock her body against the seat, my cock pounding inside her. Her skin is flushed and I want to lick it, to feel her heat on my tongue, taste the salt on her skin.

Fuck it.

I pull out of her and grab her thigh roughly, spreading them wide as I dive between her legs.

"What are you—?"

She gasps when I spread her pussy and dart my tongue into her pretty little cunt, quickly finding her clit and teasing the fuck out of that perfect little bundle. She cries out, arching against my face and clutching desperately at the seat. "Silvan!"

I love the sound of my name in her mouth when I have a mouthful of her pussy.

I eat it with abandon and hold onto her restless hips so I can lick her until she's screaming. And she does, completely fucking shameless when she comes and her pussy tightens like a vise. I pull my mouth off her while she's still breathless and panting, then I shove my dick into her hoping for a taste of it, and *fuck me*, yes, her pussy is still clamped down when I shove into it.

Fucking Christ.

Sophie is spent from her orgasm, but she looks so fucking pretty lying there boneless and unmoving, her tits bouncing as I roughly use her body.

There's something so fucking hot about fucking her after she's come, about using her body to get myself off.

Maybe it's that or the way her already impossibly tight pussy squeezes the fucking life out of my cock as I drive into her, but I can't hold on. I haven't come this fast since I was years younger, but I drive deep and let go, blasting cum deep inside her perfect little body.

After the blinding pleasure works its way through me, my muscles are fucking spent. I'm so fucking satisfied, I collapse on the seat on top of her.

She's spent, too, but she wraps her arms around my torso. For a few minutes, we lie together like that, but I start to worry I'm crushing her. I don't want to move, though. I want to stay inside her forever.

"You okay down there?" I rumble.

"Mm-hmm," she murmurs sweetly.

Christ, I love her sweetness after she's just come. I want to make her come all day long.

"You didn't use a condom again," she says after a minute.

"Yeah. If you don't want babies anytime soon, we might want to put you on some birth control."

She smiles faintly and shakes her head. "You're crazy."

I look down at her with a roguish smile. "Crazy for you."

She rolls her eyes playfully like I'm just teasing her, but I'm completely fucking serious. I've never even thought it was capable to adore someone on the level I adore this fucking girl, but I am truly fucking besotted.

I mean, I'm using words like fucking *besotted* so you know I'm a goner.

"If it's something you're worried about, you're going to have to be the one to prevent it, 'cause I gotta say, I love the idea of getting you pregnant."

"That's an absurd thing to say."

I rub her belly, not hating the idea of a little half-Silvan, half-Sophie being growing there already. I can picture her tummy growing, her excitement as it got closer to time to meet him or her.

Bet she'd stop fucking fighting being with me so hard, too.

Might not be a bad idea.

Her humor fades and she stares up at me, seeming to realize I'm not just fucking with her. "I'll make an appointment as soon as I'm unkidnapped."

"Do you want kids?" I ask.

"Yes. Just not nine months from now."

Probably not with me, either, if she's being honest, but I'm afraid that's gonna be out of her hands.

I don't know if I can make her fall in love with me this weekend, but I know I'll wear her down eventually. And hell, I'm in no rush. We have the rest of our lives to spend together, and I'm enjoying every bit of pursuing her reluctant little ass.

CHAPTER 27
SOPHIE

SILVAN HOLDS MY HAND AS HE LEADS ME THROUGH the Neiman Marcus at Copley Place.

We've been shopping for hours, and he has already bought me too many clothes I didn't ask for —only the softest sweaters because he enjoys touching me so much, a pretty Versace dress with a price tag that made me feel ill. He's taken note of the shoes I choose to try on, so I expect there will be more flats and fewer kitten heels in my future, though we made an exception today for a beautiful low heel at Jimmy Choo that I decided I could wear as long as I don't have to walk too far.

He bought me bras and new underwear, too.

"I should probably buy you extra underwear," he murmured teasingly, making me blush as the limo ride here played through my mind.

He cleaned me up in the limo with what we had available at the little bar, but I can still feel him between my thighs as we shop. I've had to be very careful trying things on so as not to dirty the clothes.

Not that it matters, I guess.

Everything I even slightly liked, he is buying for me.

As we head for the exit doors with Silvan's other hand full of stuffed shopping bags, he looks over at me and asks, "You getting hungry?"

It is around lunchtime, and we've definitely burned off breakfast. I look up at him and nod. "A bit. You?"

He nods. "There's a really good burger spot not too far from here. Sound good?"

My mouth waters, so I take that as a yes and nod vigorously.

His eyes glint with amusement and he leans over to steal a kiss before he opens the door for me.

"Such a gentleman," I say lightly.

He ruins *that* illusion by grabbing my ass on his way to wrapping his hand around my hip to keep me close. "Oh yeah, I'm an angel. Don't let anyone tell you different."

Hugh is waiting for us on the curb. He opens the door for me and takes the shopping bags from Silvan. Once he's done stowing all our purchases, he comes back to get our next location from Silvan, then dutifully closes the door and heads around to the driver's side.

"So," Silvan says, stretching out his arm on the seat behind me and making himself comfortable. "How is your first day of kidnapping?"

I nod as if considering. "Not bad. Definitely thought it would feel more murdery, but aside from all the blackmail and blatant coercion of yesterday, uh, yeah… been a pretty good experience. I wouldn't recommend it to a friend—*if I had any*—but I'd probably come again."

Silvan grins, grabbing my neck and pulling me in so he can kiss my smart mouth. "You're the best, you know that?"

I can't bite back a smile as I settle into his side

after the kiss. "So you keep telling me. Keep it up and you're gonna give me a big head."

He kisses the crown of my head. "Your head can get as big as it needs to. I'm not gonna stop hyping up my girl."

I shake my head, but I feel warm and happy all over. "You're very different from the guys I've known before."

He leans close. "Babe, you said 'better' wrong."

I laugh and he smiles. I shake my head because he's crazy, but I like when he's playful like this.

Today really feels like a day out with a guy I like. Definitely not how I saw today going yesterday, but Silvan is so easy to be with.

I mean, batshit crazy, but pretty excellent company. I don't even like people, but I can't deny I like hanging out with him.

While I'm lost in my thoughts about the surprising good time I'm having with him, his thoughts seem to be on later.

"My dad will be home for dinner tonight, so we'll eat with my parents again. That cool with you?"

My smile fades, but I nod. "Yeah."

"I know you didn't have the best time at breakfast. Sorry about him."

I don't know quite what to say. We haven't talked about it. We got a little distracted once we got in the car earlier.

"Your father is…" I pause, searching for a polite term to use.

"Traditional?" Silvan offers.

"Terrifying."

He cracks a smile. "Yeah, he can be a bit scary."

"He hates me."

"He doesn't hate you."

"When he looks at me, he sees Little Orphan

Annie dressed in rags with a panhandling cup in one hand and a pitchfork in the other."

He smirks. "He's just protective of his family, that's all."

My eyes widen. "He can't possibly think I'm a golddigger. I didn't even choose to be here!"

"It's not about that. He doesn't think you're a golddigger, he probably just thinks what he said, that our lifestyle might be a little… not what you're used to."

"I've never met a rich person with so much disdain for the less financially fortunate."

Silvan cocks an eyebrow. "How many rich people have you met?"

My mouth opens, then closes. "Well… none. But my guess is some are much less snobby about it."

He smiles faintly, shaking his head. "It's not as simple as him having an issue with you not having money. It's how *much* money my family has. I know you probably don't understand, but it puts us in a different league than most people. We're not, 'I bought a Ferrari,' rich. We're 'one of my yachts has a dirty helipad, maybe I should buy a new one' rich."

I squint at him because the levels of wealth might be more than I can grasp having just brushed with it for the first time.

"It's stupid," he assures me. "It's nothing to worry about. Like I said, we'll take all the necessary precautions to make sure there are no problems. He's just putting you through your paces, that's all. Feeling you out to make sure you're sturdy enough to make it in my family."

My lips form a pout. I've never wanted someone I dislike so vehemently to approve of me so much. "I'm plenty sturdy."

Silvan smirks, leaning in to steal a kiss. "I know you are," he murmurs against my lips. "It doesn't matter what he thinks, anyway. It only matters what I think, and I'm intent on keeping you for the long haul."

He says that so casually, just like he said the pregnancy thing earlier. Like he doesn't realize it's *a lot*, like it doesn't even cross his mind that it may be less assuring and more frightening to a girl who has just come around to admitting I don't hate his company *today*.

Maybe marriage and kids and all that seems easy to him because of the peculiar example of happiness his parents seem to have set, but that's not how it is for most people. It's certainly not how it was for my parents, or any couple I've ever met.

Maybe having money makes things easier, but surely it doesn't make that much of a difference. Plenty of rich people go through marriages like some people go through cars, ditching the old one as soon as it doesn't run like it's new anymore and trading up to a shinier model.

It's hard to explain my fears without insulting him, though.

It's hard to express that while he's painting me a perfectly lovely picture of our future together, I'm convinced he's using fingerpaints and one strong storm could wash it all away.

I like what he's selling, I just don't believe in it the way that he does.

Part of me wishes I did.

I bet it would be lovely to be so sure of something, to believe wholeheartedly in the impenetrability of a relationship with someone I've basically just met.

When my gaze drifts to his, he's watching me with a frown of concern. "You okay?"

I force a polite smile and nod even though I don't think I have to do that with him. It's an old instinct, but not an easy one to shake.

"You sure?"

I nod again, but he's closer now, invading my space like he needs to investigate so he can see for himself if I'm okay. I don't want him poking around, to be honest, so I do the thing I know will distract him.

I lean in and kiss him.

His hand slides around my neck and he pulls me in closer. He always does that, pulls me in like he can't get me close enough no matter how hard he tries.

He deepens the kiss, his grip on the back of my neck tightening before letting go. His fingers sink into my hair and he cradles the entire back of my head in his palm so he can use that to control me instead.

My heart starts to pound like it always does when he kisses me. His other hand slides up my thigh to the hem of my skirt. He slides it underneath, then higher and higher, until he's caressing my bare thigh and I'm lost in this dizzy little haze of lust he's so adept at shrouding me in.

I break away from him to catch my breath, and so things can't escalate.

I was bizarrely turned on after breakfast, so I was actually a little relieved he wanted to fuck me in the car, but just because it felt good didn't mean it didn't also hurt like hell. He was so rough with me last night, my insides feel bruised, so when my body had to stretch to accommodate him again, it wasn't the most comfortable I'd ever been in my life.

I don't know how this post-virginity thing works, exactly, but I don't want to *break* the thing, so maybe he shouldn't fuck me again at lunch time. He'll probably want to again later when we're sleeping in the same bed, so we need to at least give my body a little break before then.

He doesn't seem to mind, though.

He's satisfied with the kiss for the moment, so he settles his strong arm around my shoulders and pulls me into his side.

Before long, we're at the burger place.

I'm relieved to emerge from the hazy limousine and at least have the world open up a little bit to let in food.

He holds my hand as we walk inside, and I watch a girl at a table with another girl stop with her burger halfway to her mouth to stare at Silvan as he walks in. Her bright-eyed look droops when she sees his hand in mine, but she still looks up at his face to see if it's as good as the rest of him.

She must be so disappointed when it is.

I crack a smile, almost feeling bad for her.

Silvan notices and asks, "What are you smiling about?"

"You just attract a lot of attention in public spaces. This whole sexy Viking thing you've got going on. I think you need to cut your hair."

He smirks. "Why's that?"

"I don't know, maybe you'd be less hot," I suggest.

He nods as if considering, then pulls out his phone. I figure he's just checking it, so I search the dining area for a table off in a corner with no one around. Once I've found the perfect spot, I grab his free hand and haul him over to it.

I don't even think he's paying attention, but he stops to pull out my chair, his gaze still on his phone.

"Thank you," I murmur.

It's probably odd to feel a bit jealous of a *phone*, but usually when we're together, *I* have all of Silvan's attention.

He nods, then once I'm sitting, he holds the phone in front of me and I see what he was doing. I'm somewhat relieved to realize he wasn't distracted texting or anything like that; he was looking for a picture of himself before he grew his hair out to show me.

My gaze settles on a shot of him at the beach, shirtless and clean-shaven with short hair, laughing at something his friend is saying.

Oh, damn. He's gorgeous. He looks like he's modeling something I'd never purchase because I'd be too busy gazing at the ad to get that far.

"Not less hot. Got it."

He smirks and walks over to take the seat across from me. Now that he's shown me he's hot no matter how he styles himself, apparently, he puts his phone away and returns his full attention to me.

I try to ignore the faint burst of pleasure, but that's one of the things I really like about Silvan. He doesn't seem to have this constant need to be connected to everything but me when we're together. He's always focused on me when he's spending time with me. Most guys can't even stay off their phone on a date. It's like they're too worried about keeping up with everything else that is far more interesting to them than me.

"Can I ask you a question?"

He nods. "Of course."

"Fair warning, it's a question I hate, and I hate that I'm asking it, but… why are you single?"

He shrugs. "That's how I liked it until I met you."

"You haven't proposed marriage and babies to all the other girls you've liked?"

He laughs like the mere notion is ridiculous. "No. Actually, I think if you asked most of the girls I've gone out with, they'd be more inclined to tell you I'm a noncommittal asshole than to give a glowing review of my devotion."

That's so far from the Silvan I know, I can't entirely fathom it. "What's so different with me?" I ask earnestly.

He meets my gaze across the table. His green eyes are serious when he leans in, rests his arms on the table, and says, "Everything."

My heart skips a beat, but as lovely a sentiment as it is, it's still hard to entirely believe it.

What if he's only so attentive and determined to have me because I'm new and shiny and maybe because I've put up resistance? Seeing the responses he usually gets from other girls, I'm willing to bet he's never had to work so hard before.

If it's only the novelty of my disinterest that makes me interesting to him, what happens if I give in? Does he lose interest?

That's what I want, right?

Maybe I should play along.

I don't want to mess with his heart, though.

I don't want to mess with mine, either.

At this point, I'm not even sure what I want. For him to go away, or…?

The alternative is too crazy to even consider. Right?

Sure, he's gorgeous and interesting and funny and he actually seems devoted, which is a rare trait in anyone, let alone someone as overall appealing as he is. But he's also pushy and rapey and kind of stalkerish. I mean, he entrapped me at my professor's house and fucked me in his bed because…

Wait, how did he even come upon the notion that he needed to do that? I never got a clear answer.

"Can I ask you something else?"

He nods.

How do I even word this? "Why did you… do what you did yesterday?"

I wait for him to get defensive, but he doesn't. Calmly, he asks, "Which part?"

"Um, all of it? I mean, what made you think I'd even come?"

A glint of something hard passes through his gaze and he sits back, but he's still cool and in control. "I hoped you wouldn't come, but I knew you would. Your professor has been manipulating you. You're very easy to manipulate in certain ways."

My spine stiffens. "Oh, really?"

"I didn't mean it as an insult," he assures me. "You just have some damage in certain areas that makes it easy for a man to prey on you. He's an accomplished psychologist. Of course he fucking knows how to manipulate you, it's just pretty fucking sick that he does since he's supposed to be your teacher, someone you should be able to trust."

I can feel the anger beneath his calm as he talks about this, but it's not directed at me. My defenses lower when I realize he's not attacking *me*—I'm not sure he would ever attack me, really—but Professor DeMarco.

"I know you don't like him, and I get it. If I saw him the way you do, I wouldn't either. But I truly don't think he was trying to sleep with me. I was very confused when I got that note that I thought was from him, but was obviously from you. He told me I could come to office hours on campus if I ever needed to talk, but that's quite a stretch from inviting me to his house, to his bedroom."

"He hadn't gotten there yet," he says tightly. "He doesn't know you the way I do, and he doesn't want to get caught doing the slimy shit he does. He would have moved carefully to feel you out before he escalated things."

"I really don't think—"

"I don't want to talk about him anymore. On Monday, you'll be transferring out of his class. There's another professor—a female one—who teaches the same class at a different time. I checked your schedule, and there are no conflicts."

My jaw drops open. "You can't just—"

"Yes, I can," he states slowly and deliberately, a flash of malice in his gaze. "If you object to transferring out of his class, I'll deal with this much more aggressively and see that he never teaches anywhere ever again."

Silvan doesn't usually cut me off when I'm speaking, but he just did it twice, so he really must be getting annoyed. He's also issuing threats now, and while I like the class with the teacher I'm taking it with… I know Silvan made that video last night, and I'm not totally sure how he would use it to get Professor DeMarco fired, but I do believe he would.

"Okay. Fine. I'll switch classes. I just… I have more questions. Not about him, but… about last night."

Before I can ask them, a waitress shows up at our table with a bouncy ponytail and a big smile. "Hey, guys. Sorry about your wait. I'm Bethany and I'll be taking care of you today. Can I get you started with some drinks?"

I glance up at her, then at Silvan across the table. He's tense and we've been having such a nice day out, maybe now isn't the best time to get into it.

"We can talk about it later," I say.

Then, turning my attention to Bethany, I tell her I'd love a nice cold lemonade.

CHAPTER 28
SOPHIE

AFTER A LONG, EVENTFUL DAY, I AM BEAT.

Despite my technical role as his hostage, Silvan decides he doesn't need to lock me in the escape room and leaves me alone in the bed to curl up and relax while he takes his shower. He had some stuff to deal with, so he let me shower alone tonight.

It's a pretty comfortable kidnapping, and one I know ends when the weekend does, so I stay curled up in his bed and don't bother trying to escape.

It's crazy how comfortable I am here. I've certainly never been in any guy's bed before but being in his feels oddly natural. His mattress is insanely comfortable, too. It's hard to keep my eyes open when I'm nestled in its comfy warmth.

I must drift off while I'm lying there because one minute, I'm in bed alone and I can hear the shower in the next room. The next, there's a warm body pressed against my back, pulling me close, and Silvan's hand is splayed over my bare stomach.

He bought me night clothes while we were out today, but he didn't give me any to change into after my shower. He likes me naked in his bed, and when his cock brushes my backside, I know he's naked, too.

My heart starts to race, but I tell myself I knew this would happen.

If he *didn't* fuck me once we were in bed for the night, I would have been stunned.

His big hand slides lower, pushing between my thighs so he can cup my pussy. I twist, but I'm still held captive by the strong arm he must have snaked under my body while I slept. It's locked around my waist, keeping my body pulled flush against his.

He uses his fingers to spread my pussy open, then uses one to stroke my clit. The sensation is so sudden, I gasp and make a half-hearted attempt to wiggle away from him, but it's impossible with his firm grip on me.

"I've been thinking about touching this sweet little pussy since the moment I stopped," he rumbles in my ear. "I fucking love to touch you. To make you squirm with pleasure. To listen to you come." He moves away from the most sensitive spot to explore a little. He pumps his finger in and out slowly and steadily for several seconds before returning his attention to my clit.

He toys with me so expertly, swiftly bringing me so close to orgasm that I'm visibly shaking. He doesn't allow me to come, though, pulling his finger out of my pussy just as I start to convulse from the buildup of pleasure.

I shudder, breathing heavily, my body throbbing with need.

"Not yet," he rumbles, kissing the curve of my shoulder. At odds with his tenderness, the arm around my waist moves under me and he squeezes my jaw. I can only squirm while he nuzzles and hungrily kisses my neck, holding me captive and helping himself to my body.

I cry out when he sinks a finger back into my pussy. He shifts positions, releasing my jaw and rolling me onto my stomach. His weight crushes me, but then he moves his arm out from under me to brace his weight on one forearm. He remains mostly on top of me to keep me pinned down, and from this angle, his finger stroking my clit feels different. He brushes it and I gasp, then he fingers it more relentlessly and I can't breathe. In no time, he has me ready to come again, clutching at the pillows, my body in pleasurable torment.

Once more, he stops just before I can get there.

I groan with disappointment, sinking into the mattress.

He chuckles and kisses my shoulder blade, then he gets to his knees on the bed behind me.

My body is a mess of confused yearning, so I don't struggle when he positions me on the bed so my ass is up, my thighs spread wide. I expect him to fuck me now, so I'm surprised when he rolls onto his back and slides under me.

"What are you—?"

Before I can finish asking my question, his hot mouth is on my pussy.

I cry out at the shock, instinctively trying to move away, but he doesn't let me. He grabs my ass, pulling me into his mouth so he can devour my pussy. The electric sensation running through my body is instant and I sink into the pillow, my eyes closing and my vision fading as his tongue rubs my clit, licking and teasing until I'm whimpering, and my thighs are trembling.

Please.

I keep the word trapped in my mouth, but I'm sorely tempted to let it out. If he stops now, I might actually die. My body is hot with need and desire I don't know what to do with. My body shudders as his tongue laps at my pussy, my vision blurring at the edges.

"My god, Silvan," I moan, clawing at the sheets.

I'm so close.

His hot mouth doesn't relent and I could cry, I want it so bad.

I nearly do when he stops.

My heart hammers wildly in my chest, my skin so hot, I feel like I might catch fire.

I'm in agony as he rolls over and gets back up on the bed behind me. Every nerve ending feels raw and agitated. I've never felt need on this level, but I'm dying with it.

Please, please, please.

He fixes my positioning since I drooped a bit when he was licking my pussy, then he gets on his knees behind me and brings the swollen head of his cock to the needy spot between my thighs.

My throbbing pussy aches to be filled, so I feel relief when he pushes the head between my slick lips. I wait for him to fill me, but instead, he toys with me, rubbing his head back and forth along my dripping slit without fully entering me, driving me absolutely mad with an agonizing mix of need and anticipation.

My whole body is trembling with need. I feel sick with it.

But he only teases me further, running his cock up and down my entrance, gently parting my tender folds and rubbing the sensitive nub at my core.

When I absolutely cannot take anymore, I whisper, "Please, Silvan."

He stills. His grip on my hip tightens and he murmurs, "Please what?"

I lick my lips, begging the words to just come, but I can't.

He meets me halfway, pushing his cock against me and asking, "You want me to fuck you, baby?"

The word erupts out of me before I can even clear it with my brain. "Yes."

His hand slides over my ass approvingly, then he grips my hips, lines his cock up where I need it so desperately, and drives into me.

I'm so over-sensitized, I can't help but cry out at the invasion. He isn't gentle and doesn't ease in this time. He jams his cock into me, the violence of the impact driving the air from my lungs.

I gasp, clutching at the mattress and trying to steady myself as he draws back and pistons into me again. My pussy stings as it stretches to accommodate him, but he forces himself all the way to the hilt, then holds himself inside me for a moment. It's a relief to feel so full of him. My pussy throbs and squeezes, begging him to stay and end the torment.

He pulls out and slams into me again.

This time, it doesn't ache as much to be filled by him.

He does it again and again until I'm crying out with each thrust and feeling the emptiness of not having him deep inside me every time he draws back.

My pussy craves the brutality and pleasure tingles down my spine every time he slams his cock into me.

I pant and claw at the bedding as he fucks me. My body is awash in sensations I can't even begin to process. My pussy grips him, clutching and squeezing his cock greedily, urging him to fuck me harder.

It's like he reads my mind.

He grips my hips tighter and increases the pace, pounding into me so hard it hurts, but it feels incredible, too. The pleasure-pain only serves to heighten my senses, to leave me gasping desperately for my next breath and crying out as he slams into me, his cock going deep, his balls slapping my ass. Just when I don't think I can take anymore and I know I'm close to exploding, he reaches around and pushes a finger into me, finding my clit and rubbing.

After nearly coming three times before, that nub is so stimulated, he hardly has to do more than touch it.

I come apart and he drives deep, hard and fast, triggering a twin explosion of pleasure that erupts like hot lava inside me. I scream and cry out as wave after wave of violent pleasure assaults me. I can't handle the intensity. My body shudders and I hear the broken cries coming out of me, but I can't control it. My vision is blurred, but there's white hot pleasure and bright pops of light like little stars in the sky.

I feel like my soul has been ripped open and sucked completely out of me when I come back down. Pleasure still ripples through me, but I feel helpless and a little broken.

Silvan pulls out of me and rolls me over. He's still on top of me and still hard since he hasn't come yet. But he seems to understand how fragile I am, so he gathers me close, kissing my forehead and holding me against his body as he reaches down to push his cock back into me.

He holds me like that and uses my body to get himself off. I don't participate, but he doesn't seem to mind. When he comes, he holds me so close and so tight, I feel like I can't breathe. He releases me after a moment and sinks into the mattress with me still in his arms, my face pressed against his chest.

My body still feels oddly hollow, but I'm so grateful for that burst of blinding pleasure, I pepper his chest with soft little kisses to express my appreciation.

His arm curls around me tighter in a gesture that feels like protection and fills me with warmth.

We lay there like that for a while. Once I've regained enough of my bearings to speak, I try to pull back, but Silvan keeps me pulled tight against him, his big hand covering my tit. He nuzzles into my neck, burying his face in my hair and breathes me in. "I'm fucking obsessed with you."

My stomach flutters and my heart feels funny, but that's an intense thing to hear.

Especially when I think he might mean it.

His hand slides into my hair, gripping the back of my head and pulling me close to his chest. "I can never let you go."

The words feel raw, not like a line or even something he expects me to be particularly happy to hear. Just an admission he needs to share, maybe even a warning.

I lick my lips, but my mouth is dry. I try to think what to say.

He knows I don't feel the way he does, so I know he doesn't expect reciprocation. He also blackmailed and raped me as recently as last night, so I know I'm well within my rights to gut him while he's vulnerable if I really want to.

But I don't want to.

I may not feel the way he does, but I don't want to *hurt* Silvan. I just want him to leave me alone.

Don't I?

I can't say my feelings about it were uncomplicated when I thought he had. There was a small part of me that felt disappointed. Just because I thought he proved he was like everybody else and would drop me like I meant nothing after coming on so strong?

Or was it something else?

I don't know, but I don't even know if I can trust this obsessive feeling he has for me. What if it fades? What if he's just caught up?

I imagine how fucking crushed I would be if I overrode all my common sense about Silvan and ignored every impulse not to trust him, and then he turned out to be just like other guys. I imagine having to watch him replace me, and what an absolute fool I would feel like for lowering my guard when I had every reason to keep it up.

He's asking too much.

I'm not equipped for it.

He should have become obsessed with someone else.

There are a lot of reasons I should probably feel sad as I lie there in his arms, but the reason I do isn't any of the sensible ones.

The truth feels like a lump in my throat. I'm not even sure I want to admit it, but since he's opening himself up to me, I offer a bit of honesty back. "I don't know if I can give you what you want."

I'm tense waiting for his response. I'm not sure what I expect, but probably for him to be angry about my refusal to give in to him.

Dylan would have been angry.

Silvan isn't.

He doesn't seem fazed at all, just cradles my head in his hand and presses his lips to my forehead. "Impossible. You're already everything I want."

His words make my stomach twist. I pull back

just enough to look up at him. "How can you be sure?"

He smiles down at me like I'm the most absurd, adorable creature he's ever encountered. "I'm not as tentative as you," he says warmly. "When I'm sure of something, I don't second guess it until I'm not sure anymore."

I look down at his chest so I don't have to meet his gaze and murmur, "I don't know what to be sure of anymore."

He grabs my chin, tilting it up so I have to look at him. His green eyes are serious. "You can be sure of me."

My heart lurches, then his head dips and his lips meet mine. It's a gentle kiss, one that makes me feel loved and cherished.

When the kiss ends, he stays close and murmurs against my lips. "I will always be there for you, Sophie. Whether you want me to be or not."

CHAPTER 29
SOPHIE

Sunlight peeks through the window, but the curtains are still closed.

Silvan sits on the bed behind me in a pair of gray sweats, his legs spread so I can sit between them.

He got me a soft gray dress to wear today, but I'm not wearing it yet. I'm still naked with just the sheets and fur blanket covering me from the waist down. My breasts are bare, and Silvan periodically stops moving his fingers through my hair to reach around and palm one. To hold my in-progress braid tight and slide his hand down my stomach until it's nestled between my thighs and I'm pulled back against him.

It's taking a little longer, but I'm not complaining.

"You're gonna make us late to breakfast."

He gasps, mocking me. "Not late to breakfast."

I reach back and smack his thigh.

He chuckles, pulling my braid tight in his fist and tugging me back so he can lean in and murmur close to my ear, "They can wait."

Chills travel down my spine at his breathy rumble. I lick my lips. "I've never had a guy braid my hair before."

"I wouldn't expect you had."

"Because you think I've only dated guys with short hair?"

"Because I think you've only dated self-involved assholes."

"Oh. Well, I probably can't argue that, but I actually *have* gone out with a guy with long hair. Not for long, just a couple of weeks when I was 15. He'd been to New York City, and I'd never been anywhere, so he seemed worldly to me. He smoked cigarettes which was gross, but also kind of added to his bad boy allure. He was two years older and… well, an asshole, but he had great hair. Long and blonde, like a pretty lion."

"He sounds like an idiot."

I crack a smile at his grouchy tone. "You don't know anything about him."

"I know he let you go after two weeks. That's all the information I need."

"Maybe *I* dumped *him*, did you consider that?"

"Irrelevant. He accepted it and let you go."

"That's a normal reaction to being dumped," I inform him.

"Yeah, well, you can try dumping me and see how that works out for you."

"I feel like I tried that before I even agreed —*under coercion*—to be your girlfriend."

"Exactly." He finishes braiding my hair and wraps the tie around the bottom. "All right, all done."

I pull the braid over my shoulder so I can look at it. "Nice work. Am I allowed to get dressed now?"

"If you must."

When I throw off the blanket and crawl over to

climb off the bed, he leans forward and smacks my ass.

I shoot him a look, but judging by the smirk on his face, he's not sorry at all.

I wash up at the sink, then I pull on the soft gray dress he wants me to wear. The material is thin and I'm not wearing a bra underneath, so the outline of my breasts is clearly visible, and my nipples are inexplicably standing at attention.

I guess it *is* a little cool in here.

I can't possibly have breakfast with his parents like this, so I pop my head back into the bedroom. "Is there a robe or something I can wear over this dress?"

"You don't like it?"

"I do, it's very comfortable, but…" It's easier just to show him, so I step into the room and his gaze drops right to my nipples, standing proudly erect against the soft fabric.

Silvan smirks. "You *do* like it."

My cheeks warm and I cross my arms over my chest. "Obviously, I need more coverage than this."

"Maybe we should have breakfast in bed today," he decides, his hungry gaze locked on my tits despite my attempt to cover them.

My eyes widen. "Is that an option?"

I'd much prefer breakfast alone with Silvan than downstairs with his scary dad.

His gaze lifts to my face. "Do you want it to be?"

"Yes," I say, unable to entirely tamp down my enthusiasm.

"Then of course it's an option. And what we're doing." Leaning back, he reaches for his phone on the nightstand and shoots off what I assume is a text. "Done." He replaces the phone as soon as he's finished and pats the mattress beside him. "Now, get your pretty little ass back in bed."

"You're so good to me," I say lightly as I pull the bathroom door shut behind me and pad over to the bed. "Best kidnapper ever."

"I appreciate the acknowledgment, but I won't let my head get too big over it. That's probably a pretty easy category to win."

I slide beneath the blanket and settle it over my lap. "How does breakfast in bed work? I don't think I've ever eaten in bed except for a couple of times when I was sick as a kid and my mom made me chicken noodle soup."

"One of the servants will bring up a cart in a few minutes."

"One of the servants, he says." I shake my head at what a ridiculous notion it is.

He shrugs. "I've always had servants. It's normal to me."

"When you were a kid, did your mom bring you soup when you were sick, or did the servants?"

"A combination of both. My mom is a nurturer, so she always stepped in with the human component, but we had servants, so they helped make it easy for her. They made the soup; she sat at my bedside touching my forehead with the back of her hand and looking sad that she couldn't fix my run-of-the-mill illness for me."

I watch his face, picking up on a certain guardedness when he talks about his mom. "Are you guys close?" He looks over at me. "You and your mom?"

"Yeah, sure, we're close," he says, but even the way he says it is in a trailing off way that tells me there's more to the story.

"Spill," I command.

He cocks an eyebrow at my bossiness, but gives me a little more, anyway. "There's nothing to spill. She's a good mom."

"But?"

"No but."

He's lying, so I stare at him with my eyebrows raised expectantly.

Finally, he shrugs, looking away. "She's maybe not the best wife."

I frown because that seems utterly opposite of what I've witnessed in my short time here. She and his dad seem obscenely happy. Hell, I literally watched the woman drop everything to refill her husband's coffee like some 50s throwback. "Really? How so?"

He looks at me. "Don't say anything."

"I won't."

"She cheats."

My eyes widen. "What?"

"I know my dad's not the easiest guy to be with, but it's what she signed up for, you know? He's not the worst, either, and he does make an effort for her. It's not like he's some uncaring asshole who just doesn't give a shit, but he is who he is. And she knew who he was and supposedly loved him going into it, that's why she chose to marry him. It's supposed to be for better or worse, right? A commitment. You should be able to rely on those, but I guess someone's word is only as good as…" He shakes his head. "You've gotta consider the source. Guess she's not reliable."

I frown. None of that matches my impression of them. "They both seem happy. Your father certainly seems happy with her, and your mom seems to go out of her way for him. I would imagine layers and layers of resentment if their relationship was like the one you're describing."

"Right? Me too." He shakes his head. "Their dynamic is weird. Maybe I don't entirely get it."

"Maybe they only seemed that way to me because someone was watching. Some people are different with an audience."

"Nah. They're loved up in private, too."

"Does your dad... sleep around?"

He shakes his head. "Like I said, he only has eyes for her."

"Hm. I was gonna say, maybe they're swingers or something."

He shakes his head. "Definitely not swingers. It's cheating. There's no consent involved. My dad doesn't like it, he just... loves her too much or something, I don't know."

"Well, whatever the situation, it must work for them. Maybe we don't get it, but they're happier than any married couple I've ever seen, so they must be doing something right."

Before we can delve any deeper into the inner workings of Silvan's mom and dad's marriage, there's a knock at the door and Olena comes in pushing a cart.

Maybe it's all this talk of commitment and infidelity, but I find it even more impossible to ignore the sparkle in her eye when she brings a breakfast tray over for Silvan and starts to serve him.

"I brought coffee, orange juice, and chai tea," she tells him. "Which would you like?"

"Coffee and orange juice," he tells her, then glances over at me.

"Um, orange juice for me," I say.

She nods, grabbing two cold bottles of water off her cart and handing one to each of us. "I brought these as well, in case you needed them."

"Thank you, Olena."

She blushes prettily under his notice and says, "You're welcome, Master."

My spine stiffens. I've heard Hugh refer to him as "Master Silvan" before and it didn't bother me, but hearing it from the lips of a girl who moons at him... it feels a bit different.

Olena serves him first, then she comes over to me. She gives us ham, egg, and cheese sandwiches on warm, buttery croissants and sides of fresh fruit.

Once we have all our food, Silvan dismisses her with a warm, "Thank you, Olena," and she bows her head to him, then goes over to the cart and disappears from the room.

She's gone for approximately three seconds before I say, "She calls you *master*."

He glances over at me. "Yes." When I only continue to stare at him, he smirks. "Do you hate it?"

"Yes, I hate it," I blurt.

"It's not personal," he says dismissively. "The house she was in before ours, the husband liked for her to call him master."

"I wonder how his wife liked it," I mutter.

Still amused, he grabs his glass of orange juice. "Not much. Why do you think she's with us now? Official story is it wasn't a good fit, but Mom says the wife found a condom wrapper between the couch cushions and demanded she go."

My eyes are wide. "Have you slept with her?"

He shakes his head. I don't know why I feel a small measure of relief. "I don't fuck the help. Neither does my dad, so having her here wasn't a problem."

"I'm surprised your mom's comfortable having her here knowing that."

"Why?" He looks over at me. "Olena's willingness to fuck married men poses no threat to her.

My dad's not a cheater. Men *are* completely capable of keeping their dicks in their pants around willing women, Sophie. If the only reason he isn't cheating is a lack of opportunity, better to find out while you're young and can find someone better."

"I guess that's true. Still, seems like needless temptation."

He shrugs. "He's not tempted. Besides, the other man who was interested in her wouldn't have treated her well. At least she's safe here."

My brow furrows. "Couldn't she just opt not to work for someone who would mistreat her?"

"Her options are limited. She's working off a debt. Not hers, her family's, but... whether or not she wants to do something isn't of the utmost importance."

My frown deepens. "That doesn't sound legal."

He cracks a smile and looks over at me as if he finds me adorable. Nodding at my plate, he says, "Eat your breakfast."

After a delicious breakfast, the rest of our lazy Saturday just seems to drift away.

Hugh brought my school bag, but I didn't have time to do it yesterday. Today, we lie around on Silvan's bed with textbooks and notebooks open doing our homework together.

It's kind of nice.

Then for lunch, Olena brings us these chicken salads with kale and quinoa. I'm not terribly excited about eating it as I watch Silvan squeeze a lemon wedge over his and then mimic his movements, but I'm sold after the first bite.

Whatever indentured servitude is going on in this place, the food is damn good.

Once we've finished with our schoolwork, we laze around and watch some television. I text Mom —under Silvan's careful scrutiny—and get so comfy, I almost fall asleep.

But then somehow, it's dinnertime already, and Silvan locks his arms around my waist and pulls me back against him, murmuring, "We need to shower and get dressed for dinner."

I've never had to get dressed for dinner on a lazy day at home before, but things at Silvan's house aren't remotely like things at mine.

This time, we shower together.

Silvan goes down on me in the shower, then turns me around and spreads my ass cheeks apart. I shudder as warm water hits my lower back, gasp as he teases my hole with his finger. Looking back at him, I whisper, "Please..."

He can tell I'm reluctant.

That doesn't always stop him, but right now, it seems to. He releases my cheeks and runs a firm hand over the curve of my ass. Kissing my wet shoulder blade, he rumbles, "Later."

A threat, a promise—whatever it is, it reminds me that he has access to me however and whenever he wants it as long as I'm here in his domain.

But I won't be for much longer.

Tomorrow is Sunday, and judging by things he has said, it seems like he'll let me get back to my regularly scheduled life—*minus Professor DeMarco's class, of course*—come Monday.

As we're both getting dressed for dinner with his parents, I ask, "Do I get to go home tomorrow?"

His hand stills on the collar of his shirt briefly, then he shrugs to adjust the fit and finishes the process of buttoning up. "Eager to leave me, are you?"

The way he says it makes me feel a pinch of guilt, which I know is absurd.

I'm not really being mistreated, and I know I'm not in any danger, but I am still here because he made me be here. Not because I wanted to be. "I just need to get ready for the start of a new week. I have school... a new class, apparently."

His jaw locks at even the peripheral mention of Professor DeMarco.

"I just need to get myself prepared. I haven't even been able to check my school email since I've been here, and sometimes my teachers will email me about preparations I need to make for class. If I haven't checked it before Monday morning and I miss something important, they won't think, 'oh, she was probably kidnapped this weekend and didn't have access to her laptop,' they'll just think I'm being a slacker."

He's quiet as he grabs his leather belt off the counter and puts it on.

"My father may ask you questions at dinner. If he does, don't express your impatience to leave. Act like you like me more than you do, and make it as clear as you must that you have no desire to tell anyone about this weekend or get me in trouble."

I don't know if it's his words or his monotone delivery of them, but guilt pinches me when he grabs my hand and hauls me out of the bathroom. I flick off the light and follow after him, but I can't seem to outrun the icky feeling.

When we get to the hall outside his bedroom, I tug on his hand and slow down.

He turns to look back at me.

I don't know what to say.

My lips part, but no words come.

Instead of offering up words, I offer up the only

thing I can think of that I know he wants: me. With my gaze locked on his, I back up against the wall.

His eyes narrow, but his predator's instincts are engaged. He has to stalk me and close in on me like he has to breathe. He grabs my waist with one hand and my neck with the other, pulling me against his body, then pressing me back against the wall.

My heart pounds so hard, I can hear it in my ears. I know I invited this, but it makes it no less intense when he claims my mouth. His hunger for me is overwhelming, and while I wanted to offer a kiss to make up for possibly hurting his feelings, he seems intent on taking much more.

"Silvan," I say desperately, breaking away from his lips as he hikes up my dress, his big hands moving possessively between my thighs.

He doesn't say anything and doesn't stop. Instead, he rips my panties away from my body and shoves his hand between my legs. I try to squeeze my thighs together to stop him, but he just releases my waist and grabs my thigh, lifting it and wrapping my leg around his hip.

"Stop," I say, grabbing his wrist and the hem of my dress to try shoving it down. "We have to meet your parents for dinner."

"Fuck dinner."

"Silvan..."

The sound of his zipper makes my heart lurch, then start to beat harder. I look down the hall to make sure we're at least alone, then grab his shoulders on instinct as he lifts me.

I meet his gaze fleetingly as his cock meets my entrance. I'm not ready for him, but he shoves into me, anyway.

Fuck.

I whine as I stretch to fit him, trying to move

away from his intruding cock but also terrified he'll drop me if I move too much. He grips my ass possessively, pulling me hard against him as he forces himself deeper inside me.

"I fucking love having you on my cock," he growls. "I'd keep you here all goddamn day if I could."

I drop one hand from his shoulder to brace it on the wall behind me as he shifts our positions, easing back so he can ram into me again. I cry out, but he ignores my protest and smashes me against the wall, grabbing a rough handful of my hair and crushing his mouth against mine. I can scarcely breathe as he ravages my mouth, driving his cock deep into my aching pussy. It's a brutal invasion, and it feels like it's meant to be one.

I can feel every inch of his thick, hard cock as he pounds into me again and again, using my pussy, making me take him. He's not worried about my pleasure this time, only using me to get himself off.

Clearly, there's something very wrong with me because his roughness, the way he's using me... pleasure starts to build. From the friction, from the violence of it? I flash back to the shower, his expert tongue lapping at my pussy until I cried out, convulsing beneath the shower's spray, and now he's gripping me so tight I'm sure my skin will bruise and driving into my pussy like he's determined to break it.

"Silvan," I cry out breathlessly as he pounds into me. "Oh, God..."

"You like that, baby? You like to be fucking used?"

Yes. God, yes.

His lips are at my ear, and he murmurs, "I'm going to ruin you for anyone else, you know that?"

Joke's on him. I'm already ruined.

I give him all the proof he should need when he drives his cock deep and I explode around him, gasping and whining through my orgasm as he continues to fuck me.

I close my eyes and take it, trying to catch my breath as I come down from my own orgasm. My pussy takes a beating, then he drives deep and pumps me full of his cum.

I feel fucking filthy but also strangely alive when he finishes with me. He pulls his cock out of me and I feel his cum leak out and trail down my thigh.

My legs are shaky as he puts me back down.

"Get on your knees."

I do. I sink to them so fast, I should be ashamed.

"Take my cock in your mouth and clean me up."

I grip his hip and lean in, opening my mouth and taking him between my lips. He watches me, pushing his fingers through my hair to reward me as I suck him clean.

I don't know what's wrong with me, but I want to keep sucking him. I want him to get hard again and make me please him. I want him inside me again. I want him to make me hurt, and then make me come.

I think he broke something in my brain.

I try to shake it off as I finish cleaning him and ease back, but when I look up at him, I think he can see it. He caresses my face, then shoves his thumb into my mouth. I suck it, holding his gaze.

"Mm. You're fucking perfect, you know that?"

I didn't feel perfect a moment ago, but I do now.

The feeling is fleeting, and so is the intensely

confusing cloud of lust I'm momentarily shrouded in.

He pops his thumb out of my mouth and gives me his hand to help me stand.

My legs feel hollow and unreliable as I get my feet back on the ground beneath me.

"You can clean yourself up in the bathroom. I'll wait out here."

I must look as wobbly as I feel because before he lets me go, he grabs my waist, pulls me close, and gives me a long, tender kiss to steady me.

CHAPTER 30
SILVAN

WE'RE LATE TO DINNER.

Mom and dad are finishing up the soup and salad course when we come in.

"Nice of you to join us," Dad says wryly.

Mom's bright gaze hits Sophie trailing behind me, holding my hand. "Oh, that's a pretty dress."

"Thanks," Sophie murmurs shyly.

She's softer now that she's been fucked. I didn't plan to fuck her before dinner, but it's probably good that I did.

I pull out Sophie's chair for her. She thanks me, but I can tell she's nervous about sitting across from my father again after last time.

I'm not thrilled about it, either.

I don't know if he'll grill her, and I don't know what she'll say if he does.

Ilona brings in salads for us. Sophie's cheeks burn like she'll know why we're late and judge her for it, but of course, the maid doesn't give a single fuck. The cook made cauliflower soup with a bread crumb topping, so we each get a cup of that as well.

We've thrown off the rhythm of dinner by being so late. Sophie tries to eat quickly to catch up because she's considerate like that. I eat a little quicker, too, but for a different reason.

I can feel Dad watching Sophie. Tension gathers in my shoulders.

I'm just waiting for him to say something and hoping we can get through dinner quickly before anything can go wrong.

For several minutes, the only sound is silverware clinking against China as we eat. The maids bring in the main course for Mom and Dad, then come over to clear our plates so they can bring ours in next.

"So," Dad finally says, reaching for his wine glass and regarding Sophie across the table. "Have you had a nice weekend?"

I barely resist the temptation to reach beneath the table and grab her thigh to subtly pressure her to give the right answers. The only reason I don't is my dad would notice, so it would defeat the purpose.

After a pause that feels to me like three fucking years, Sophie finally says, "Yes." She pauses again, then adds, "Thank you for having me."

My soul lightens with relief.

Maybe she's going to play ball.

I didn't say as much as I could have about how important it is that my dad come out of this weekend reassured that she won't cause trouble, but I didn't want to make her more nervous than I knew she would be.

"Haven't spent much time in the escape room, have you?" he continues.

I feel her wanting to look over at me, but she keeps her gaze on the table and forces a faint smile. "No. I've been a good little hostage."

I flinch a bit at her using that word, afraid he'll

latch onto it, but before anything else can be said, Ilona brings in our main course.

A frown flickers across Sophie's face as she thanks her, then she asks softly, "What is it?"

"Veal with a balsamic-tomato sauce," the maid answers.

"Thank you."

Ilona nods and returns to the kitchen.

Sophie reaches over her plate and grabs the wine glass that's been filled for her. Dad watches her drink, then she hesitates, probably wondering if she was supposed to do that. I know Sophie's only 19 and I'm sure he does by now, too, but he's not going to care about a glass of wine with dinner.

She doesn't know that, though, so she flushes, probably thinking she's done something wrong. I grab my glass and take a sip hoping she'll see she hasn't, but she's too flustered to notice.

"How would you feel about staying a few more days?" Dad asks.

Sophie's eyes widen. "Oh… I couldn't. I stay in a dorm, I have roommates. They're probably already miffed I skipped out on my share of the chores this weekend. They'll kill me if I skip grocery shopping, too," she says lightly.

His lips tug up faintly. "We have a staff. We can send someone to meet your obligations for you so you can stay."

"That's a generous offer," she says uneasily, looking down at her plate. Pushing it away from her, she goes on. "I sort of have a routine at home that I'm pretty fond of, though, so I should really be getting back."

"It seems to me your routine is quite fluid," he says smoothly, cutting into his veal. "Sometimes you're at your dorm, sometimes you're at your mother's. Seems it would be easy for you to disappear for a while without anyone noticing." He takes a bite and meets her gaze across the table.

Sophie pales and starts to reach for her wine glass again but seems to think better of it and drops her hands. They're in her lap and I have to resist the urge to reach over and grab one to reassure her.

I trust Sophie to handle my father without my help, and I suspect he'll respect her more if she can.

If it goes bad, I'll do damage control, but I want to give her a chance and see how she does on her own first.

"Is there something wrong with the veal?" he asks evenly since she hasn't touched it and has now pushed the plate away from her as if finished.

She clears her throat, grabbing the water goblet and taking a drink instead. "I don't eat veal."

"Why not?"

"Because... when I look at it, I see a baby cow that hasn't even had a chance to live its life." Dead silence greets her, so she continues. "They're separated from their mothers at birth and raised solely to be consumed, so the calves are kept confined under cruel conditions in order to keep their flesh tender for the consumer. They're not allowed to wander around and graze or socialize like an animal should; they're kept in veal crates so they can't move to keep their muscles weak. Some are so weak, they can't even make the walk to the slaughter line, and I just... It's an unspeakably cruel way to treat a living thing, and I'm not going to eat it."

"It's already dead."

"I understand, and if anyone else would like it, please take it. I hate for the poor baby cow to be treated horribly and then slaughtered for no reason, but I feel ill even thinking about taking a bite, so… I'm not going to."

Dad slices off another piece of his abused baby cow and pops it into his mouth, unbothered. "You're not a vegetarian?"

"I'm not. Just no veal, and I do try to only buy meat I know is cruelty-free. Living things shouldn't be treated the way—" She stops herself, shaking her head. "You don't care."

"No," he murmurs.

"But I do, so no veal for me."

Dad's gaze drifts to me. "Excellent job, son. You've brought home a humanitarian."

I crack a smile, but before I can say anything, Sophie does.

"I know, I know. Super annoying to care about things. Sorry," she says, sounding not sorry at all.

"I never thought about it that way before," Mom says, frowning down at her plate. "I don't think we should have veal anymore, honey. I don't want to eat baby cows."

"Why don't I fund a farm where baby cows can live their best lives before we butcher them for their meat?"

"Oh, yes," Mom says, smiling. "That would be nice."

"I was joking, sweetheart."

"Oh." Mom drops her fork. "Well, I still think it sounds nice." Looking across the table at Sophie, she says, "I'm going to the kitchen to see if I can get us something else to eat. Would you like to come with me?"

Sophie blinks in surprise, then nods her head. "Sure."

Dad and I watch the women head for the kitchen, then he looks at me across the table.

"You couldn't have brought home a nice

shallow girl who only cares about shopping and social media?"

I crack a smile and slice into my veal so I can eat it before Sophie comes back. "Sorry."

"This one's going to be a pain in the ass," he warns me.

I shake my head, pulling her plate over so I can take the meat so she doesn't have to look at it anymore. "Not to me. I respect her values. She's not like the people I usually hang out with."

"That's by design," he says dryly. "If you're going to keep her around, I'd like to limit the time she spends with your mother."

I frown. "Why?"

"Your mother is easily influenced." He drags her plate over to take her meat like I'm doing with Sophie's since Mom is now a convert to the no-veal club. "As it is, I'm not going to have a meal I enjoy for a good long time because of your troublesome girlfriend. I'd like to keep her from causing any further disruptions to my life."

"Speaking of disruptions..." I finish clearing Sophie's plate and slide it under mine, then I look at him across the table. "Shame about that investment banker, isn't it?"

His gaze is empty when he meets mine as if he hasn't the slightest idea what I'm talking about.

"I saw in that paper you had me throw away that one of Mom's friends died."

"Mm. Turned out, he wasn't such a good friend. He took advantage of her gentle nature, tried to take things that didn't belong to him." He pulls off a bit of meat, then meets my gaze, smiling noncommittally. "Sometimes, people get what they deserve."

Dad and I never openly acknowledge Mom's temporary distractions, but since I'm fairly certain he murdered her most recent lover, my curiosity is piqued. Why this one? "Is that the only friend you've felt the need to… unfriend for her?"

"No. There have been a few over the years."

"Does she know about any of them?"

He shakes his head, slicing off another piece of meat. "That would make her sad," he says before popping it into his mouth.

A frown flickers across my face. "Not to be an asshole, but don't you think maybe she deserves to be a little sad about it? Maybe she'd take it as a warning and stop doing it."

"I do what must be done to punish *the men*, Silvan, not your mother."

"Why?"

"Melanie is exactly who I want her to be. The last thing I would ever want is to change or damage her. It's not her fault other men have noticed her easy nature and snuck in from time to time. If that's anyone's fault, it's mine for getting too busy and not keeping a good enough eye on her."

I'm not sure that entirely makes sense to me, but before another word can be said about it, we hear chattering and then Mom and Sophie come in with second salad plates.

Mom is cheerful and Sophie seems to be in good spirits, too. I watch Dad look up at his wife as she runs a hand over the back of his neck fondly before sitting down. "Have a nice girls' trip to the kitchen?" he asks lightly.

"Yes, we did," Mom says happily, setting her plate down.

"I see you found some nice cruelty-free lettuce."

Mom waves off his teasing, but Sophie rolls her

eyes. I smirk when she shoots me a look and squeeze her thigh under the table.

I know she and my father won't be besties anytime soon. I'll happily settle for them not being enemies because my father is not a good enemy to have.

At least Sophie seems more comfortable when she settles in, and I watch her happily eat her salad.

We get through the rest of dinner and dessert without incident.

While I was initially cautious about the possibility of them butting heads, I'm glad they did. He might personally consider caring about people and creatures that can do nothing for him idealistic and foolish, but I think now that my father has slid Sophie into a "caring" category of people, he'll be less concerned about releasing her back into the world. It's clear that she doesn't hate me, so when I assure him she won't cause trouble, I think he'll be inclined to believe me.

After all, Sophie doesn't make waves just to be difficult. She only does it over something she's truly passionate about.

Defending herself has never made that list.

I don't love what assholes like Dylan Prescott have gotten away with because of it, but now that she's mine, no one will ever get one over on her again.

I'll make damn sure of it.

While I still don't entirely understand my parents' relationship, what Dad said while the girls were in the kitchen stirred memories of a couple of nights ago.

Was I pissed that Sophie showed up at his house? Fuck yes.

Would I have lost her over it?

Not a fucking chance.

Dad and I may not agree on forgoing her punishment completely—if anything *had* happened between them, I would have gone scorched fucking earth—but maybe we're more alike than I thought.

And she may not have chosen this life, but Sophie can fit in here. Maybe not seamlessly with no friction, but she can fit.

When we get back upstairs, as I'm helping her unzip her dress, Sophie tells me, "I'm sorry to tell you this, but I am *not* on your side when it comes to this whole situation with your mom. I think she's the sweetest person I've ever met, and I don't know *how* she puts up with your father. If I were her, I'd cheat on him too, just to piss him off."

I smirk, tugging the material of her dress apart and exposing her lovely back. "I believe that's why he never would have married you. Would've ended badly."

"I can't believe he managed to marry her. She's just so lovely and he's so... not. Was it a hostage situation? Is this a Stockholm marriage or something?"

I kiss her bare back. "The men in my family *are* pretty ruthless when it comes to locking down the woman they desire, but as far as I know, there was no kidnapping involved in their courtship."

She shakes her head. "I don't understand."

I shrug. "Opposites attract. Sometimes," I add, since obviously *she* and my father do not attract at all.

"I feel like adopting her so I can rescue her from his dastardly clutches."

That melts the smile right off my face. I'm sure she's joking, but I'm also sure there's a kernel of truth to what she says. "That's one thing you can never do," I tell her. "My father can be a bit of a bastard, but there's no one he loves more than her. He'd never tolerate someone trying to separate them."

She peeks at me over her shoulder. "Even if it's a noble humanitarian effort?"

I nod solemnly. "He's more villain than hero. He wouldn't empathize and doesn't care about any human who isn't her."

She cracks a smile. "What about you?"

"I'm second or third on the list. She has her own separate sheet of paper because she's so far above everyone else. It's not even close."

"Hmm."

I kiss her shoulder. "He's also already pegged you as a potential problem, so do us both a favor and please don't give him any more reason to believe that. My father isn't a nice man, Sophie. All jokes aside, he's not someone you want to cross."

With a frown marring her pretty brow, she looks back at me. "Did you ever tell me what it was your father does for a living?"

I lean in and brush a kiss across her lips. "I didn't."

Her eyebrows rise. "Could you?"

I kiss her again, lingering close to her mouth. "He makes a lot of money. That's all you need to know."

"I disagree," she says, but then she gasps when I swat her on the ass. "Hey!"

I grin and grab her hand, dragging her back into the bedroom. "Come on. It's time for bed."

"But it's only…" She looks around for a clock, but fails to find one. "Well, I'm not sure, but it's not *bedtime*."

"I didn't say we're going to sleep."

CHAPTER 31
SOPHIE

I'M HAVING THE ODDEST DREAM.

My brain is sometimes hateful when I'm asleep and unable to defend myself. It forces me to deal with things I'm too well-guarded to allow in when I'm awake.

Since I met Silvan, he's taken my life over to such a degree that even my brain stopped pulling its shit while I slept.

Tonight, it disturbs me by putting me in the passenger seat of a car that Dylan Prescott is driving. I look over at him, a bit foggy on why he's there, but in my dream state, not fully possessing all my faculties, either. All I can feel is the confusion at first, and then a strong sense of dread.

I don't want to go anywhere with him.

I don't want him driving my car.

I glance in the backseat and see my wedding dress hanging up. Not a real wedding dress, not white and lovely like I would *want* my wedding dress to be. It's a plain dress that only falls to the knee, a pale purple color, and despite the sense that it's new, the fabric is already pilling.

"I told you, you should have bought a different

one," he says even though I haven't brought any attention to it.

My stomach feels sick.

Dread swallows me up. I look out the front windshield and see a bleak sky. We're driving down an empty highway. "Where are you taking me?"

He looks over at me and smiles. "To our wedding."

I jerk awake with a gasp, panic swelling up in my chest because I can't breathe and I feel—

Full.

Before I can wake up enough to recognize why my body feels so thoroughly possessed, I register a man's weight on top of me and fingers wrapped around my throat.

I'm blurry and confused, but Silvan's deep voice is like an anchor thrown ashore, jerking me from the fog and bringing me fully into his still-dark bedroom.

His hand is locked around my throat tight enough to trigger a small wave of panic. "What did you just say?" he growls.

My heart slams forward in my chest. I grab his wrist, trying to pull it from my throat. "I... I... I don't know. I was asleep."

"You said a name."

My heart sinks.

"I—I said Silvan," I lie on impulse.

"Really?" he asks silkily. "Because it sounded an awful lot like *Dylan*."

I gulp, and with his hand wrapped so tightly around my throat, I know he feels it. "I... Those names sound similar enough. You must have misheard."

His eyes narrow to slits. He's thoroughly un-convinced, but rather than press the issue with words, he pulls his hips back and drives into me harder.

I gasp as my body stretches around his cock. That full feeling, it's this.

He started fucking me while I was asleep.

My heart pounds furiously as I become aware of the assault on my body. I can't escape the feeling of fear, but I know I won't be able to stop him if I fight, so even though I want to in this moment, I don't. I hold onto his wrist and he holds onto my throat while he fucks me roughly, keeping me pinned to his bed, even my breaths controlled by his firm grip.

The message is clear: my body belongs to him.

He doesn't even need my permission to use it.

The sick part of me responds to his ruthless domination. It craves the times he fucks me when he's angry at me because he does it without care, using my body in such a way that I know I don't stand a chance fighting him, so I don't have to.

He releases my throat and pulls out of me, but my relief—*disappointment?*—is short-lived. He rolls me over so I'm facedown on the bed, then pulls my hips up, spreading my thighs wide and positioning himself between my legs.

My pussy throbs, waiting for him. My heart hammers because *what's wrong with me?*

Then he grabs my hips, his hands rough and unforgiving.

He brings his cock to my entrance and shoves in hard, making me cry out at the merciless intrusion.

He fucks me without guilt or concern for my comfort. Every thrust is deep, hard, and relentless. My body scurries to accommodate the invasion of his. I must have been slick when he first entered me because while I feel the familiar tugging and friction as my skin stretches to accommodate him, it's not painful.

"You're enjoying this, aren't you?"

His voice is a little mean and makes my heart flip over in my chest.

I don't want him to be mean to me.

Panic swells up as he eases down, sliding his hand around my throat, forcing me close as he comes down on top of me.

"Who do you belong to, Sophie?"

"You," I whisper.

It feels like an absolute betrayal to myself, but I know it's what he wants to hear, and I want to give him what he wants so he isn't mean to me.

The warmth in his voice drizzles through my veins and kindles heat between my thighs. "Mm, that's a good girl. That's exactly what I wanted to hear. But you knew that, didn't you? You're always willing to placate me when I scare the living fuck out of you."

That's an uncomfortable thing to hear, but I guess it's not untrue.

"I'm never sure you mean it, though, that's the thing. Can I trust you once the words have been spoken? Or are you just saying whatever you have to say to get away with as little damage as possible? Are we running in circles, Sophie?"

I swallow, but don't say a word.

Taking my silence as insufficient reassurance, apparently, he speaks again, his breath hot against my ear. "Do you know what I would do to a man if he touched you?"

His voice is like poisoned silk held over my mouth, the toxicity invading my senses and making me light-headed. I swallow, but I can't speak.

"I would rip him limb from limb. I don't mean

that metaphorically, either. I would literally sever any part of him that touched you from his fucking body."

His words intensify my fear but pull me closer to him as if seeking his protection.

From him?

Absurd, but it feels reliable.

He's angry right now, but I'm not truly afraid he would hurt me. Whatever faults he has, I know how much Silvan values me. Even though it feels mildly psychotic to admit this even to myself, I even believe he might love me.

Or at least think he does.

And I know Silvan would protect me from any threat. I know that in my bones.

Maybe that's why I feel the rush of fear and the familiar tightness in my chest, but it never escalates to a full-blown panic attack. Mere memories can send me into one, but actually being held down, threatened, and used by Silvan doesn't.

"Now, I'm not going to keep repeating myself, Sophie. I'm going to tell you this once, so I suggest you remember it, because my promise has no expiration date. You belong to me, and I'm an only child, baby; I can't share for shit. If another man ever touches you, I will torture him and make you watch. Depending on how thoroughly you've pissed me off, I might let you leave the room before the grand finale, but know that it would end with me cutting off all the parts of him you might have liked and then standing on his throat as he gurgled his own blood. His last fucking words would be begging me for mercy, and I would not feel one single bit of fucking remorse as I withheld it and watched him die. I would come to you and fuck you with his blood spatter still on my body, so please, Sophie, for your sake, take me seriously. I don't have my father's patience, and I don't want to break you."

His words stir images that make me feel queasy.

I might not believe most guys saying something so crazy, but I believe him.

From that first night when he was dressed up as a Viking, I sensed something authentically brutal in him. It's not something that's overbearing most of the time, but it comes awake when he feels threatened.

I'm his prized possession, the thing he'll defend at all costs. Kill for if he must.

That shouldn't turn me on, but I can't deny the aching need I feel for him in this moment.

When he pulls his hips back and drives into me again, I gasp, reaching back to grab his neck and pull him closer. He growls with approval, scraping the sensitive skin along the back of my neck with his teeth as he bites me, then kisses me all over. Leaning his face into the curve of my neck, he breathes me in.

"You smell like me," he whispers, then he licks my skin and his hot tongue ignites my nerve endings, triggering an explosion of white-hot lust in my brain.

His words resonate through my body, that possessive, proprietary tone of his that makes me feel owned. He fucks me harder, and I feel it everywhere. I feel suffocated by him, overwhelmed by him, but it's oddly reassuring.

He'll never let me leave.

The thought bubbles up in my mind but my senses are too wrapped around him to deal with it, so I shove it away and focus on breathing. My breaths are coming quick and shallow, my heart pounding as he dominates my pussy.

When he yanks my hair to pull my head back, I take his punishing kiss. I don't realize how close I am until he tears his lips from mine, grips my throat tight, and growls, "Come for me, baby."

Pleasure explodes as he continues to ram my pussy, dragging out the pleasure as I cry out, my pussy spasming and clenching around his cock. His greedy hand roams my body, squeezing my tits as he holds me against him by the throat.

I feel… indescribable.

I feel free.

There's a constant weight I carry, but I feel none of it now. I'm free as a bird, wings spread, flying on the breeze of sheer bliss.

I feel him still pounding inside me, hear his sounds of strain and groans of pleasure. I want to give it to him. I want him to feel at least a fraction of the pleasure he gave to me.

Rationally, I think he's dangerous and a little crazy.

But there's no room for rationality in this bed right now.

I squeeze my pussy muscles tight around him, keeping my ass up the way I know he likes.

He always says sexy things that make the sex more intense for me, but I don't have the first clue what I could say that would do that for him.

I guess I know what he likes, though. And I know he's close.

The thought of him coming in my pussy without a condom on again makes me shiver, but it's the first thing I can think of. He'll do it whether I tell him to or not, anyway, and my defenses are down from that orgasm, so the invitation just slips out of my mouth.

"Come inside me, Silvan."

His cock jerks and his grip on my throat tightens. "You want it, baby?"

"Yes. Please," I add, remembering he liked that before.

"Fuck." He growls, squeezing my throat hard enough to make me gasp.

He drives deep and his body goes rigid. I feel the warm spurts of his seed filling my pussy and I know I should be worried about it, but I'm too spent to care right now.

Silvan collapses on top of me at first, but moves off me onto the bed beside me as soon as he's able. He pulls me close, kissing the side of my face and settling my body against his warm muscled chest.

I nuzzle into him and close my eyes.

Absently, he caresses my face and kisses my hair.

We lay like that for a while just enjoying each other's company, the mindless bliss.

When it fades and reality starts to pull me back to its side, the horror of it all settles in on me.

It isn't sexy that he talks like a madman about possessing me because we don't agree on that point. I don't want to be his. That's what he wants. It's not like I was in any hurry to date anybody else when we met, but as long as he thinks I belong to him, that door is closed to me, and that's not fair. I'm not his to claim.

It's definitely not okay for him to keep coming inside me. I can't believe I got so carried away and said that to him. My god, what was I thinking?

As crazy as he is about keeping me locked down now, imagine if he actually managed to get me pregnant.

I need to get away from him, but I don't know how.

The weekend's over so I don't have to play the

polite captive anymore, but I don't know how to get back to my life when he won't let me.

Maybe I wasn't living my best life before him, but at least it was mine.

I pull out of his embrace and roll out of bed. I head to the bathroom to clean myself up and so he'll think that's why I'm moving away from him, but when I get back into bed, I stay on my own side.

I don't know how I fooled myself into believing he might not notice if I was slick about it. My move fails to accomplish anything. When I come back and stay on my side of the bed, Silvan just scoots over into my space, locks his arms around my waist, and pulls me back against him.

"What are you thinking?" he asks.

"Lots of things," I answer honestly.

My stomach is twisted up in knots. I want to pull out of his embrace again, but he's left me nowhere to go. If I move any farther toward the edge of the bed, I'll fall off.

And then he'll just pick my ass up and pull me back into his arms on the bed.

"I need to go home tomorrow."

"Why?"

He asks casually enough, but his question surprises me. "I've already told you."

"You've given me all the bullshit reasons, yeah. Not the real one."

"You know the real one, Silvan. I haven't made it a secret, have I? I don't…"

I don't know what to say. Anything I could say that's true feels mean.

I don't want to be with you.

Mean.

I'm only here because you forced me to be. As soon as you stop forcing me to be, I won't be here anymore.

Also feels mean.

The thought of saying anything like that to him makes me sad which I guess is absurd, but despite his forcefulness in pursuing me, Silvan isn't really *mean* to me. I don't want to be mean to him, either.

I just want to be let go.

"When I was a little girl, I loved *Beauty and the Beast*."

His lips tug up. "Yeah?"

I nod. "It was my favorite movie. I'd watch it in any form, but the Disney cartoon was my favorite. I'd watch it over and over again."

"When we have a little girl, we'll have to watch it with her."

Oh my god, Silvan.

"We're not having a little girl."

He shrugs his shoulders, but doesn't let me go. "With our son, then."

Despite myself, I find myself thinking about it too much. "Actually, I think if I have a daughter, I'll navigate her away from the classics for a good long while. She's starting off with *Frozen*. Sneaky villains preying on sheltered princesses so you learn not to trust so quickly, not falling for the kidnapper. Just in case that shit got in early," I say, tapping my head.

Silvan laughs, squeezing me a little tighter. He kisses the side of my face and rumbles, "That mean you're falling for me, farm girl?"

My stomach flutters. I swallow. "No. Where I was going with that before you distracted me with talk of babies was... Have you seen the movie?"

He nods. "When I was a kid."

"Well, obviously, she started falling for him while she was still his captive."

"Right."

"But it wasn't until he let her go and she was

able to come back to him that... she was really able to *choose* him. If he'd never let her go, how would we have ever really known it was her choice? Maybe she was just making the best of a bad situation."

He cracks a smile. "That's funny."

"What?"

"We watched that movie very differently. Even as a kid, I was like, 'What's this asshole doing sending the girl he loves out into a snowy forest at night to help her dad all by herself?' He's a prince, for god's sake. Keep her there and send someone to bring her bumbling father back to her. Or, hell, go with her and bring him back yourself. It's no reason to let her go."

I laugh. "Oh my god. Of course, you didn't think Beast was kidnappy *enough*."

He grins. "He wasn't. Fuck that guy. I'm not an 'if you love something, let it go' kind of person. I'm more, 'if you love something, why the fuck would you let it go? Hold on tighter so it doesn't go anywhere.'"

I shouldn't be so delighted, but I shake my head, finding myself reluctantly charmed. "You're crazy."

"Maybe," he says, but he's obviously sharing in my amusement.

I shake my head. "I must say, as your current captive, this isn't very encouraging."

"Might as well give up," he agrees.

I tilt my head to look back at him. "Are you really going to let me leave tomorrow?"

He brushes my hair back from my face, then runs his knuckles along my jawline. "You won't be going far."

"Will you miss having me in your bed?"

"Every night." He kisses the corner of my

mouth. "I'll be sad." He kisses a little lower. "Lonely." Another kiss, this time on my lips. "I'll reach out for you in the dead of night, and you won't be there. Heartbreaking shit."

My fool heart drops even though I know he's deliberately tugging on the strings. "Don't say that."

He smirks faintly, tracing the curve of my lips with his fingertip. "You don't wanna break my heart?"

"No," I murmur, but it feels like a shameful admission. Like I shouldn't care, I just… do.

He's quiet for a moment, then in a more sober tone, he says, "You're allowed to like me, you know?"

I don't think I am, but I don't say that.

I don't say anything else.

I'm already pulled so close I'm nearly facing him, so I turn in his arms the rest of the way and drape an arm over his shoulder.

He closes the distance between us. My heart skitters, but I know I invited it this time. His lips find mine in the dark and my eyes drift closed as a swarm of butterflies burst free in my stomach.

It's so easy to get swept up in his kisses. I wrap my thigh around his hip as he rolls on top of me. Since we just fucked, there's no urgency to do it again. We're just lazily kissing and touching. I slide my hand around his side and grab his back, keeping his body close to mine.

I very much enjoy the feel of his body beneath my hands. He has a very nice body, so I'm sure I'm not the first girl who has.

The thought of other girls touching him leaves an unpleasant feeling in my gut, but I try to push it away. He tangles his fingers in my hair and angles my face, dominating my mouth, leaving me breathless.

He breaks away to come up for air, but he keeps my head cradled in his hand.

I lick my lips and look down.

He pulls me in, resting his forehead against mine.

"You're a very good kisser," I tell him.

"I know. I've had a lot of practice."

I roll my eyes and try to push him away, but he just laughs.

"I'm kidding."

"No, you're not."

He smirks, yanking me closer since I tried to push him away. "You're the only girl I want to kiss now, so you don't have to sound so salty about it."

He's arrogant and far too audacious, but I settle in and enjoy this last cuddle, anyway.

It is our last night together, after all.

I know I'll still see him, I'm even sure he'll still have sex with me, but it won't be like this.

All weekend, he's had unlimited access to me.

Tomorrow, we'll go back to him only seeing me when he can arrange it—and I'm learning all his tricks, so I like to think I'll be able to do a better job of avoiding him when I don't want to see him.

I wonder how he'll cope with that.

I know Silvan is accustomed to always getting his way, so if I had to put money on it, I'd say not well.

CHAPTER 32
SOPHIE

SILVAN MAKES THE MOST OF HIS LAST DAY WITH ME AT his place.

We skip breakfast downstairs in favor of breakfast in bed again.

We binge Disney movies so he can further critique Beast's moves and find out what *Frozen* is.

Since he knows this is probably his last day before I make an emergency appointment with my OB-GYN to get some birth control in my body, he does his very best to impregnate me.

He's crazy.

It's not news, I just feel the need to remind myself every now and then since being with him is so strangely nice and comfortable sometimes, I let myself forget.

We shower together and get dressed for dinner with his parents. After we eat, he says Hugh will come pick us up so he can take me home. I mostly believe him, but I'm still cautious when we head downstairs and I know I'll have to see his father.

I half-expect dinner tonight to be veal with a side of veal and veal for dessert just to spite me, but since Silvan's mom's eyes were opened to the cruelty of the meat, I don't think she'll want veal on any future menus.

I don't know how well she'd hold up if her husband exerted any pressure, but I don't know if he will, either. Their relationship is still a bit of an enigma to me.

There's no veal tonight, but there is salmon. I don't eat that either.

I hope his dad doesn't call me out on it. Fortunately, he gets a call he has to step out of the room to take just after the main course is brought out.

Silvan and his mom are both watching him leave the room frowning with confusion. I take advantage of his absence to grab my plate and make quick work of unloading my salmon onto Silvan's.

"You don't like salmon, either?"

"We're going to have to watch *The Little Mermaid* so I can introduce you to my cute little fish friends."

He smirks, shaking his head. "Do you want another salad?"

"No, I want to pretend I cleared my plate and only eat the vegetables so your dad leaves me alone."

"That's odd," Melanie says, her gaze drifting to Silvan. "Your father never takes calls at dinnertime. I hope everything's all right."

"I'm sure it's fine." To me, he says, "You're going to have to give me a list of all the foods you don't like so I can keep them off the menu when I'm feeding you."

"Can't you just make nice, simple chicken? What's wrong with chicken?"

Silvan smirks about my plebeian tastebuds but before he has to answer, his father comes back into the room and takes his seat across from me.

"Is everything all right?" Melanie asks, placing her hand on his arm.

He glances over at her and smiles faintly. "Yes, sweetheart. Everything's fine." He leans over to give her a kiss, then grabs his silverware and cuts into his salmon.

His word is her gospel, apparently, so Melanie's worry eases, and she goes back to enjoying her meal.

We don't have coffee tonight, but we do have water goblets and a pitcher of water kept on the table for refills. When Melanie notices her husband's has emptied, she puts down her fork and stands to grab the pitcher and refill his glass.

It reminds me to check on Silvan's. I'm horrified a moment after I've had the impulse, but I can't shake the sense that I need to earn brownie points with Silvan's dad, either, so when Melanie puts the pitcher down, I grab it so I can refill Silvan's cup.

The action certainly grabs his father's attention. I feel his gaze on me, but I don't look back at him as I put the pitcher down and take my seat.

"You seem to be a fast-learner," he remarks. His gaze drops to my plate and his eyebrows rise. "You also seem to be quite hungry tonight."

I lick my lips, unsure what to say.

Good thing I didn't lie because his gaze drifts to Silvan's plate next and he smirks when he sees he has two pieces of salmon.

"Don't have the heart to eat a dead fish, either?" he asks with mocking solemnity.

I tip my chin up and grab my fork and knife so I can cut into the tender glazed carrot. "I don't enjoy the texture of salmon."

I don't enjoy *him*, either. I'm glad I only have

one more course to get through before I hopefully never have to see him again.

When the last plate is cleared, it feels like the end of my stay. I tell Silvan I'm going to run upstairs to grab my things, and he says he'll let Hugh know I'm ready for a ride home.

"Why don't you stay for a bit longer?" Richard suggests, but it's not really a suggestion.

Silvan frowns at the command and his gaze flickers to me.

"I should really be going," I say a touch awkwardly.

"You'll stay for a drink first," he says, and that's the end of the debate.

I was nervous about Silvan possibly dragging his feet about me leaving, but I wasn't prepared for his father to do it.

Silvan nods toward the stairs. "Go up and get your things. You can meet us in Dad's study. One drink, then she really has to go home."

It makes me even more uneasy that Silvan is suddenly pushing me out the door. I know it's not because he *wants* me to go. I think it's because his father doesn't, and for Silvan to be uneasy about it makes me think I'm right to be as well.

A memory of the call at dinner resurfaces.

I don't know what to make of any of it because I don't *know* these people. Silvan won't even give me the bare minimum of details about them.

I need to Google them when I get home.

Although, I suppose if they are into shady dealings and none of them are in jail, Google probably won't know about it.

I go upstairs alone, my heart beating a little too hard.

I think about sneaking out.

On one hand, it feels silly to have stayed the

whole weekend just to sneak out and beg someone for a ride home moments before they're sending a car to pick me up.

On the other, Silvan's dad scares me, and Silvan has been evasive enough about him to make me think the fear isn't entirely irrational.

There's also the scope of Silvan's entitlements. He's not just spoiled in the sense that if he wants something, he thinks he can buy it. He also thinks it's perfectly acceptable to kidnap a reluctant girl he wants to date and threaten maiming and murder to any man she likes who isn't him. He does things like what he did the other night at my professor's house. He was completely comfortable breaking and entering, like it was no big deal at all.

I may not have met many, but I can't imagine that being the norm for elitist rich boys.

There are certain aspects to Silvan's behaviors that are… well, very casually criminal. If he was raised in a family where criminal activity was normalized, that might explain it.

That's too much to think about.

It's scary enough that someone with his financial resources has zeroed in on me, but if he has resources like those behind him, too…

My god.

Nope, not going to think about it.

Nope, nope, nope.

I'm just imagining things, that's all.

I'm sure casual felonies and armored cars are perfectly normal among the elite.

So, so normal. Definitely not criminal and scary at all.

I still feel sick when I head back downstairs.

Since I snuck around Silvan's house checking the place out the night of his party, I know the way to the study, but I pause outside of it, considering sneaking out once more.

My instincts are telling me to sneak out. I have a love-hate relationship with them, but maybe I should listen this time.

Once more, I ignore my screaming instincts and step inside the room.

It's not because I'm sure my instincts are wrong, but because even if they're right, I believe Silvan will protect me.

It's an impressive study, intimate in size but with high walls and a spiral staircase up to the second level which is only there so you can access the tops of the bookshelves. He has so many books. Since we just watched the movie today, it feels a little reminiscent of the one in *Beauty and the Beast*, but without so much natural lighting. It's a warmly decorated dark room. Maybe more befitting a vampire version of *Beauty and the Beast*.

Maybe they're vampires.

The silly thought makes me smile, but it's not the first time Silvan's made me think of them. Back when I was convinced he was creeping in my bedroom while I slept, I was like, *Get it together, Sophie. He's not a lovesick Edward Cullen; he's a pushy asshole who forced himself on you.*

At least I'm smiling when Silvan's father looks at me.

"Happy to get away?"

"No, I was just thinking about *Twilight*."

He frowns. "What?"

Silvan chokes. "It's a movie, Dad. Or a book. Both. It's nothing, she was joking."

"Vampires are always rich because they've been around for so long," I inform him. "I mean, if they haven't managed to acquire wealth over the course of several lifetimes..."

"We're not vampires," Silvan assures me.

I obviously don't believe in vampires, but I narrow my eyes at him, anyway. "That's just what a vampire would say."

He smirks and grabs my waist, pulling me against him. "You're crazy."

My lips form a pout. "And now I kinda want to watch *Twilight*."

Putting a hand on my hip and guiding me toward a red leather chair, he says, "Later. Right now, let's get this drink and get you out of here."

"Melanie, fetch Sophie a drink."

As I take my seat, my gaze flickers to Silvan's mom on her way over to the alcohol cart.

Something about him specifying the drink she's getting is for me—*paired with my existing paranoia about him*—doesn't sit right with me. "Actually, I'm not thirsty. I'll hang out while you guys drink, though."

"You sure?" his dad asks, watching me. "I've got the good stuff."

I shake my head. "Thank you, anyway."

His mom comes back with two glasses and gives one to her husband and one to Silvan, then she sits down on her husband's lap as if without thought.

He keeps his gaze trained on me as he settles his wife on his lap. I lick my lips, wishing I had that drink, but also glad I turned it down. I think Silvan's mom is super sweet and unlikely to poison me, but I also think if her not-at-all sweet husband told her to do something, she'd do it with no questions asked.

Seeming to understand I was afraid of being drugged, Silvan takes a single sip of his drink, then passes it to me.

"Thank you," I murmur, taking a greedy sip.

The breath is sucked from my lungs as I swallow. It burns like hell all the way down my throat.

I don't know what it is, but damn, it is strong.

Maybe they didn't have to drug me. One glass of this and I'll be on my ass.

I hand the glass back to Silvan.

I need to keep a clear head.

"How was your weekend?" Richard asks me.

It feels like a trick, so I keep my answer concise. "Good."

"Did my son kidnap you?"

My heart stops. He asks it so casually, and I don't know what to say. I'm the one who originally said he did…

I don't know what answer he's expecting, so I hedge my bets. "Kind of…"

"It's a yes or no question, Sophie."

My heart skitters and my palms start to sweat. I don't know if he wants me to lie or tell the truth. "Well, yes. Yes, he did."

"How?"

I glance over at Silvan, unsure how much I should share.

Silvan's frowning, but he nods and I take it to mean I can tell him.

"He…"

I stop, though, because I don't *want* to.

I'm afraid of getting him in trouble. What parent would be fine with his son breaking into a professor's house and doing all the stuff Silvan did to me?

Then again, what parent co-hosts a kidnapping for their son?

I don't understand this family at all.

"He used some stuff to blackmail me," I answer vaguely.

"And that was enough to keep you?"

"He locked me in the escape room that first night, but yeah. I didn't choose to come here, but I wasn't really trying to leave."

"Why not?"

"I... I don't know. It was only for the weekend."

Richard nods, taking a sip of his drink. "What else did he do to you?"

My stomach twists and my hands clench. His question makes my skin crawl more than any of the stuff Silvan actually did to me.

When I don't answer, his voice turns harder, and he cuts to the chase. "Did he rape you?"

Silvan's used that word before and it didn't trigger me, but hearing his father say it does. It feels much more like an interrogation and reminds me of last year with Dylan.

A moment ago, I cared about things like making some kind of impression on his father, but right now, all I care about is getting out of here.

I squeeze my eyes shut and try to breathe. My fists are clenched so painfully tight, my knuckles hurt.

Silvan grabs my shoulder. I shrug it off before I can think about it.

"Sophie?"

"I want to leave."

"All right." He puts his glass down on the table. "This is done," he tells his father.

"Not yet," his father says, his tone hard. "I'd like a moment alone with Sophie."

My eyes pop open and widen. "What?" I look up at Silvan, horrified to find him thinking about it. I launch up and grab his shirt. "No. Silvan, don't leave me here with him."

Silvan grabs my shoulders to steady me. I can see he's conflicted, but I don't understand why.

Melanie stands, but she looks conflicted, too. That worries me even more. She leans down to whisper something in her husband's ear, then she kisses the corner of his mouth the way Silvan kisses mine and comes over to get her son.

"Come on, honey. Just give them a moment. She'll be fine."

"Don't leave me here," I beg, clinging to Silvan's shirt. "Please. I want to go home."

Silvan looks distraught, but he pulls me in for a tight hug. He kisses the side of my head, then says softly, "I have to let him talk to you or I'm afraid he won't let you leave at all. You'll be fine, all right? Just let him know we're good, and you'll be fine."

Are you serious?

I don't say the words, but he can see the betrayal written all over my face.

He grabs my face and pulls me in for a fierce kiss. "I would never let anything happen to you, Sophie."

I want to believe that, but I do *not* want to be in a room alone with his father.

My wants don't matter right now, apparently, because Silvan's mom grabs his wrist to lead him out of the room.

And he lets her.

CHAPTER 33
SOPHIE

THE STUDY DOOR CLOSES, THE METALLIC CLICK OF THE door's latch feeling like a lock sealing my fate.

We're alone together, and that is intensely more awkward after trying so hard not to be.

I glance in Richard's direction, but he doesn't appear to be offended by my desperation not to be alone with him. It's as if he gets that reaction all the time.

I don't sit back down on the chair. I don't know if I have more of an advantage standing, but I feel like it'd be easier to run screaming for help without losing the fraction of a second it would take me to stand.

His tone sadistically amused, Richard says, "You can come closer."

"No, thank you."

He shrugs as if it doesn't matter to him one way or the other, then he takes a slow sip of his drink. "Do you have a family, Sophie? People you love?"

I feel like he already knows, but I answer him anyway. "Sure. I have a mom."

"That's it?"

I shrug uneasily.

"Well, for someone who seems to care quite

easily, I might expect the list of people you love to be a bit longer. Perhaps I should ask this about animals instead," he says dryly.

"Animals tend to be more loyal than people," I mutter. "I don't love a lot of people, I guess, but I... care about people."

"Do you care about Silvan?"

"Yes."

At least I don't have to negotiate that answer. The truth will do just fine.

He nods slowly, watching me. "So do I. The list of people I care about is quite small as well, but the people who make that list fall under my protection. There is *nothing* I would not do to protect them."

"I understand."

"Do you?"

I nod. "If that's what you're worried about, I'm not going to say anything about... any of this."

"That's good. I value discretion. Would you like compensation for your silence?"

"No." I swallow. "Is that all? Can I go now?"

He smiles faintly, but doesn't bother to answer. "Did Silvan tell you anything about me?"

"No. Not really."

"No? Well," he sets his drink down, "what he should have told you is that I am *fiercely* protective of my family. A long time ago, someone very foolish did something to harm my family. The goal was to harm me, but they used my family to do it. They had tried to shake me down, and it didn't work. That made them angry. They knew the family I came from and assumed I was some soft-bellied fuck who'd inherited my part of the family fortune and couldn't defend myself. Must not have considered that I don't spring from the main tree. I hail from the bastard branch, and my father was certainly a man capable of violence."

I swallow again but don't say anything.

"That man landed a solid hit. I'm not invincible, after all. It was a sucker punch, and I didn't see it coming. But I felt it once it had happened. The pain radiated. He hurt the only thing I'd ever truly loved just to get at me, and that... that was a mistake. He succeeded in punishing me if that's what he wanted." He slides his hand across the smooth mahogany of his desk, then raises his gaze back to mine. "But once I recovered from that sucker punch, I killed him with my bare hands and took over his operation."

I feel myself lose a shade of color, but having someone I'm in a room alone with casually confess to murder is... a lot.

"I gave his wife to my men—*they were my men, then*—and dragged his corpse to a chair with a view so he could watch them defile her. So, while he may have landed a hit, it wasn't worth it. In the end, I won. In the end, I will always win."

He pauses for a moment to let that sink in, then he goes on, an edge of malice in his voice.

"That man was a feared criminal, Sophie. You are a college student with too tender a heart to eat baby cows. I promise you, if you cross me, I will fucking obliterate you. I'll convince Silvan it was a nice, clean death, but it won't be. I'll give you to the meanest son of a bitch I know and make him feed you nothing but veal until you kill yourself or die from your injuries. My son may not be your first choice, but you are his, and let's be honest, he's a much better catch than you ever could have landed, anyway."

My skin is as pale as parchment, my eyes as wide as saucers.

"If you play ball, you'll have a nice life. You're not the kind of girl I would have picked out for Silvan, but I don't have a problem with you. I'll accept you if you're what he wants. Who my son loves is of little consequence to me as long as she's not too much of a troublemaker. But you'll have to learn the art of compromising. Maybe Silvan's methods in capturing your attention have been a little unconventional, but his motives are pure. He's utterly infatuated with you. Will it last? I can't say for sure, but I'd put my money on yes. I love my wife more today than I did the day I married her, and I already loved her an awful lot. The men in my family tend to be laser-focused, and while Silvan is a touch more impulsive than the rest of us, he's not fickle. He's also still young. He might grow out of it. If he grows out of *you*, then we'll take good care of you, set you up with your own place, a job you enjoy, and a nice little nest egg. But if he remains determined to keep you, then he will, and if you prove more trouble than you're worth, I will personally see to it that you are jettisoned from all our lives—permanently. Silvan will be crushed, of course, but debutantes prettier and more obedient than you will line up down the street waiting for their turn to make him feel better. I promise you, he will eventually recover."

My jaw is on the floor when his steely gaze meets mine.

"Consider your choices, Sophie. You could do much worse than someone who's willing to do absolutely anything to keep you. Most of the people you'll call friends in your lifetime won't care about you at all. When you find the ones that truly do, hold on to them, even if they aren't perfect."

I don't speak. I don't think I can. In the last few minutes, this man has just admitted to murder and other atrocities, threatened *me* with murder and those other atrocities, and essentially demanded that I accept his son—or else.

I can scarcely *breathe*.

"So, will you play ball, Sophie?"

I nod my head.

Is there any other answer?

He smiles. "Good." He stands, pushing back his chair and moving around the desk.

On instinct, I back away from him.

His smile transforms into a smirk that reminds me a bit of Silvan, but a much, much meaner Silvan. "You don't have to be afraid of me, Sophie. As long as you make my son happy, you're part of my family. I won't hurt you unless you give me a reason to. Your destiny is really in your own hands." He meets my gaze. "Everybody serves a master whether they realize it or not. At least you know who yours is."

I gasp softly when he drapes an arm around my shoulders. My leg muscles feel wobbly when he leads me toward the door.

It's like I'm not in control of my own body. Someone else is walking. I can't even feel the weight of his arm around me, but I can see it as if I'm floating outside myself.

I think maybe I'm in shock.

This is reminiscent of how I felt the night I left Dylan.

This assault was a lot different than that one.

Richard opens the door and Silvan is waiting anxiously outside. His gaze darts to his father's arm around my shoulder and confusion flickers across his face. Richard releases me and heads back to his wife's side, sliding an arm around her waist.

Silvan grabs my face and searches it. "Are you all right? You look pale."

I nod, but I still can't speak.

"She's fine," Richard says, his tone even like nothing is amiss.

I want to rally and pretend the same thing, I just can't. I've reached capacity for what I can endure tonight, and I just want to climb into bed and sleep it off.

"Sophie's part of the family now," he says easily. "As long as she's with you, anyway. Had to give her a formal welcome."

Silvan slides his father a look to let him know he's displeased as he curls an arm protectively around me. "Come on, let's get out of here."

I'm more than happy to leave.

Richard and Melanie follow us out. The sight of Hugh standing outside the limo pierces the fog and relief slips in through the pinprick hole.

A noise from somewhere off to our left destroys it. Especially when I look and it's not an animal or my imagination. Two hulking, shady-looking men stand in the shadows.

I grab Silvan's arm and his gaze snaps in that direction to see what's startled me.

His hand finds the small of my back and he pushes me toward the car. "It's all right," he murmurs lowly. "They work for my dad."

That doesn't feel like an "it's all right" to me, but he said the same thing about his friend the other night. I don't think Silvan's "it's all right," means "those men aren't dangerous." Just, "those dangerous men are under our control, so you don't have to be afraid unless I want you to be."

What have I gotten myself into?

I guess I didn't really get myself into it.

All I did was go to a stupid party.

I knew going to parties was a shitty idea.

I'm never going to a party again.

I get into the car where at least I feel safe. Silvan

joins me and wraps an arm around me, pulling me into his arms. As soon as the door is shut, he asks, "Are you okay?"

"Yeah."

"What did he say to you?"

"That he's a murderer. Some other stuff, but… that part stuck."

"Jesus. Well, I didn't want to share anything I shouldn't, but if he told you himself, I guess it's okay. I'm sure this goes without saying, but…"

"I won't say anything. I'm not trying to get your murdery dad after me."

His lips curve up faintly and he brushes my hair back. "Good. I also don't want my murdery father after you. No way that ends well."

Tell me about it.

His threats echo in my memory. He doesn't even know me, and somehow, he zeroed in on my biggest fears to tailor threats around them.

Silvan is observant, too.

Like father, like son, I guess.

Silvan asks if I want to go to my dorm or my mom's house. I don't feel like there's a right answer.

I don't want to have to talk to my mom right now, but I want to be alone most of all and while there's a chance she could be out or I can slip by her with an excuse about homework or being tired, I share a bedroom with three other girls. There is no shot in hell I'll be alone in my dorm.

He takes me to my mom's house. My car isn't there, so he tells me he'll send Hugh to pick me up for school in the morning. I don't want him to come inside because I'm not ready to introduce him to my mom, but he insists on walking me to the door.

We stop under the porch light. He pulls me in

for another hug, and when we part a bit, he still cradles my head in his hand and looks down at me.

"I'm sorry my dad traumatized you."

I shrug. "I'll get over it."

He shakes his head and caresses my face with his thumb. "I hated the way you looked at me back there. I wasn't handing you over to fend for yourself. I hope you know that. I just know our life will be a lot easier with his approval, and he needed to see for himself that you'll…"

"Cover your ass?"

He nods. "Yeah."

"And what if I wouldn't?"

"Well, then I wouldn't have left you with him."

Those men outside resurface in my mind. The call at dinner. The threats he made.

Would he have handed me off to them right there?

My chest starts to feel tight as my imagination travels further down that road. I picture myself ripped from Silvan's arms, ripped from life as I know it in a much scarier way than when Silvan was the one stealing me.

Maybe he's a lunatic, but it sure could be worse.

I hug him again. He's surprised I'm the one initiating, but he must know I need it because he hugs me tight. "I'm safe with you, right?" I murmur against his chest.

His grip on me tightens protectively. "Always," he rumbles. "As long as you're mine, no one else will ever hurt you."

There it is.

An echo of what his father said.

I'm safe, as long as I'm his.

As long as I cooperate.

I swallow, pushing the thoughts away.

I don't want to think about it anymore tonight. I'm too numb to know how I feel, anyway.

When I lean back, Silvan tucks a lock of hair behind my ear and leans close so I can feel his breath on my lips. "I'll see you tomorrow?"

I guess so.

There's an "or else" that hangs over my head making me wonder if I'll ever feel free again.

If I'll ever *be* free again.

I guess the only way out of this that doesn't go badly for me is if *Silvan* changes his mind and lets me go. His father already said that would be okay.

He gives me a goodnight kiss, then takes a step back.

He stays on the porch until I'm safely inside the house with the door locked.

I watch out the window as he walks back to the limo.

Seeing those two guys at his dad's house has made me paranoid, so I watch for another minute or so after the limo pulls away to make sure no other cars pull up.

I guess they don't have a reason to.

I agreed to "play ball," whatever that means.

When I'm satisfied that no scary goons are coming to kidnap me, I finally leave the entryway. The house is dark, so Mom must be out.

I'm relieved.

I go to my bedroom and drop my bags, then I strip off my nice clothes and the new bra Silvan bought me and pull on a comfy sleep shirt.

Despite the overall numbness, I do feel a little lonely when I slip between my cool sheets and settle my blankets around me and I don't feel Silvan's lush fur beneath my fingers or his strong arms wrapped around my waist.

I miss his heat.

Maybe I just miss him.

Clearly, my brain is too broken for proper thinking tonight, so I close my eyes, forcing all the unpleasant thoughts away and tell myself to just go to sleep.

Tomorrow is a new day. A calmer day.

Tomorrow, I get to go back to some semblance of my real life.

CHAPTER 34
SOPHIE

I SLEEP IN A LITTLE SINCE I KNOW SILVAN IS SENDING a car to pick me up.

My whole vibe this morning is very low-effort. I shower and blow out my hair, but only because it's cold outside. I tie my hair in lazy low pigtail buns and brush on a little lip gloss and mascara. I wear comfy jeans and a shirt baggy enough that I can get away with not wearing a bra, then I grab my bag and head out to the limo.

Breakfast waits for me on a tray in the car. I sigh happily as I grab the cold bottle of water and stuff it in my bag, then have a sweet sip of my spiced latte.

Heaven.

And it only comes with every string imaginable.

What a bargain.

I smile faintly, grabbing my warm breakfast sandwich and devouring it. Silvan must know I've been picked up because he shoots off a text that reads, "How is my pretty girl this morning?"

"Not so pretty," I shoot back. "I'm being lazy this morning."

"Lies. You're always beautiful."

"Thank you for sending the car. I did not have the zeal to make myself food this morning."

"Are you feeling all right?"

"Yeah. Just a little tired."

That reminds me, I need to call my doctor. I swipe away from his texts and search up the number for my OB-GYN's office. Unfortunately, she's booked solid and can't get me in for a couple of weeks.

That won't do at all.

Plan B. I look up student health services and give them a call to see if they can get me in today.

Once I have all that handled, I do a little studying before I get to campus. I gave myself a little extra time since I have to hustle to get a new class schedule so I know where my new class is, but when Hugh opens the door and lets me out, he holds out a crisp white sheet of paper.

"Your schedule."

I blink, then take it. "Oh. Thank you."

"Master Silvan printed one off for you this morning. He wasn't sure you'd have time before class."

I crack a smile. "Is that his way of saying I'm always on the verge of being late?"

"I believe in Master Silvan's opinion, anytime you appear to be late, it's the other party's fault for not waiting for you."

I thank him again, hoist my bag on my shoulder, and make my way toward my first class of the day.

I'm on my way out of the student health center when I see Silvan standing at the information desk, talking to the nurse.

My heart skips a beat and my steps slow. "Silvan?"

He turns toward me, an easy smile on his handsome face. "Hey."

My gaze drifts to the nurse behind the desk. She avoids my gaze and looks a little flustered, shuffling papers around the desk to look busy.

My eyes narrow with suspicion but before I can watch to see what she does next, Silvan is in front of me, grabbing my wrist with one hand, my chin with the other. His touch is gentle enough, but he forces me to meet his gaze.

"What are you doing here?" I ask.

"Thought I'd see if you wanted to grab a bite to eat now that you're done."

"I didn't tell you I was coming here today. How did you know I'd be—?" I stop myself with a sigh. "Goddammit, Hugh. There's no privacy with that man around."

Silvan smirks, leaning in to kiss me. "There's no privacy anywhere." Taking my hand, he hauls me toward the door. "Come on."

I sigh heavily. "I'm not hungry. And I need to go to a pharmacy so I can fill this prescription."

"I'll take care of it for you. We've got an appointment in a few minutes, that'll eat up some time. We'll grab some dinner after. Maybe you'll be hungry by then."

I frown, following him out the door. "What kind of appointment?"

He looks back and shoots me an enigmatic smile. "You'll see."

Hugh is waiting for us by the limo. I shoot him

a dirty look as I climb into the car. "We need to talk about you being a major narc."

His mustache twitches. "I'm sure I don't know what you mean, Miss Bradwell."

"Mm-hmm," I murmur, making it clear I don't believe him.

Silvan settles in and smirks. "Thanks, Hugh."

About 15 minutes later, we drive past Boston Commons and pull up outside of a beautiful white brick building. The bottom floor houses an upscale Italian restaurant and there are five stories above it.

I assume we're here to eat, but he said we had an appointment somewhere first.

Rather than explain himself, he hands off my birth control prescription to Hugh. "Get this taken care of while we're here, will you."

"Of course," he says dutifully as I step out onto the sidewalk.

I look ahead at the man and woman walking out of the restaurant. She's wearing heels and a tight green dress. He's wearing a suit and shiny loafers.

I look down at my comfy outfit. "Um, I don't think I'm dressed for this place."

He takes my hand, leading me past the restaurant and down the small side street the side of the building faces. We stop about halfway down at a pair of double doors beneath an overhang.

He scans a card to gain access to the building, then pulls the door open and gestures for me to walk inside.

The place is very white and for a horrifying moment, I wonder if he's brought me to a wedding dress shop. There's a lot of empty space and gleaming floors. Light blue couches are set up in a few spots, well spaces out to give anyone sitting in them privacy.

No dresses that I can see.

There's a woman behind a marble counter with straight brown hair in a navy blue skirt suit. Silvan takes my hand and hauls me over to her.

"We're seeing unit 1209."

She smiles brightly. "Of course. Your father said you'd be here." She grabs a white envelope off the desk, slides a stapled packet of papers inside, then closes it and slides it across the smooth surface.

Silvan takes it. "Thank you."

"You'll want to take the elevator up to the top floor. Let me know if you have any questions."

I do.

I wait until we're past the receptionist on our way to the elevator before I ask any. "Your *father* is sending us somewhere? Should I brace myself?"

"No, it's a nice thing," he assures me.

I eye him as suspiciously as Hugh. "Your father isn't nice."

"To his family, he is. Sometimes," he adds.

We take the elevator up to the top floor and exit into a hallway with a door on the left side and a door on the right side. The one on the right says 1209 in gleaming gold above the door.

"Here we are."

Silvan takes a key out of the folder and uses it to open the door.

"Where is here, exactly?" I murmur as he steps inside, and I follow.

My eyes widen as I step into a beautifully decorated apartment. It's massive with light-colored hardwood floors, marble accents, and gleaming white surfaces everywhere I look.

Off to the right is a dining area and a huge kitchen with white marble countertops and a marble island to match. There's a wine cooler behind the table and a second sink and counter area for making drinks.

Across the open floorplan room on our right is a seating area, white leather couches with a gray fur blanket thrown over the back. A white marble table sits between the couches with an ottoman in front and a big screen TV on the wall it's facing.

Beyond that seating area, I see a second living area with plush gray couches set up in front of a white marble fireplace, but what steals my attention is the wall of windows to my right. There are no window treatments so you can see out to the view of Boston Commons and the city skyline.

I stop in front of the window to look out at downtown, my jaw open.

Silvan comes up behind me and locks his arms around my waist. "Nice view, huh?"

"I'll say."

"Come on." He takes my hand and pulls me through the living area with the gray couches toward the hallway.

There are four bedrooms, three and a half bathrooms, and a study. One of the bedrooms has a couple of built-in shelves, though, and he says we could make that one my study if I wanted to.

My study?

I'm hesitant as he leads me back down the hall toward the main area.

"So, do you like it?"

"Of course I like it." I'd have to be crazy not to like it. "It's beautiful."

"It's ours if we want it."

I tear my gaze away from the view out the window to look back at him. "What?"

His lips tug up. "Turns out, the idea of even one night without you in my bed… I'm not into it. My dad thought we might like to have our own place a little closer to school. He owns this building, and this unit happened to be available, so…"

"You want to move in together?" I demand, somehow shocked despite my more logical side telling me every single thing I know about him should have led me to frankly *expect* this lunacy.

I can't move in with him. I've barely swallowed agreeing to date *him.*

But do I really have a choice?

His dad is giving us his stamp of approval letting us live here, and yeah, it's a gorgeous apartment, more than I ever dreamed of, but…

"Silvan, do you really think we're ready to move in together?"

"I know it's fast, but I like having you in my bed every night. And your living situation is far from ideal." He comes up behind me, wrapping his arms around my waist and pulling me back against him. "Can you really tell me you'd rather live in a shared bedroom with three roommates than here with me?"

No.

Not without lying my ass off, anyway.

"You liked spending the weekend with me, didn't you?"

"Yes," I murmur. "But don't you think…"

He gives me a minute, and when I don't finish the thought, he prods me. "Don't I think…?"

I lick my lips, my skin a bit warm. "Don't you think you might get sick of me? I mean, living together is a huge step from dating and we were barely doing that."

His lips find the curve of my neck. "Sophie, that is the most absurd fucking thing you have ever said."

"It isn't."

"It is. Keep saying shit like that, and I'm going

to drag you on a private plane to Vegas and marry your little ass to show you how serious I am."

"You are not."

"Mm-hmm. Watch me," he murmurs, nipping lightly at my neck and sending shivers down my spine. "I *want* to live with you. I want to go to sleep with you every night and wake up with you every morning. I want to know what you're doing every moment of every day in-between. Haven't you figured it out by now? I'm fucking obsessed with you."

I sigh with pleasure, tilting my neck to give him more access.

"I want us to be a team," he murmurs against my skin. "I want us to be a family. I'm not testing the waters with you, Sophie. I'm all in."

His lips feel so good on the sensitive skin of my neck, it's hard to think clearly. He takes advantage of the mental fog to spin me around and push me down onto the soft gray couch.

There's a devious tilt to his lips and a matching glint of mischief in his pretty green eyes as he sinks to his knees.

"What are you doing?" I ask, but I already know.

My heart jumps when he reaches for the button of my jeans.

"Silvan, we can't. This isn't our apartment."

"It will be."

"I haven't said yes."

"You haven't said no, either," he points out.

I cut him a dry look. "What's the point? You don't seem to be familiar with that word."

He smirks, utterly shameless, and yanks down my jeans.

"Oh, my god," I say covering my face with my hands.

"Let's try it out," he says as he hooks his fingers into the waistband of my panties and drags those down, too. "See if this place feels like home."

Before I can utter another objection, he parts my thighs and gazes at my pussy like a hungry lion anticipating a nice, juicy meal.

"Hello, beautiful," he says, making me nearly die before he drops his head between my thighs and latches on.

My back arches off the couch and he takes advantage to slide his hand under my ass, pulling me closer to the edge. Pleasure lances through me as he feasts on my pussy, licking and sucking and drawing sounds out of me no human should make.

I groan when he slides two fingers inside me as he continues to lick and suck on my clit. He pumps them in and out, in and out, and I writhe, unable to keep still.

"Silvan."

His tongue brushes my clit at the same time he jams his fingers in my pussy and I grab the edge of the couch, needing something to hold onto.

It's not what I want, though.

I let go and reach between my legs, sinking my finger into his hair. I tug on it and he growls against my pussy, his fingers biting into my ass. He attacks my pussy with more force and I shudder, my skin so hot, I'm afraid I might explode.

And then I do, pleasure bursting free inside me and sending ripples of ecstasy through my body. Trembling, I try to close my legs around his head as I cry out, but his steely grip on my thighs makes it impossible.

I'm a puddle on the couch in the wake of that orgasm. I couldn't move if the place suddenly caught fire.

Silvan kisses my pussy before pulling back and

closing my legs, then he sits on the couch next to me and pulls me against him.

I'm boneless, but I sink against his strong body and close my eyes.

I lay on him for a few minutes until I regain a sense of strength in my extremities. When I finally look up at him, I find a satisfied grin on his face. "I think this place is going to work out just fine."

CHAPTER 35
SOPHIE

WHEN I GET BACK TO MY DORM, IT'S DARK.

It gets darker earlier these days, though. It's not really that late.

We had dinner at some Italian place—not the one beneath the apartment, but one within walking distance. There's a lot of stuff in walking distance of that apartment.

I don't want to think about the dream apartment, though. I take out my key to unlock the door, but I get a strong whiff of sautéed garlic coming from inside my dorm room, so I know someone is home.

I drop my key back into my purse and open the door.

Instant chaos.

Everyone is home and the place is small—*feels smaller now that I've just been through that massive apartment with Silvan*—so the room feels crowded.

"There she is," Rumi says, glancing over her shoulder as she uses her spatula to move something around in the skillet.

"I guess she isn't ghosting us after all," Sabrina says, cocking an unimpressed eyebrow at me.

"Sorry," I say, shutting the door. "I know I haven't been home all weekend. It's a long story."

"Seems like it, but that's not why we're mad."

"You really went and got a new place without even telling us?" Rumi demands.

"I know having roommates isn't your favorite, but I thought we all got along," Sabrina agrees. "I can't believe you didn't even have the decency to tell us."

My jaw drops open. "What are you talking about?"

Before anyone has a chance to answer me, two huge men come out of the bedroom and down the hall in my direction. My eyes widen as I take in the boxes they're carrying. I step out of the way so as not to get trampled, but I'm completely confused.

"What are they doing?"

Kendra stares at me. "Moving your shit, Sophie. What do you think they're doing?"

My heart sinks. "Already?"

Kendra frowns. "What do you mean, already? Isn't that what you've been doing this weekend?"

"No! I just went through the apartment like an hour ago. I didn't know..."

It won't make any sense if I explain myself, will it?

I'll sound like a liar.

"Your roommates helped us get everything boxed up," the moving guy tells me as he heads for the door. "Might want to take a look around, see if we missed anything."

Sabrina glares at his back but waits until he walks out to mutter, "Like she has anything worth stealing."

"Sabrina," Rumi says.

"What? I'm pissed."

"Look, I get it," I say. "I understand you probably don't believe me, but I had no idea he was moving my stuff out tonight. I had no idea moving was even a thing that was happening until after school today. I wouldn't have left you high and dry like this."

"Who's 'he'?" Rumi asks, her curiosity getting the better of her. "You're not talking about Silvan?"

I nod. "He's moving into this apartment, and he wants me to move in with him."

Sabrina's eyes practically pop out of her skull. "Seriously? You guys have been dating for like five minutes."

A short laugh escapes me. "Yeah, I know."

Sabrina cuts a look at Rumi. "If I text a guy too many times, he ghosts me. Meanwhile she has the richest guy on campus literally falling at her feet after knowing her for like two days."

"Green is not a cute color on you," Kendra informs her, then cuts her gaze back to me, frowning. "You seriously didn't know?"

"I bet his apartment is awesome," Rumi says.

"I'm just really trying to wrap my head around how this man *moved your shit* out of your apartment without your knowledge, let alone your consent," Kendra says, touching her temples. "This does not compute for me."

"It's a long story." Since I'm not going to hang around and tell it, I head down the hall to see what the movers have packed.

Since the dorm is so small and I didn't want to take up more than my fair share of the space, most of my stuff is at my mom's house. I only kept the essentials here.

Looks like they got everything.

Is this the last time I'll be here? All my stuff is out, so I guess so. I got along fine with my roommates, but realistically, I don't see myself going out of my way to see any of them again. It's the kind of thing people say they'll do but never actually do. I tend not to make the promise in the first place.

I take one last look around because, while I have no particular fondness for this place, I know it's the last bit of separation I had between me and Silvan. When I lived here, I could come and go as I pleased, and I don't know what that's going to look like now. Honestly, I can't see him being cool with me not coming home one random day because I decided to go sleep at my mom's.

He'll want to know where I am at all times, like he said today. His wording was more romantic, but the gist was the same.

His words from this past weekend resurface in my mind.

"Am I free now?"

"No. Just moving you to a comfier cage."

I move my arm and pull my cell phone out of the back pocket of my Marc Jacobs bag. There are no new texts from Silvan, but I pull up our chain of messages and type one out to him.

"So… I guess my stuff is all packed and… wherever those men took it."

"Good. Come home."

Home.

I bite down on my bottom lip uncertainly.

"Is Hugh coming back for me?"

"He never left," Silvan answers. "Once you've said goodbye to your old roommates, go downstairs and he'll bring you to me."

"Do I need to do anything here? Talk to the movers?"

"Nope, I've handled everything. All you have to do is get in the car."

I'm relieved I don't have to deal with this move I never asked for, at least. Maybe he picked up my world and moved it, but at least he didn't also leave me with a to-do list.

"Thank you," I type back.

"You're welcome. Now, I miss you. Get your pretty ass downstairs."

I crack a smile and darken the screen, slipping my phone back into my bag and heading back to the kitchen.

Rumi is distributing food to three plates. Since they're about to eat, this is probably a good time to make my exit.

"Well, I'm sorry for the abrupt departure. It's been cool living with you guys this semester, and I hope your next roommate is an awesome fit."

Sabrina must have simmered down—or at least realized she couldn't fish for an invitation if she was still mad at me—because she says, "Well, you better have us over."

"And if Silvan has any similarly hot, rich friends in the market for a live-in girlfriend, hook a girl up."

I crack a smile. "I'll keep you in mind. I've only briefly met one of his friends, and he's definitely taken."

"Are you sure you're not moving too fast?" Kendra asks me. "You haven't even met this man's friends. Girl, what are you doing?"

I offer a little smile and, in an uncharacteristic move, give her a quick hug. "Thanks for looking out for me. I appreciate it, but I'll be okay."

She pulls back and her dark eyes meet mine. "You sure? Hot guys can be crazy, too."

I nod. "Believe me, I know."

"Well, we're just a text away if you need us."

In the car on the way to Silvan's new apartment, I debate texting my mom, but I don't know what to say. I need to let her know my address has changed, but I have no idea how to explain it.

It might be easier than I'm expecting. She has made terrible choices for guys over the years, so maybe moving in with someone after a week and a half won't seem that crazy to her. Or, if it does, at least a relatable kind of crazy and not the sort where she schedules an intervention.

Before I can talk myself into it, we pull up on the side road Hugh didn't pull onto earlier where the front entry doors are.

When Hugh lets me out of the car, he hands me a key card like the one Silvan used to scan in earlier. "This is a very secure building, so you'll need this to get in."

"Thanks, Hugh."

He nods, looking past me. "As I'm sure Master Silvan has already told you, each card is registered to its resident, so there will be a log of when you specifically come and go."

My heart sinks and my gaze darts to him. He's still looking ahead at the door, his posture stiff and proper.

I recognize he probably wasn't supposed to tell me that, so I offer a small smile. "Thanks, Hugh."

My expression is grim as I scan my key card over the reader before opening the door.

I knew this place would come with strings.

I head for the elevators and get out on the top floor.

I go right and try to imagine coming home to this every day.

I feel like I should be here to clean or something, not to live.

I don't have a key, so I almost knock on the door, but I decide to try turning the knob first.

It's open.

I let myself inside and lock it behind me.

Silvan is standing at the counter in the dining area with a bottle of champagne, pouring it into two glasses.

I wonder if he knew I was here because Hugh told him, or because he gets some notification when I scan into the building.

He's only wearing a pair of gray sweats, so his chest is bare. My gaze gets caught on his muscular arms and when he turns, I feel a stray butterfly flutter through my stomach.

"Welcome home," he says, handing me a glass.

It's easy to forget his creepy, controlling tendencies when I'm looking at him.

"Thank you," I say, taking the glass and taking a sip.

He nods toward the white marble table at his right, my left. "I got you a present."

I look over and find a big white box with a gray silk bow on top. "You did?"

"Mm-hmm. A new home requires a new present. Plus, I didn't want you to worry about unpacking tonight. You can do that tomorrow when you get home from school, or I'll have Ilona come over and do it for you if you'd like."

"That's okay, I'd prefer to unpack my own things." I put my champagne flute down on the table and take the lid off the box. Inside, there's a pair of blue pajamas made of the softest silk. I grab them and rub the fabric against my face, it's so nice. "Oh, these are awesome." I shoot him a playful look over my shoulder. "I thought you wanted me to sleep naked."

"I do." He smirks. "Those are for lounging around the apartment *before* bed and in the morning when you wake up. No curtains out here.

Can't have the birds checking out my girl's ass every morning."

I laugh because he's so ridiculous.

I feel him come up behind me and rest my body against his, locking his arms around my waist. "I think you missed something."

I peer into the box and see there was something hidden beneath the pajamas. My brow furrows with good-natured confusion when I see a microwavable packet of extra butter popcorn, then I move it aside and see a cloudy gray background with a brooding vampire and his clumsy beloved.

It's a Blu-ray of *Twilight*.

"You didn't!" I laugh, delighted. I grab the movie case out of the box and hug it, then I look back at him, still grinning. "You messed up, buddy. I'm gonna make you watch it with me now."

He grins, kissing my neck. "What do you think we're doing tonight?" He lets go of me and snatches the popcorn out of the box, then he smacks my ass before heading for the kitchen. "I'll make the popcorn. You go put on your new pajamas."

I can't stop grinning as I take my gifts and head for the hall, but I stop in the kitchen to give him a hug first.

"Thank you," I say seriously. It's a silly gift, but it's also thoughtful and one more example of how he's always listening to everything I say. "I was joking about the movie, but I'm actually really excited to make you watch it."

He smirks. "I can survive a bad movie. I just like making you smile."

My heart tugs. "You do. A lot." I give him one more hug, then I hand him the movie so he can get it set up, and I go to our new bedroom to get changed into something much more comfortable.

CHAPTER 36
SOPHIE

THE BEDROOM IS DARK WHEN I OPEN MY EYES, BUT that doesn't mean anything. Our new bedroom has the same massive windows as the living area, but there are shades in here to block the sun and make the room dark as night.

I can smell bacon cooking down the hall so I know it must be morning.

I'm surprised Silvan cooks since he's had a staff all his life, but it's a pleasant surprise.

I give myself one more minute to lie there with my eyes closed, soaking up the comfort of our massive king bed, then I drag myself out of it and head for the bathroom.

It's a school day and I don't know what our morning routine is going to look like now. I assume since Silvan and I are coming from the same place and going to the same place, we'll probably ride together.

That reminds me, my car is still at the dorm. I'll need to ask him about parking so I can bring it here.

I search the medicine cabinet for my new pack of birth control pills, but I don't see them. I meant to take the first one last night, but I'm not in the habit yet, so I forgot. I'm supposed to take them at the same time every day, so I'd rather take them in the evening when I know I'll be awake. On non-school days, I like to sleep in.

I slip on my pajamas since I need to shower before school, but Silvan is already making breakfast. I don't want it to get cold, so I'll eat with him first.

"Hey, what did you do with the birth control Hugh got for me yesterday?"

I halt at the end of the hall when instead of seeing Silvan at the stove making breakfast, I see him sitting at the island *waiting for* breakfast.

My gaze drifts to Olena at the stove and my lips thin.

I look back at him and cock an eyebrow.

"It's in my school bag. I'll grab it," he says, hopping off the chair.

I follow him, keeping my voice low. "You really brought the maid that wants to bang you?"

He smirks. "Gotta keep you on your toes."

"How dare you."

He laughs and grabs me, pulling me in for a kiss. "I'm just teasing. You know I'm only interested in you."

"Yeah, that's great, but I am not as trusting as your mom."

"No one's as trusting as my mom," he says lightly as he lets me go and reaches into his bag.

"We do not need a maid," I tell him.

"We don't need *a* maid, or we don't need *that* maid?"

"Either. Both. I don't know. I'm perfectly capable of cooking and cleaning. Do you know how to cook?"

"Nope."

"Then I'll show you. It'll be fun."

"I'm fine with that, but I don't see why either of

us should waste our time cleaning. Why don't we have her over a couple of times a week at least to keep the place in order?"

"If we must have someone come once or twice a week, can it at least be the maid who doesn't call you master like she'd rather be working off her debt tied to your bed than cooking us breakfast?"

Silvan smirks. "Sure. If it makes you feel better, I'll tell Ilona to come next time."

"Thank you."

He hands me the birth control, his amused gaze never leaving mine. "You're welcome."

Silvan's classes run later than mine on Tuesday, so Hugh brings me home alone.

As soon as I scan in to enter the building, though, all I can think about is if Silvan is being notified.

He has completely taken over my life and hasn't left even a sliver of it alone. I don't like the idea that I'm unable to come and go without him knowing, so I hatched an idea between classes today.

Rather than go directly upstairs, I hoist my bag on my shoulder and approach the receptionist.

She beams me a big smile. "Hello, Miss Bradwell. Are you enjoying your new apartment?"

"Yes, it's lovely, thank you." I flash her a pleasant smile. "I was hoping you could help me with something, though."

She nods, eager to help. "Of course."

"This morning, Silvan had a maid come over to make us breakfast and clean up the apartment while we were out. Does she have a building key?"

She shakes her head. "No, Mr. Koch called down and requested that I let her in."

I nod. "*Is* there something like a service key card for the doors?"

"Of course. Would you like one?"

"Yes, please."

"Only one, or will there be more staff coming?"

"Just one for now. We are planning to hire a part-time housekeeper, but we won't need that one just yet. Silvan might still ask you to let people in until we've decided on someone, then we'll get her a key of her own."

"Not a problem. Anytime you need to add or remove someone's access to the building, just let me know and we'll get a card made for them."

I grab the card she slides across the counter. "Thank you so much."

I feel a tenuous tie to the freedom I've felt slipping away with this key card in hand, but I'm not sure where to put it where Silvan won't find it. I'd keep it in my purse, but I don't want it to be detected every time my card is scanned when I leave the building. If Silvan has access to the log and he notices that, he'll know I have another card.

I don't know how sophisticated the system is or who monitors it, but since Silvan's dad owns the building, it stands to reason Silvan can see it if he wants to even if he doesn't get notified directly of my comings and goings.

All I know is I don't have to scan anything to open the door leaving the building, but Hugh said there would be a log of my coming *and* goings, so that must mean the card is still detected somehow.

I unload my school bag on the counter and walk around the apartment in search of a hiding space. Since he wants someone to come and clean, it has to be somewhere no one else will stumble across it, either.

There's a box of stuff in the bathroom that I need to unpack from my dorm room. I reach in and pull out a box of pantyliners I use sometimes at the tail end of my period.

He won't look in here.

I don't want it to rattle around if he moves it, so I dig around my boxes until I find the Scotch tape, then I tape the secret key card to the inside of the box.

Perfect.

Maybe I'll never even use it, but I like knowing I have the option.

Silvan still isn't home when I finish unpacking, but he had a white desk built in the room he said we could make my study while I was at school today. The bed is still in here since it was set up to be a bedroom, so I fling my school bag down on it and unpack what I need to get started on my homework.

When I sit down at the desk, I realize I forgot to grab my pen pouch. I would get up and get it, but Silvan already has a little rose gold pen cup on the desk for me and it has all the writing utensils I need.

I grab the yellow highlighter and a pen, but when I grab the pen, I frown, realizing it's one of the black and gray ones I found in my pen pouch last week and thought I must have stolen from somewhere.

I stole it from Silvan?

That doesn't make sense. Silvan and I never even did homework together until this past weekend, and that was after I found the pen. When else would I have had access to one of his pens to steal it?

If I didn't steal the pen, but it's his… he must have put it there.

I don't know when he would have slipped a pen into my pen pouch or—more importantly —*why* he would have slipped a pen into my pouch…

A batshit crazy thought surfaces but it's too crazy.

Isn't it?

I rotate the pen, looking at the clicky part. I set it aside for a second and grab my cell phone, peeling off the bottom of the case so I can see the microphone holes.

I grab the pen and hold it clicky side up beside the bottom of my phone so I can compare them.

They look the same.

There's something that looks like a metal screen inside the clicky hole, and now, try as I might to convince myself I'm imagining things, I can't believe it.

I think it's a microphone.

Is he spying on me?

I feel even crazier thinking this than I felt imagining he might get some kind of "Sophie is leaving!" or "Sophie is home now!" notifications on his phone when he had the champagne ready as soon as I stepped inside the apartment last night, but there are things it would explain.

That conversation I had with Professor De-Marco at the coffee shop. There's no way he should have known what was said that day, but he knew he invited me to office hours or he wouldn't have known to fake that letter from him. He seemed to know what we talked about, too, judging by the things he said when he had me in his bedroom.

What would even make him think I might like Professor DeMarco in the first place? He can't crawl inside my head and literally know what I'm thinking, and I know for a fact I never mentioned my professor to Silvan, let alone indicated any kind of interest in him.

Is it a spy pen?

That's too crazy to consider... isn't it?

Maybe it would be crazy *not* to consider it. This is Silvan we're talking about, after all.

I want to know if he's spying on me, but I don't want to ask. If he knows I'm onto him and I'm right, he'll just find another way. Maybe one I won't figure out.

Besides, I could be wrong.

Maybe my imagination is getting the better of me.

Maybe he doesn't even know when I'm coming or going, and that's just a standard security measure since this is an upscale place and they want to make sure residents aren't getting robbed.

Maybe he only knew about Professor DeMarco inviting me to office hours because...

Actually, no, I can't think of another explanation for that.

On impulse, I put the pen down and grab my phone. I pull up my internet app and search "spy pen" to see if I can find this one.

I can't, but I am startled by how easy it is to buy them. You can get them on Amazon, for Christ's sake.

I should order some kind of spy thing to spy on him and see how he likes it.

I give up looking for the pens and tell myself to stop thinking about this and just get going on my homework. It's not like I'm doing anything he can't know about, anyway, it's just the absolute invasion of my privacy to keep dibs on me so thoroughly. It's not like I've given him a reason to. I'm living here with him in this lovely cage, after all.

This cage where he might keep track of my every single move.

He says he wants a partner, but he watches me like I'm his pet.

And not even a well-behaved pet, but one he expects to fuck everything up. He keeps careful watch so he can step in and prevent any of my possible missteps.

A pet he has no faith in.

Maybe it's not even a spy pen and I'm getting upset over nothing.

But I don't believe that, not really.

I want to *know* if he's listening to me.

I think about saying something in front of the pen that I know will get a reaction out of him if he's listening, but if I just talk into the pen when I'm in the apartment by myself, he'll know I'm suspicious. He can either acknowledge it, too, and switch his spying tactics to using some other household item or pretend he didn't hear anything so I think I'm crazy and it's *not* a spy pen and then I don't suspect it anymore.

No, I need to be more subtle than that. I need to say something I wouldn't want him to hear, but I need to make sure he doesn't realize I'm onto him.

A phone call.

I'll fake a phone call.

From who?

I remember the other night when he woke me up with his hand around my throat and fire in his eyes because I said Dylan's name in my sleep.

A normal guy might never believe I'd have a

romantic fuck to give about Dylan after what he did to me last year, but Silvan knows I'm living with *him* after what *he* has done to me *this* year.

Silvan might be convinced.

It's a mean thing to do, but he's done plenty of mean things.

Besides, I won't let it drag on.

If he comes home pissed and fucks me like he does when I've pissed him off... well, I'll let him do that first, but once he confronts me about Dylan, I'll confront *him* about the spy pens and reassure him that nothing is going on.

I don't want to play games like these. If we're going to be in a relationship, I want to know he trusts me. Maybe we need to talk about it. I guess we haven't really defined our relationship, he just keeps doing insane things like trying to impregnate me, marry me, and move me in with him.

We'll have hot sex and then we'll have the talk and I'll tell him I don't want him spying on me anymore. If he wants to be my boyfriend, then he should act like a boyfriend—*not* a warden.

I pick up the pen and click it, then I start jotting down notes from this page of my textbook.

After a few minutes, when it feels natural, I put the pen down and grab my cell phone.

"Hello?" I pause briefly, then look over my shoulder even though I'm alone since that's what I feel my character would do. "Why are you calling me? I told you Silvan moved me in with him. You can't do that anymore." I pause again, trying to think where to take this since I'm fully winging it. "No, Dylan, I cannot *meet you* tonight. Are you crazy? Look, if you want to talk, you're going to have to text me during school hours. He's a senior and we have different concentrations, so we don't have any of the same classes. You can't text me when I'm at his place, though. It's too risky."

That last line is almost too much, and I don't want to tip my hand, so I decide to end my call with pretend Dylan.

"Look, I have to go. I have homework and he could be home any minute." I pause briefly. "Yeah, I'll talk to you later. Bye."

I tap the screen to end my pretend call, then put the phone down.

My heart is racing a bit now that it's done. There's no taking that back.

I have to know, though. One way or the other.

CHAPTER 37
SOPHIE

WHEN SILVAN GETS HOME, I'M NOT SURE WHAT TO expect.

It's evening, already dark outside.

I feel a little jumpy so I'm up off the couch and heading for the kitchen to greet him like an eager pup when its owner gets home.

My eagerness is less excitement he's here, though, and more anxiety about how he'll respond —*if* he'll respond—to what I did earlier.

I don't know how the whole spy pen, watching my every move thing works. He has school and his own shit to do, so does he spy on me in real time, or is it something he'll review later? He may not have heard the phone call yet.

I search his face for some sign of anger. He isn't looking at me, though, he's busy putting down the stuff he brought home.

He sets a bottle of wine on the counter and starts unpacking a paper bag full of groceries.

"What do we have here?" I ask, eyeing up the fresh pack of cage-free chicken and package of fresh pasta on the counter.

"Groceries. I bought stuff to make dinner."

"Ooh. What are we having?"

"I don't know. You'll have to look at what I bought and see what we can make with it."

I crack a smile. "Hey, I'm sure many delicious dinners were made that way."

"We have the essentials in the cabinets already, anyway. Olena did some shopping for us earlier."

"Well, I've never made this kind of pasta before, so let's see how to prepare it." I pull aside the bag of carrots and the fresh loaf of Italian bread. "We'll definitely use these. I'm thinking maybe pasta primavera. That's a good 'throw it all together' kind of dish."

He slides a container of freshly grated parmesan cheese across the counter.

"Thank you. Did you happen to get peas?"

He grabs a bag of them and slides it to me.

"Nice. You did really good for a spoiled rich boy who's never cooked a day in his life," I tease.

He smirks, abandoning the bag and coming over to wrap his arms around me from behind. "And how was your day?"

My heart skips a beat. Of course he would stand behind me—where I can't see his face—to ask about my day. "Not bad. Yours?"

"It's better now." He kisses my neck. "What do you need me to do for dinner?"

"Um… You can put a pot of water on to cook the pasta. Have you done that before?"

He lets me go and heads to the cupboards, opening a couple before he finds the one with the pots. "Nope."

"Make sure you salt it."

"Salt what?"

I crack a smile. "The water."

He reaches into the upper cabinet for the salt. "Are you enjoying your new psych class?"

I pause since he's now indirectly referencing

the class he made me drop with Professor De-Marco. "Yeah, it seems good so far."

He's salting the pasta water, so his back is still to me.

"Did anything else happen today?" he asks idly.

My stomach rocks. Is this it? *Did* he hear the call and now he's fishing for me to tell him about it?

"Um… I don't think so, not really." I clear my throat and shuffle ingredients around on the counter, then I look over at him again, but he's putting the freaking salt *away* now so I still can't see his face.

When he finally turns, he leans against the counter and crosses his arms. He's watching me, but I can't read his expression. I can't tell if he's shielding something, or there's just nothing to shield. "Nothing else?"

I lick my lips. His words carry the weight of expectation, so I'm braced for him to say something about it.

He watches me, waiting. When I don't say anything, he says, "You didn't get any… strange follow requests?"

What?

Then it hits me.

I was so preoccupied with my thing, I completely forgot his mom followed me on social media today.

Well, that settles it.

He hasn't had a chance to review his tapes or whatever. He doesn't know about the phone call.

I feel strangely relieved. The bulk of the anxiety melts out of me, and I smile, triggering an answering smirk from him.

"Oh, yeah. I completely forgot about that. Your mom and I are social media buddies now. She liked a bunch of my old pictures like a total stalker. Is a follow request from your dad coming next?" I joke.

He shakes his head, pushing off the counter and coming to join me at the island. "As you might expect, he doesn't do social media. I think he has a profile somewhere that his assistant set up for him so she could tag him in certain things, but it has zero posts, and he has never logged into it."

"I can't even imagine your father on social media. I can't even picture him on a computer. Your dad is frozen in the 1920's in my head, reading his physical newspapers and entertaining sketchy people at the family restaurant with his devoted moll by his side."

"Yeah, they're kind of throwbacks."

"Probably why you're so… unique."

He laughs. "That's a word."

An odd swell of protectiveness wells up inside me. I don't know where it comes from. His words might be playfully self-deprecating, but it's not like I'm unaware of his ego. I know he's perfectly fine with who he is.

Even the joking sense that he isn't bothers me, though. It makes not one bit of sense.

I look over at him. "Can I ask you something?"

He loses the smile, sensing I'm serious, and nods. "Of course."

"It's personal. I'm just curious. We've never really talked about it. I'm not even sure how exactly to ask."

His brows draw together fleetingly and he kind of smiles like I'm being weird. Which is fair because I am. "All right…"

"Um… Well, surely you realize your courting habits are a bit odd."

His lips quirk. "Sure. Unique is the word I think we decided to use," he adds with a wink.

I shoot him a look, but I still feel awkward. It occurs to me that it's absurd that he feels perfectly comfortable kidnapping me, yet I feel awkward bringing up the anti-social qualities of his behavior.

"And you said you're not usually like that with other girls you've dated."

"No."

"But I feel like, while I get that maybe I have different qualities that triggered different behaviors, I couldn't have created them, you know? Those impulses must have already been alive inside you. And while I'm not in your head so I can't know for sure, it doesn't seem like anything you've been remotely surprised by or conflicted over, so it doesn't feel like this is the first time they've emerged. I'm not calling you a liar or anything," I add quickly, before he takes it the wrong way. "But if I'm not the first girl you've felt this way toward… if there have been others… I'd like to know how it ended with them so I can form a better idea of what to expect."

He's silent for so long, I'm not sure he's going to answer me. His palms are braced on the island, his jaw locked and his shoulders tense.

I feel immensely awkward and think about trying to walk it back, but before I can land on anything, he finally speaks.

"Sophie, I don't know how I could possibly be clearer about my intentions."

"I understand your intentions. Everybody starts out with good intentions. Well, maybe not everybody, but mostly everybody. Intentions aren't reliable predictors of the future. The past is, so I'm just wondering if there are any possible roadmaps you've already traveled that I could have a look at."

"Okay, you're right. Intentions don't mean shit, but *actions* do," he states, looking over at me. "Where in my actions could you have possibly found a corner to peel up to convince yourself I'm unreliable and I'm going to bail on you at some point? I have gone far outside the lines of legality *and* morality to lock you down. I feel like I've proven how much I want you."

"I know, but it's all still very new. You've only recently acquired me, so I wouldn't expect your passions to cool yet. I'm wondering what comes next now that you have me."

He stares at me. "Now, I enjoy *having* your crazy little ass."

I bite down on my lip to stifle a smile at his annoyance. "Right. But after that."

He stares at me for another moment, then he takes out his cell phone. I frown but wait for him to finish texting. Then, he grabs the chicken and puts it in the fridge. He turns the stovetop off.

"What are you doing?" I ask. "We need to make dinner."

"No, we don't. I have servants and an inheritance so large I could buy a small country if I wanted one. You don't have to lift a goddamn finger to do anything ever again if you don't want to. I'm not indulging your self-sufficient bullshit tonight."

My jaw drops. "Excuse me?"

"You heard me." He grabs my wrist and hauls me out of the kitchen. "I want to make a few things very clear. First, it isn't your fault I zeroed in on you. It's not your fault guys like Dylan or your professor did, either. Belief in a just world is a fairytale that people tell themselves so they can feel safer. 'That could never happen to me because I wouldn't do the things she did.' It's self-soothing bullshit for people who can't cope with reality. The world isn't just. Bad things can happen to anyone, and you can't always protect yourself. There are much worse fates than being vulnerable to hurt, Sophie. Being hurtable does not mean there's something wrong with you, and having something bad happen to you is not an indictment of your inability to protect yourself." He stops in the hall to look back at me. "There is nothing you could have done to protect yourself from me. There is nothing you did wrong to catch my attention. If you would have dropped out of school Monday morning and moved away, I would have hired an entire team of people to find you. If you would have gone underground, I would have razed the city and searched the rubble until I had located you. I'm glad you've bent as much as you have because I prefer your happiness, but not having you was not an option. If you had fought me tooth and nail at every turn, I wouldn't have given up and released you, I would just put you in smaller and smaller cages until you eventually gave up. These aren't healthy impulses. I know that. But I don't care. I feel a certainty when it comes to you that I wish I could share with you because if you could step inside my mind for a single minute, you would never again doubt my devotion to you. I'm not going anywhere, Sophie. Whether you believe it or not, that's the truth. It's okay if you don't trust it yet. It annoys me because I don't understand why you think you're so easy to leave, but time will show you I mean what I say. I adore you. I worship every cell of your being. I will never let you go. This feels like too ordinary a phrase to even bother saying, but I love you, Sophie, and I always will. There are no roadmaps I can show you to ease your mind because I've never traveled this road before, and I never will again.

You're it for me. You're my path. There is no alternate route."

He grabs my waist and pulls me close. His eyes are green flames as he speaks to fears, desires, and needs I don't even fully understand.

"You can rely on me, Sophie. I promise. I'll be here for you, loving you, until I draw my last breath." He slides his hand into my hair and pulls me closer.

I wrap my arms around his neck and rest my body fully against his.

"I know you don't always ask for what you want. I wish you would. You can ask me for anything and it's yours. But since I know you won't and I want to take good care of you, I have to pay close attention. Every time I figure out what it is that you want, I'm going to give it to you." He tugs my hair to pull me back and looks down at me. "Have you ever heard the saying 'closed mouths don't get fed?'"

I shake my head.

"No? Well, it reminds me of you." He presses down on my bottom lip, then leans in and kisses me. "Fortunately for you," he murmurs with our faces still close together, "I've found pretty effective ways of opening this pretty little mouth. Going forward, I'll make sure to find a few more."

My cheeks heat, but it's the pleasure his words stoke more than the mild embarrassment I'm most full of.

Not just pleasure because now he's hauling me into the bedroom and I know orgasms are forthcoming, but because he gets me in a way no one ever has.

Maybe I *am* looking for trouble where there isn't any.

Our relationship may have its dysfunctional

qualities, but regardless of how it started, I can't deny that I feel truly loved by him.

Maybe I'm crazy to have butterflies in my tummy as my one-time stalkerish kidnapper hauls me to our shared bedroom for pre-dinner sex, and maybe he's crazy for being willing to chase and stalk me when by all rights, he should already have me locked down.

But maybe we're the right kinds of crazy for each other and that's okay.

CHAPTER 38
SOPHIE

MOONLIGHT FILLS THE ROOM WHEN MY EYES OPEN.

I'm lying on the floor with Silvan sprawled beside me. We watched a movie last night and fell asleep on the couch. I woke up to him nibbling on my breasts and only moments later, his cock was inside me.

We ended up on the floor—*thank god this rug is so soft*—and I guess we fell asleep here.

I try to muster the gumption to wake up Silvan so we can go to our room, but his body is so warm and comfy, I just lie here sprawled naked on the floor with my body pressed against his.

A notification causes his phone to light up.

It's late and I'm curious, so I check that he's still asleep, then I peer over at the screen to see what it says.

It's just a notification about some new follower on Instagram, but my eyes widen and my stomach drops when I read the one below it, a text from someone named Leslie.

"Maybe you need a new girl then."

What the fuck.

I grab the phone without thinking and try to swipe the screen, but of course, he has a pass code.

What am I even doing?

I put the phone down and try to stop thinking about it, but I can't.

A moment later, I grab the phone again and try to think what Silvan's pass code would be.

I nearly jump out of my skin when his sleepy voice rumbles, "It's 1031."

My guilty gaze jumps to his. At first, I think he means the time, but it's much later than that.

"My pass code," he clarifies, rubbing his eyes. "What time is it?"

"Um... almost 3AM."

He locks his arm around my waist and pulls me down on top of him. "Guess we fell asleep, huh?"

He doesn't even care that I was just snooping in his phone?

Or trying to, anyway.

"I was just... Your phone woke me up."

He smirks faintly. "Anything interesting?"

I cock an eyebrow. "Yes, actually. Someone named Leslie telling you she thinks you need a new girlfriend."

He laughs and shakes his head. "Leslie's a guy, babe. Go ahead. See for yourself."

Well, if he's going to invite me to look...

"What'd you say the code was again?"

"It's 1031. Halloween," he adds, absently palming one of my breasts.

I still feel a little crazy as I swipe his screen and input his pass code, but he told me I could, so I waste no time opening his messages to see why this Leslie person isn't a fan.

I don't feel the sense of anxiety and doom I felt when I saw the message on the screen since he's inviting me to read it, but I'm still relieved when I see the exchange.

LESLIE: You coming out tonight or what?

SILVAN: Nah, my girl's a homebody. We're gonna stay in and take it easy tonight.

Then the last message Leslie sent but Silvan never bothered to even read.

My lips form a natural pout and I look down at Silvan's smug, handsome face. "Find what you were looking for?"

"Yes."

"Since we're exchanging passwords, I'd like the one to your computer," he tells me.

My initial impulse is to say no, but I guess there's no reason to. It's not like I have anything top-secret on my laptop. "Binx389."

"Binx?"

I nod, "Like the cat in *Hocus Pocus*. I had a black cat named that when I was a kid."

His lips curve up. "You like cats?"

"I do."

"Maybe we should get one."

My eyes light up. "Really?"

He nods. "Why not?"

He hauls me aside so he can sit up. My gaze drifts down to his cock hanging between his thighs and I have to stifle the urge to touch it.

"Why were you cool with giving me your pass code?" I ask instead, redirecting my attention to more important matters.

"Why not?" He stands up, absently rubs his abdomen, then heads for the kitchen. "You want a cold water?"

"Yes, please." I gasp, realizing I forgot to take my stupid birth control again. "Shoot," I mutter to myself, standing and heading for the bathroom so I can get it.

Is it better to take it six hours late or to skip a day and take it tomorrow?

Stupid pills.

I open the little case they came in and draw one of the rounded rectangular tablets out. The pill casing is sweet, so I don't mind leaving it on my tongue as I head back to the kitchen.

"Everything okay?" Silvan asks, handing me the water he grabbed for me.

I nod, uncapping it and taking a sip to wash the pill down. "I keep forgetting about my birth control. I'm not in the habit of taking it yet. I really wish you'd wear condoms at least until I get better at this and get it working in my system."

He locks an arm around my waist, pulling me close and walking me backward. "Why?"

"Because we should probably have a cat before we have a baby."

He smirks. "But you're finally coming around to the acceptance that we're *going* to have a baby someday. I'm calling it progress."

"I'm calling you crazy," I return lightly.

"Maybe." He leans down and steals a kiss, still walking me backward. "What kind of cat are we getting?"

"I don't know. We'll go to a shelter. Plenty of abandoned kitties in need of homes. Can we get one before Christmas?"

"We'll go next weekend."

"Why not this weekend?"

"I have something planned this weekend."

"Oh yeah? Am I invited to this something?"

He smirks. "You are. My family has some property up in New Hampshire, we like to visit around this time of year for hunting trips. They won't be there this weekend, but I thought we'd head up Friday night and spend the weekend there, enjoy a little uninterrupted alone time."

"How long's the drive?"

"About an hour."

I crack a smile. "Our first mini road trip."

A mysterious smile tugs at his lips, but he doesn't say anything. We're in the bedroom now, so he kicks the door closed behind us and walks me over to the bed.

"But right now, I think these lovely tits want my attention."

"Oh, do they?" I murmur as he picks me up and places me on the bed, climbing on with me and then hauling me closer to the middle.

"Mm-hmm," he murmurs, dipping down and kissing the soft swell of my breasts.

I sigh with pleasure, but still tease him. "I think they get an awful lot of your attention."

"They deserve it."

I laugh softly and then my eyes widen as he slides a hand down between my thighs. His insatiable fingers find my wetness and I grab his wrist to stop him. "Silvan Koch."

"Sophie Bradwell," he tosses right back in a playfully mocking tone.

"You do not need to fuck me again. It's bedtime."

"Need? Maybe not. Want…?"

"Silvan, don't you dare," I say on a squeal as he tickles me, then drops down and pries my clenched thighs apart.

My playful objections fall on deaf ears, and moments later, I'm too swept up to care.

Wednesday comes and goes without a single change in his behavior, then Thursday does, too.

By Friday, I'm convinced he doesn't actually listen to whatever the spy pens pick up, or maybe they're not even spy pens to begin with. I suppose it's possible my mind was playing tricks on me, that I was imagining a microphone when really it was just a part of the pen.

Whatever the case, my anxiety about the fake phone call eases and I allow myself to just enjoy my new favorite pens instead of being suspicious of them. I did want to order more of those pens for myself, anyway. Maybe it was just Silvan noticing I liked those pens and providing more of them for me in true Silvan style.

I don't have class on Friday, but Silvan has to head to campus for some meeting of some club he's in. Once he's dressed and ready to leave, he climbs back into bed with me and locks his arm around my waist, pulling me back against him.

I'm still sleeping, but I don't object to a quick cuddle before he goes.

"After the meeting, I've got some loose ends to tie up before we leave for the weekend," he tells me.

"Mm. Okay."

His free hand slides down to grab my ass. "Sleep all you want, but when you wake up, pack a bag for the weekend. Bring your schoolbooks if you have homework to do while we're there."

"When will you be back?"

His hand slides around and he presses his warm palm against my smooth stomach. "I'm gonna drive up ahead of you so I can set some stuff up. I'll send a car for you."

If I were more awake, I might have questions. I thought we were going to drive up together, and it's a long enough ride that I'm surprised he'd send me with Hugh instead.

But he kept me up half the night, so I'm sleepy, and the room is so dark, the bed so comfy...

My eyes get heavy. I fade out for a second but wake up to feel Silvan's lips pressed to the corner of my mouth. "I'll see you tonight, pretty girl."

"Mm. See you tonight," I murmur, dragging my pillow closer and cuddling with it since he won't be in bed with me anymore.

"I love you, Sophie."

If I were more awake, I might find that odd, too.

Silvan loves me, but he doesn't say it all that much. He doesn't say the words out of habit, repeating them so many times they lose their meaning. He only says it when he feels the genuine need to tell me he loves me.

<hr>

Silvan has bought me lots of pretty clothes since he barged into my life and took it over, but for the car ride up to New Hampshire, I want to wear something cute-verging-on-sexy but also *comfy*, and I can't find what I'm looking for in any of the new stuff.

I have most of the clothes I didn't pack strewn across the bed, but I end up digging out an outfit from high school—the before times.

I had this cute mini skirt the color of red wine with a dark textured overlay that I used to wear all the time. It was my favorite skirt, but since it *was* my favorite skirt, I'd worn it out with Dylan a couple of times and caught him looking at my exposed legs a little too long. Before that night, I didn't care that much. I was used to the male gaze landing on me. It didn't bother me.

After that night, it did.

I benched the skirt for the rest of high school, but I brought it with me to college since I had these big dreams about college being different, about *me* being different and getting comfortable in my own skin again. Surely, I could at least reclaim a favorite article of my own clothing.

Silly Sophie.

Still, it's a really pretty skirt and I always felt beautiful in it, so I guess it's a good choice for a romantic weekend away with my boyfriend.

My tummy flutters.

That feels weird to think.

I dig out this great pair of brown boots I also bought in high school that look so cute with the skirt. They have a low heel, so I don't wear them a ton, but they're comfortable enough, and since we're going to some house Silvan's family owns, it's not like I'll be walking in them a ton, anyway. Probably just from the car to the house, and once Silvan sees me in my whole outfit, I'll take the boots off since we'll be inside.

I wonder what the house is like.

Big, probably. He said they take hunting trips there, so probably lots of land.

I need to finish getting dressed so I can get out of here.

I zip up my skirt and turn in the mirror to check my reflection as I smooth down the material. The skirt rides low on my hips and I grab a soft V-neck T-shirt that's cropped so some of my stomach shows.

Since Silvan has gone to the trouble of setting up a romantic getaway for us this weekend, I want to at least put in some effort. I so seldom do, and he never seems to care, bless him.

I grab a lightweight navy-blue jacket and pull it on over my cute outfit, then I pull my blonde hair out of the coat and let it hang free. I look myself over in the mirror and think I look super cute, so with a smile and one last glance around the bathroom to make sure I'm not forgetting anything, I head for the bedroom to grab my bag so I can get downstairs and meet Hugh.

"Oh, shoot."

Damn birth control.

I run back to the bathroom to grab it and shove it in my purse since I already packed my toiletry bag. I shove my bottle of water in my purse, too, and then I'm ready to go.

There's an extra pep in my step as I turn off all the lights in the apartment and head out the door with my bags. My cute heeled boots make more sound than the comfier shoes I usually favor. I feel like I'm going out on a date for the first time in a lifetime, and it actually feels… good.

I smile and look at my pretty painted nails as I tap out a text to Silvan. "Heading to meet Hugh now!"

A strong gust of wind hits me as soon as I step out of the building.

Of course, it's windy when I'm dressed like a girl.

I flush as I juggle my bags to free up a hand so I can push my skirt down, then I look around for Hugh intending to make a joke about putting on a show for him, but… he isn't here yet.

There's a black car parked on the street, but I wasn't paying it any mind since I was looking for a stretch limo. Hugh has only ever picked me up in a stretch limo.

The front door on the driver's side opens and a

guy gets out. I'm only half paying attention because that's clearly not my ride, but then the guy turns around and my stomach drops to my toes. I recognize him.

Joker.

I'm frozen in place as he heads toward me. There's something naturally predatory about him that makes me uneasy, but then my gaze lands on his hands and my fear spikes.

He's wearing black leather gloves.

Move!

My instincts wake up a little too late and I stumble back a step in my stupid heeled boots.

Of course, the day I wear heeled boots is the day I get an impulse to run for my life.

I'm 5'9" so I'm hardly short, but he's taller than I am with a longer stride, so before I can gather my wits and choreograph my getaway, he's closing in on me. "You must be Sophie."

"Nope," I chirp, backing away from him.

He grabs my arm to stop me, shoots a look behind me to survey the scene (and note any potential witnesses?), then brings his gaze back to me.

Not suspicious *at all.*

"I'm here to give you a ride," he says.

I try to pull my arm free, but his grip is too firm. "No, thank you."

"Silvan sent me," he adds as if that will reassure me.

"He usually sends someone else."

"Yeah, well… today he sent me."

That is not encouraging.

I shake my head. "I'm suddenly feeling a bit sick. I think I'll stay home."

"Better take a Tums 'cause that's not an option," he says simply, then he snatches my weekend bag with his other hand and hauls me over to his car.

My heart kicks up several speeds. "Let me go. I don't want to scream and make a scene, but I will. I don't know you; I am not getting into a car with you."

"You've seen me before."

"At a crime scene. Oddly enough, that doesn't make me want to get into a car with you."

"Silvan said you might have some objections. He also said to tell you he invited a friend of yours out to the New Hampshire house tonight to have a little chat, and if you'd like a chance to say goodbye to him, then you should really get in the car."

Say goodbye.

To *him*?

I don't have any male friends. Hell, I hardly have female friends.

My mouth opens and closes, and then a thought passes through my mind.

Professor DeMarco?

He wouldn't… right? He has no reason to! I transferred out of his class. I haven't even seen the man since.

I look up and meet a pair of cool brown eyes that make my stomach sink all over again. There's something unsettling about them, but his clear disinterest when he looks at me neutralizes the unease a bit.

I can't imagine having him coming at you like that *with* interest in his eyes.

It would be terrifying.

"Did he… tell you the friend's name?"

"If you want any more information, you'll have to get in the car."

I bite down on my lip, my gaze flitting to the

open car door on the passenger side. I very much do not want to get in... but surely Silvan wouldn't have sent this guy to pick me up if he didn't trust him.

Also, despite putting in actual effort to look cute and having more exposed skin than I've shown in public in about two years, the man could not be less interested. His gaze hasn't lingered for a millisecond. Even his touch felt clinical when he grabbed my arm.

I'm not overly worried about him pouncing on me, but I *am* still uncomfortable getting into his car.

I do it, anyway.

I don't understand why Silvan sent his illegal activities friend to get me instead of Hugh, but the only rational explanation I can glom onto with the limited information I have is that he's doing something too illegal to involve Hugh in. Obviously, Silvan has access to professional criminals through his father, yet he's opted to go with this friend of his instead.

Like the night at Professor DeMarco's house.

So maybe he doesn't want his dad to know about the stuff he's doing to Professor DeMarco. I guess this is a game he only wants to play with me, and using his friend keeps it between us. When Silvan's father gets involved, sometimes he grabs the reins, and I'm sure Silvan doesn't like that.

He wants me at *his* mercy, not his father's.

I just don't understand why he's doing this without any provocation. I'd understand if I had put up a fight and refused to transfer out of his class or something, but I've done exactly what he...

The computer password.

I haven't seen Silvan use my computer since I gave it to him, but sometimes he wakes up before me to work out and shower before school. I know he had expressed concern about me that day in the coffee shop, and then I suddenly dropped his class. Could Professor DeMarco have sent me an email that Silvan intercepted, and I never saw?

I want to text him and ask what's going on, but I also don't want to say anything incriminating in case he's being a lunatic.

God. Just when I was settling into the idea of being in an actual relationship with him. I thought we were having a nice romantic weekend, not... whatever this is.

I fold my arms over my chest and sulk as Silvan's friend closes my car door and pops the trunk to throw my bag in.

I kept my purse up here with me and I think about texting Silvan just to make sure he did send this guy, but I don't really have enough doubt to go through with it. I know they're friends since he came last time Silvan got all crazy, and why else would this guy who is so clearly not interested in me be abducting me if not because my psycho boyfriend told him to? It just doesn't check out.

I glance over at him when he gets in and shuts his door. "Do you work for Silvan or something?"

He shakes his head. "Just friends with similar interests."

"When most people say that, they mean shopping or pilates," I mutter.

He smirks faintly and reaches for the gear shift, but before he shifts into drive, he seems to remember something. "Can you do me a favor? Reach into the glove compartment and grab my phone. I need to put the address in the GPS."

"Sure." Without thought, I drop my purse in the floor and lean forward to unlatch the glove compartment door.

As soon as my hands are close together, he grabs them. I yelp, fighting to pull away, but before I can, he locks handcuffs around both hands and secures them. He reaches between my legs and I scream, but he's not touching me, he's only grabbing a chain on the floor and attaching it to the chain linking the cuffs. I yank and yank, but I must be chained to something under the seat because I can't move my hands higher than my lap.

Wide-eyed and belligerent, I say, "What the hell?"

He ignores me and grabs my purse from the floor. He opens the middle section first and looks inside. When he doesn't find what he's looking for, he closes it and pulls open the back part, finding my phone. He grabs it and tosses it into the backseat so I won't be able to reach it.

"Are you *kidnapping* me?"

Now that I'm bound, he seems to find me even less significant than before. I don't think he'll even bother answering me, but he finally says, "I'm taking you to Silvan, like I said."

"To ransom me? Because if Silvan sent you, I can't believe he would want me transported this way. When he finds out how you're treating me, he's going to be *pissed*."

I expect my words to get through a little bit. If he and Silvan are good enough friends for Silvan to trust him with the things he trusts him with, surely, he knows how much Silvan cares about me.

Rather than look the least bit scared, though, the bastard smirks at me. "Maybe before your little phone call. But Silvan has pretty strong opinions about unfaithful women. Right now, I think he could be convinced that you needed to be... punished."

When he delivers the last line, he reaches over

and traces the curve of my jaw with one gloved finger. My breath hitches and a thrill of sheer terror shoots down my spine because I know how helpless I am to defend myself right now.

Just stay calm. Don't panic. He's *certainly not going to calm you down.*

My chest is getting tighter, but I breathe through it.

I lick my lips, but they're dry.

I wish I would have taken a sip of my water before I put it in my bag.

If Silvan were the one kidnapping me, he would somehow sense my thirst. He would grab my bottle of water out of my purse and give me a sip to satisfy my needs even while he's mad at me.

But this isn't Silvan, and this guy doesn't give a single fuck about my needs or my comfort.

The thought makes me a little sad.

I miss Silvan.

I really didn't think he'd heard the call. I stopped thinking about it because his behavior hadn't changed. I'm honestly stunned that's what this is about.

Surely, there should have been some indication that he was mad at me.

My mind races through the past few days searching for something, anything that felt off, but I can't think of a single thing. We've been… happy.

Silvan's friend shifts his car into drive. Before we take off, he looks over at me. "How are you at following rules, Sophie?"

I lick my dry lips again. "I'd say pretty good."

"Good. I like girls who can follow the rules. My rules are simple, and as long as you follow them, we'll get along just fine." His dark gaze locks with mine, a flicker of malice glinting in their otherwise empty-looking depths. "Don't fight back. Don't piss me off. And don't be a troublemaker." He holds my gaze for a moment before digging in on that one. "I don't like troublemakers."

I have a feeling his bad side is a scary place to be, so I assure him, "Don't worry. I'll be a good little hostage."

"Good." He flashes me a charming smile that makes him look almost normal, then his expression goes blank, his attention shifts back to the road, and he cuts the wheel to pull away from the curb.

CHAPTER 39
SOPHIE

AFTER THE LONGEST HOUR OF MY LIFE, WE FINALLY pull into a long gated driveway.

I'm relieved, honestly.

When he turned down this road, I started to get scared that this guy has been lying to me the whole time and he's taking me somewhere to kill me. I don't know why he would want to kill me, but I'm sure plenty of people about to be murdered have no idea why it's going to happen.

The guy is wearing black leather gloves, for fuck's sake. That strikes me as very murdery.

This road is also dropped in the middle of the woods with no streetlights and no other cars traveling it in either direction. The only light is from his headlights, and I haven't seen another driveway in several miles.

Riddled with anxiety, I kept stealing looks over at him to see if some big villain reveal was coming, but he maintained his utter ambivalence toward me and didn't even bother glancing over when I'm sure he could feel me staring.

I guess it wouldn't have been a big reveal, honestly. The guy oozes villain vibes, he's just not mine.

Poor Harley.

I guess she must be into that, though.

To each their own. If I had to wake up in bed next to him every day, the stress would kill me if *he* didn't.

I expect for Silvan's family house to be lit up with him inside, but the house is dark and cold. I only get a glimpse of the dark structure when the headlights hit it as we're making our way down the driveway.

It definitely doesn't look like anyone is home.

And I don't see Silvan's car...

Something isn't right.

Fear creeps down my spine all over again and makes me ice cold. I regret my outfit choice as gooseflesh erupt across my skin and so much of it is uncovered.

"You're sure Silvan's here?" I ask uneasily, watching as we drive past the house. The unease grows when he keeps driving past the driveway, down a dirt path toward the woods.

Oh my god.

I cannot disappear into the woods with this man. I will never come back out.

"Um, I think... I have to pee," I lie, grasping desperately for some reason to get out of the car. On instinct, I pull on the chain trying to break free, but it's useless.

"We're almost there," he murmurs, watching the path ahead as the lane narrows.

We are *driving into the woods.*

I'm going to die.

I don't know why, I don't understand what's happening, but this is the kind of deserted, scary place you take a person you're going to kill, not someone you want to have a romantic weekend with.

"Please just let me out of the car. I don't know what's going on here, I don't know where Silvan is… I don't believe he's okay with this, even if he did hear that phone call. And it was a fake phone call!" I add, realizing I haven't defended myself yet. "I wasn't really going to meet anybody, I just thought Silvan was spying on me and it made me feel some type of way, so I wanted to know for sure if he was. I thought if I made a fake phone call to this guy I had history with, it would make him mad enough to like… throw me around the bedroom during sex, but I didn't think he would just *not even fucking mention it* and then sentence me to be murdered which it feels a little like is what's happening here. Call Silvan, let me tell him what I did. It was dumb and I'm sorry and I'll never do it again."

Joker's smirking by the time I'm done begging for my life, but he doesn't say anything. He just keeps driving slowly down the path into the woods.

Oh my god oh my god oh my god.

I don't want to die.

I haven't even lived yet. I've wasted the last couple of years imprisoned by trauma. I haven't even had a chance to fall in love.

I'm angry at myself for letting Dylan hold me back the way he did. I've done plenty of coping and surviving since he pushed my life off course, but damn, I wish I would have done more healing. I need more time. I want to be brave.

There's a break in the darkness up ahead.

I see a small structure with windows lit by an orangish glow. By my standards, it's a small house, but not by Silvan's. I doubt he has ever stepped foot in a place like this once in his whole life.

This is a creepy cabin in the woods.

This is definitely a place for torture or murdering someone where no one can hear them scream. Not a place for romance.

"Please don't kill me."

"I'm not here to kill you. As far as I know, anyway. If I *am* here to kill you, it won't be before you've seen Silvan and had a chance to plead your case. The guy's fucking obsessed with you, so I like your chances." He puts the car in park, then kills the engine.

"We're getting out here? At the creepy murder cabin?"

"That's our destination," he confirms.

"Maybe you didn't hear me. I *don't* want to be murdered. I RSVPd for staying alive. You can take me back to the main house."

Amusement tugs at his lips. I think it's genuine, but he's getting out of the car, so I can't see his eyes to be sure.

His murdery dead eyes.

I pout. "I don't want to get murdered by him."

He opens my door a couple of seconds later. He doesn't have my weekend bag which further worries me. If I'm staying in this horror movie cabin with Silvan, he should be bringing my things. Silvan told me to remember to bring my books so I could do homework, which strongly suggested I would make it home alive, but Silvan would definitely think about small details like that. If he planned to murder someone but didn't want them to know yet, he would *definitely* tell them something like that to keep them from getting suspicious.

He's so smart. I really like that about him. Why didn't I tell him that?

He probably wouldn't have let his friend murder me if I told him that.

He's not going to let this guy kill you, Sophie. Calm down.

But it's hard to because the guy did imply he wasn't 100% *sure* he wasn't here to kill me, and again, he is not getting my bag out of his trunk. Is he just going to take my stuff? Is he going to put rocks in my bag and toss it in the river they'll dump my body in later? Maybe have a nice bonfire with it so there isn't so much evidence?

This *sucks.*

Once he's freed me from the handcuffs, I grab my purse. He grabs my arm and hauls me out of the car.

I want to tell him I can get out of the car myself, but it sounds like something a "troublemaker" might say. He doesn't let go once I'm out, anyway, so I don't think he'd care. He still looks bored to death by me, he's probably just afraid if he lets me go, I'll make a mad dash into the woods, and he'll have to hunt me down.

Yikes. That's a terrifying enough thought that I wouldn't do it even if I *didn't* think I'd surely get lost in the forest and die of hypothermia.

Every scenario seems to end really badly for me. I hate it here.

I'm going to be so mad if I played by all his rules and still end up floating down the Merrimack, but I'm holding onto hope this cabin is lit up because Silvan is inside. If Silvan is inside, I'll be okay. I can convince him not to hurt me even if he wants to right now. We have a system. I'm excellent at bargaining with him. I like to think he wouldn't go to this much effort, including his scary friend in the whole thing, just to put me in a position where I have to plead for his mercy again, but it's not outside the realm of possibility.

I'll let him win, too. I'll do anything he wants

me to do. As long as I escape this night without being murdered, I'm calling it a win for me.

Joker hauls me up the porch steps—I should really get his name—and raps on the wood door.

Hope blossoms in my chest. He's knocking. That means…

The door opens and a burst of warmth hits us from the heated cabin. My knees nearly buckle, but it's not because of the heat.

Silvan.

Joker propels me toward him and I open my arms, throwing myself against him and wrapping my arms around his neck.

"Whoa," he says, chuckling at the enthusiasm of my greeting.

"I'm so happy to see you."

"I'm happy to see you, too," he says, but I can hear the surprise in his voice. "This is a nice surprise."

Amusement warming his otherwise cool voice, Joker says, "You're welcome."

"What is this guy's name?" I murmur against Silvan's shoulder.

"Dare."

How fitting.

"I keep calling him Joker, and he's scary enough without his sole identity in my head being a Batman villain."

"You sound grumpy."

"I thought your friend was going to kill me!"

Silvan leans back. I'm not ready to quit the hug, but I lean back, anyway, so I can meet his gaze. "Why?" he asks.

My eyes widen. "That stupid phone call! It was a fake phone call. I didn't really call anybody. I was going to tell you as soon as you brought it up, but then you never did so I thought it wasn't a spy pen after all. I was just testing it out to see if you were spying on me, Silvan, I wasn't really sneaking out to meet anybody, especially him. Never him. Ew, ew, ew. Ew forever."

Silvan smirks and kisses my forehead. "Why don't you come inside." Looking past me at his friend, he says, "Thanks for bringing her to me."

I glance back to shoot this Dare guy a dirty look, but he doesn't even bother looking at me. He just nods at Silvan and turns to head back to his car.

"Wait, he has my stuff in his trunk."

"I know," Silvan says. "He's going to take it to the main house for you."

"He's the worst bellboy ever. I hope you don't give him a tip," I mutter.

He smirks and pulls me in for another kiss, this time on the lips. "Sounds like you had a great drive up."

"I did not. He *handcuffed* me to his—" I stop dead in my tracks, the words falling right off my tongue, when I lay eyes on the display in the living room.

Dylan Prescott is on his hands and knees on the floor, bound at the wrists and ankles, stripped down to his tighty-whities, with a gag in his mouth. His face is pale and splotchy at the same time.

My stomach was already roiling from the car ride up here and then the scary setting of this god-forsaken cabin in the woods, but now, at the sight of a nearly naked Dylan tied up on the floor...

I am at a loss.

"What. The. Fuck. Silvan?"

He takes my hand and hauls me into the living room—and toward Dylan. Everything in my whole body screams against going near him, but

Silvan drags me in there and drops my hand in front of the couch. He sits, sprawling out and leaning back with his muscular arms spread out like a… well, like a Viking who's just come home after a good pillaging and wants to put his feet up and relax.

And then he does. Dylan cries out and flinches as Silvan props his booted feet up on Dylan's back like he's a piece of furniture.

"Come here, baby," Silvan says, patting the cushion beside him. "You've had a long day. Sit down with your man and relax. Put your feet up," he adds, nodding at his human ottoman.

I'm too horrified to move.

Silvan pats the couch more assertively, his eyes hardening.

Something like fear jumps in my stomach. I have no frame of reference for what to do and I think I'm kind of in shock, so I just do as Silvan says. I sit down on the edge of the couch and put my purse on my lap. I look at Dylan's body, pale but with bruises and scrapes all over.

It's clear Silvan wasn't gentle with him when he… ripped his clothes off, bound him, gagged him, and then propped him up in the living room of this murder cabin like a footstool?

"Silvan. Baby. Can I just ask… what the fuck is happening? Because I'm super confused."

He opens his mouth like he's going to answer me, but then his gaze drifts to Dylan and his eyes go cold. He sits forward and drops his feet, giving Dylan a hard kick to the ribs that sends him halfway across the room.

I jump, startled.

"You don't look at her," he tells Dylan. "We talked about this before she got here. Did I fucking stutter, piggy? Lay your slimy fucking eyeballs on my girl one more time and I'll cut them out to make sure you never do it again."

Dylan whines pitifully in a sideways heap on the floor. It's hard to watch, honestly.

"Fucking pathetic," Silvan spits, shaking his head. He stands and walks over to grab Dylan by the hair, pulling him back up on his hands and knees. "Get the fuck up, you worthless piece of shit." Leaning down, he gets in Dylan's face and tells him, "You are an object, not a person. You're a fucking ottoman, you understand? Objects sit where the fuck they're put and take whatever is doled out to them until and unless they break, then they're tossed aside and easily replaced because they don't matter. That's what you are now. That's what you are unless I decide otherwise, and let me assure you that glaring at my fucking woman, looking at her at all? Not how you get there. Nod that you understand me."

Sniveling and snotty, Dylan nods his head.

Yuck.

I'm grimacing when Silvan straightens and looks back at me. A smirk plays across his lips as he slowly walks over to me. He's shirtless and wearing just a pair of black sweats. He looks yummy and reminds me more than ever of the night we met when he was a sexy Viking and I was his captive slave girl.

He stops in front of me, looking down at me still sitting on the edge of the couch. His gaze is dark and hooded. I want to touch him, so I do. Tentatively, I reach out and touch his hips. I look up and watch his face to see his reaction, then I palm his cock through the soft fabric.

It hardens beneath my hand. He slides his fingers through my hair, rough and tender at the same time. On pure animal instinct, I slide to the floor, dumping my purse upside down, and get on my knees for Silvan.

He backs up just enough to make room for me, his lips tugging up with quiet approval as I tug his sweats down, then his black boxer-briefs. His cock is hard and springs free right in my face. I grab it with one hand and lean in to kiss it, then I open up and take him into my mouth.

He grabs the other side of my head with his other hand, cradling it, stabilizing me as I take his cock deeper. I'm hungry for it. I want to please him. I stroke his shaft, my lips working their way up and down his impressive length. I look up at him as I work to make sure he still looks pleased with me, and the warmth on his handsome face warms *me* right up.

"Did I forget to tell you how beautiful you look tonight?" he asks idly, sliding one hand around to the back of my head. "Because you're fucking stunning." He pushes my head forward. "Even prettier with that perfect mouth full of my cock."

He takes control and I let him. I'm happy to have my mouth used for his pleasure.

"Maybe I'll spend the night fucking your face, baby. Just like this."

I whimper around his cock at the thought of it. I want that. But I want more, too. I can feel the wetness gathering between my legs just from sucking him, and as he gets rougher taking what he wants from me, I get wetter.

He fucks my throat, controlling how deep he goes, how hard. It's a struggle for me to breathe, but his firm hand on the back of my head keeps me from pulling back unless he wants me to.

When he pulls out of me, I sit back on my heels and watch him stroke his cock.

"You want this, baby?"

I nod eagerly. "Yes, please."

He smiles. "Take your panties off. Leave the skirt on, though. I like the skirt."

So does Dylan.

I feel a sick thrill at the thought of him having to listen from over there as Silvan gets on the floor behind me, peels up that skirt Dylan has gawked at me in so many times, and shoves his cock into me. He peels my coat off and tosses it on the couch, then he grabs my hips and holds on so he can push himself deeper.

"Fuck, baby. Always so goddamn tight."

I've never felt so turned on in my life. I push my ass back against him to take him deeper, faster. I want him all the way inside me. I want him to fucking wreck me.

"Silvan, please." I brace my palms on the hardwood floor. I always let him control the pace, but I want it so bad right now, I'm tempted to ask for it.

As usual, though, Silvan anticipates my needs before I have to.

This isn't a slow, tender lovemaking, it's a primal claiming, a show of exactly who the fuck I belong to in front of the only other male who has ever put his hands on me.

He grabs my hair, gripping it tight enough to hurt a little. "You're mine," he says, thrusting into me from behind. "Tell him."

"I'm his," I say on a groan as his cock fills me.

I'm overwhelmed with how much I mean it.

I *am* his. I'm *happy* to be his.

He pumps into me harder and faster, every stroke a claiming. I can feel the pressure building inside me with every brutal thrust.

"Say it," he growls, gripping my hair tighter and slamming into me. "Say who the fuck you belong to."

"You," I say breathlessly, already teetering on the edge of climax.

"Who?" he demands, leaning over me and angling my head so he can reach my mouth as he slides deep into my pussy.

"You!" I cry out against his lips. "Oh, God, Silvan!"

He grunts as he fucks me, his mouth claiming mine for a hard kiss before he uses my hair to pull me back. "Who does that tight little cunt belong to, Sophie?"

"You!" I gasp, arching up to get closer to him. "All of me belongs to you, Silvan. All of me."

I must have found the right combination of words because his voice is warm with approval when he rumbles, "That's my good girl." His grip on my hair eases, but then he pushes my face against the floor, holding me there and driving his cock deep and hard into my pussy.

This angle is so incredible, I can scarcely breathe.

With one final thrust, I'm coming so hard, chills shoot down my spine and I nearly burst into tears. I cry out sharply as I come all over his cock, moaning and whimpering and making sounds I didn't even know I could make.

Silvan keeps fucking me, chasing his own orgasm as he groans and curses through mine.

I feel a savage spark of satisfaction when I look over at Dylan's red face and see his eyes focused straight ahead because he knows my boyfriend will beat his ass if he looks this way.

I have the best boyfriend.

He's exactly what I never knew I needed.

I feel warmth as Silvan reaches his climax and shoots his cum deep in my pussy. I've never wanted it as much as I do right now.

He drops to the floor beside me and pulls me into his arms in one smooth motion. I curl up close, feeling my exposed stomach press against his hot skin.

"That was amazing," I say, though it probably goes without saying.

The corners of his mouth tug up. "Agreed."

I don't want to mention Dylan and risk spoiling the moment, but I've never had sex with an audience before and the realization of what we just did —what *I* initiated—makes my skin hot. I wonder what Silvan must think of me, if he's surprised.

I don't know what came over me. Seeing him dominate and humiliate Dylan… I wanted to serve him. I needed his cock right then and there.

"I can't believe we had sex in front of him."

"I'm glad we did," he says, curling his arm around my back to pull me closer and glancing menacingly in Dylan's direction. "Now the little fucker finally knows what it looks like when you want it."

CHAPTER 40
SILVAN

SOPHIE SNUGGLES UP NEXT TO ME ON THE FLOOR, HER soft hand absently caressing my chest, her perfect little lips kissing my left pec and along my shoulder.

She's soft as hell right now, her body—and sense of vengeance, perhaps—satisfied.

Not mine, though.

I won't tell her that right now. I just want to enjoy her. I told Dare he was welcome to put a little fear into her as long as he didn't hurt her because I know fear always warms Sophie up, but I didn't expect her to be *this* warmed up.

As we lie tangled together on the floor, she confesses all about the fake phone call she made acting like it's the worst thing anyone has ever done. I smirk at her because, hell, it's not even the worst thing someone *in this room* has done. But she apologizes to me anyway, and I let her. I kiss her pretty, apologetic lips and smile when she adds that since it was all a mix-up, we should probably let slimy Dylan go. Make him sign an NDA or something so he doesn't go blabbing about all this.

She's adorable.

While she was clearly down to fuck in front of

the bastard, I'm not so sure she'll be down for the rest of what I have planned, and I want to enjoy her company a bit before I do anything that could ruin it.

So, I order our ottoman back over to the couch and make us a bowl of popcorn. I turn on a movie and cuddle up with Sophie on the couch. I even make her put her feet up for a while. She seems to feel guilty about it at first since—unlike me and Dylan—she's not comfortable treating human beings like pieces of shit, but Dylan's going to learn what it's like to be helpless and humiliated before I put him out of his misery later, and I'm not letting him out of it just because she's a colossally better person than either one of us.

I knew Sophie was faking the phone call.

I didn't catch the call on the pen recording. I put more of the pens out because she seemed to like them. From the moment she found my pen in her bag, it's the one she used for everything.

But I watched her sit there and inspect the pen on the feed from the cameras in the apartment. I watched her compare it to her phone, and then, mysteriously, a few minutes later she got her phone call. Only there was no call on the screen, and it was lit up when she put it to her ear and put it back down.

I know what a phone call looks like on an iPhone.

Of course, she didn't know I was watching *video* footage. Maybe if I'd been listening to just an audio recording, it would have worked.

In any case, I explicitly told Sophie what would happen if I caught her fucking around with some other guy, and then she turned around and made an effort to make it look like she was.

Clearly, she wanted me to go after the guy.

Maybe it's an unconscious thing. Maybe she doesn't even realize it's what she wants.

But *I* realize it, so I'm gonna give it to her.

I don't like the idea of Dylan existing in the world, anyway. Not only did he touch my girl when she didn't want him to, but he disrespected her time and time again, and that's not something I can let him get away with.

Hugh said he disrespected me, too, but I couldn't give fewer fucks what he thinks about me. Still, I guess it's mildly satisfying to show him what a dorky fucking loser Sophie's new man is, after all.

He was boiling mad after I fucked her in that short little skirt and he couldn't do shit about it. Couldn't even watch without risking fucking body parts.

I figured he would be. I had a hunch from the stuff Hugh had relayed to me and my own digging that this guy liked Sophie and was probably bitter he never caught her.

I'm not surprised, though. Sophie requires meticulous care and he's far too self-involved to be able to offer it to her.

She can be cornered and pushed around for a short time if you know the right buttons to push, but if you want to *keep* her, that's not nearly as easy. She's slippery, and it takes a lot of effort to find out what she needs to be happy. I don't know if it's how she was raised, the shit she's been through, or just her natural inclination, but Sophie is very reluctant to express—or even admit—her desires. It's like there was never room for her wants and needs to be a priority so she got into the habit of pretending she didn't have any to not inconvenience anybody else.

I'd like to break her of it eventually, but in the

meantime, I'm happy to stalk her little ass and figure out what she needs that way.

Dylan couldn't cut it with Sophie. Most guys probably couldn't, but it's their loss because she's worth every bit of the effort.

Right now, her needs are very well met, so she's curled up beside me on the couch with her arms around my waist, her head resting on my shoulder, watching *Snow White*. She mutters about the Huntsman, and I laugh at her disgruntled tone.

"Too fresh?" I tease.

"I almost had to run for my life into the woods. You're lucky I didn't dress warmer. I might have."

"You better not." I pull her closer. "We've got a lot of land out here. You could get lost or eaten by an animal."

"It wasn't nature's furry predators I was worried about," she murmurs. "I thought your friend would chase me if I ran, so I didn't."

"Nah. If someone's gonna chase your pretty little ass through the woods, it's gonna be me."

"Sounds kinda sexy when you put it that way."

"Mm-hmm." I lean in and kiss her neck, feeling the thrum of her pulse beneath my lips. "You should see how sexy it would be when I caught you."

Her heart rate kicks up a little.

She likes to be a little afraid, so I bet she likes that idea.

We'll have to play that game sometime, too.

Satisfaction washes over me and I wrap my arms around her middle to give her a hug. "I love you, Sophie."

I don't expect her to say anything back. She never does, and that's fine. I know the score.

So, it's like someone scoops out my soul when

she threads her fingers through my hair and says, "I love you, too."

I tip my head and look up at her. "Oh, yeah?"

She smiles. "Mm-hmm."

"This is a new development."

"Near death experiences have a way of bringing things into quick perspective."

I smirk. "You sure it's not because I've made your *Beauty and the Beast* fantasies come true?"

Her brow furrows with confusion and she cocks her head.

I let go of her waist with one hand to make a sweeping gesture toward our cursed ottoman. "I suppose I could have put a tablecloth over him to make it a little clearer. I'll make him sing for you if you want. You know 'Be Our Guest', piggy? Sophie's a big *Beauty and the Beast* fan."

Her gaze flickers to Dylan the ottoman and she covers her face with her hands, but I think it's to hide her smile. "You are being rather beastly."

"Wait until I fuck you in the main house library later." I bring my hand back in and slide it up under her tiny T-shirt so I can squeeze her tits.

"This is the most twisted Disney date ever."

She doesn't add that she loves it, but I'm pretty sure she does.

I don't need her to admit it.

I push her shirt up so I can kiss her pretty tits for a little while, enjoying the sounds of her sighs and the feeling of her fingers in my hair. We make out on the couch while the rest of the movie plays, but then I get carried away and have to eat her pussy. I just want to make her come, but the inevitable result of her sexy little mewls is that I start wanting to fuck her again, and that's not the plan.

I guess it's time to deal with Dylan so we can

get on with our evening. I'm just hoping I don't scare her off.

Sophie is fine with me fucking with her head a little and manipulating her surroundings to give her a scare, but in the face of it actually happening, I'm not sure she'll be okay with someone getting hurt—even if it *is* Dylan.

I told her what would happen, though, and she knows I'm not some asshole who talks just to hear his own voice. I think she knows I mean what I say, so even if rationally she didn't intend to unleash me on him, I think deep down, she did.

And that's fucking fine. She doesn't have to forgive a single goddamn person who steps on her toes, least of all this asshole. If she wants me to mow through her past fucking up everyone who's ever hurt her, I am more than happy to do so.

Sophie's my queen, and she can order as many heads chopped off as she pleases.

In an adorable—but absurd—fit of shyness, she looks up at me with her flushed cheeks and twinkling eyes and tugs her shirt back down to cover her tits.

I love her so fucking much.

Tearing myself away from her is torture, but I sit back and pull her up with me.

She's docile and very much in the mood to be fucked so she makes it harder. I could do anything I want to her right now and she'd love it.

I really, really want to fuck her.

I look at the time, though.

I don't want to keep Dare here all night. He's doing me a favor, but I know he has his own girl to get home to. I don't want to be an asshole when he's helping me out.

Fucking her will have to wait.

It's Dylan's turn.

Heaving a sigh of regret, I tear myself away from Sophie and head over to the closet to grab the thick plastic drop cloth I stashed in there earlier when we were setting up.

"Now, I'm not gonna lie to you, baby, this next part's gonna get pretty messy. I know I told you I'd make you watch, but as we've established, the phone call was fake and you were never really going to meet this guy. I'm not doing this to punish you. I'm doing it to punish *him*." I unfold the sheet and throw it across the wood floor. "If you'd prefer not to watch, I'll have Dare come back and get you. He can take you to the main house to wait for me."

Sophie's starting to get nervous. Her gaze flits from the thick plastic sheet I just spread out on the floor to Dylan, wide-eyed and pale, bound like a good little piggy on the floor.

Pitiful.

The idea of this fuck ever manipulating Sophie makes me so mad, I want to kick him in the face.

So I do.

Sophie gasps and curls her legs back behind her on the couch. "Silvan... what are you doing? I thought you were just embarrassing him before you let him go."

I thought that might be the case. "I could do that," I say. "I told him I might. See, I wanted to let the sorry bastard cling to hope. The same hope you clung to that night when you thought maybe you could bargain your way out of a scary situation." I open a drawer to grab a pair of gloves and a roll of duct tape. "But the truth is, Sophie, that's not good enough for me. This bastard harmed you. He did it willfully, and to be frank, he rubbed your fucking face in it. He refused to apologize, then he insulted and humiliated you on top of everything else. That just doesn't sit right with me. I think he wants to fuck you, but I also think he dislikes you. I think maybe he hates you. It's probably a basic case of misogyny and not you, personally, but *I* take it *very* personally. You're my girl and I think you walk on fucking water, so the fact that this asshole thinks he can treat you like shit..." I sigh and look over at her. "It offends me, Sophie. It really does."

Her eyes are wide, but even though she can definitely see where I'm going with this, she doesn't look afraid. Alarmed, but not afraid.

"Anyway, I don't think the world will miss him, and frankly, I don't care if it does. I want him gone." I walk over and look down at her kneeling on the couch. So fucking pretty. I grab her jaw and lean in to kiss her pretty mouth. "I can't erase what he did to you, Sophie, but I can erase *him*. And I'm going to." My hand slides down to grip her throat. I can feel her pulse thundering in her neck.

Her pretty little tits rise and fall beneath her shirt, her breaths fast and shallow. "What... what exactly are you going to do to him?"

I lean in and kiss the corner of her mouth. "Well, he broke your heart, so I think it's only fair that I take his." I release her throat and reach over into the side table drawer. I draw out a small jewelry box and open it. It's a delicate gold chain with a gold key dangling from it. "I had this made for you."

She looks at the necklace. "It's beautiful."

I crack a smile, then grab the gleaming wood box off the table. Inspired by Snow White's evil queen and the Viking pumpkin from the last room of the escape room the night we met, I had it built so Sophie's key has to be inserted into the heart to open the box.

I impale the heart with the key and twist. The

box opens. There's a bed of deep red velvet lining the interior. It's sealed so nothing can seep out.

The perfect place for a worthless treasure.

Sophie's breathless. Speechless.

Turned on.

I can see the fire in her pretty blue and brown eyes when she looks up into mine.

I see something I've never seen there before.

Devotion.

She's mine now.

She wants to be.

I kiss her to make sure I'm not just seeing what I want to see, but her answering hunger tells me I'm not. My dirty soul dances with her much purer one. She needed to be dirtied up a little. She needed *me*.

She's panting when she pulls away.

"I think I'll wait for you at the main house."

I nod. "Okay."

Dylan does not find our bonding experience nearly as precious as I do. When I stand up to let Sophie off the couch, he's watching us like we're both monsters.

Fucking normie.

No wonder Sophie didn't like his boring ass.

I text Dare to let him know Sophie needs a ride back to the house, then put her coat back on her so she doesn't get cold. She gets on her hands and knees to collect the spilled items from her purse. Something rolled under the couch, so she pops her pretty little ass up and shoves her hand under the couch to reach it. Once she sees what it is, she sits back on her heels with a sigh, looking forlornly at the case of pills I gave her.

"Dammit, I forgot again."

She takes one out and uncaps her water so she can take it.

As often as she forgets, I wonder if she really *wants* to be taking birth control at all, or if she just feels like it's what she *should* want. I think if she really worried that much about getting pregnant, she might've gone with an IUD, something that would take effect immediately since she knew I wasn't going to use a condom.

At some point, I should probably tell her it's not birth control.

Maybe later.

Right now, I've got my hands full killing a pig so I can deliver its heart to my lovely queen.

Besides, she probably already knows. Sophie's no idiot and prenatal vitamins don't look a damn thing like birth control pills.

She knew the risks when she let *me* fill her birth control prescription.

Headlights appear through the kitchen window, so I know Dare's here.

I walk Sophie to the front door and give her a kiss before I open it.

Dare is standing on the other side, waiting.

Sophie slides her hands over my shoulder, then winds her arms around my neck for a hug. "You'll be okay, right?"

"Baby, don't insult me. I could take him blindfolded and armed with a fly swatter."

She laughs and buries her face in my neck.

Christ, I love her.

She pulls back and I let her go to follow Dare outside.

Before they step off the porch, I hear him say, "Thought there'd be more tears."

"From me?" Sophie looks back over her shoulder, her eyes glinting with warmth when her gaze meets mine. "What have I got to cry about?"

CHAPTER 41
SOPHIE

I REMEMBER WHAT HAPPINESS FEELS LIKE.

The curse feels broken.

That sense of freedom Silvan has brought me to in the bedroom doesn't end when the orgasm fog fades.

I thought the beast had to let me go to give me my freedom back, but I was wrong. My mind wasn't open enough. I was thinking too small.

I was pretending Silvan was the only beast I'd ever been imprisoned by.

Now, I don't have to pretend.

Only one beast remains, and it's the one that loves me.

I've never been freer than I am right now, locked against Silvan's naked body with his arm thrown around my waist.

His hand moves across my tummy and I think he might be about to start things up again. He's been ravenous since he came back from the cabin. I don't know if he's chasing demons or just as amped up as I was, but the result has been a marathon fucking session that reminds me I need to ask if he has some cranberry juice in the morning.

"We should shower," he rumbles.

We probably should.

The bedroom was dark when he came in. He'd put a hoodie on since it's cold outside, but I don't know if he had it on when he was handling his business. At the very least, I'm sure he got sweaty, and he didn't shower when he came in. He ripped off his hoodie, kicked off his pants, then climbed on the bed and pried open my thighs. We've been fucking pretty much nonstop ever since.

We haven't unpacked. Dare brought my stuff in, so I don't even know where anything is.

I guess it doesn't matter. I follow Silvan into the bathroom, and he flicks on the light.

I gasp, startled at the sight of smeared blood on *my* body.

My gaze drifts to his hands. His muscled chest. His toned abdomen. Even his cock is smeared with blood. I don't know if that's Dylan's or mine. He got pretty rough with me.

I guess I don't really care.

We're both getting clean now.

I follow Silvan into the shower and welcome the piping hot spray as it hits my skin.

He rinses off quickly, then he pours some shampoo in his palm and turns me around. I close my eyes and enjoy the sensation of his hands in my hair as he lathers me up. He pushes me under the spray when he's finished and leans in to kiss me, letting the sudsy water run down over both of us.

I'm breathless when he pulls back. My pussy's going to be exceptionally sore tomorrow, but I want it again.

His eyes twinkle with arrogance to let me know he's aware, but he's not done cleaning me. He works some conditioner into my hair, then rinses his hands and reaches for the body wash.

He grabs a soft cloth and lathers it up, then he soaps up my tits and washes my stomach. He pushes it between my legs, and I rest my head back against his strong shoulder as he drags the cloth over my pussy and cleans my thighs.

He takes care of me like he always does.

When he's done, he hands me the cloth.

Your turn.

He doesn't say it, but he doesn't have to. I take the cloth and get to work. It's not like I'm going to say no to another chance to touch him.

I run the cloth over his chest, his abs, his cock, his thighs. I scrub every flake of dried blood off his magnificent body.

It feels like a baptism. A fresh start. A chance to open myself up to things I was too afraid of before.

I don't feel afraid with him beside me, and he'll always be beside me.

We're in this together now. Our souls are twisted around each other, and they'll continue to grow that way for the rest of our lives.

He's been trying to tell me that, but I couldn't believe him. I believe him now.

He pins me to the shower wall and kisses me. He runs his knuckles over the curve of my jaw before grabbing my throat.

I feel my pulse beating in my throat where his hand rests.

He smiles.

He feels it, too.

Never one to deny me the things I want, he slides his hand down to grab my thigh. He lifts it, wraps it around his hip, and guides his cock to my entrance.

I hiss as he pushes into me. My flesh is bruised and tender. It stings, but it feels so good.

"I love you, Silvan."

I just felt the need to tell him.

He pulls back just enough to look at me. His lips quirk. "I love you, too."

───────

We spend Friday night and Saturday in New Hampshire, but Silvan drives us home Sunday afternoon. His parents invited us over for Sunday night dinner, and while I didn't much enjoy the last one, I figure we should probably go.

I'll have to get over Silvan's dad threatening my life and get more comfortable being around him because I'll be part of the family in a much more official capacity soon.

Silvan gave me a ring before we left the New Hampshire house. His grandma's ring.

It's a darkly beautiful ring with an unhappy history, but I think we can breathe new life into it and improve upon its legacy.

He said when his grandfather married his grandmother, he didn't marry her because he loved her. He married her because his brother did.

She was his trophy, a wrathful token he could snatch away from the kid who had unknowingly stolen his birthright.

A wrathful and proud man, he had this ring custom made for his stolen bride to serve as an endless taunt. He bought her the biggest, most expensive ruby he could find. Silvan said they call it a pigeon's blood ruby, that it's the most coveted ruby in the world because of how rare they are. He had the stone cut and crafted in this shape suggestive of a heart and set in a particular and peculiar way, with a smaller band underneath to symbolize her, and a slightly thicker, more dominant band above it, like arms gripping the stolen heart and keeping it—and her —captive.

Silvan said James wanted her to wear this ring as a constant reminder that he kept her heart in a cage, that she belonged to him and always would.

I guess she still had unresolved feelings for the brother he had ripped her away from, and Silvan's grandfather must've been similarly bad at sharing his wife's affections.

It's an extremely valuable ring, but one Silvan's father hated. When his mother died, he wouldn't give it to Melanie and sully her lovely finger with it because it was a ring crafted by hate and vengeance.

I think it's perfect.

Maybe it wasn't meant to be, but I even think it's romantic that they're both holding the same heart.

Whatever dark legacy this ring was born from, it's one-of-a-kind, just like the man I'm marrying.

I'm nervous on my way over to the mansion, my tummy aching and tumbling.

Silvan wants to tell his parents our good news, but as understanding as they've been about the whiplash pace of our courtship so far, I think they might have some objections about us getting engaged so quickly. His dad might even take issue with Silvan giving me his mother's ring.

I look down at it now, the dark glint of the moonlight hitting the rare stone.

I wonder what the woman who wore it before me felt when she looked down at this ring. For a split second, I can almost feel it. A claustrophobic feeling, colossal regret. Fear. Anguish.

What have I done?

Silvan's hand finds my thigh and pulls me from my pondering. I look over at him with one hand on the wheel, the other on my leg. It's so weird that he's driving. "You feeling okay?"

I nod. "Yeah. Just thinking."

"About what."

"Your family." I crack a smile. "I know you're not worried, but I really don't think your parents are going to pop open the champagne when we tell them this news."

He smirks. "It'll be fine. Stop worrying. Your mom wasn't mad when you told her, and she hasn't even met me yet," he points out.

I slide him a look. "Because you moved me into a $14 million mansion, *not* because she believes it will last. I'm pretty sure she looks at this marriage as a wild opportunity that will fizzle out before I've graduated college and she just wants me to take what I can get out of it. Like when a celebrity gets wasted and marries some rando in Vegas. We all know they'll be divorced in a few months, tops, but at least you got to see your picture in *People* magazine. That kind of thing. *Your* family isn't going to see it that way. *I'm* not all upside."

He cracks a smile. "Neither am I; your mom just hasn't met me yet."

"She'll love you," I say, rolling my eyes. "She's not hard to please. Now your dad *is* going to think I'm being a golddigger."

"Even if he did, he wouldn't care. If someone wants to forego love for money, he'd say that's their business. Since when do you care so much about my dad's opinion, anyway? This isn't because of that shit he said, is it? I told you, you don't have to be afraid of him. I'd never let him hurt you."

"No," I say, waving him off. "It's not that. I don't know, he accessed that part of my brain. He scares me, but I still weirdly want his approval. I think I have a grudging respect for him or something. I'm not sure what's wrong with me."

He chuckles, putting his hand over mine. "All the right things," he says lightly.

Since we drove tonight, I get the now-novel experience of letting *myself* out of the car. Silvan takes my hand, and we walk inside together.

His mom has brought in the Christmas trees in the time since I've been gone. There's a massive one in the entry way, all decked out in white. I spot a red one and a gold one before we get to the dining room. Dinner isn't ready quite yet, so Silvan takes me to his father's study where his parents are waiting for us.

I do not expect to see a tree in here since I'm quite certain Silvan's dad couldn't be less interested in Christmas trees if he tried to be, but Melanie must have wanted to dust her Christmas spirit in every room, even his, because there's a tall skinny tree in the corner decked out in red and gold.

The last time I saw them, I didn't even really want to *be* with Silvan, but there's no reflection of that brief reality on Melanie's face when she rushes over to hug me like I'm her daughter already. She tells me how pretty I look as she looks over my dress, and before I can even think to move it, her gaze lands on my left hand.

She gasps and brings a hand to her chest. Wide-eyed, she looks from me to Silvan.

"Surprise," he says.

"Oh, Richard, they're engaged." She grabs her husband's arm, then turns back to us, bursting with more joy than I've ever seen in a human being. "Oh, that's such wonderful news."

Is it?

I'm floored and expecting the more grounded

half of this duo to have more reservations, but when I look to Silvan's father, he merely smiles blandly and says, "I suppose congratulations are in order."

"Let me have a look at that ring," Melanie says, grabbing my hand.

My gaze is locked on her husband and my heart sinks when his polite if mildly disinterested smile disappears completely.

At the same time he realizes it, Melanie says, "Isn't this your mother's ring?"

"I know you didn't want it," Silvan says.

"Interesting choice," his father says, already recovered from his surprise. "I'd have bought something new."

"It's a lovely ring," Melanie says. "So unique. I've always thought so."

"Sophie likes it."

His father lifts his drink and takes a slow sip, holding my gaze over the rim. "Well, I hope you have better luck with it than she did."

"Have you set a date yet?" Melanie asks.

I open my mouth to say not yet, but Silvan speaks before I can. "Soon. I'd like to be married before the year's end."

My eyes widen and my gaze snaps to his. "*This* year?"

He smirks. "Yes."

His mother clasps her hands together. "A December wedding, then. Oh, it will be beautiful. I'll make some calls tomorrow to see what will need to be moved around to ensure you get the venue you'd like. Do you know where you'd like to be married?"

I shake my head. I didn't even know I *was* getting married so soon. Since the engagement happened so quickly, I figured we would take our time walking down the aisle. "I don't know what we'll be able to get on such short notice. My bridal knowledge consists of only what I've seen in rom-coms, but aren't places usually booked like a year out?"

Melanie waves me off. "Richard will make sure that's not a problem, won't you, dear?"

"I'll handle it," he confirms.

My gaze flits to him. I can't help being suspicious. "You're just going to convince people who have spent a whole year planning their wedding to move it?"

He smirks at me. "I'm pretty persuasive."

That's true.

Melanie goes on. "We host a big Christmas party every year, so I'm already working with a great team of vendors and event planners. We can use them for the wedding, too. They do excellent work so I know everything will run smoothly for you. Richard and I got married at a beautiful historic church downtown, the same one his parents were married at. Would you like to see pictures?"

"Oh. Sure." I nod and smile, trying to keep up with her enthusiasm. She heads toward the bookshelves and opens a bottom cabinet to pull out a leatherbound book.

"Would you like to see a picture of Katherine? It's her ring Silvan gave you."

"Oh, yes. Please. I'm heavily invested in their story."

Richard cocks an eyebrow like that's an odd thing to say.

"Not that… your parents' marriage is a story," I add awkwardly. "But Silvan told me a little bit about them, and…"

"She's a big *Beauty and the Beast* fan," Silvan says by way of explanation.

My face heats. I look over at him. "Thanks, babe. Big help."

"He was a beast, all right," Richard murmurs, glancing back at his wife as she comes at us with an armful of family photo albums.

"And she was a beauty," she says, carefully dropping the treasured books on her husband's desk and flipping the first one open. I walk over as she turns the pages until she finds the one she's looking for. "There she is."

I lean in and peer at a portrait of a beautiful brunette with thick dark eyebrows and piercing eyes. She's alone in the photograph wearing an ivory satin wedding gown with a matching stole draped around her slender shoulders. She's the picture of luxury, no doubt the envy of her friends, but there's something lonely and fearful in her eyes, something that echoes the thought I had earlier about her regretting the life she got pulled into.

"She's lovely," I say softly.

Melanie nods her agreement.

Then she turns the page. "And this is James."

The breath is momentarily sucked from my lungs when I lay eyes on the man who created the emotional problems of all the people in this room.

I can see so much of Silvan in him, with Richard's aura of danger—but amplified because this man's danger isn't quiet and capable of catching you by surprise. One look at him and you know he'll absolutely ruin your life, but there's something that draws you in, anyway. His handsomeness, sure, but there's more to it than that. A sense that he's wounded, that he's a man who's never known happiness.

The temptation to believe he can be fixed is so strong, I feel it even though I know how the story ended.

Some version of it, anyway.

I suppose I only know how their relationship looked to certain others, much like Silvan judges his parents' relationship one way, but when I look at it, I see a much different picture. I didn't come in at the same moment he did, and the image I have of their relationship is two people deeply in love who would do anything for one another.

There's a picture of the bride and groom together on the next page, and maybe it's the romantic in me, but I see his possessive grip on her waist and wonder if there was more to the story than what I've heard.

I think of Silvan's brutal side, the ruthless Viking spirit I can't help but enjoy. I can see it coming from this man. His lips look like they've never smiled. His eyebrows are set at a fearsome slant that leaves no doubt that he is, in fact, a beast.

I certainly wouldn't fuck with him.

I mean, I can see why Katherine let him ruin her life, no question, but yikes. Big scary vibes.

"Well, at least I don't have to worry our kids will be ugly," I say lightly.

Melanie's eyes sparkle knowingly. "He looks much less handsome once you've met him," she says with a little wink.

"And here I thought you liked them mean," I tease.

Her eyes sparkle and she looks over her shoulder at her husband. "He isn't mean to *me*."

Closing that book, she opens a second one and shows me pictures of her wedding to Richard at the church where James and Katherine got married. It's a gorgeous cathedral to be sure, but it's the kind of place I'm certain is booked several years out, and I don't want Richard pulling strings to open a place up for us. I'd rather just have our wedding somewhere that's available without threats and intimidation.

Melanie is so excited about planning my wedding, I can see the location is out of my hands and at this point she's set on it being this church for the ceremony. It's a tradition at this point, one she'd like to keep going.

"I very much appreciate your enthusiasm and your help, but I think my mom will probably also want to be involved with the planning."

"Oh." The light in her eyes dims a bit, not deliberately, she just seems to wear her heart right on her sleeve and can't hide her true feelings. "Of course. Look at me, prattling on like you're *my* daughter. Of course, you'll want to make plans with your own mother."

The study door opens, and I hear the maid announcing that dinner is ready and we should head to the dining room. My gaze catches on Richard watching me, his eyes narrowed with displeasure.

My heart skips a beat.

What did I do?

I look at Melanie closing her photo albums and taking them back to the cabinet. I didn't mean to hurt her feelings, but I think maybe I did.

I open my mouth searching for something to say, but I can't come up with anything. All I said was that my mom would want to help plan the wedding.

I feel bad for dimming her excitement, though. I want to fix it even before I realize that's probably why Richard was looking at me that way. He's clearly very protective of his wife.

Melanie takes Richard's arm, and he leans in to give her a kiss. She brightens a bit and leans her head on his arm, then they lead the way out of the study.

I fall in next to Silvan and he slides a hand around my waist.

"I think I upset your mom," I whisper.

He nods grimly. "Probably. She's not great at sharing, either."

I watch Richard's back wordlessly as we leave the study.

I feel crazy even suggesting it, but the entire fabric of Silvan's family seems to be stitched together by sheer insanity, so I give voice to my thoughts. "You don't think your dad would... do anything to get my mom out of the way just so Melanie would be my only wedding planner, do you?"

Silvan's head rocks from side to side as he considers. "I mean, it's not *not* something he would do. You weren't mean, though, all you said was you want your mom involved." He observes his parents for a couple of seconds. "She can be a little sensitive, though. Just make sure she doesn't feel left out, and you should be okay."

My stomach hollows out.

He's betting an awful lot on a maybe.

As soon as we enter the dining room and take our seats, I tell Melanie I'd love to set up a lunch this week so she can meet my mom and clue her in on all the wedding plans. I make it very clear I'm totally onboard with Melanie's choices, I just want my mom to be along for the ride so she can experience it with us.

That seems to be the right compromise. Melanie perks back up and starts telling me all her ideas about a beautiful snow-dusted ballroom with Christmas trees placed around the room and glittery, glowing lanterns suspended above the round tables surrounding the dance floor. I nod and smile and tell her how much I love all her ideas, and when I glance at Richard, he offers me a faint smile of approval laced lightly with amusement.

This family is very temperamental and a little high maintenance, but I think I'm beginning to learn the ropes around here.

I didn't ask Silvan ahead of time what they were having for dinner, so I hold my breath when the plates are brought out.

"Grilled chicken with pesto and penne," Ilona says as she puts my plate down in front of me.

I breathe a sigh of relief. "Thank you, Ilona."

She nods and puts Silvan's plate on the table in front of him, then heads back to the kitchen.

I grab my silverware to cut into my food so I can mix it all up when suddenly the strong scent of the pesto sauce wafts to my nose and makes me feel instantly ill.

Unable to keep from grimacing, I sit back, trying to put distance between the plate and my nostrils and press a hand against my stomach.

Richard's dry tone brings my gaze up. "What's wrong now? Silvan told us you like chicken. Are you afraid we were mean to the basil?"

I crack a smile and shake my head. "No, it's not that. I just… I don't know, I feel a little sick. Does the pesto smell really strong to anyone else?"

Richard's gaze flickers to Silvan.

I'm moments from throwing up but I refuse to do it, so I grab a water goblet and take a few sips to keep it down.

Then Silvan's mom asks, "Could you be pregnant?" and I nearly choke.

No!

I open my mouth to deny the possibility, but I can't. Silvan has come inside me so many times, I think I have more of his DNA in my body than mine.

My hesitation is all the confirmation they need, apparently.

"Oh, my goodness. Should we get you a test? I can send someone out now, you'll have it by the time dinner's over. Ilona," she calls.

I shake my head. "I can't be. I mean, it's not impossible, but I wouldn't know this soon…"

"You might," she says, bright-eyed. "With Silvan I didn't know right away, but I was young and didn't really know what to look out for. With my second pregnancy, I was ill from the very beginning. I knew within days."

I blink in surprise. "Isn't Silvan an only child?"

Melanie's eyes widen and she looks over at Richard. "Yes. Yes, what I meant was—"

He cuts in with a decisive, "She lost it." He holds my gaze for a beat, then says, "It's a painful memory she doesn't like to revisit."

No questions. Got it.

That makes sense to me, anyway. I'm sure if I miscarried, it would hurt to talk about, and I'm not nearly as sensitive as Melanie is.

She clears her throat. "Have you had any soreness in your breasts? Felt extra tired? Perhaps a little more emotional than usual?"

I have no idea.

I mean, yes, but I attributed those things to falling in love with her son and the physical aftermath of our bedroom activities. We had a *lot* of sex this weekend, and he very much enjoys playing with my breasts. I figured that's why they were a little sore when I was getting dressed for dinner.

Obviously, I cannot say that.

"Oh, this is so exciting," she says. Too eager to wait for Ilona to come back, she gets up and goes to the kitchen to get her.

Once she's gone, Silvan looks at his dad. "I didn't know Mom had a miscarriage."

Richard spears a piece of chicken. "You were young. And, as I said, she doesn't like to talk about it."

I look over at Silvan, shaking my head. "I can't be pregnant. It's too soon."

He reaches over and takes my hand. He doesn't say anything, but I can tell he's not anxious about it like I am.

His mom comes back moments later, telling Ilona to get several packages of pregnancy tests so we can be sure. "Make sure you get the early detection ones!"

The nausea passes and I'm able to eat, but I'm on autopilot and can't really focus on a thing until Ilona comes back with a white plastic bag full of pregnancy tests.

I want to scold Silvan that I warned him this could happen and why couldn't he just put on a damn condom? But my scolding would fall on deaf ears because, inexplicably, I'm the only one at the table even remotely bothered by the idea of having a baby with a man I've known for less than a month.

I mean, yes, we're getting married, but my god, this is fast.

I take the bag of tests to the bathroom as soon as the dessert plates are cleared. I open several packages and read through all the directions. I set up a pregnancy test assembly line on the counter and then I wait for the first one to show results.

I have my cell phone timer set for a different test, so I do a mental count for the first one. At the last second, I grab the stick off the counter and check the little window.

I tell myself there will be one lonely line. There

has to be. There's no way Silvan got me pregnant so quickly. No way.

Only there are two lines.

My eyes widen and I grab the next test.

Same result.

My cell phone alarm goes off and I press stop, then I grab the third test and look, but I already know what it's going to say.

Pregnant.

I feel as if I've swallowed my heart. It beats in my throat and my head starts buzzing.

I jump when Silvan raps on the door. "Sophie?"

I clear my throat and try to get the hollow, terrified feeling out of my stomach, then I open the door.

His attentive gaze is on me, searching. "Well?"

"I'm pregnant," I say softly.

His reaction is delayed by about a millisecond, but then he grins and grabs me around the waist, pulling me in and holding me tight. "That's great fucking news."

Is it?

I'm still a little unsure.

It still feels surreal, but I wrap my arms around his middle and rest my face on his chest. He feels so strong and reliable, so sure in the face of my uncertainty that some of the dread melts out of me.

"You're really happy?" I murmur.

"Are you kidding me? I get to have a baby with my favorite person. What's not to be happy about?"

My heart gives and flutters and more of my doubt falls away. "You don't think it's way too soon?"

"Nah, I'd say we're right on schedule."

I crack a smile and tip my head back to look up at him. "You're crazy."

He smirks. "That's why you love me."

I open my mouth to argue, but he catches my protest on his lips and makes me forget what I wanted to say. His hand cradles my face, then slides into my hair. He unleashes all the butterflies and cages up all the doubt, and when we head back to his parents hand in hand, I feel a crazy little burst of excitement.

We're going to have a baby.

Melanie is overjoyed to find out her baby is having a baby, and Richard assures me I shouldn't feel bad, that pregnant brides are a Koch family tradition.

I should have really known I couldn't rely on any of them to be the sane one in this whole ordeal.

I guess no one has to be the sane one.

I'll be a Koch soon, myself, and I already have the next generation growing in my womb.

We're in the car on the way home and I'm fishing around for my lip balm when I come across my case of birth control pills.

"Guess I don't need to remember to take these anymore."

Silvan glances over. "Actually, you should probably keep taking those."

My brows furrow with confusion.

"I had Hugh buy you prenatal vitamins, not birth control."

My eyes widen.

"Hey, I wanted to make sure you were well-nourished, just in case."

"Silvan! Those were supposed to stop me from getting pregnant, not prep my womb to be optimal living accommodations. What am I going to do with you?"

His eyes twinkle and his handsome mouth tugs up in a charming little smirk. "Love me forever?"

I sigh and shake my head. I feel like I should be angrier at him, but I also feel like I probably should have Googled it when I opened that case of pills and there were no calendar slots to tell me what day to take which pill like all the birth control I had seen before.

Oh well.

It's done now, and I *do* love babies.

An image of a little half me, half Silvan baby wearing a onesie and kicking its adorable little legs and giving me a big, gummy smile fills my mind and that small burst of excitement from earlier explodes a little. I look over at him.

"You can be excited, Sophie."

It's like he can read my mind.

I love that about him.

"We're so young. This was very irresponsible."

"I'm very rich. We can hire all the help we need. And look at it this way: we'll be hot grandparents."

"Oh my god," I say, covering my face with my hands but unable to stifle a little smile.

He's shameless.

But I love that about him, too.

CHAPTER 42
SILVAN

"How could I possibly be expected to get just one?"

Ahead of me, Sophie bends over giving me a very nice view of her ass as she plays with a pair of gray kittens in a cage. One is lazing in the corner watching while the other stretches up to paw at her finger.

"We need to adopt them all," she informs me.

"You know I'd adopt a thousand cats for you if that's what would make you happy," I say, coming to survey the runt she's playing with, "but since we are having a baby, I don't think we should fill the apartment with cats."

She pouts and my cock jumps at the sight of those pretty lips it's so fucking fond of. "But I love them all. And they're homeless. Right before Christmas," she adds, giving me giant puppy dog eyes I couldn't possibly resist.

"How about this? Give me the cat."

She looks over her shoulder as if she's unsure she's allowed to just reach in and grab it, but then she does. She's getting more used to the idea that she can do whatever she wants.

The kitten's claws come out and cling to her sweater.

There's probably little chance we're not taking this guy home, but the lady said these two needed to be homed together, and I really do not want two cats right now.

"Now get the lazy one."

She scoops the sleepy one out. It blinks at her, but otherwise remains in a ball of unmoving fluff. I juggle their flexible little bodies so I'm snuggling both of them, then I pass Sophie my phone.

"Take a picture."

She's got the big, wobbly anime eyes looking at me so I'm pretty sure it's a good pose. "If you hadn't already put a baby in me..."

I laugh and she snaps a couple of pictures. I take the phone back and hand off the kittens, then I make a quick post blatantly shilling for them and tag the shelter we're browsing for our kitten. "There," I tell her before slipping my phone back into my pocket. "They'll be adopted by the end of the day."

She lowers the lazy cat back to its sleeping spot and nuzzles the playful one. "You know, ordinarily, I would take issue with you posting thirst traps like that, but I appreciate you using your hotness for a good cause."

"Yeah, yeah, yeah. I love all that save the world shit you're into. Now, can you put that cat down so we can look at the ones we can actually adopt?"

She catches the kitten's tiny paws in her hand. "I want to, it's just… he's so cute I could die."

Since prying her away from this kitten isn't going to be an easy task, I take a lap to see what other cute kittens I can find to draw her attention away from that one.

There's a whole litter of tabbies frolicking

around that she hasn't even made it to yet. I'll have to put a blindfold on her to get her past all that cuteness.

Past the tabbies, in a cage by itself, I see a cute little white and gray ball of fur. Its coloring looks like it got dropped into a mud puddle and shook itself off but little bursts of gray remained.

He looks attentive. I like that, so I walk closer to get a better look at him.

He sees me coming and takes a cautious step toward me to check me out, too.

"Hey, little guy. You in the market for a mommy?"

The kitten walks forward and brushes up against the cage.

This one seems more selective than the easy charmer Sophie's playing with. I can see why her head got turned—she doesn't have the best taste in guys, after all—but this guy's got the attention span. I feel like you'd have to win him over, but once you do, he's loyal for life.

"Come here, you." I open his cage and scoop him out. He sits on my hand and watches curiously as I bring him up to my chest, then he ventures closer, gently walks his little paws up to stand on me, and claws the fuck out of me.

I can't help laughing. I like his spirit.

"Yeah, I think you can beat that other cat for her attention. Let's go find out."

I cradle the kitten so he doesn't fall and break his little neck, then I sneak up on Sophie. She put the other kitten back in his cage, but she's still playing with him.

"What about this one?"

She turns around and gasps, leaning down so she can visit with this ball of cuteness. "Aww, aren't you a handsome boy?"

He likes her. He goes strutting toward her and when she picks him up, he gazes at her the way I do.

"I think he looks like a Snowball."

"Are you a Snowball?" she asks in the cutesy voice she uses to talk to baby animals. The kitten flops over on his back and bats at her finger as she dangles it for him. "Oh, he's so *cute*." She looks up at me, bright-eyed. "Good find, baby."

I grab her waist and tug her in for a forehead kiss. "I've got a good eye," I murmur teasingly.

She carries the kitten around getting to know him a little better while we track down the lady we talked to before to ask about him. I figure we should make sure he's not an asshole, but the woman mirrors my impression of him and says she thinks he'll be an excellent pet for a family that makes time to foster a connection with him.

I fill out the papers and pay the adoption fee while Sophie bonds with her kitty. They're well on their way to love a hell of a lot faster than I was able to get her there, but I try not to be offended. He is a cute little bastard, after all.

Hugh is waiting for us by the curb when we emerge with the newest member of the family. Sophie is cuddling him, but she stops to show him off to Hugh before we get in the car.

"What a fine choice," Hugh tells her.

"We're going to spoil him rotten," she says, nuzzling his fluffy little head. "To the pet store!"

It's the end of our first night as new cat parents.

Sophie's lying on the floor where Snowball fell asleep, absently petting his soft fur.

I don't like her being so far away from me, so I abandon the couch to join her on the rug.

She looks back at me, her face peaceful, and smiles. "Hey, you."

I pull back enough of her robe so I can kiss her bare shoulder. "Hey, right back."

"I'm sleepy."

"I can see that. You ready to pass him off to Ilona so we can go to bed?"

Ilona is staying here with us for a while. I figured that would be easier while we're training the kitten. Plus, then he won't feel abandoned during the day when we're at school.

"I just love cuddling him," she says.

"And I love cuddling *you*."

She smiles. "All right, all right. Twist my arm, why don't you?"

I take the sleepy cat off her hands and carry him down the hall to the room Ilona's staying in for the time being.

Sophie's waiting in the bathroom to brush her teeth since we always get ready for bed together. Now that we're in the privacy of our rooms, we strip off our clothes and climb into bed.

"Do you think we'll be good cat parents?" Sophie asks, yawning.

"Yeah."

She misses a beat, then rests her hand on her tummy. "Do you think we'll be good human parents, too?"

I crack a smile, sliding my hand around to splay it over hers on her tummy. "I'm pretty certain we will be."

"If we have a boy, he's not allowed to grow up to be a kidnapper."

"I make no promises."

"And if we have a girl, we should teach her

kidnapping is bad and to adamantly avoid boys who try to kidnap her."

I lock my arms around her tighter, pulling her back against me and kissing her neck. "Mm, I don't know. I feel like we should take it on a case-by-case basis. Maybe she takes after her mother and left him little choice."

She rolls her eyes. "As if you tried to pursue any other avenue. You didn't even ask me on a date until after you'd kidnapped me the first time."

"If I did, you would have said no. I just skipped a few steps."

"Skipping steps is your favorite," she murmurs.

"Are you still meeting our moms to try on wedding dresses tomorrow?"

"Oh! Yes. Will you set an alarm for me? If I try to move… I won't be able to."

I smother a laugh. "Clever turn of phrase."

"Listen, the baby is eating my brain. I can't be expected to grow a human *and* come up with snappy comebacks."

"Good thing I love you for your looks," I tease.

"I'm going to murder you."

I laugh and give her a kiss. "You can't. You'd miss me too much." I give her another kiss along her temple. "You're tired. Why don't you close those pretty eyes and get some sleep?"

"But I promised to let you put a baby in me tonight."

"I already did that."

"You don't want to practice, anyway?"

"I do. But you know how much I like waking you up with my cock."

"Mm, I do," she murmurs thickly.

I nod and lean in to kiss her lips. "So," I murmur leadingly, "why don't you go to sleep."

"Okay." She smiles softly, rolling over so she's

facing me. "Thank you for taking me to get a kitten today."

"You're welcome."

She locks her arms around me, then drapes a leg over my hips, pulling our pelvises closer. "Thank you for making me marry you, too."

My cock starts to wake up sensing her nearness. I crack a smile, shifting my hips to adjust a little. "Anytime."

Then, to be a perfectly troublesome little minx, she gets close enough to grind her pussy against me.

"Good night, Silvan," she says sweetly.

I push on her ass to force her closer so my cock can stay close to her sweet pussy until it's time to fuck it. "Good night, baby." I kiss the corner of her mouth. "I'll see you soon."

EPILOGUE

SOPHIE

I'M TOWEL-DRYING MY HAIR AFTER A SHOWER, TRYING my best not to be frazzled in the last of my solitary moments for the day when I'm startled by the sound of someone pounding on the door to my bridal suite.

My eyes widen and I walk over to it, but before I can say anything, my future husband's voice rumbles, "Let me in."

I lean close to the door and call back playfully, "Who is it?"

"You know who it is."

"Hmm… nope."

"It's the only man who better be trying to get in your dressing room when you're half-naked. Now, open the damn door."

"Isn't it bad luck to see the bride on the wedding day?"

"If I believed in superstitions, I wouldn't have given you a cursed ring. Now, let me in before I break down the damn door."

I crack a smile and open the door to my bridal suite so Silvan can step inside. "So beastly," I say with playful reprimand.

"Just the way you like me."

I'm not dressed yet, but I'm fresh from a shower, wearing a white satin robe as I wait for my wedding entourage to show up.

Silvan smiles down at me like I'm the most gorgeous creature to ever exist. He slides his arms around my waist and pulls me close. "There's my beautiful bride."

I smile and lock my arms around his neck. "There's my handsome groom."

"What do you say we blow this whole thing off and go find a soft surface I can fuck you on instead?"

I cover his mouth with my hand. "Silvan, you can't say that word in a church."

He moves his mouth, keeping his gaze locked on me. Rather than move my hand, he grabs it and kisses the sensitive skin along my inner wrist.

My stomach flutters.

Other parts of my body feel fluttery, too.

He makes it *so* hard not to fuck him.

These damn pregnancy hormones aren't helping matters.

I sigh and hug him, needing not to look at his stupid handsome face. "Be gone, beast. I have a wedding to get ready for. You can't ravish me until later."

"That's quitter talk," he murmurs, kissing my forehead.

I smile and tip my head to look up at him. "What did you need?"

He frowns, uncomprehending.

My eyebrows rise. "The urgent matter which required me opening the door to my private bridal sanctum and letting you inside?"

"Oh. Nothing. I just missed you."

My heart gives a little and I lean up to give him

a kiss. "I'm really glad I'm marrying you, you know that?"

He locks his arm around my waist to keep me close and leans in, his lips lingering near mine. "You better be," he teases.

The door opens and several girls I hardly know all come in together. They're girlfriends of Silvan's friends. Since they'll constitute Silvan's side of the wedding party, I just invited the girlfriends to be mine. I don't have any close friends other than Silvan, so there was no one I really needed to ask.

I thought about asking Kendra since she is sort of the one who introduced us, but when I bumped into her on campus and told her I was engaged, she looked at me like I'd lost my damn mind.

Which is fair.

Still, not the energy I wanted at my wedding.

Luckily, Silvan's friends have a whole team of enablers. Right now, Harley Quinn is leading the charge, hauling my wedding dress over her shoulder.

I guess I should call her Aubrey now, but they'll always be Harley and Joker to me.

"Whoa, you're not supposed to be in here," she says, cocking an eyebrow at Silvan.

"He's a dirty rotten rule-breaker," I tell her.

She nods. "I know the type. You can break all the rules later, buddy. We've got a bride to build."

Silvan smirks and reluctantly lets me go. "I guess I'll have to share you today, huh?"

I nod and give him one last pre-wedding kiss. "It'll be good practice for parenthood."

He holds onto me for a moment longer when I try to pull back and murmurs against my lips, "I guess I'll do it, but I don't have to like it."

I roll my eyes at him and give him one last kiss, then I shoo him out the door.

Once my groom has been banished from the bridal suite, I head back over to Aubrey. She's talking to one of the other girls about a photo they should pose me for. The photographer will be here in a few minutes to get shots of me getting ready for Melanie's photo album.

"We're sure this fits, right? We don't need to send anyone out for emergency shapewear?"

I shake my head. "I haven't gained any weight yet. We should be good."

Aubrey and I aren't friends, exactly, but it's not because we don't like each other. It's because both of our boyfriends are godawful at giving up time with us.

When we got back from New Hampshire and Silvan was leaving me home one night so he could go meet Dare, I asked if I could tag along.

He cocked an eyebrow. "You want to hang out with Dare?"

"God, no. No, the Joker's all yours, but maybe I could keep Harley company," I suggested, remembering our almost friendship before Silvan intervened the night of the Halloween party.

Well, it was an almost-friendship in my head, anyway.

I'd save her from Batman, she'd thank me for the save, and we'd be sipping lattes in a coffee shop together at some point later when I felt like socializing.

Instead, we both wound up pinned to walls by our respective troublemakers.

Literally *and* figuratively.

Silvan told me she wouldn't be there that night and I couldn't come because he had to introduce Dare to a couple of his dad's guys, and that wasn't anything he wanted me around for. When I told him he should set something up another time so we could meet formally instead of just waving at each other when our boyfriends were doing crime together, he said Dare didn't really let her have friends.

"Sounds healthy," I snarked, not realizing I was in the same position until he leaned in to steal a kiss and murmured wryly, "Some people might think the same about us."

I guess friends from a distance are good, too.

More my style, really.

Having limited access to a whole girl team lends the feeling—and illusion—that I have friends, even if I know the only person I ever really hang out with is Silvan. At least on a day like today, I have a ready supply of bridesmaids.

Thanks to the girls and the stylists, I'm gussied up and ready to go when I should be. Silvan knows I have a tendency to not be on time, so he tasked Aubrey with keeping things moving.

He must have also told her I'm an introvert and that today would be challenging for me because she makes sure there's enough time for me to have a moment alone to recharge before we have to head for the aisle. She chases all the other girls out of the room so I can have a moment of peace and quiet.

She grabs her bouquet. "Do you need anything else before I go?"

I shake my head. "No. Thank you for all your help."

"Of course." She sees me standing in the mirror, so she grabs the only bouquet that's left and brings it over to me. "Don't forget this."

I smile and take the bouquet, then I look at my reflection in the mirror.

"I feel pretty."

She smiles. "You look radiant. Silvan won't know what hit him."

My smile widens. "I hope so."

I do love my bridal look.

Silvan isn't as in the dark about it as grooms are supposed to be. He hasn't seen it all put together, but I showed him my dress. He even picked out part of it.

He noticed I really liked his grandma's wedding look with her sexy satin dress and the fur stole she was wrapped in. My dress isn't satin or ivory like hers, it's snow white with a much more modest cut, but he bought me a white fur mantle (ethically sourced, of course) to wear to our winter wedding. It completes the look and fits the theme —and the groom—perfectly. It'll also keep me nice and warm when we're leaving the ceremony and running to the car Hugh will have waiting for us once we've said our vows.

A burst of excitement wells up.

It's happening.

It's time.

We're getting married today.

Crazy.

Good crazy, though. Just like the groom.

And the bride, too, I guess.

I smile at my reflection because the thought fuels no anxiety. I'm more at peace with myself than I ever have been, and more than ready to commit the rest of my life to a man I met two months ago.

Let's do this.

Time to become Mrs. Silvan Koch.

I leave the mirror and the bridal suite to join my seven pretend friends outside the doors to the room where everyone is gathered, waiting to watch me walk down the aisle.

That thought fuels some anxiety, but before I can worry too much about it, my new father-in-law steals my attention. His gaze flickers over me impassively, then he offers his arm. "Ready?"

I nod and swallow. "I think so."

He's still a little scary and maybe not my first choice of person to give me away at my wedding, but Melanie thought it would be nice, so here we both are.

"Any last words of wisdom?" I ask lightly.

"Try not to trip."

I'm caught off-guard by his joke so a startled laugh slips out of me. "Got it. Excellent advice, thank you."

"No need to pretend my *advice* will end at your wedding," he says silkily. "You're my family now. You'll hear my input as often as I want to give it."

That's less funny because I know how true it is. I never thought I would marry a man with so many strings attached to him, but as volatile as they are, I really enjoy all of Silvan's family. None of them are quite what they seem upon first impression and they're *all* a little scary, but I really do feel like I've been welcomed into the fold with open arms.

After all that "I'll kill you if you step out of line" business, anyway.

The girls go down the aisle ahead of us, and then it's our turn.

The music swells and a grin of anticipation splits my face, then I walk with Silvan's dad to the mouth of the aisle.

I feel like a princess—on the arm of a scary king, on the way to my happily ever after with my own dark prince.

Silvan's gaze hits mine and his chest puffs up. I

can see his pleasure at the mere sight of me, feel it fill me up with sheer joy.

So this is love.

I don't feel any of the hundreds of eyes I know are trained on me. There's no swell of self-consciousness or anxiety like I expected.

When he looks at me like that, it's just me and Silvan, and that's not scary.

I was unnerved anticipating it, though, and I'm overcome with emotion as I join Silvan on the altar. My hands are trembling when he takes mine, but his are firm and steady.

Everyone takes their seat, and the pastor starts speaking, but it's all white noise until we get to make our vows.

"And do you Sophie take Silvan to be your husband, to live together in holy matrimony, to love him, to honor him, to comfort and cherish him all the days of your life?"

I smile at Silvan, and he gives my hands a little squeeze. "I do."

I feel like I mean it more than most brides do.

Like I have to.

I want to, as well, but I'm under no illusions that I ever really had a choice. My desiring this outcome is just a stroke of good fortune and clever planning on Silvan's part.

Meeting Silvan was a little like surviving a natural disaster, but coming out with a better life because of it. He wasn't in my plan and there was little warning he would strike and wipe out life as I knew it, but because he did, I have a life I never even knew to dream of. One I never would have asked for.

And now, we're going to live happily ever after.

Or else.

ALSO BY SAM MARIANO

If you're a **series reader**, be sure to check out her super binge-able Morelli family series! It's dark and twisty mafia romance, and the first book is *Accidental Witness*

ABOUT THE AUTHOR
SAM MARIANO

Sam Mariano has a soft spot for the bad guys (in fiction, anyway). She loves to write edgy, twisty reads with complicated characters you're left thinking about long after you turn the last page. Her favorite thing about indie publishing is the ability to play by your own rules! If she isn't writing her next book, playing with her mischievous pup, or hanging out with her lovely daughter… actually, that's about all she has time for these days.

Feel free to find Sam on Facebook (Sam Mariano's General Reader Group), Goodreads, Instagram, or her blog—she loves hearing from readers! She's also available on TikTok now @sammarianobooks. You can sign up for her totally-not-spammy newsletter HERE

If you have the time and inclination to leave a review, however short or long, she would greatly appreciate it! :)

ABOUT THE AUTHOR

LAURA LOVETT

Laura Lovett is new to the romance writing scene, but she's a lifelong romantic with a penchant for the bad boys. Laura writes steamy romance featuring bad boy heroes sure to melt your panties.

You can find Laura on Facebook or Instagram, and make sure you follow her on Amazon so you don't miss her Seahorse Tavern series!

Made in the USA
Columbia, SC
01 January 2023

75222593R00250